STCKR: platonic panic - 2

For my dogs and cat, the trees that were paper for this, anyone I bothered trying to explain the story to, nick for trying to read it, my bed, and funky music.

Made with many hours and even more mistaks.

STCKR: PLATONIC PANIC
EPISODE 1: FNTSY

STCKR: PLATONIC PANIC
EPISODE 2: CLRS

STCKR: PLATONIC PANIC
EPISODE 3: RBTTL

STCKR: PLATONIC PANIC
EPISODE 4: TYPHN

STCKR: PLATONIC PANIC
EPISODE 5: RNFLL

STCKR: PLATONIC PANIC
EPISODE 6: JNGL

STCKR: PLATONIC PANIC
EPISODE 1: FNTSY

CHAPTER 1: SCHOOL AT SUNSET

Marcus Alvarado was hungry. It was the first period and he was sprawled rather than sitting, leaning onto his desk and obfuscating the sight but not the sound of his gurgling stomach. His rich tan skin may have actually drained a shade paler if anyone had bothered to turn toward his direction but no one did in the end. So he sat there at his desk and tried to remember if he had eaten that morning or not. There were many things that the boy that was Marcus Alvarado did not know. Similarly, but much less in number, were things that he did not understand, only because of the condition of the prior fact being so prevalent. He was not an ignorant child though, make no mistake about that. Ignorance was bliss and Marcus was, if anything, someone who experienced bliss in his life. It started in a morning, not the morning, but his morning. One where he woke up rigid from the cold or sweating in the heat of his blankets but never in between. Two steps within fantasy only to be followed by one foot outside so he had enough focus to recognize the familiarities between each of his days. His hair was always a mess just like the first day he had bleached and dyed it blue, a color that had still refused to fully separate and leave his normal brown. For no particular reason that he could remember he had decided to make all of his outfits clash in color, something he may have cared about if he spent more time looking in the mirror. In the end, all the focus he could manage to expend was enough to pat his hair down to an acceptable mess, giving up on most of the cowlicks in the back, and letting the long strands from the front fall just above his eye line. All of which was in thanks to the haphazard at-home haircut he continued to fail at. The rest could be considered a blur. A school uniform a size too small, old white sneakers stained a different hue from use. The same walk to school each day and the same seat in the same class. Until the semester changed. Until summer started. Until senior year started. There is something that is absolutely integral to the psyche that is Marcus Alvarado. That being: terror. Not the healthy kind either. Not something that could motivate him nor could it bring out any strong actions or emotions for that matter. It was unnatural, unnecessary, and unneeded. How afraid was he that he might go unpunished rather than to be punished? For example, not a single head turned to look at the frozen boy as his stomach imitated the mating calls of whales. He couldn't remember if he remembered to eat that morning. Another thing about Marcus Alvarado: he did not talk that much. Although he was fully equipped with a voice deeper than one would assume from his less-than-average stature and a sufficient, if not limited, vocabulary to match. His lips were thick with a sharp cupid's bow, but rarely parted to depart any sounds from them during the day, the act of which would have been reason enough for a classmate to turn that morning in surprise at the occasion of noise. Today though, just like most mornings, no one batted an eye towards his direction. It was something that had yet to properly occur within the unholy sanctum that was his first period classroom. In regards to the mornings and Marcus Alvarado it would be foolhardy to further the discussion of his character without first describing the topic which has been continuously walked around: his fantasy. One of which was filled-

"Can you shut it up in there?"

Lauren was the single brightest golden student within the entirety of La Barranca High. Not only because of her platinum blonde hair, making her the only other in the class to experiment with their natural colors, but because she was the pride and prestige of the faculty and students alike. Quite literally her words were worth their weight in gold within these halls, and Marcus was penniless. So when her warm breath brushed against the back of his left earlobe like mittens in a snowstorm he could only turn around in shock. How could-

"I mean it," she glared, leaning over her desk so her soft whisper would reach him. "At least try to focus."

Glare wasn't the right word, but it certainly was the right intensity though. Behind her glasses were miniature forests of green that were fixated not so much on his stomach but on his head. She didn't even know how hungry he was, not like she would care if she did know.

"Sure," he mumbled and turned back around to continue to not focus on the lecture.

Lauren was not the type to stare daggers into a person but nonetheless, she could have bore tunnels through the back of Marcus's skull by the end of class each day. School had only started a few days ago but she had been preparing with club and committee meetings far earlier in the summer. It was readily apparent that the robin's blue of the idiot's head before her was a flagrant distraction she had yet to fully overcome. Annoying. The word was often overused if she had to suggest so, but in this case she couldn't help but admit that it was most accurate. It had only been a few hours in total that she had ever seen him before, at least to the degree that she could associate a name to a face. Better put, it had only been a little since she knew Marcus to the degree that she was conscious that there was even a person known as Marcus Alvarado. However, in those few hours within the days she was quick to catch onto her classmates' lethargic and introspective temperament.

She was, above all else, well-spoken. And to be so involved required, if anything, perceptive eyes. The latter of which she liked to jokingly accredit to her prescription lenses when in reality it had nothing to do with her eyes and more to do with her heart. If she was more well-versed in that kind of vocabulary then maybe she could have formulated her feelings into an arrangement of words and understood just what she was doing at that moment, but in the end she could not tell. The silent boy in front of her rarely talked, but she had no evidence to assume it was from some acute affliction of timidity or shyness. Marcus Alvarado, with rich skin like the dark shades of fresh clay. Hair like watercolor blue skies, but dark brown along the roots and spots along the back that he missed. Brown eyes like old and aged oak, framed by heavy and long eyelashes that pulled down his eyelids and made him appear half awake as if he was caught in a daydream rather than class. He was shorter than her, like most people, and had puffy cheeks that met at a small but pronounced chin giving him the expression of a natural frown. Lauren was not the type to ignore nor disregard her classmates, but even so, she couldn't quite explain to herself the fascination that she held for the social outcast. Someone like him had survived four years in high school while it seemed like a single word could topple him. Disappointment seemed to come so naturally to him. And for some inane reason, she wanted to know why.

"Do you want a granola bar?"

Marcus looked up from his desk where he was priorly looking at nothing in particular waiting for the minutes to tick by. So enveloped was he in his task that he forgot to notice the bell nor Lauren's hand offering the wrapped bar. He didn't bother meeting those two miniature forests again.

She had green eyes. Blue framed glasses. Platinum blonde hair. The front of which swooped to the right and settled behind her ears. The ends of which were sectioned into two braids in the back. Golden tan skin. White straight teeth. She wore a beige vest. White button shirt. And black pants just like him. It was the uniform after all. She was tall. Taller than most in the class. Standing at least a whole head length above him and she probably could have picked him up too. Her nails were not colored. There was a little less hair on her arms than there was on his. Her first name was Lauren. She was smart.

"You should try eating more. One day you could even grow up as big and strong as me," she interrupted his silence. It was lunch and Marcus was once again in his favorite seat which was really any open one next to the window in an empty classroom. A lunch alone just so he could have a view of the city toward the ocean. Even from the second-story view above miles of houses and streets, all that could be made out from this distance was the shadowy shades of blue that made up the vague outlines of the few islands far off.

"I'm sorry to disappoint you then but I'm afraid I have already peaked in life," he answered turning to face her.

"So it's a war of attrition?"

"What's that supposed to mean?"

Lauren didn't so much as bother to waste a glance of approval or permission before she pulled up the nearest chair to his desk and set down the snack.

It meant he was stubborn, but she didn't plan on losing.

Marcus, who did not know the girl that was Lauren, the girl that was before him, and the girl that was famous within these halls, hardly had any reason to disagree with the generosity. But that didn't stop him. Solitude was comfortable. It wrapped him like a blanket and left him in a fragile but pleasant peace. Good enough at least that if he stopped thinking altogether he could forget the headaches in class from his regular malnutrition for just long enough. The girl that was Lauren had her eyes on him once again though. She probably did many times now that he thought about it, being as she sat behind him and all, but he was intimately aware that she had her eyes on him now. And she was aware that he was aware that she was aware, refraining from eating until he picked the first bar.

"Are you always this combative when you first introduce yourself to people?" he pointed out rather than asked, tearing off the smallest portion he could manage from the single messy bar.

"Introductions are hardly needed given that our reputations precede us," she paused. "That and roll call helps."

"You're talking down to me." He meant to ask rather than point out this time but was distracted in-between bites. Lauren waited for him to swallow before finally picking up her own snack. She didn't know him long, but Marcus seemed like the type to choke on his food easily.

"Negative reinforcement seems to work better with you."

"You haven't even tried positive reinforcement yet."

"Please I would never stoop that low for me."

Annoying. That would probably be the best word he had to describe his interactions with her although Marcus' own vocabulary was relatively limited. With that sort of sarcastic attitude and genuine smile, it was enough to make his head hurt, or at least remind himself his head was hurting. Aggravating was also another way to describe it, probably the kind of fancy word he expected Lauren herself to use. He had to give her props. Her tongue had the precision of a scalpel. Lauren would have her autopsy. And far before the walls of the cavity that was his personal space broke down for those around to uncover a surprisingly lively and still beating heart the sour woman with platinum-fried hair divided his brain in half. She took mental notes, studying him, trying to understand the anomaly that Marcus Alvarado was to her when in comparison he was so little to everyone else. As much as she cut around it there was no blade sharp enough that seemed to pierce right past his pericardium and into the center to remind him that he too bled.

Lauren poked him with a pencil in the arm as if checking a cut of meat. " You seem a lot more lively for someone who is the textbook image of rigor mortis."

"If anything is giving me a reason to die it's you right now," he shot back.

"As of yet, you still haven't answered my questions. I have had better conversations with my late aunt than this."

"Talking lightly of the dead is a bad habit to have."

"What would you know about good habits?"

It was slow, like most things in your last year of high school. Far too slow to enjoy in the moment and then only the fastest of memories when you reflect on them through the years. But it was in the days after, in one another's company and on a morning that had been grayed by a recurring overcast trapping the cold to the ground and the people to the confines of workplaces, homes, and classrooms that Lauren had surmounted a compiling report of Marcus. Having successfully pulled back every layer of skin, peered into every cavity, documented every organ she retrieved, extracted his bones for records, and sliced every tendon of muscle tissue to free any memory trapped inside. Her comprehension was a culmination of the minute and minuscule details. All of which laid out the information for each and every brushstroke of the portrait in oil paints that she could make in her mind for her to analyze. For as much objectivity as she searched for, there was none. Between finished and unfinished sentences alike Lauren had extrapolated all the details necessary for her to realize the answer to her question that had been left ignored. Anything less of her would be to let down the expectations she had set for herself.

Now it would be foolhardy to discuss Marcus Alvarado without describing the topic of most importance. Evident enough from her investigations Lauren knew full and well that there was one thing integral to his being: terror. Indeed, both of them spent their time in school hallways for the majority of their days to much of their own dismay. But in fact, they did not walk the very same halls. As the morning fog rolled in, unnaturally as ever, the clouds hung low with guilt and shame, threatening to confide in the earth with teardrops.

Now it would be foolhardy to understand Marcus Alvarado without understanding one thing about him: fantasy. The type that had no escape and did not act as such. It was the one thing that he could not ignore, as much as he was adept with such a skill honed through nearly every day of his life. It was the kind of fantasy that made Lauren paint in oranges. Her halls were white with linoleum floors, his were stained the colors of citrus. She looked out the window to the depressing sight of doldrum mornings, Marcus' day was perpetually ending with the ocean pulled in far closer so he could see the sun setting in the citrus expanse of the sky. The city was exact, but not quite. The sun's rays struck through the window. The sky was painted.

And when called it had no other option but to answer.

Lauren had dissected the boy in mere moments, had pulled apart his tongue, and realized he had only tasted that of his own decaying mouth.

What words were there to describe it? She searched for it nonetheless.

That of which was not real. Without fact. Without taste. Without substance.

Marcus shifted in his seat one day a few lunches later, stuck in the same scene as per usual. He looked at Lauren looking at him. He felt the flavor in his mouth, unusual and unfamiliar at first. For a moment the orange dream was sweeter like syrup.

A fantasy, wasn't it?

CHAPTER 2: THOSE WHO WATCH BUGS

The city of San Anlos was not always titled as such, at least in regard to the spectrum of Marcus' life. It didn't really have a name to it, nothing to recognize nor bother paying true attention to. There was nothing he wanted to pay attention to at least. His tendency to ignore the reality of San Anlos is the factual evidence to explain why he took no true notice of the truly peculiar happenings within his home blocks. Suffering from a reignited case of inspiration, his routine was simple just as it had always been. A sun had kissed both his mind, his body, and his town within his mental space. The only one that seemed to be exempt from the parade was the one sun he had been chasing.

Around him, crawling along the sidewalk with scuttling legs and joints creaking with every rapid movement, were the bugs. It was the insects. It was the filth. It was with their rough exteriors, matte black against the sunlight and offering no reflection, that they took selfishly within their bodies the essence of the citrus light. Their undersides were covered with dirt and dung-stricken hair. Their exact genus went unnoted. Rather unnecessary really. What was supposed to be noted was the people, or rather what was supposedly people, or rather at least their forms, or rather their lack of proper ones. Where the people should have walked on the sidewalk, scuttled through crosswalks, and paced around cars and doorways, the insects lived about the city. Until all details of a person were rendered obscured and thereby irrelevant and it was Marcus alone with his sun.

"Look at our little pretentious king," the animal whined in an affectionate tone with such fervor that her repulsion couldn't be masked. "He's so pathetic it's almost adorable."

Almost.

There was a predator beast that had entered the unrestful city known as San Anlos, tracking prey of the rarest kind. The scent was stronger in recent days, enough to call from one's planet to across the cosmos leading her to these streets. Marcus, too caught up in his casual pursuits of delusion, took no notice of the imminent danger posed by the proximity to the king of the food chain that was on the prowl. Her breath was hot and heavy, shaking from an anticipation sparked by oncoming violence she could taste in the air. San Anlos was truly a home for monsters of the highest caliber.

"How lucky I am then."

From within a stalking limousine enveloped in a singular shade of black along every exterior until it was nearly a shadow along the asphalt, two animals in business suits sat.

"Do you know how to gauge someone's character?" the woman asked from the comfort of the cabin.

Tired bags greeted her gaze from the rearview mirror before his eyes could follow. "This is the kind of question where my answer is less important than yours," the driver responded.

She gazed out the window, unbothered as sunbeams glinted off the glass and cast rays all along herself. The same black of her suit and suitcase was alight for only a moment. Her business formal attire would have been uninteresting if not for her odd choice in black thigh-high sneakers embellished with green laces that zig-zagged all along the length of them and, of course, her hair. Exorbitant amounts, cascading off her head and folding in on itself as it filled up the available space along each side of hers. Those details were far less important and far less interesting when standing in comparison to the figure of the plain boy that her eyes were closing in on. Someone completely oblivious to the cat-like purr of the limousine that had followed him through his routines.

"It's to watch how they reach for their dreams. When the goal is literally the one sought after concept they have. It's complete individuality. The opposition to society. No matter what, there will be prying hands, eyes, and mouths trying to take it from you. Trying to change it permanently. To truly achieve that kind of dream is to be covetous." She let her eyes hover just above the boy's head, between him and the sunset truly present. "That kind of person has to be disgusting." The last part was said with a smile that did little more than what a snarl would have achieved.

"I understand your tenacity, but please try not to forget there is a standard protocol for these types of things," the driver reminded her, inching the vehicle forward slightly.

"Protocol is just an official way of saying formalities," she scoffed. "If I had to assume, it seems like you just want to waste your time in this city for a bit longer." The last line was very brash thinking coming from someone that was currently lounging about in the comfort of the furnishings that was the limousine's interior. "I understand your concern though," she conceded, although her sincerity suggested anything but. "The timing of execution still needs to be perfect in order for this job to be considered anything near the success we want it to be. However, I would argue that wasting our margin of error doing nothing isn't going to help either. After all, you want to know just as bad as I do."

He let up on the brakes a little more, keeping a close eye on both the task before him as well as the volatile one in his backseat. Little more than a glance from the man was all of an answer that could be offered. He was dressed similarly in a suit and matching colored pants. The only outstanding difference was his elongated white tie that reached past his belt and the leather

color that buckled right over his adam's apple. He was hardly
interesting. Neither was she. Not when there was a panoply of
melons, berries, and citrus that littered the car's cabin and
provided a better audience than her chauffeur that was only ever
confined to the same workspace as her, a reality that she was
accustomed to. Along every surface within the cabin, sitting in
disorganized rows was the harvest. The swathes of fruit were
already withering with a give in their surface and mushiness to
their fiber from the heat of the city letting sweet juices fall onto
the carpeted floor and velvet cushions. They waited attentively at
her feet, under her hair, to her side, before her, and around.

Her new audience would not be in attendance for much
longer.

The only reason for filling up the space between her and
her co-conspirator was an appetite.

Her limbs were a blur caught throughout the clench of her
fingers and the glint of feral canines among other teeth digging
into the assembly members. Her silhouette from the afternoon
light through the window was amorphous. Her hair swung behind
her with each sudden and violent movement. In and out between
momentary stills of motion was her hungry figure as her muscles
themselves trembled from the sensation of ravenous abandon.
She tore into the fruit with the feverous hunger of wild dogs, their
insides now outsides and their outsides clinging to every surface
of the cabin they were discarded onto. Soft cavities, hard pods of
seeds, stiff rines, and sweet juices alike.

She could only hope that the insides of her dreams were as
delicious and ripe as she hoped.

Among the mounting pile of discarded carcasses the
demon dressed in business formal attire loomed. Or rather,
loomed as much as she could have in the small vehicle, half bent

was her back as she easily surpassed the dimensions in height. But oppressive was her figure nonetheless. The black silk web that was her hair in the afternoon stuck to every surface of sticky sweet nectar interweaving in and out of each other following the succession of destruction she had completed until the shadows found more space to occupy than before.

"But you never really know until that final very moment."

There was a particular melon she had saved for last, cradled in her hands against her chest. Her finger clasped tightly. And tighter. And tighter. And tighter. And tighter. And tighter. And tighter. And tighter. And tighter. And tighter. And tighter. And tighter. And tighter. And tighter. And tighter. And tighter. And tighter.

Until they were carving into its very core. Fingertips mingling with the seedy insides. Gold tinted slimy juices poured out from its wounds. All of which culminated with the moment she tore it clean in half exposing the melon's sunset hued center.

"Not until you have first seen their insides for yourself."

Among the deceased members that were once her inhuman audience, she stood with her head leaning back and arms limp. She allowed herself to let a sigh of exhaustion and relief slip through her lips after such a manic state. All that was left now was to wait while her knotting anticipation and wonder mounted. Would his insides be ripe for the bounty, or were they expired as she expected?

In the faux afternoon sunlight that no one had corrected for him yet, Marcus was not only oblivious to new threats like a violently shaking and tinted vehicle behind his steps, but also threats of the old nature as well. The continuation of his trance and daydream only resulted within the betterment of the rampant industrialization around him. Changes in the identity that was his city as a whole began to occur. The era that had transfixed the city of San Anlos was the post-consumerism of the 2000s, a town lost between suburbs, rundown blocks, and gentrified hills. In the span of a few decades of revitalization it had become the definition of a mixed message, less than a mile away from the beach was an overpriced main street that most couldn't afford, and beyond that were blocks of closed businesses or ones nearly there. Bookmarking the end of it all was the small outcropping of a public peachy beach littered with trash, beachgoers, and people finding a place to sleep. Most of the rest of the coast, both north and south, had been reserved for wildlife sanctuaries brimming with greenery and tidepools.

For a city that prided both itself and its expenditures on the few blocks of the coast it allocated for public use it still fared on the decrepit side of the spectrum, only a slight improvement from the rest of the city. A hike a few blocks further inland and one would find themselves surrounded by chain-linked fenced yards, family dogs roaming the streets, and most empty lots waiting for hopeless or hopeful entrepreneurs. Grocery stores with an adequate lack of branding for their neighborly audience were squeezed between houses and liquor stores, beckoning people towards an oasis of food among the desert that had become what was once their home. San Anlos was alive and breathing in those moments against all odds. It was the other sides of city streets that wanted to finish with the suffocation.

Among the ancient artifacts of families and homes that rested warmly underneath the ground, waiting for generations of later, was a society of plastics and trash that divided the people from the true earth. The lead support and advocate for the prevalence of this issue being generous enough to line the shelves of every previously described store desperate enough to have open space with a plethora of faulty toys and malfunctioning gadgets. A sure buy for anyone looking for the gift of disappointment.

Their presence: omnipresent.

Their reach: near infinite.

Their name: Tandem Tantrum Toys and Co.

The origin of its predatory abuse of labor and goods was unknown. Perhaps the swindling bloodbath of corporate capitalism had leaked into its international waters. Maybe the tyrannical level of power it levied abroad had found its way back home. Or possibly the roles were perpetually inverted. Nevertheless, the vision of corporate executives and T.T.T.&Co. remained synonymous among its many branches: the complete domination of survival. Inherently contradictory in nature, their business really was a mad balancing act that teetered towards collapse at one moment but then towards the dystopian power of surveillance and control of society the next. In a roundabout way, there was a fortress of plastic that was slowly but surely constructing itself. It was encaging the city of San Anlos from within, and Marcus took no concern or note of the open maw he stepped towards every day. Days just like this one. As every mechanical surface developed a need for ears and eyes to listen and watch, but no mouth to speak its agenda, he felt comfortable just like many others do in the warm homely arms of a corporate captor that becomes a corporate friend.

As the days passed with his eyes transfixed on a citrus sky ever-present for him and no one else, there were eyes fixated from every kind of watcher.

Documenting.

Recording.

Yearning.

Observing.
Watching.

CHAPTER 3:   BROKEN GLASS IN THE HOUSE

Within the ocean bleached leftovers that were San Anlos' southernmost tip of the coast, so desolate and drab that no one ever visited for fear of the boredom that it offered, was an abandoned oil refinery. However, within the confines of San Anlos' city limits nothing stayed dead for very long. The reanimated corpse of industry was more active and productive than ever before. So much so that citizens had hardly questioned why such a facility still allocated work when the city had announced its closure years ago. Regardless, as the average and unaverage citizen alike ignored the factory remains as it continued to regurgitate clouds of water droplets and less obvious non-water droplets from its tower's mouths. Mornings began to stop gracing San Anlos with its presence long ago, instead replaced with what some would consider a fog. A select few knew what it was most certainly. Very soon people altogether forgot what morning really looked liked and accepted a new artificial gray time of day that was recognized as the start. The remnants of the factory did belong to someone still, new property owners who had become expected for more egregious actions such as these.

Tandem Tantrum Toys and Co.

Within the steel reinforced walls of the industrial behemoth work continued at a frantic pace. However contrary to what one would assume there was only ever one lone employee present.

"Annoying."

One singular employee who had lost the memory of daylight's touch far before any other resident had. Downsizing, layoffs, and pay cuts were all he had felt in a long time as Tandem

Tantrum Toys and Co. learned that a mechanical corporate heart was neither fit nor capable of any warm emotions.

"Stupid," he hissed.

Within the top of a spiral staircase within the pitch black void of a workroom was a singular manned workforce. Within the consciousness of only that man, save for a few others, was the name Christopher Abadie, along with the knowledge of the person that went along with it.

"Good for nothing," his teeth creaked under the stress of his clenched jaw as the words escaped through the small gaps.

On a night where summer air was replaced with a crisp fall breeze, Christopher was alive with panic and anger.

"Useless idiotic dumb worthless absolute trash waste of space forgettable dunce irrelevant has-been aggravating insect no good alien."

He spewed curse after curse for no one to hear but himself while flipping switches, turning dials, pulling levers, and typing one security code after another into his computer. All at a familiar frantic pace. Company standard.

The whole shadow of his office space was awash in the obnoxious red light of alarms and sound of sirens that he had neither the time nor knowledge to expend on shutting up. His lean, short, pale, freckled figure was bathed in the color red which could be considered fine for the time being as it matched his mood. The grating reflection bouncing off his wire framed glasses and into his eyes could not be considered so. Instead, it could be considered more akin to spears of light sinking into the very back of his retinas, blood red spilling directly into his vision. The deafening mechanical shrieks were only a fraction as strong as the anger he harbored. Such sensory details were something extremely valuable because they made him productive and were

desperately needed for his current assignment. He leaned only
further into his desk and placed his face mere inches from the
large screen that was really haphazardly made up of multiple
monitors. Corporate only gave him one size so he ordered more to
make do. In fact, corporate had determined a lot of things for
him. His personality had largely been trimmed and scrubbed
away accordingly with corporate protocol. The only signifiers of
his prior self were the dark leather gloves he wore reminding him
of his prior years as a mechanic and his permanently aching
pinky finger from being crushed one too many times. Cues for
emotions and such were sometimes needed after everything
about him including his purple sneakers, black cuffed pants, and
light blue uniform shirt had been dictated by company
expectations. In that sense, the red lights could probably be
considered helpful.

 Undervalued.

 Understaffed.

 Underpaid.

 Something beyond the uproar of sight and sound caught
his attention for just a second. It caught enough of his attention to
convince him to betray productivity standards and workplace
policy. His eyes strained searching for it again along the pixels.
His fingers hovered just above the keys in anticipation. And he
found it again. His own reflection, distorted but there. More
ragged from what he remembered with larger bags under his
eyes. He was somehow a shade paler than before if that was
possible, only accentuating his freckles. On a normal day he
would have been running through regular diagnostic checks and
performing the maintenance an old facility like this would have
required with his mechanical expertise. Beyond that, well, he
couldn't remember that much about what he would have been

doing at this time of night before he started working. It was a shame then that corporate only gave him the esteemed title of senior retail associate and compensated him accordingly.

A vibration shook through the handheld game console on his lap reminding him of the reason that his panic had ensued. Even within one office there had to be an entire system of remotes and controls until it was sufficiently confusing. Of course security camera footage, an otherwise necessary provision under the San Anlos office practice, had to be trivialized as per Tandem Tantrum Toys and Co. culture. Negligence and abuse is fun when it had bright colors to announce it, and so he quickly pivoted the joysticks to focus on the new window. Christopher's tired eyes squinted on the footage that was obsfucated with an on screen pop up. Another alert sounded, starting the systems of alarms and sirens all over again as Tandem Tantrum Toys and Co. found another sighting of public enemy number one of the Southern California District. Surmising all the restraint laid in reserve within his body he held himself from acting on a more primal response of aggression which culminated the desire to split whatever he was holding, in this case his controller, into two separate pieces.

For the first time in a long time Christopher felt his pulse pounding and his lungs breathing. He took one hot shaky breath after another, warding off the chill of the night air. The cloud of vapor that dispersed after each exhale may as well have been smoke.

A sole desire that had been wanted so many times throughout history would be wanted again. That of a head on a silver platter. In this case: Isabella Luna.

Bella was not an ignorant woman. She was petty, narcissistic, greedy, and cruel, but she remained free of the high crime of idiocy. Standing above the shards of evidence that indicated her uninvited entry through the front window and waiting for the commotion that her entrances always seemed to call in response, she took keen notice of the eyes that were watching her at that moment. In reality, she was more disappointed than surprised that more people were not aware of the blatant and brash avenues of intrusion that such a company was deciding to take now. "Lens Fwends" was hardly a good enough excuse from a marketing department to set up a teddy bear with a literal camera jutting out of its forehead. Focus groups for the latest product ideas must have been getting lazy. Well aware that within the metal catacombs along the coast a bull had just seen red she continued to do her job. That which consisted of already reducing two individuals to literal puddles of cracked eggs with the power of transmutation that resided within the stickers she was armed to the teeth with.

The stickers are important. Very important.

She knew full and well how outlandish and incomprehensible it was to the dull Marcus who had watched it all unfold, let alone how hard it would be for an average person of better intelligence to understand the latest string of events. But he would have no other choice but to bare with her a bit longer if he wanted to find out any truths. More importantly, Bella was aware that while she stood above broken glass and the bodies of creatures that were once parents threat defense protocols were being issued to kill on site.

Christopher hated her, but he hated it more when she broke his toys.

CHAPTER 4: CHOKING ON MY WORDS

The meeting between Marcus Alvarado and Isabella Luna had been star-crossed since she had crossed stars to exist in the same stratosphere. It was late at night, the time of day that intruders liked to act, when the front window of a particular house along Rosewood Street was shattered. It was broken into, loudly and with theatrics without the slightest hesitation that would accompany the fear of punishment that went along with actions such as these. Isabella surveyed the room with a nonchalant attitude that was more common in the aisles of a grocery store than a home invasion. Marcus avoided the old wooden step in the stairs that had agreed to creak every time weight was placed upon it. In doing so he descended slowly in a crouch behind the little cover that the white banisters offered, peaking through the baluster pegs to see the shadows cast from the kitchen.

His parents must have heard the sound before him. Or rather, he was hoping his parents had heard the sound before him, he didn't really want to deal with a problem like a home invasion nor did he have any inkling as to how one would go about so. For a brief moment there were the distinct shadows of his legal guardians, tall and upright, plastered along the white walls next to the television. Then on cue with the sound of two slaps they disappeared. No, that wasn't right actually. They didn't disappear. The shape of the shadows performed what could only be described as melting. In the manner of seconds they were liquefying. Marcus' mind couldn't fully comprehend that though, so it opted to forget the idea altogether and fill the gaps with a disappearing act.

Something jostled through the contents of the refrigerator, shifting through it rather aggressively.

Under normal circumstances someone may have found themselves in the grips of fear. It's possible that their heart would be fluttering in their chest at a frantic pace. Maybe their hands would tremble. Maybe their lips would pale. It certainly would have been the normal response conditioned into the brain as an innate action for self preservation. A healthy sense of fear has remained the necessary survival instinct allowing for humans to prosper for so many years. Marcus Alvarado waltzed downstairs.

"My sweet prince, you are far too old to be sitting on that throne of yours."

The house had remained dark, nearly pitch black for the late hour of the night it had been. The only light poured out from the open door of the stainless steel refrigerator into the kitchen casting Isabella's figure in a silhouette that left only the outline of her presence. She didn't bother to greet him formally, turning her head to recognize his presence only after sufficiently searching through the contents of the refrigerator. Her tall frame was bent so she could look in, her lengthy hair piling over her shoulder. When she finally turned to greet him it was with her head only at first, letting her eyes peek through the strands of bangs like a hunter in the grass. The smile that spread across her lips was far too friendly to be genuine. Marcus had ignored any and all signals that would have been ingrained in another person and was drawn towards the woman like a moth towards the most ravenous flame. The only real contributing factor in his somewhat lacking decision process was a curiosity that was derived from a laughable sense of silent idiocy that he was well acquainted with. His feeble mind wasn't adept enough to imagine the possibility of dangers on top of his permanent visions painted orange.

"Who are you?" Groggy and unawake, his reply was simple.

"Strange that would be your first concern." Isabella noted. She stepped toward him, pressing the soles of her thigh high sneakers into the heads of two yellow yolk-like figures with features familiar enough to the sleepy Marcus that he could recognize them as the remnants of his parents. "Without any guiding voice of instruction you're almost like a ghost. Haunting these walls rather than living in them."

The cracked eggs that were once Mrs. and Mr. Alavarado laid on the floor with cartoonish faces, smiling content, two dots and a line, losing familiarity by the second. They were gelatinous messes without proper form, barely sturdy enough to support the surface tension that held Isabella. And she was standing directly on top of the piled two. Their useless insides were slowly becoming even more useless outsides as the yolk broke trickling down the sides and along the whites of Isabella's sneakers.

"Shouldn't you be more concerned about your parents? Or possibly..." She took another step, placing her right in front of him. Marcus watched as her fingers wrapped around his throat delicately lifting him up with a single hand in a slow but methodical fashion. "...shouldn't you worry for yourself?"

No introductions were truly needed in this moment as Marcus had already become well acquainted with the insides of Bellas's clenched hand in a greeting he was not accustomed to. Nonetheless, he was still flattered.

"You're. Choking. Me." he gasped or attempted to at least. Obvious reasons inhibited him from exercising his surprise fully. With his feet aloft from the floor the air seemed even further out of reach as he struggled to draw much needed oxygen with every labored breath.

"I can hardly see how that is a matter of your concern," she replied matter of factly. "In a few moments, you will be dead and won't have to worry about anything at all ever again. I am going to be the one who is going to have to deal with this entire mess that will be left behind." Or at least she would be if she actually took her job seriously, but that part didn't need to be spoken aloud.

Marcus' face was a shade of blue that would remind someone of a rich vast sky to soar in. His eyes were already rolling back into his skull and into the comfort of nothingness. Isabella frowned at the sight of it. She had expected her words to not make a dent in his psyche, but to see it play out in reality was all the more humiliating. If there was going to be any chance to impart him with some wisdom it was a quickly fleeting window of opportunity. So she pulled him close towards herself. Careful not to release her grip because admitting her mistakes would be an unimaginable mistake in such a routine task.

His earlobe against her lips. Her breath against his skin. His throat between her touch. Her voice within his brain.

Sweet nothings in all the senses of the word were whispered with the intimacy of lovers between the folds of blankets. Her words had no precision, but were rather a force of nature that encompassed all that stood in her way.

"You're not someone with opinions of your own so this will escape you, but it's in my best judgment that you can be near perfect for me. Make no mistake, I harbor no affection for someone like you, but such a promised chance is too good to not pass up."

The effect of her words had already escaped him, having slipped into a place between consciousness and that which went without it. Regardless, Marcus did not deserve the benefit of the doubt in his ability to understand any message even if he was in a sound headspace of mind.

Bella was ready to do the unthinkable to a man she barely knew only because the unthinkable was her profession.

"So panic for me."

A career so focused in atrocious weaponry commonly entailed such drastic actions for the best results. Marcus was no different, the only exception to this was that his forceful mental stasis would pose an adequate hurdle in achieving satisfactory results.

"Break down for me," she snarled.

Strangling the boy in the same indifferent manner as she performed any manual labor she was reminded of the many lessons taught to her in class for such occasions. All because her moon had deemed it so. Luna Cultivation Procedures, Chapter 83 paragraph 130 line 32 if she had to pin it exactly, although she did her best not to. Her hand clenched a little too hard for comfort. Her comfort, at least.

"Languish."

Her words were already transcendent in his ears. His mind was empty within a purgatory as every single syllable was a phantasm coalescing with his innermost thoughts. The experience was utterly transfixing. In that instance, and for an instance only, the pollutant filled fog of confusion and ignorance seemed to lift from his peripherals. His signature offense had a stay of execution by silent peers for only a night, but a night enough to understand what it meant to be aware of his surroundings. As his ears wrung themselves out with pain and his diaphragm contorted trying to squeeze in remnants of air, he immortalized all the sensations in their finality as the memory of his final moments. Fitting that it's only nearing the end that he was able to catch a glimpse of the night sky for the first true time. When he could feel the crisp air that had no hints of sugar on his tongue. See the street lamps and car lights shining through a broken window, glittering as infinite reflections within the shattered glass.

An important note about Marcus Alvarado and integral to his psyche was one thing: he was not one afraid of death.

He saw the view just above his body. And there were so many walls.

He was just about his block. And there were so many houses.

He was higher into the night. And there were so many stars.

He left the sight of a world his own. And there was so much space.

Sundown and sunset had become synonymous. There was a moon but she lacked compassion. His vision was cleared in the last moments of a murder that he could understand as his death, which was like his life in that it was indifferent. It was enough to make him blush. Whether he was mangled, crushed, or burned at the stake, there was the knowledge that the earth would continue to move on, the sun would set and rise. His screams penetrated nowhere, heard by no one.

It was unfamiliarly familiar, like someone he did not know but needed no introduction nonetheless. He praised the fantasy of a being shielded from his view by cloth. The diety's face was protected, not out of courtesy nor formality, but complete irrelevancy. If his fortune continued he could truly take in the details of such a god. 'Smite me' he would scream for no one to hear. And the infanticide would be complete.

Then the veil lifted and the hollowed out eyes of orange light turned. Suddenly Marcus Alvarado was no longer alone in the chasm of space, but in the presence of something. Certainly something.

Lessons went unlearned.

As fleeting as the moment started, the bear trap grip loosened around his trachea. Finger by finger, in a slow methodical manner. Marcus' consciousness came plummeting through orbit- The sky was orange - burning upon atmosphere entry - the time was twilight - plunging through the clear skies - something was there - crashing through the ceiling of both his house and skull until he was a collapsed pile of bricks against the floor.

As he laid his parents to bed later into the night both their forms and color slowly retracted into a proper shade of health for the Alvarados. Little thought was actually expended into the effort that would seem to be most prevalent for many others, that being desperate attempts to understand the nature of recent events. Even as he tidied his room and prepared for a sleep that would not come, the only activity within the mind of Marcus was a continuous playback. Reliving the singular moment. In the same vein as everything else in life up until that point there was a failure in articulation. Where one was expected to voice themselves to protect the bare minimum of self-worth, Marcus conceded. Even after turning blue in the hands of a woman he had never met it was not her grip that he choked on, but rather his own words. He was smiling well into the morning. That night the final word of parting that would fall into the silence after could only ever be hers.

"Pathetic."

CHAPTER 5: FURTHER EVENTS

During the event of a post break in the Alvarado household one could attest to a sense of calm, something that one more critical of their surroundings would have gone as far as to suggest had never before been experienced within the walls. The uptight and constricted atmosphere of the house had finally deflated into something that was more than a reasonable degree of comfort. A window was open in Marcus' room letting out the warm and compressed air that the battery stripped fire alarm might have argued contained a little too much CO_2 presently. Mr. and Mrs. Alavarado lounged in the T.V. room sofa with the screen door open for the last of a summer breeze to circulate in before the chills of fall could ruin the moment. For the first time during the season it felt like summer. Fresh air found its way from the second floor, exiting the room of Marcus and descending the stairs, sweeping through the kitchen and T.V. room, and leaving in the same instant through either the screen door or the same entrance that Isabella took.

"It's broken. Still."

Lauren frowned staring down at the face of Marcus who was laying upside down off the side of his bed because it offered a better view of the sky from his window.

"Has the whole Alvarado family finally forgotten their survival instincts as a unit now?"

The detail was glaring enough that even Marcus was well aware of what exactly she was referencing.

"If we always resorted to drastic actions when someone let themselves into the house then you would have to be convicted too then," he breathed out in less than a reply. Careless thought blew through his head like an open window was installed on his skull and not his room.

It was a very roundabout way of saying that neither Alejandro nor Amelia Alvarado found reason urgent enough to file a police report for recent invasions of privacy and security alike, let alone fix the window. No talk of intruders or fear was present in the already sparse conversations among the hallways and rooms. To the contrary, since their post metamorphosis states from the time as absolute eggs the elder Alvarado's had never been so unbothered before. The parents were relaxed to such a degree that they held no recollection of the events and any evidence in relation to them. The contents of the fridge had always been disorganized, the front door had always been bruised and beaten, the window next to it had always been punched through, and Marcus' skin had never seemed so healthy around his neck. Only a vague collection of sensation, visuals, sounds, and scents wrapped themselves into a bundle of incomprehension taking refuge right behind their most immediate memories.

With the sweeping temperament of warm rivers coasting through the halls, even the shell that was Marcus' mind was not impervious to such waves. It had only been two days or so, but they had begun to pass with a lethargic focus on the sky outside his window. By the end of each day there was no one left to worry within the household. Except for Lauren, having made more than enough visits to and from the Alvarado house to no longer describe it as a rare occasion. She checked in on Marcus the moment she heard the news. She made sure he got to school safely. She made sure he got back home. She went back and forth from her house to his when her concern wouldn't subside from merely not looking at the boy. Her worry not only manifested in journeys to the strange home, but also in the knot of her brow, tremors in her gut, and the most concerning effect on her tongue.

"Don't try to waste too much thought on trying to make sense. I wouldn't want to be responsible for burning out your only brain cells left this early on in life," she jabbed.

Marcus let out an easy laugh that left his mouth and dispersed through the air, leaving as easily as it came.

"What about your parents?" Lauren continued. "Aren't they worried at least, understandably terrified at most?"

The laughing stopped.

Truthfully Lauren had slowly been fostering a worry that started from mere suspicion. One that grew within the womb of her mouth, underneath her tongue so she couldn't find the right ways to make the words fit. It developed and matured until it slowly continued to dominate a disproportionate amount of attention. Her tongue dulled to the point it could no longer cut paper let alone stone. It was heavy and unwieldy, always at odds with the natural forms of her mouth.

Marcus had finally rolled over to lounge in his bed properly. "What do you think? Worried about missing work maybe, but what else would it be?" Against all the odds the stars aligned and for a second and a second only Marcus was actually able to read the room, specifically the obvious concern that swelled in Lauren's eyes looking down on him. "If there is anyone that would be able to catch the criminal it's this neighborhood of chismosos. Plus with your four eyes, big head, and even bigger brain on the case there is no way we can lose." Malicious contempt was always a good remedy for concern. Lauren was already smiling with a friendly desire to break another window with the boy's limp body, deciding instead in that last moment to take a seat on his bed and seethe.

"Resorting to juvenile insults?" she remarked condescendingly.

"What, don't tell me they are getting to you."

"I could shove you down the garbage disposal and no one would even notice."

"Yes, put me down the munchy drain, make a fleshy custard," he applauded sheepishly and excitedly while somehow managing to find a way to sink even further into his mattress.

Needless to say, he was not providing the responses she had wanted from him. Lauren frowned again, hard enough through a mixture of disappointment and awkwardness with her body that it could have left a permanent crease at the corners of her lips. Reaching over for a simple tug let her know that everything about Marcus' being seemed to be far too malleable to the displeasure of hers and pleasure of his.

"I don't like this new self deprecating tactic that you seemed to have acquired."

"Why, because it's working?"

She responded with a disapproving squint, even if he was far too enveloped in his pillows to see. As much as it pained her to agree, Marcus did actually have a point to his incoherency. One that she would still contest as not an adequate measure of safety or distance from the recent terrifying invasion, but a solid point nonetheless that she couldn't deny. On her many trips that carried her over the cracked sidewalk, slabs lifted and disjointed from the rise of tree roots far larger than expected, beyond the yards of patchy grass and weeds, above the concrete, atop the splintered wood porches, between termite ridden doorways, behind dirt stained glass windows, they were there. In the identical rundown houses lining streets like soldiers at attention. Each and every single one similar in design and separated by its own breed of wear and tear.

Plots of land were little more than sentries, houses nothing more than jars for the many eyes inside, or at least in regard to her. That was not entirely true. It was better to say that such an audience occured in regards to anything that could be in association with the famed problem child Marcus and the Alvarado household. There was little need, if any, for Lauren to exert a strong mind or keen ear to decipher words that were whispered from the houses alone.

"He's finally broken his parents."

Not an unfounded idea, she posited, but certainly an unjust one. Based solely on accusatory blame for the odd. An odd which peeked out from the corners of the burial between pillows of his bed. She readied to leave, but before that leaned over the edge of the mattress and the nearly sleeping boy to flick his forehead.

"I know we joke about the morbid a lot, but I'm serious when I tell you that you should be taking this far more seriously."

"You really think so?" he asked.

"I don't need to think so. It's common sense."

From the closed eyes and beyond the expanse of comfort he found it in him to answer. "I will probably have to trust you on that, you have a record for knowing everything." Words recited without the slightest hint of sarcasm that had always been foreign from his mouth. A statement completely invasive and blunt, both because of the other.

Lauren was not the outlier of the populace that was not accustomed to change, it was a reality far more prevalent in the untethered San Anlos in comparison to any other city. Yet there was something in how the walls sighed as they walked to the door that discomforted her. The common words trespassed some sort of bounds when spoken by Marcus.

"Hey Marcus, if you're so close to your lady friend then you should treat her to a night out one of these days," proclaimed Alejandro Alvarado on the living room sofa, sudden and alert as if disturbed awake from his sleep. Most likely because he was. Without the slightest change in tone or demeanor Marcus answered as if the man wasn't even there in the first place even though he was talking directly to him.

"Understood."

Lauren should have noticed that her friend's face ran pale when the words crawled up his spine and into his ears. Or she should have picked up on the fact that for as many visits that she had made to the house had barely talked, or introduced herself for that matter, to the Alvarado parents. Or she should have known that in that moment parents should be more focused on their children's safety than amicable arrangements.

She didn't. What she did know was that her face flushed a color bright red that it burnt at her cheeks and ears while her breath tripped in her throat and caught on itself.

CHAPTER 6: LOVEBIRDS DON'T FLY

The evening of the momentous occasion that was dinner for two was a cool one, in which Marcus and Lauren situated themselves only a half block away from the small stretch of coast available to the public. They sat in the middle of one of the few shopping plazas that existed within city limits. When there were so few options anyone would have been lost in the headspace of indecision. However, for the broke lifestyle of high school students, they acted in almost protest to the plethora of choices present. Instead, they dined on delicacies only possible through the catering of a nearby dollar store while sitting atop the side of a stone rim lining the planter containing mostly dying bushes. Between the two of them was an unsung agreement.

This would be good enough.

Marcus was glad there were no complications towards such mighty events in his rather timid and deservingly barren life. Similarly, there were no qualms on behalf of Lauren who was excited and flustered at the turn of events. After certain ideas continued to make themselves present in her head, spoken into her consciousness with the observations even a half asleep Mr. Alvarado could make, she struggled to contain herself. There was something that made it impossible to not trip over her words that she could not pin down exactly. Her assumption and running theory for the time was that she was experiencing an emotion along the lines of extreme excitement or joy. Contentedness perhaps? How does one measure how content they are?

Looking before her now, and looking back through the years of her life, everything seemed altered in some way that escaped all the words readily available in her vocabulary to understand. In the cold of the night her glasses frosted, making it hard to see the details of the city that was seemingly so familiar for her. Change had been creeping in far in a far slower manner beforehand, in ways words spoken had no need.

"How disgusting," she would tell herself during the nights she couldn't go to sleep. "You have to be sick."

She was worse off than sick. She was smitten, in all aspects of her life. On the nights when sleep had refrained from the usual visits she laid there in her bed and dreamed so incredibly vividly and dreamed so incredibly vaguely. Infected with an illness of the most common kind, Lauren was rendered defenseless and impressionable. Since meeting Marcus all her memories felt unconcrete and noticeably empty, more akin to fever dreams than anything else. Everything she felt had an open space to it. Nothing was complete.

Sitting in a plaza completely open to the cruelty and affection that the world had to offer the ailment was presenting itself once again. In regards to the most recurring symptom Lauren squeezed her abdomen which contained a multitude of organs, but the problematic one in this case was the fluttering stomach neither appeased by measures of starvation nor consumption. It continued to be unresolved as much as she tried to eat gummy worms and chocolates at selective moments. Luckily, sparing her embarrassment alone, Marcus was not the type of person that routinely took acute notice of anything, let alone the sometimes not so subtle subtleties of a person's body language.

"The sky is so much larger when it is dark isn't it?" he asked staring up at the infinite darkening sky above them and speaking in a manner only capable of Marcus.

"Your judgment is just relative, in proportion to whatever standard you're comparing it to," she managed to respond.

She didn't know why she liked him, he was annoying most of the time and more than a burden during the rest. That being said, she couldn't help but worry for him, and if she worried for him there must be something in him worth worrying for. She couldn't help but like him for some reason. She liked it when he was quiet. She also liked when he spoke, his thoughts seemingly untempered. That night Lauren came to understand that she could not understand most sorts of things. Like what Marcus truly meant most times that he spoke, why they had bought so much cheap candy, what she was feeling, what he was feeling, or what the point was for a night like this.

"Like in color?" he asked, stars reflecting in his eyes. "Like how the black is vast but the blue is smothering?"

Her most pressing concern was the failure to understand why she reached for his hand, soft and smooth as if it were an incorporeal being not of this plane of existence rather than a person.

"Or maybe distance? In the day you are occupied with clouds but on nights like these you can peer into the stars," she remarked. "Maybe it's one distance compared to another?"

Marcus' eyes were pointed up, as per usual ignoring the events unraveling before him. If he had spared a moment's attention the importance might have set in for him to realize that when he looked up there was no perpetual orange fantasy or the something that resided within it hanging over.

What there was in his world was the stars, the infinite sky, the remnants of sugar in his mouth, the cool sea breeze on his back, and the warm touch of Lauren at his side.

And it was all very real.

"How my sparrows have lost the taste for freedom under their wings," Isabella cooed through clenched teeth and bared fangs.

Marcus' eyes opened wide, catching every detail possible before him. He was focused not on the closed gap between him and Lauren, but the sudden intimacy there was in space between him and the villain of the utmost tenacity. The spotlight of the moon was set as the stage pivoted in a fell swoop from one of tenderness to one that was something not of this world. Marcus did not know what to think. Lauren did not know what was happening. But the audience of stars knew everything necessary as they twinkled with uproarious applause.

"No indeed, lovebirds truly do not fly. All the better for me that death alone can do you part."

Isabella's voice had no need to raise in volume or tone, traveling through the air between them with a perfect clarity as its own force of nature overtaking all else. It only took a moment for her presence across the plaza to overwhelm all senses. In another moment she covered the distance between them in a similar manner with encompassing strides that could overcome mountain ranges and footsteps that crushed hearts.

"When you are pulled low into the filth of your imaginations the overly exerted lovers can't keep things up for too long."

She stopped a moment towering above the two with her unnatural height, her pale slender hand reaching behind her neck and lost in the folds of her hair.

"Tell me, did that statement sound like a euphemism or an omen? Chained together is chained all the same. Make no mistake, I harbor nothing but respect and adoration for such constraints. But first, let me make sure these shackles are true and these bonds can hold."

The woman with both suit and suitcase finally extended the pleasantry of introductions although her far exceeding presence had made such a formality null and void. With full honesty, Isabella couldn't care less if the words organized themselves into nonsense or sense when spoken from her condescending mouth. It was all prose and rhetoric premeditated and loosely ingrained in a similar practice to how a student knows their ABCs. Lesson 3 of Standard Productions in the course mandated per Luna curriculum for Class I individuals: samples are inherently curious in nature and a crafted aura of mystery is greatly encouraged to confuse for easy manipulation, entrapment, and cultivation. She couldn't remember the exact punctuations to the line recited but it originated from chapter 152, paragraph 33 to be precise.

Lauren's hand tightened around Marcus' along with the knot deep in her gut from reasonable instinct. "Who is that?" she asked him. Isabella answered instead.

"When does he ever know what's before him?" she spat.

However it was not verbal abuse that hurt so much as the very real physical one. There was a single swift movement in which Bella was able to achieve a multitude of things, no doubt in part to the many hundred instances of experiences reiterated upon and communicated through a single second. With the absence of any effort for such a feat she brandished two stickers from the sheathes of her hair. Stickers that were applied with a satisfying slap to each of the couple's sweaty hands presently in the process of more than a platonic embrace.

The stickers are important.

In this case their pink color seeped out diluting the very skin that they resided on. Bright pink shades that dominated the identical images of double scooped ice cream cones of strawberry and vanilla with the reds of cartoon candy hearts atop began to mix with their own pigments until both their hands were a similar unnatural color. However, that was not the most remarkable or concerning phenomena that pulled at their attention. The couple's anxieties largely consisted of a suddenly surreal and all too tangible transmutation of their flesh, morphing into a thick, wet, and sticky substance wherever their skin turned a strawberry shade of pink. The affectionate symbol of hand holding quickly turned into a disgusting mess as their two stretchy amorphous, heavy, gooey, gelatinous, warm, slimy, globules of pink appendages stuck fast to each other. Each attempt to pull away only drew out long strings that collapsed back into one another furthering the mixture against the best of their efforts to retract their numb phalanges.

Isabella produced a single screw with a rounded phillips head that appeared like miniature plus signs from the inside of her black suitcase. Balancing the item delicately on her middle fingertip she paused for a moment in thought and admired her work.

But only for a moment.

The screw flicked into the sloshy soup of pink before her leaving only a mere glint of light as evidence of its travel. The metal fastener spiraled as it made contact, further blending the two separated shades into one singular mess, and at the sight of which Isabella let herself smile for a job done quickly.

"Lovebirds weren't meant to be freed. They were meant to be cooked."

CHAPTER 7: RISING ACTION

A normally darkened void of a room inside the corpse of a building was struck again with enough electricity to bring it to life once more. Red light once again, strong enough to stain the walls a shade indicative of blood. Every screen, even screens that had never been taken into account before, screamed with alarms and popup alerts for the rising action currently taking place. Time had run out and Christopher, who had resorted to soundproof earmuffs in response to the many incessant horns he lacked authority to shut off, was busy ignoring already ignored emails. His reports and appeals to higher management for advanced access to on site resources would have to be approved after the fact as his quick fingers and, at this point, mostly broken keyboards were occupied bypassing the strictest password walls and security protocols that management had made him install himself. His mouth closed and teeth clenched with such a grasp around his bottom lip that blood was all but waiting to be drawn as his focus could only fixate on the pixels of a figure he knew far too well standing over another set of victims.

"I will wipe you off the face of the earth with enough firepower to burn hell over twice, you pale egotistical glutton!" he yelled at his computer screen. Or at least it's what he intended, what came out was more of an incoherent screech littered with far too many expletives to sustain reasonable clarity.

There was a heat lamp fixed on the toy city now. The only question left to ask is whether San Anlos could withstand it or not.

Her worst fears had been manifested and actualized in the flesh. Bella's delicate but suffocating presence loomed over the melting bodies of Marcus and Lauren. The two of which pooled there, totally collapsed on the cold concrete. There were very few details that were actually obtainable for Marcus to process and even fewer that he would be able to retain within his memory which would later prove to be only a muddled mess. However, there would be one distinct fact that he could never forget, having emblazoned itself into his recollection. The eyes of Isabella. Bright silver light. Reflective, like the moon to the sun. Devoid of any evidence that would suggest pupils. Missing anything remotely human.

"Please don't tell me that you are actually this useless Marcus," she pleaded with an incredulous echo rising in her voice. His response, communicated back to her in an eloquent groan, illustrated the bare minimum comprehension that was present.

The world froze over. The air hung still in anticipation. All were waiting to bear witness to her next actions. Long waves of hair were left suspended in the air giving Isabella the oppressive silhouette of a bird of prey. All while she processed the rampant disappointment and the rush of many other emotions that may or may not have been part of the standard job experience. She couldn't remember at this point, her mind was reeling. Her smile was through gritted teeth that nearly held back both air and sound from escaping, the act creating more of a sign of danger. Before her, all that she looked at was cattle.

"Don't worry Marcus," she murmured. "You're a young boy. Stamina is a very hard talent that only comes with experience." The hunger in her was rapturous, it ate at the walls along her stomach and demanded to be satisfied. The hate she felt at the hands that withheld her most desired was far more powerful. "Now if you would just mature a little faster. Some of us, unlike you, have expectations with no margin for failure left."

The words she spoke consisted of letters organized in a way to console, but everything else about them smoldered with a violence bound in red rope to each syllable. Slowly, gathering enough about him to recognize when being spoken to, Marcus nudged his face over to the side. It was currently in the process of trying to bite a chunk of concrete with a limp jaw, but caught sight of his pink gelatinous arm detached from both screw and a larger mass of melted pink slime next to him. Across was the unrecognizable figure of what was once a human named Lauren, now consisting of a bucket load of melting pink and white ice cream, a cracked waffle cone-like torso, similar appendages, and a red candy heart with a crude face of her's printed on in the area that most would assume was a head. More so now than any time before in his life, Marcus was at a loss for words. Lauren, or what was left of her, certainly had no capacity to formulate a single thought about her current state. Thankfully there was no demand necessary for either of them to open their mouths, although Marcus' was hanging open nonetheless.

Isabella steadied herself for a moment, one arm held her suitcase, the other was placed against her chest holding her still and letting her hair fall against her back. The pace of her heartbeat slowed and she let herself take a slow, concentrated, and subdued breath of quivering cool air. And then she flung her head back letting out a guttural scream which reverberated through the air and tore its way past people's eardrums contesting with the immediate ringing it brought on. Her back bent at an angle painful and inhuman carrying all her motion and weight that was thrown into the effort as if she had been shot from point blank. The long storm of her dark hair engulfed her head, shooting upward in the movement and obscuring her face. It was a deep scream that fought for every moment to escape, beating against her own throat. One that would appeal to both wounded and those responsible for such wounds alike. However, her shriek strong enough to send quakes through the earth would be the least astounding event to come.

More immediate and remarkable in spectacle was the multitude of stickers in infinite supply that manifested with no discernable source in sight. The flurry of papers enveloped her body, migrating up from the earth and sailing into the air at vulgar velocities. Like a typhoon of the most unusual breed, it descended on the plaza and soon buried the entire area in the torrents of its havoc. It would have been a magnificent sight if not for the malevolent epicenter that demanded otherwise.

Christopher had run out of reserves for expletives and insults to fuel his rage, compromising to work in a silent methodical animosity with a focus on his task instead.

Complete Destruction of Isabella Luna.

Passing the last security lock and successfully initiating the Tandem Tantrum Toys and Co. San Anlos Prototype City Defense Infrastructure he quite literally got his hands on enough cannon, laser, turret, and missile backed fire power to level a city. In this case it would be just enough to intercept and render the whirling masses of stickers into ash and char, but not enough to be recorded in the reports as a successful defense. Within minutes the air of the blocks just before the small public bay of San Anlos was on fire from hidden weapons of destruction. From their homes underneath sidewalk, within walls, atop buildings, and constructed into the very fabric of the city unbeknownst to many the unmanned firearms rose. Barrels of weapons propped themselves forward from every surface already charged to fire.

With the sky smothered in a sufficient layer of smoke the hurricane of paper had already begun mingling with the panicked citizens within a block radius. Through hundreds of simultaneous feeds Christopher could watch as confused and nervous people struck with the flashy designs of colorful tags were rendered into jelly puddles of sludgy homunculus.

Marcus was watching it all, but in a far more distant and detached perspective as his consciousness and body both rejected the unrequited transmutation of a pink sticker. Slowly but surely he returned to a form that could now be considered mostly normal. He watched as Isabella slowly stepped out of the inverse of a storm's eye and made towards the nearby bystanders caught in the incident. From his perspective, everyone present was melted into piles of different colors but in a similar state to that of Laurens. And each and every one was tossed aside by the tall woman's hand with a dissatisfied grimace after inspecting them.

Somehow bruting the force of the paper and fire monsoon came a limousine parting papers against its windshield wipers set to full power. It came to a confident stop about twenty feet from Isabella. From the long black vehicle was a shockingly tall man, somehow taller than the already giant Isabella. He was athletically built and fit but it was hard to tell as he let his body bend when he stood, hunched over letting his tar black hair fall into his olive skin face. He dressed in a matching set of formal attire, same as Isabella's save for a black leather choker around his neck and his needlessly long white tie more akin to a lease. There were large bags under his eyes and the impressions of wrinkles along his forehead, although he didn't seem that old. His eyes were half awake even now, he apparently could not be bothered enough to shave his five o'clock shadow along his chin let alone open his eyes fully.

"Do you really think this was the smartest idea?" the man yelled from permanent grimaced teeth, trying to make his voice reach over the roaring winds and artillery fire.

"Shut up Eve," Isabella yelled back with a fanatic pace of work. "I only need to find one more. There has to be at least someone here that will work."

The man apparently called Eve had no time to let out a sigh to go along with his disapproving glance from sleep deprived eyes. Isabella did not have time to find a sufficient enough victim. Marcus had no time to understand the action that was only rising.

In that moment a fleet of military grade missiles collided with the earth in front of them welcoming a massive green mech through the flames.

CHAPTER 8: EMPTY HEADS CONNECTED

There is no point to the concept of a clear mind. That's actually kind of the point of it. There was no sum of its parts. There was no larger meaning to the action of it. What there was in meaning was only positive or negative association out of connotation and based on a perspective rather than any reality. It was the attachment of emotions and words to vague ideas that lacked the harsh objectivity present to it. However, there was no misdeed nor sin in doing so. There was no point to that of Christina's clear mind. That was kind of the point of it.

Christina Zheng, daughter of Samantha Lei Zheng, child of the second generation of immigrants, was a descendent of open minded and empty headed individuals. True to what many would hope to ever achieve was her illustrious state a mind. It was a life at peace. A single data point, chosen and stretched over an infinite amount of days until everything was painted with the same color. Christina had the fortune of never experiencing anything strong, passionate, or emotional to any general standard of measure. There were beliefs that someone could have prescribed to her, but her lack of intent rendered all surroundings null and void. Of course she could never describe and realize such ideas herself. It was not a peace that she felt, nor the rest of her lineage for that matter. Instead, it was a slumber of the deepest kinds.

She was comatose walking.

There was a dark blue night sky with no stars to guide it. There was a sea with no waves to wake it. Without any intention behind the actions the existence was a happenstance.

It was a happenstance that made Christina cancel on a movie trip for her friend's 18th birthday to make dinner for her grandma instead. The backfire of which, brought her to a classroom fueled by many reasons for arguments. Something could be said about the cruel words that were dumped from each individual's mouth or the faces of her friends that always seemed to construct a wall facing her, but she would not be the one to say such things. In fact, she was hardly the type of person to pay close attention to anything when the answer was always in plain sight. It was no surprise to her that two tickets to make up for time lost was enough to smooth things over, that of which brought them to a theater with a broken projector that couldn't survive past the previews. All of which culminated in refunds, sour faces, and a walk outside to salvage the night.

It was absent minded happenstance that steered course for most of her path, leading her to enjoy a sea breeze as the moon disappeared while she looked out, waiting for some answer to her problems to present itself. Now her worries consisted of how to fix not only the night, but her friend as well. Everywhere she looked people were reduced to puddles amid a current of airborne paper. One paper, just like any other save for its unique design, struck against her own cheek with a resounding slap.

Several of the many incognito cameras placed haphazardly throughout the city were recording the disaster, letting Christopher succumb to drowning in his own untempered rage. That was until the shock of a blue light pierced the red burnt room, silently drawing attention to a sudden change in brain chemistry that was in response to contact with foreign material. It was enough to hook him and reel him forward.

"Impossible."

Christina said nothing. As usual, she had no thoughts to voice the inside of the thick concrete block that was her skull. However, regardless of what she did or did not say, neutrals would continue to align in a perfect formation that accessed more power in her life than someone would ever find a need for. Alarms upon alarms began to blare within a small room as system control was totally lost. Meanwhile, in a vacant skull four bars popped up. A connection was established. That empty head of hers could be filled yet, if only temporarily. Far above a plastic city with far too much going on for its own good a satellite began reorienting itself in the vacuum of space. With a fearsome pinpoint exactness that machines are only expected of a blue beam of light shot from its dish, destined to make it to earth.

Christopher had a head about him, one that could confidently claim to have been rendered speechless twice in his life that he could remember. Once for love, the second for hate. Now he could mark this day as his third foray into the experience. One for curiosity. He couldn't help but gawk at the data on the screen. The girl was unassuming, she hardly stood out in a crowd. Black short hair, blank brown eyes, a black crop top sweater over a blue shirt tucked into black jeans cuffed right above blue sneakers. Christopher could hardly pay attention just looking at her and yet.

"A perfect null type zero server connection."

Corporate labeled scientific jargon really, but enough words to occupy his mind so that the embarrassment lessened as the outside connection completed the override of security checks and authorized its own release of a defense set with a matching ID neural code. With the sticker attached her fleshy brain was empty enough to fit space for a wireless connection and human processing power. Human bluetooth. The perfect processing power to match any requirements necessary for dangerous company property. The actual results of all those words was the electrification of the small body of Christina's and her even smaller brain. Pure electricity coursed through her, the sticker sizzling against the skin and falling off, limp and useless. Her knees buckled from the power, her eyes rolled back, and her head turned up towards the sky as a blue beam of light shot directly into her mouth filling her form with a perpetual sense of waiting. Or rather, it was-

'LOADING...' read white text along her blue luminescent eyes.

A single data point was on the screen and blinked viciously reflecting off of Christopher's glasses and wide eyes. With a few clicks of the keyboard all three hanger doors were open and the clearance was ready for an aerial shipment.

Hangar doors groaned when there should not have been any and within seconds autopilot missiles shot off from the runway within the dead factory's remains carrying precious cargo labeled under the file name: Barrage Unit Defense Model Type 3. The action itself was against all lessons in protocol, workplace behavior standards, corporate responsibility, and immediate warnings. But as Christopher put it.

"Screw work."

CHAPTER 9: SUNSETS AND NIGHT SKIES

"He's not dead is he?" Eve asked, looking up while unbending his long body to finally stand up straight. Both he and Isabella watched disinterestedly as the limp figure of Marcus was made airbourne.

"No less than before," Isabella sighed, looking up as well before abruptly shifting her focus to Eve. "The only one that has a right to kill that idiot is me."

The formally attired duo stood amidst a riot of chaos, chattering with a bitter tone the way friends do, completely oblivious in care to the rocket shells and all manner of projectiles attempting to send them to oblivion. Neither Isabella nor Eve could really be blamed for their lukewarm reactions, if anyone was to be forced into a sudden awareness of their close encounters with death then their first reaction would very well be heightened attention. But given time, and hundreds of years of it, the two could sharpen the acquired skill of willful imperception to a higher degree possible so that nothing fazed them.

Ignoring the fact that they were already ignoring so much, Isabella shielded her eyes while braving the tapestry of fire and ash that painted the sky making out the singular speck of a once again unconscious Marcus among the countless other specks of debris currently tossed upwards as well. As to how in particular Marcus had happened to experience said circumstances the details were unknown to everyone presently preoccupied with blinding lights from the immediate explosions searing into their retinas. It was only afterwards, with an open space that was missing a child, that the two realized their person of interest was tasting a familiar dish of suspected brain damage on a new platter that was the comfort of a free fall. Late perhaps, but in all frankness Marcus' wellbeing was not at the top in their list of priorities. Isabella's top interest was finding a suitable sample to mix with Marcus so her job could be finished. Eve was more distracted with a quiet eagerness that diluted his insomniac mind. However, priority zero of anyone bearing the Luna name was a strict punctuality, one both could only follow for so long.

"You couldn't honestly have thought that throwing a fit like this was going to work did you?" Eve questioned as he held the limousine cabin door open for Isabella to take a seat.

"I'm doing it for work so it has to."

He pulled the door open wide as she tried to shut it herself. It was not so much as a glare he gave her, but the usual stare from his half awake eyes. "Don't try to brush this problem off. You have a bad habit of drawing attention with your kind of temperament."

Her long hair spilled out over into the space of the seats next to her as she narrowed her eyes in contempt. "Then I'm lucky it's your job to keep these things under wraps."

"You know what my job is."

"Then why don't you start doing it," she snarled pulling at his white tie until her teeth were nearly around his throat. She held him there for a moment before pushing him out of the doorway and giving him a chance to take a seat behind the wheel before she continued. "Having lovestruck eyes that look every way but forward is no way to go about your business driver, let alone mine." The ground shook punctually for her. "So don't."

He refused to respond, letting the silence fill the car that was not possible with the earthquake from explosions just beyond a metal divider of doors. They waited.

"I don't mean to kill the angry mood we have going for us but if that boy explodes against the concrete both of our arguments are pretty much useless," he finally answered.

Leaning over his shoulder and pointing out the windshield to Marcus' exact spot in the sky, Bella barked a single order that someone like herself had no right nor authority to give.

"Go fetch."

"You're sure someone as blind as me is good to drive."

Marcus hit the corner of the movie theater rooftop and continued his fall.

"With your skill I know even crashing would get us there," she sighed, falling back into her seat.

Lovestruck and heartbroken once again in a manner of minutes, Christopher strangled the purple game controller in his hands and vied for control of a lumbering green mech. From beyond a wall of burning stickers that encased the entire plaza a hulking mass of green metal outfitted with missile launchers on its shoulder pads, a 360 degree camera headset, and a fully mobilized land and aerial transportation equipment fired. It was military grade, colored military green to match, and military use was the main reason for production. However, the line never did reach beyond the testing phase. Kinks had yet to be wrung out of the machine. Its hulkish design was roundish with an oculus head and an inverse trapezoidal chest that gave way to titanium peg legs fitted with wheels. The only source of movement came from these and the rocket powered boosters along the legs and back. Because of this the painted humanlike armor and the titanium skeleton rig inside was a lumbering beast to control. Wrangling against the poorly optimized system autopilot that continued to fire off its heaviest weaponry through a targeting system obfuscated from the outside of a paper blizzard Christopher instead decided to bulldozer through, soaring through an opening burned by the firepower of machine guns that fit in the fingertips alone before entering the eye of the storm to catch a fleeting glimpse of a black limousine.

Currently, the Barrage Unit Defense Model Type 3 assembly had launched with no hiccups in code, only the minor collateral damage of a few home walls in transit, but notably not a single casualty since the start up of the mecha.exe program. The last two details were still quite positive, but Christopher's goals had already diverged from the company standards. The entire fiasco was already a major victory for corporate who received notification immediately with a message that the sidelined mecha initiative had become active with a successful impossible-to-obtain brain sync. Temporarily, it was enough grandeur to ignore the fact that the San Anlos location had no directive nor authority to use or tamper with company property as evidence would naturally make one suspect.

No one knew how the mechanical unit was finally operative after repeated and proven failures of the necessary processing power and storage space to make the piloted machine feasible. No one except for the tender fleshy heart inside. However, at present circumstances her spacious skull was being used at 100% for running diagnostics, integrating processed information into code, and general system maintenance with no room for new memory of the scenario she was in. So it was unlikely even the fleshy tender heart inside was aware.

The empty void of synapse space was alive with the lighting of electric charges of ion motion, as axon bridges and terminals were bullet trains carrying more information in a millisecond than Christina would ever be able to comprehend in her entire life. All she had to do was listen and respond in a half awake manner to the communicated directions from a distant and safe operating location.

So as she aligned the multidirectional cameras within the head onto the highlighted targets ascending the side of a building in a lengthy black vehicle against the laws of gravity, it was not truly her in action. And although it was her arm that was held aloft readied with missiles, it wasn't really her doing so. And even though it was technically her who unleashed enough fire and fury to make the firestorm around them look like a campfire by comparison, it was not really of her own volition, choice, nor decision.

Marcus had begun to question if what he was experiencing was reality or another fantasy that had taken up far too much space in his head. Better yet, the tantalizing and very real third option: that it was likely the byproduct of serious brain damage he had just acquired. Any fear he had of delusions was dashed after slowly blinking away the unknowing loss of mental capacity to be present. He did so just in time to catch sight of the business formal devil in her metal chariot, still without full comprehension of the divine punishment of a free fall he was locked into.

True enough, he wasn't fully present. He was only registering the broadest strokes possible. He had taken no notice of the stoic and tired face of Eve behind the wheel with his usual gritted teeth, hand over hand as he struggled between totaling the car and evading the impact of oncoming missiles trailing behind them. In the back, completely unperturbed by both the fact that the limo she was riding in was driving vertically up the wall of the unfortunate movie theater and the addition of imminent dangers as chunks of said wall exploded around them, sat Isabella.

"What time was it again?" he wondered.

Priorities all mixed up and inside out, Marcus was unlucky enough to witness the spectacle as one overachieving missile from an overachieving aim proved properly placed in the path of the usually overachieving but now underachieving Eve. Against all his effort the force of the explosion underneath the wheel sent the vehicle somersaulting through the busy air. With each flip, as the windshield gave way to the back, and so on and so on, Marcus stared. Caught in his free fall. The earth was ever approaching. The limousine blocked out his vision. And with each flip there was a change of film as the sky rotated between an afternoon orange and a night blue, caught in the battle between dream and basic survival.

Against the backdrop of a tired sun at twilight was the silhouette of Isabella, standing atop the tossed vehicle, arms outstretched to balance against the wind. Effortlessly she walked along the roof of the limo as it spun through the air, approaching the front end whether gravity wanted to permit or not. Her hair whipped around in the air, caught in the force of the motion of rotation that should have affected her entire body.

Already familiar with the fire singed oxygen escaping his lungs, wind battering against his face, and the dangerous welcome of a fast nearing earth, Marcus' attention was drawn to the soft voice that called for him.

"Marcus Alvarado."

The catapulted mass of black metal was on him in an instant, only giving him the briefest glimpse to process before a hand reached out inches from his face. He desperately wanted to take it, but the world cared not for one man, and Isabella did not care for him as she grasped his head. There was enough force between her fingers that his first surprise was not having his brains crushed from her tectonic grip.

"You're disgusting."

It was enough to make him blush.

CHAPTER 10: JUVENILE NAUSEA

There was the distinct soft skin of Bella's against Marcus' face. There was lightning coursing through a girl named Christina's brain. There was anger frothing at Christopher's mouth. There were fireworks with a destructive agenda closing in on Eve. There were always bugs with a desire no other than that of the fecal nature. There was another sensation between two fingers, the fineness of paper behind Isabella's neck.

It was only after the sudden lack of downward momentum tugging at his life, now more than ever, that Marcus noticed he was not plummeting but still very much at the whims of gravity. Any fear that was related to such a revelation was a distant relative to the reunion as anxiety and fear were still slowly creeping up on him. Instead he was lost among the gasps of air and the course of a shadowed galleon that was the limo sailing through the sky at speeds that could race towards infinity. He himself was transfixed to a minor, confined, miniscule infinity as Bella spoke to him. Marcus was lost in the starry night sky of her hair that enveloped the two, shielded from the hellish chaos and prying eyes and ears, manufactured and organic alike.

He would have prefered for her words to be sweet nothings. Even if they had sharp edges and were punctuated with razor blades meant for slitting wrists and throats. At this point, exposed flesh and deep cuts were a new form of friendship for him. He would have liked for her to quote the readings of Lunar Explotation Techniques, Section 348: Executionary Words for Purposes of Psychological Disturbances, Paragraph 72. He would have liked to be immune to harsh truths.

"What do you want from me?" he asked without the slightest hint of a meaningful intention in his voice. A tragic smile broke across Isabella's face. Even in a time of danger like this he could only think about one thing.

"Should I speak to not disturb your ego?" she asked in response, her voice gentle and caressing. "Is that what you think I want to do? Should I explain to you the basic fundamentals of life within a universe like this for your simple mind and let it seem like something new? Do you think you could handle that? Do you think I could handle that?"

There was no time to respond. Her voice dropped to a growl, losing any emotion it had except for a thick coating of contempt around each word.

"I had to hope on the hopeless against my better intuition. My little despot, understand I do not crush the housefly when it will lead me to fruit. But this city has developed a taste for the rotted, infested, and expired. How long are you going to continue to stay in this stasis of failure? Is it something that fills you up inside? Are you not full yet?"

Her fingertips dug deep into his cranium and he could hear the crack and snap of bone.

"Listen to these words I say."

Knots of hair wound around his neck slowly tightening. Her voice was inhuman. There was a quality of her voice not from this world, harmonizing with the unnatural everytime she spoke.

"You're not deserving of my inattention. For once, I want your worthlessness to be beaten into your understanding. I want you to bleed out your failures. I want your every second in that flesh of yours to be an embarrassment."

Out of the multitude of emotions that Marcus would spend a lifetime or two discussing with no one but himself, the lesson posed this night could actually be considered short in comparison. However it is one continuously reiterated upon and repeated, unable to scratch the exact itch of an epiphany needed.

He was after all, nothing but a ragged stray with only the echoes of disappointment to reverberate through him, threatening to split his head open. A simple phrase was enough to initiate disappointment of the most guttural caliber. The words were like daggers in his ears and retracted with the splashing beads of cold sweat on his forehead.

From her free hand, not presently crushing bone, Isabella presented the small green sticker she had retrieved from behind her neck. Delicately she placed it over his lips without his slightest notice, having been reduced to mess by a sentence not of death but of failure. He made no effort to be keen on his surroundings, oblivious to the detail of a green baby that wore a skull on its head, all surrounded by a massive crown that now covered his mouth.

"You deserve to be nauseous."

He grabbed at his throbbing head in his usual futile effort, begging with pawing hands to release his brain now swelling against his skull for the freedom of open air. He wanted to beat his panic into submission, and if not that, then a feeble and incapacitated complancency. A breathless fervor descended through his body.

Isabella let her vicious grip loosen and slip away, casting Marcus into a fate of descension. He fell from his perch amid the sailing car, tumbling through the fiery air colliding with paper and flame. The wind battered and beat him, the air escaped from his lungs, the earth only ever greeted him harshly. His impact against the concrete of the plaza center was a ruthless embrace, bouncing his body high off the ground after the initial crash which was strong enough to send ripples of cracks through both the ground below and the bones inside him. Ribs collided with ribs and organs alike, piercing all manner of precious. It started in his stomach, it bubbled and festered into a worry that he could not control and fought for its way up his esophagus and into his mouth. All his revolting, disgusting, vehement, odious vomit shot out through his mouth and upon meeting the green gatekeeping sticker blocking their escape warped. The remarkably detested creation of stomach fluid and art did not simply destroy one another, but spilled out of his mouth in a luminescent green-like slime, glowing in the night as it shot into the air and caught Marcus' near lifeless body in a puddle by the time he landed again. In seconds the substance enveloped his entire being and inflated like a bubble until the tops of power lines, palm trees, and nearby buildings could not hide it.

A luminescent green baby, feeble and infantile, filled the entire plaza with its chubby body and overly large head adorned with a skull on the outside that morphed into a crown at its very top. A swollen placenta traced from its belly button deep inside to a comatose Marcus. Fat green drops of saliva dripped from the creature's mouth as it struggled to balance the weight of its cranium, the globules extinguishing the fires it fell upon with a childlike hate and acidic touch. There was only Christopher and Eve left in opposition to wonder together: how does one tame the childlike animosity? Isabella on the other hand was overjoyed at the sight of the inflated infant. She shook with energy, barely able to contain herself. She wanted to run to him and give the baby and hug, but when she spoke it was obvious that her heart was dry of any maternal sentiment.

"I can't wait to see you grow."

CHAPTER 11: KNIGHTS AND MONARCHS

Christina was fighting a losing battle against children's tantrums of enormous proportion and giant globs of green spit, at no fault of her own of course. Not immune to the attacks either, Christopher's lungs tightened in embarrassment and humiliation with every drop of drool that struck the mecha's armor. Each acidic spit peeled the military green paint job from the metal with corrosive ease sending burning steam into the air everywhere it landed.

Victory had sounded so sweet to him, even if it had to be played in proverbial minor key, but now as he let out one wave of screeching hellfire after another directed at the creation of the moonchild Isabella, all he could hear was his own heartbeat drumming in his ears. The army encased in the steel structure of a single mecha unit was more than capable in sinking fleets, but was futile in any attempt to injure the amorphous mass of pitiful goo. It absorbed each bombardment of missiles against its surface with astonishing elasticity. The most he could achieve now was a continuous state of evasion and barrages against the onslaught of the immense weight of fluids flung with wails and whines from the creature. Dancing between the acidic droplets of spit through the air, he was stuck letting loose more futile volleys of gunfire, one after another, only to explode without results.

Christopher grinded his teeth, feeling the muscles tense in frustration while an aggressive desperation from ineffectuality kicked in. The baby flung and screamed, swinging its oversized head side to side cleanly toppling through the movie theater before it. Debris hailed from above and Christopher twisted his thumb and joystick setting in a series of spins to avoid the incoming object. The acidic spittle came out, lit strings of goo sailed through the air in need of breaking up, and faltering in his dance with danger was Christopher's gloved index finger squeezing against the right and left bumpers of his controller multiple times over. The plastic was poorly made and he could only mash it so many times, unloading all manner of ammunition, until the controller broke in his hands. The Barrage Unit Defense Model Type 3, left limp and still in the air without direction, soon was engulfed in a green slime that bubbled and popped with hisses against its surface while eating away at any and all metal that it could.

Crushed between the alien substance and a familiar earth the impact was enough to send a military grade weapon in all directions in the form of loose metal scraps, completely broken and disassembled. Years of progress on behalf of shady executives and unquestioning, but eager, engineers laid in pieces around the unresponsive body of Christina, only remarkable because she was more responsive than usual. Surrounding her was the bouquet of metal waste adorning the ground like a funeral wreath of non-biodegradable flowers.

All to which Christopher could surmise poetically in a single sentence. As each and every last one of the camera feeds went down to collateral damage by drool or rocket power so did his frustrations in a matter of fact type of shock.

"Well shit."

Laying in a similar state of disarray, not too far off, was the crushed remains of a once luxurious limousine that could not find a way to escape the brutal hands of physics any longer. Its hood was compacted into the asphalt of what was left of the road so that it stood straight up on its head, back wheels high in the air and still letting out a pathetic rotation. Meanwhile, Eve sat in the driver seat slumped over the steering wheel, not in pain but certainly fatigue, while Bella perched herself on the back end high above to watch the scene unfold. In this case the perspective was to see, in all its glory, the monolithic green toddler flailing on its belly taking out buildings, street lights, and palm trees along with it. Flailing, but like most others in life, in a spectacular way.

"Eve," she called down sweetly. "I know that you're particularly tired, more so than usual, but don't worry. The only question now is one about compatibility."

A muted grunt against the leather of the wheel creeped its way up in response. Leaning over in her perch, her eyes fell on the passed out girl that had stolen the show. Indeed the fruits of their labors were nearly in reach.

Like a crow to the bygone and deserted strewn across highways, she descended from her enst to stand before and slightly above the casket display of Christina. It was a serene ceremony of beauty among war, as her body was laid inside a shell of metal. A 21st century mural of the immaculate, innocence, and purity present to a fault. The sight of moonlight kissing the girl's cheek while she brushed her hair gently in reflection was familiar enough to remind Isabella of her own childhood.

A colorless memory laying among the itchy blades of synthetic grass with nothing but the sound of running water and the warmth of sunlight. The water of course, from a nearby public fountain, and the sunlight of course, the artificial product of a vast amount of LED screens and heating lamps. Nonetheless the sentiment was still there even if the memories were tainted with a bitter taste of knowledge and heat of anger stored over the period of years. Perfect regardless of their implications, or rather, perfect exactly because of them. Knowledge allowed the worn out filter of nostalgia to be fixed permanently over these short minutes of her life.

Head tilted and held in one hand, Bella let out a sigh to reminisce on the imagery among the current onslaught of carnage. There Christina lay, ignoring the world as always.

"She's so quiet and it's beautiful."

Then Isabella released enough force through her fist into Christina's gut with a single punch that even the dead would flinch in pain.

"But I don't need beauty," she hissed.

Stronger in fortitude than many, Christina only let out the slightest cough of blood in acknowledgment without breaking her sleep. With a touch sweeter than a kiss Isabella reached behind her neck. Delicate fingers placed around an even more delicate sticker as she placed the paper on the girl's lips in a similar fashion as she did with Marcus. As saliva and blood trickled out from the corner of her lips in a slow fragile stream it passed through the paper and transformed into a glowing white substance. The sticker displayed the blue design of a sea anemone with white tendrils and a sick cartoon face. The same white tendrils encased her body in a web slowly solidifying. In moments, lengthy and filled with anticipation, Christina found herself in a suit of blue substance with a rare white stripe on each side that stretched from her head to toe. Her fingers stretched out to be claws, her body and limbs elongated to unnatural lengths so that each section was a inch or two too much. Bends and ends jutted out from her body that was taught and emaciated. Engulfing her head was a mane of white anemone tendrils sprouting from her collarbone and obscuring her face entirely. And all along her white circles speckled her body which glowed in the night much like her tendrils. In the inverse of the natural it was beautiful through spectacle alone. The way something can be beautiful in the complete disorientation of the human form.

A scene like this would have been more than enough for anyone else, but for Isabella's appetite it was nothing but lacking.

"Learn to listen girl!" she roared with exasperation devoid of any and all patience or concern. Once again she thrust her fist deep into the abdomen of the creature that once was the human Christina Zheng. Deep enough to threaten snapping the sea monster in half. Once again the lifeform that would have otherwise been a normal teenage girl coughed blood. Red shot from the head of the beast falling down on itself like rainfall and staining any white that was previously present. And it was stained in her own blood, stumbling backwards and screeching, that she saw the king.

CHAPTER 12: BRIGHT FIREWORKS

"In all aspects of production the mixture must be perfect."
It's the motto that had dragged her eyelids awake each night,
barricaded itself incessantly within her thought, and were the
exact words that she whispered to herself each day.

"Is it perfect Isabella?"

No, it certainly was not. And nothing except exceptional
was to be expected.

However, there was a gleam to her smile, a message in her
eyes, and a desire to be had in the chaos of the night. Things were
far from perfect, but the stars were already watching and she
would make them aghast and disgusted with this city of filth. Each
agonizing second she could feel eyes on her work, watching in
abhorrence as she flailed and floundered in distress with no
knowledge of the full destruction that was caused. She wanted the
stars to whisper among themselves until words slipped through to
the moon. And then she wanted to remind the pale mistress
herself that they were no better, they were no different.

Isabella dreamed so hard that she lost contact with her
surroundings. Her only tether being the taste of an approximation
to blood filling her mouth that reigned her back. That, at least,
was no fantasy she reminded herself and realized she was
regressing into old habits of a bitten tongue. Bella reached into
her mouth to touch the wound and see a color almost the same
red as blood at the tips of her fingertips. Red enough to elicit a
laugh.

Fantasies were cathartic, but the light of the night was a
brighter relief to reach. As cathartic as it was she knew better
than to be lost in the limbo of possibilities and beginnings that
her stay had become in San Anlos. There was work to be done and

she still had a job to complete with a flourish no less than perfection. As she had always done for herself.

Reaching deeper, far deeper that possibility recommended or necessity demanded, she extracted from her black leather suitcase: a philips screw. A large one. So large in fact that her grip on the head was the same that one would grip a melon.

Meanwhile, the walking sea anemone began its approach towards the colossal slime child that had begun to squirm out from its entrapment between buildings at all sides, the babies drool coating the entire plaza underneath it in a slick pool of acid. The monarch's enormous frame dwarfed the land abiding sea life much like it did all else. Even the attention of Eve, someone who was often thought to be deficient in energy for any number of feats, was intent on watching with full curiosity at what might occur before him.

It was the culmination of all events proceeding, the perfect mixture in action, the summation of all their intents and actions. And the ruling was a harsh sentence of violence as the two creature, noticing each other finally, began to attack like animals. The infant steamed with an unjustified rage and sputtered waves of acidic slime at the small blue creature. Far more agile in build, the sea anemone dropped to all fours and dodged the incoming assault to the screeching displeasure of the child. Bounding towards the green monstrosity the sea life took its turn to vomit red intestinal innards, tubule and whiplike, stretching far and winding around the giant green mass like a net. The child let out thunderous yelps coughing up more spittle, buildings quaked and shook from the force of the tantrum while the surface of the creature squeezed like a water balloon ready to pop. Flailing with a newfound desperation against the digestive threads the baby was near close to pullings the insides out with a strong enough move.

It was a sight of a battle. It was a sight of destruction. It was a sight of climax. It was a sight of intimacy.

The scene should have been awash in the insides of both amalgamations involved. Instead Isabella faltered in intervening, choosing to wait and watch the most unusual display. Cooing that should have been wails and affectionate pink innards that should have been blood red anger around the green child had replaced the battle. A cathartic fantasy was playing out before her.

"It's a complete synthesis," she gasped in awe. "A once in a lifetime phenomenon." With a life as long as hers she had seen it plenty. A natural compatibility with possibility far greater than her talents of cultivation.

From a crumpled driver's seat Eve watched in a similar astonishment, even though he did not show it through the wide eyes and a slack jaw as his coworder did.

"It's weird that something so important can be happening regardless of the input we give it," Eve called from behind her, still sitting in the wreckage of the driver seat.

"I mean it with full sincerity. This is not the time for your annoying observations."

"My interruptions are for your benefit. Fireworks like these can only be set off once, remember that. So be prepared to entertain the spectacle when the spectacle does occur."

His words were meant to be words of encouragement for her to act, himself already tired of the amount of effort that went into this job alone. However, Isabella listened to them in the right order only to come upon a different conclusion. There was much more to be done than this job alone. A behavior that was long ago abandoned and disciplined in a sterile room, to the point her mind forgot the motions to replicate it, had resurfaced.

Isabella dreamed once again. A whole new dream. A simple dream that she wanted to bring to fruition. She saw the sunlight of an open field. And she saw a beast so far beyond control that it would offer nothing but disruption.

The wind lifted her hair and pushed her forward. Eve was correct, for her at least, fireworks like these did not come often. They could not be wasted just now. She looked back over her shoulder with a genuine smile for once that was not out of place.

"Eve, good thing you're here to catch my mistakes.

On a normal night Isabella would combine the two mixtures, fulfilling her specific capabilities and role as per Luna business. With the proper disturbance in samples in place, they would be compacted and compounded into a weapon that could level the city at minimum and eviscerate the surface of earth on average. But wondrous warheads from Babylon was not what she was searching for tonight. She couldn't taste it or see it, but there was something her she was hungry for. In the streets. Under the skin. Within her heart. Inside San Anlos.

She just had to carve it out.

There was nothing left for him to do but let out another conflicted sigh, the idea of an unfinished job weighing down on him. Bella replaced the philips screw with a standard flat one, the kind with a single notch that appeared like a subtraction symbol, equally large and procured from her suitcase as well.

Left leg high in the air, readied like a pitcher, Isabella prepared to break the barriers of sound. Lurching forward with a booming release that sent not only wind and dust but ripped up pieces of concrete and asphalt rocketing around her, she let go of the screw directly towards the entanglement of absurdity before her. With the release she put spin to the object, letting it twist as it cut through the air. Twirling with razor edges it eviscerated its way into the combining creatures, leaving nothing but an explosive escape of air along with substances colored green and blue.

Christina and Marcus laid there unconscious in piles of goo letting out deep groans in their unresponsive state.

The perfect mixture, but not just yet.

STCKR: PLATONIC PANIC
EPISODE 2: CLRS

CHAPTER 1: REDOS

It was little more than lazy afternoons set adrift in the sea. Set up against such vast obstacles of distance there were a number of manners in which one could go about travel. Continent makers or leaders in people and thought often set out to embark in galleons and armadas in a desperate attempt to tame the currents to their own will. How feeble was this such grandeur in comparison to the weight of its actions. Alternatively, you could struggle for survival in a fight against the salted water that offered only sickness and rot, strong enough to send aches through your vessels that creaked with pain like whispers between bandits at night. Waiting. Patiently. Perhaps you were an adventurer sailing through the turmoil, blinded by passion and fantasy to forget there was no land to discover. That the air you breathed could not be possessed. That the sea you stood above did not belong to you but to the schools of fish, life, and lessons from sunken corpses of those like minded before you. None of these navigations were set by Christina, who did not think for herself but instead with a general lethargy and apathy. Her only deviations were in thoughts of nothing in particular instead of exertion of the muscles and the strain of sweat. What was it to revel in the soft relations that was to be adrift without course, without struggle, without knowledge, and most importantly without care?

The words of comfort and patience held so much meaning to her that she was drowning in the definition themselves.

This was to say that Christina had no regard for any present circumstances, out of touch and unconstrained by the conventions of reality that most others abided by at any present moment. Her continual state of dissociation was so vast that the only true evidence that such a girl named Christina Zheng existed was her birth certificate. Christina was certainly present in terms of physical space. Though not much else.

The space between her eyes started to feel fuzzy like teal polka dots bouncing. Her hand squeezed into the space of her tight jeans pockets to finagle out her phone before it even began to vibrate from the call. Grandma's contact had popped up waiting for her to answer, which was weird considering that she was doing her best to stand right next to her, however hunched that effort might be.

"Getting your attention really shouldn't be this difficult," Grandma Xiaodan pointed out with disappointment, but not quite disapproval. Phone in hand. "While you have it out, check which street we need to follow."

Regrettably, in stark contrast to all else, was the talent wasted on Christina. Specifically a skill for remaining in the present when she really should not be able to. Perceptively present. To a degree that definition and meaning was less important than the abstractions while everyday fixations made themselves more apparent to her.

She saw colors.

Personal interpretations that held her hand. In her ability to perceive, she herself had become imperceptible so as to only be described as pleasant, respectful, good mannered, and on rare occasions even docile. It was less rare than someone would have liked.

None of these interpretations were faulty or touted misinformation either. All were accurate in the process of classifying in words that of which could not be. To call for the name of Christina was to wait for no response. A fruitless endeavor that showcases the furthest extension of the capabilities that words possess.

Or so Grandma Xiaodan was finding out. At this point she could at least say with confidence that she was used to the usual temperament of Christina when she was in moods like today, so she didn't need to find a reason to frown. Even though it was hot standing on the sidewalk where there was no shade from nearby trees she waited. Without a frown. One thing about her precious granddaughter was that she was bright. So needless to say, she was content to stay there waiting, perpetually falling forward onto her walker while she waited for her little girl's response.

"You don't need to take all day though," she grunted.

Whatever words of encouragement they were, they did not make it to Christina's eardrums for her to make them out. Her mind was solely focused on the task at hand to focus as minimally as possible. And to do that she followed the greens. Thickets of it, like bushes that grew in the air to ensnare them and lead them to the left. She didn't need to bother with directions on her phone.

"It's left until we get to where the old library was and then just down that street. Remember?" She never bothered to learn the street names.

All of which was no matter to mind in that of hers. Names weren't something she had to take note of. Nor was it something people had to take note of from her. She knew full and well what kind of impression she had. How when people said her name it was with the same milky blue that one remembers childhood accounts of a spring sky. Temporary and remarkable for its lack of. If anything, to see any color but that was a shock to her, to the point that in the fourth grade when her aggravated teacher had called on her the words escaped from Mrs. Hillson's mouth to hang in the air as a noxious cloud of a magenta stain and Christina had cried like never before. Crystal tears of silver innocence poured like streams from her eyes without an end that classmates and their parents began to suspect that she was afflicted with a fragile persona as that of her mother. Luckily the orange fire lashings of her grandmother's kind words were enough to dry out her only reservoir of sadness so that she would not shed another tear.

Somewhere out there in the vast hurricanes of blue Christina found herself this gift. Colors lay behind each and every corner that she encountered. There to tell her the correct path, a scripted line for each conversation, who she should talk to, and most importantly who to avoid. That was how she came to find the most violent red of tenacity one summer night that bled into autumn. After calamity befell and she was gifted with vague memories of mechas, babies, and deadly screws, Christina woke up in the cot of an emergency medical response team in a caravan of white canopies and bedspreads. All of the latter were donated and staffed by the charity of Tandem Tantrum Toys and Co.

Having learned no lesson in particular from the night before, she had decided to sneak away from the fanfare of disaster relief equipped with hazmat suits and a mischievous plotting shade of vibrant bubblegum pink. Against her better judgment and wishes, Christina would no longer be in the vast blue she was comfortable in ever since a limo had entered the same stratosphere.

And she was plainly unaware of such changes. There was no sign to spell it out for her. Christina had continued to persevere through the subtle changes of her life the same way she had always gone about. Trips from the house without much purpose, daylight spent in a classroom that left her with migraines to occupy her time until she went back home, and a home at which she spoke hushedly or not at all in order to refrain from upsetting her mom.

Her mother. A woman who was a portrait of the serene suffering of penance. Such was the nature of Samantha Lei Zheng, who contained enough worry in her small frail frame that the winds lost direction or the energy to fly, as the grass before her feet depressed in honor of her sacrifice and pain, whose mere presence was whispered about in a gossip because the air blanketed her name and face in an unnatural fog in attempts to hide her white diamond tears among earthly secrets. Christina never stayed in the worn out iris violets of her mother's kitchen for long. She was quick to pass the corrosive silence of her father's room and greet the smoldering orange gaze of her watchful grandma.

"Wrong way grandma," Christina called out just as Ms. Xiaodan started to turn down on the first corner they reached.

"Just give me a street name," she huffed, far too focused on trying to place her walker correctly along the upturned and nearly demolished concrete slabs of sidewalk to pay attention to where she was going.

Grandma was a vibrant character. Xiaodan Lin was a woman of incomprehensible character and steadfastness, refusing to let calamity, struggle, or even age render her capable of weakness. It was said among her friends and family that when she emigrated to San Francisco the ship would not sink for fear that it would have to face Xiaodan's scrutiny. Waiting until 1965 for the U.S. government to catch up with her plans was patience consuming enough. Xiaodan was dare not touched by any further calamities. Such was the strength of her character that even when her dear friend Yina Zheng died of sudden appendicitis in the company of her newly familiar bedroom with both friend and child, Xiaodan's only response was to raise the daughter as her own.

The memories of San Francisco did not deserve to house the Lin and Zheng names any longer, so it was south to San Anlos where she continued to raise both daughters and echoes with her bold, confident, and enterprising attitude. With promise from no other but her own, she raised and ran the illustrious Local Zheng Market until the fateful day she had to sell ownership to pay the way for the rest of Samantha Zheng's education.

Now she stood there hunched, nearly crippled, and dependent on a walker to her displeasure. But before her granddaughter, Xiaodan still carried herself with the remnants of her pride and passion. Even now, she was sure to still support the legacy of her shop and was more than grateful for the good owners after her.

"It doesn't mean they need to sell out for cheap goods though," she complained, waiting next to the glass doors for Christina to catch up. Despite her stature, Xiaodan still managed to outpace her tired granddaughter's stride easily. Her perceptive granddaughter didn't need to hear the words leave her mouth to understand what she said.

"Stop the act grandma, just be happy it's open."

Xiaodan's fire was orange but bright. She wore a thin smile that spoke more history and pain than a frown could ever as she watched with each eventual morning the state of San Anlos deteriorate and her beloved shop along with it.

It was days like these that Christina enjoyed the most. Potent enough in the basic comfort she surrounded herself that even now she could repress the disturbing memories of what she was beginning to believe was a set of hallucinations and make her way inside. Strolling down the rather short aisles, looking for the random assortment of food that Xiaodan considered groceries: jasmine rice, one watermelon, twinkies, etc. Christina slowly wandered off absent mindedly. Luckily the summer sun still radiated a friendly warmth that postponed the oncoming aches and pains of her grandma's bones during the cold temperature, well enough that she could keep the fire in her lungs at rest. Xiaodan was already ahead on her own accord like always. Christina took time perusing the shelves for useless toys and trinkets she couldn't see anywhere else but here or in a landfill. As always she made sure to look at nothing in particular too hard.

White.

When, unlike always, she was caught off guard.

Light.

By something truly astonishing.

Blinding milk refrigerators.

Except they were not exceptionally bright nor notable in any way, not to anyone else at least. The same plastic doors before rows of milk and milk produce lined the back wall in the same manner it always had, if not a little more disorderly than usual. But there, while she looked into the semi-frigid world of processed dairy, she saw it plainly. White light snaked out from the corners of the door's gap like a neon wire following the length of the wall. Rising and falling. Twisting in on itself and contorting until it overlapped in some parts. Her intuition told her one thing. Spelled plainly and brightly that it had caught her attention. Like always.

'Enter.'

And from within the gaps of milk produce came a white gloved hand. Reaching out. Unlike always.

CHAPTER 2: FAULTY LINE OF QUESTIONING

There was more to the city than just a retired factory and a dangerous intake of pollutant smog. After all, San Anlos was built on the backbreaking labor of culture and history. Gentrification and assimilation worked hard as well, righteous in its unequal application of duty and punishment. Nevertheless, the forgotten echoes of a proud city and people still reverberated through the sidewalk and walls. Rest assured though. This slack in the binds of indoctrination was picked up by a harbinger and messiah of corporate philosophy and violence for violence capitalism, that which is Tandem Tantrum Toys and Co.

This was the culture of San Anlos.

It was in one of these new sites of vast importance, an arcade room, that captured the intangible feeling of existential dread birthed by monotony as any joy or wonder perspired from happy token carriers had managed to drip down the floor drain. A drain pipe just as these rooms were accustomed to having fitted per corporate policy. In the meantime Christopher had situated the room in such a fashion that all the arcade machines were pushed to the back against the plain white walls. Meanwhile, the only chair and table sat in the cold cone of a single lightbulb dangling above. All these pieces of solitary furniture were placed in the centermost point, near perfect symmetry but slightly off.

Christopher had found enough notes of flavor in his cocktail of emotions: passion, panic, wrath, etc. to find his way out from his makeshift fortress of steel and into society. Against protocol he was losing a conditioned fear of public spaces which was the mandatory standard for employee training. As much as this ordeal was major for his personal character neither the limelight nor the eyes of keen observers were situated on him.

"So where is he?" Christopher asked standing in the previously described spotlight, his gloved hands pressed against the metal tabletop as if he was emulating the posture of detective archetype characters from the movies.

He was.

It was all an impromptu interrogation. The featured star of this show was none other than the girl now famed within circles higher than she would ever achieve. None other than Lauren sat before him, with her posture straight against the harsh bends of the metal chair.

"Mr. Abadie, it is nice to finally get a chance to meet you," she smiled. Up until then their correspondence about the intern position had only been through email.

The silence was quizzical.

Lauren, whose last name was not important, had been waiting for this opportunity. There was much to the long list according to what Tandem Tantrum Toys and Co. deemed essential prior to her employment. These included genealogy, age, address, family, body type, first language, criminal history, drug use, disabilities, previous employment, eye color, hobbies, pet peeves, online accounts, blood type, credit score, political affiliation, favorite color, etc. However, the only information important to her as well as the only information Christopher had on hand was the single highlighted sentence printed on the center of the paper on his clipboard.

'CLOSE ACQUAINTANCES WITH MARCUS ALVARADO.'

"This would be your turn to respond, Christopher."

She couldn't really make heads or tails of the pale freckled faced man that barely towered over her even as she sat and he stood. The whole situation didn't seem to initiate her fight or flight response like she would have assumed something like this would, false pretenses and misleading invitations and all. There was the air of smooth jazz but played by a recorder. A childlike interpretation of what events should be like in such a scenario. Her coolness in such times was to a degree it made her shiver and could have been confused for nervousness against her own logic. It made her laugh, naturally and freely with a smile as she leaned into the table with her folded hands.

Her tongue was newly sharpened from grinding against pain and, worst yet, embarrassment.

Christopher's teeth and hands clenched and he refused to move let alone look up. In all honesty, he really had no idea how to handle any acts of disobedience, let alone ones through complete complacency like this.

"You're so eloquent," he tisked. How annoying it was in front of his supervisors.

He would be the first to admit that the false pretense of a possible internship was only bait concocted with the usual pairing of mixed intentions as anything else he did. However, any good faith or unequal power dynamics he could have leveraged were already lost. Without any other avenues to take he still had one tried and true tactic.

"Mam. Please don't embarrass me in front of my superiors," he begged in a hushed tone, careful to not let the sight of his lips or the sound of his voice travel far. Behind the light's glare along his glasses he pointed to the side only with the darting of his eyes letting Lauren follow his gaze. She participated more out of pure curiosity than any generosity left within her. It only made sense of sorts as to why the arcade screens were displaying anonymous user profile pictures above redacted names. Her eyes moved up above the screen to the familiar red dot of an actively recording camera.

"The internship is still on the table if you want to comply." He whisper yelled the words at her.

"You literally called me in here about that in the first place," she whisper yelled back.

"I can add a minor salary with it."

"I never said I was going to turn it down in the first place."

"Full time employee benefits are also on the table now."

"You're bad at negotiating."

"What's your answer then."

Lauren leaned back exasperated. "I was going to say yes in the first place. You're the one making this into a creepy interrogation about Marcus."

"That's the thing." Christopher looked up as if just remembering what exactly the meeting was for. "All I need to know is the current location of Marcus Alvarado. With as few questions as possible preferably."

He waited.

The truth was silence was the only bargaining point available, but such folding on his part wouldn't be seen as a total defeat in the eyes of his supervisors if he could make the deal land. In recent days, after waking up alone in a canopy of medical workers and white tents Lauren had no other option but to assume that perhaps they also realized what she had.

Of course she was smarter than to completely believe that line of doubt, squashing what little internal conspiracy that festered within the hunger of her gut. But she couldn't kill it. Silence was the only means of existence now as her tongue was sharpened to a point never before, double sided to each syllable and pressing just as deeply into herself as she did to others. That is to say that as she described how Marcus had not bothered to contact her and how after her own investigations she discovered he had decided to follow around the annoying prominent woman Isabella, it hurt her just as much as it would hurt the future of Marcus Alvarado.

Her mouth tasted of blood and all she could focus on was its slow descent down her throat while she watched realization strike Christopher as he pulled out his phone to answer a call. Body parts. It sounded like body parts because he was ordering body parts over the phone in between the cursing.

CHAPTER 3: SOUR MOUTHED DOGS

Any goodwill or charity that was established in surplus among the Alvarado household had completely run dry by the time Marcus had arrived the next morning after being picked up from the medical tents. He did not know it and would continue to remain oblivious to this fact, as he did with any other fact, but even in his moments of crushing lows in both ego and awareness Marcus was lucky.

If there was anything about the Alvarado household it was this: the house was built upon little words spoken.

It was precisely because of his departure in attention after such exhausting events that the gaze of Alejandro Alvarado, which had the same effect that the dry hot air had on the desert, did little in regard to Marcus. Instead of the usual iron maiden of silence and social etiquette taboo, Marcus was prescribed with a splitting headache and the task of holding down past meals of only candy. The latter of which he was now regretting.

How terrifying, was it not? To be in the sights of a god. Within the grasp of a deity. The breath of something holy. Celestial splendor, a shape ever changing in the light of a permanent sunset that remained the only constant in his mind. His only desire for months and years even had been to catch up to that figure caught within the twilight of the perpetual setting sun. He had lost track of exactly when the dream became so detailed and specific. It had started with sunset strolls with his mom along the beach after his soccer practice early on in grade school. He was still young in comparison to the age of most others, but even now those days felt like forever ago.

Much had changed.

He hadn't. Not in a remarkable way at least.

Now it hung in the hallway, peering in from the windows and behind the closed doors just as he entered the house. He could act like he didn't notice. That he couldn't feel the cold light of the gaze he had so often searched for coalescing with his skin, his clothes, his hair, his face. Meeting his eyes. Traversing his household was easy enough. Marcus could do it in a sprint if he really wanted to, which he did want, but ultimately he did not. Not in the end of things, regardless of the face of a sunsetting god who chased him down the near bare and empty halls. It was peeking, just as the orange light did through the edges of the curtains. Peering over the fence of the backyard, looking in through the glass doors. It framed itself along the few pictures that landmarked the indistinguishable blank void that was the house, covering the images with the reflection of its holy glare. So it was a race through the halls each and every time, trying to reach the finish line that he couldn't find with a terror behind his steps. There was no safety in his room. There was no safety in the house. There were no expectations met by standing still when all eyes were focused.

So he ran. It just happened that he really didn't know any other direction than toward Isabella.

Such pleasantries in timidness and obscurity were not tolerated by any Luna name, let alone Bella. That is to say, the constant shadow that was Marcus' awkward figure failing to trail her was more annoying than amusing. So Marcus found himself in a prison of his most desired. He was situated in a dog collar and in a limo that was actually more of a cage now. The smell of citrus was overwhelming even though there was no discernable source that could be made out. And of course, Bella was there watching her new pup with a pleased expression.

"Look at the stray we caught," she remarked, although her body language demanded that there be no response. An order which Eve followed perfectly from the comfortable distance removed in the driver's seat.

The sun was closer than ever before, although only Marcus was there to witness it. It painted the world in a single shade of orange, casting the insides of the limo into a cobweb of silhouettes. The god was peering in through the windows. Eyes luminous. Around the edges the veil drifted away from its marble face. A marble face that stopped at the lip. No need for a mouth when there was no need for words. But Marcus did have a mouth and a need for words. However, he was at a loss for them.

Instead, he adjusted in his squishy velvet seat to speak up which was hard to achieve given the rather tightly fixed dog collar making his heartbeat echo against its leather. In the end, breathing was a minor feat in itself. That day, more specifically that exact moment in time, there were a lot of feats to bear witness to. The other ones were mainly by Isabella as she moved herself effortlessly through the cabin of the moving car to personally shush him with a single hand.

The first of these feats was the navigation alone through the spider's nest of chains that stood taut with tension inside the limo. Caught on every edge and corner of surface available within the vehicle they darkened the insides from sheer volume. They wrapped around themselves, metal upon metal, until they reached the leather and flesh that was the collar and Marcus' throat. Yet Isabella walked towards the boy from the opposite end as if the dizzying mess had no bearing on her actions whatsoever, picking her path without hesitancy.

The second of these feats was the waves of lemon wafts that erupted with each of her movements. Not so much from the woman herself, but the presence that entered the room and his brain through the cracks in the doors, pounding along the cabin walls. The lemon. A discomfort in leisure. A comfortable nuisance to a degree that its total net worth was counted in delight. The waves of scent hit Marcus hard enough he could taste the flavor after it had stabbed the back of his nose and lined his throat. Yellow crushing waves of yellow scent, like the harsh light of an eye's gaze.

Her fingers were soft like before. Softer than he remembered. All it took was one, placed along his lips so gently that for a moment he almost mistook the creature before him as compassionate. The moment of rampant comfort was strong enough to strip him of all defenses so that when he looked up at her he forgot he would have to meet her gaze. Staring at him. The lemon stabbed his mouth so strongly he could taste it. And he loved every moment of it.

"Marcus, you're going to have to develop a better work ethic my dear," Isabella requested. "We can't be preserving you forever you know."

Among many things, such as warning signs and the most momentous occasions in his life, Marcus did not notice the cooler filled with ice and liquor that was installed directly into the vehicle along the wall to his right. He also did not realize that this car should have already been destroyed from the other day.

Something stung against his lips, interrupting the silence of the room and errant meddlings of his thoughts. Without contest he let the ice slip through as Isabella pressed a single cube into his mouth, feeding him a treat like a dog.

Eyes focused on his lips. Intently.

As per her prescription, the ice cooled any stray thoughts bubbling with unanswered questions, possible reservations, and concerns inside the microcosm of an ecosystem in which he found himself. He instead sat there letting the cube dissolve on his tongue.

Eyes were no longer focused on him. Instead, Bella doubled over, elated in a burst of furious laughter. Uncontrollable and without end.

Marcus couldn't understand the person that was before him. Her actions didn't seem to make any sense to him, or rather maybe he had never tried so hard to make sense out of a person before. Why was she laughing? No. That wasn't the right way to ask it.

"Why are you laughing?"

He finally spoke.

The laughter immediately stopped. The action of halting itself stopped with such a force, like a vacuum in the small space, that his breath caught and the array of chain links around them clinked against each other.

"Drink some of this fido." She barked the order while pulling a chilled bottle of vodka from the ice chest behind to her side.

Marcus was in the throes of rejections trying to formulate some kind of argument as to why he shouldn't, which was composed of facts about laws, his age, and overall morals, but deep down he knew his defenses were severely compromised already. Isabella towered over him, frost in her hand only slightly less cold than her voice.

"That's not what this part is about Marcus. Your Marcus Alvarado. The Marcus Alvarado that barely thinks but never speaks. The one that monologues in long winded run-on sentences without end or meaning. The one whose words are a wall of text that are sluggish and boring to trek through. There are platitudes and abstractions that you bother with and now you have the audacity for a request. Wasting your breath only to waste mine. How dare you. Spending your time with useless words only to speak now."

She didn't take a step forward. She didn't bother with the advance. Her figure still loomed larger. Her hair rose around her blocking out the light except for the gray of her irises.

"How about some lemonade then, you mutt."

A pale hand extended from the shadows with a wet can of cold lemonade.

Blue skies and spare clouds had filled the windows, but for Marcus Alvarado his words could describe nothing more than the colors that were orange. He deserved no more in the end. After a flash of dominance and her simple command it was more than enough to bring the god closer than before, almost at an embrace. Peering right at him.

A size indiscernible but discernibly massive, a flesh bruised in color but dense with strength, a face of marble mask but incomplete just above the bottom lip, a halo of holy tangible gold wielded into its head, a veil of white cast aside. A smell stronger than lemons.

The smell hurt more than the taste of sour lemonade in his mouth.

"Look how domesticated you are," Bella murmured.

CHAPTER 4: LUST ON THE RADIO

Eve had successfully managed to park the limousine at their destination in the same uneventful manner in which he had scaled a wall and crashed it a few nights ago. In all sincerity, under his unconscious hands of his and manipulation it was an achievement unto itself arriving anywhere, deserving of abundant praise.

This is all because of the lacking way in which he was resolved to approach all tasks in his life such as chauffeuring unwieldy attendants and other assignments that entailed much more. Today was a rich blue sky dotted with occasional clouds, remarkable for the lasting effect on people's memories it would have being the image they recalled to embody the ordinary and normal. Eve spared no attention, focused on maintaining the unusual metal cage of a vehicle that he and Isabella kept themselves in. When all was said and done, it could perhaps be a coffin for a life of jobs successful.

Any surplus of life that a world outside of this had to offer was not welcomed nor needed. Eve remained contradictory to his nature as a class E individual. The prospects of such children were admired for their remarkable perceptiveness which often posed to be problematic. Deficient in aspirations or desires, he was a man of concrete brutalist reality even though his own was absurd. These qualifications, vigorous exercises of both mental and physical aptitude, and questionable experiments had fulfilled the exact requirements to be assigned compatriot, comrade, and largely unwilling partner to Isabella. Constantly at odds, his distaste for work and the exhaustion that came with any exercise of existence made every moment picturesquely contrast with

Isabella's innate nature to cause more work from one scene of destruction to another. As she was expected.

Nonetheless, her Class I nature did not offer any personal salvation from Eve's sighs of desperation and disapproval, a man who had resigned to being an enabler in an effort to consolidate energy and influence against the waves of insatiable forces and primal urges that belonged to Isabella. She could rarely take no for an answer. As long as he could prod her along in an orderly fashion he hoped enough free time could be enjoyed between intergalactic jobs that he could definitively say his was a life well lived, before his corpse was sent hurtling into a star for a traditional retirement.

As he watched the figure of his one and only friend and compatriot walk away to cause what can only be described as utter havoc, he began issuing his own string of minor terror, turning towards the backseat to look at Marcus.

"I'm giving you one chance to run for it."

"You talk?" Marcus asked, reminded about the fact that Eve was even there, let alone the car had a chauffeur. The said chauffeur's eyes closed for a moment in pure and untainted disappointment, but not for a moment too long for risk of sleep overtaking his already minuscule reserve of willpower.

"Get out of my car."

"Can't really." He was an idiot but Marcus' answer wasn't without calculation, evident as he pointed at the collar and chain around his neck.

"Yeah, you can."

Through the small window to the cabin the single black chain threaded itself into the similarly black suitcase that was cracked open and resting on the passenger seat in a rather uninteresting way. Despite appearances at first glance, the endless quantity of black chain present was pulled into the shallow insides of the business appropriate compartment as if buy unknown reels. Marcus could only stare in an amazement that was harder to find as each and every day tried that particular expression more and more. He watched until he realized that the chain pulling taught was the same one still attached to his neck, link by link, in an obsidian blur.

The metal wall and reinforced windows would probably bruise him pretty badly if Marcus was the type of person to both take note of or care about that kind of information. Instead, he stuck to the small divider wall that he collided with like a dead fly unfortunately caught inside. Eve undid the collar's clip with a simple snap of his fingers and then took it off of his neck himself.

"What was that?" Marcus gasped.

"A bequeath for me," Eve grunted, snapping the suitcase latches shut. "Unfortunately for you, all I can offer is freedom this once."

Uncharacteristically energetic to act in such a lessened lethargy, Eve had calculated in that moment to risk any progress they made in San Anlos in exchange to set Bella right. He had no idea what excursion from the usual job this one was building towards. What he did know was that in the wake of her journey there was only cataclysm and more work to be done. It was a gamble, bet mostly on the gifts lady luck has for beginners. But he made sure not to bother with expending any care to hold his breath for the next decisions. From the short but near complete character profile of Marcus, the belief that the boy would make the right choice in this moment was exactly that, based near completely in faith. His newest business partner, compatriot, and freed man that was Marcus Alvarado fulfilled every disappointingly low expectation set before him and more by failing far greater than previously thought possible, fumbling out the limo door in a bolt towards the fresh trail of Isabella. A straight line was destined for him through the small parking lot of cracked asphalt into the rundown and near abandoned Local Mart entrance like it was the gates to paradise. As for whether the boy was looking forward to heaven or hell Eve could not tell. There was too much of the usual ailment of disappointment to bother with. To some degree, maybe, he could understand the infatuated fool.

In the end of things, he was once again alone.

Stuck in his automotive workspace he had nothing but the minimal necessities to comfort him from his most recent failure. The liquor wasn't for him, but an incentive to keep Bella in one place at a time, as were the luxury seats and furnished cabin. However, Eve made sure the ice was purposefully bountiful.

Alone in his cramped leather seat with ice to chew on and a radio that played mostly static, but sometimes stations. A place only for him. A sound just for his ears. Perhaps because no one else bothered to listen, or maybe perhaps it was because he bothered to listen in the first place.

Indeed it was enough for Eve Luna.

If he was the kind of person to reflect on situations with intention he would have been taken aback to the monotonous monochrome memories of school days when he recited phrase after phrase.

"Ask not the caged dog for its keys to freedom."

Then again, even if he was the type to bother to remember old vintage details so clearly, wasting the energy to listen past the static to echoes, there was little value in doing so. The only lesson actually present would be to point out matter-of-factly that he doubted even a freed dog understood the concept of a key and lock sufficiently, let alone how to manipulate such with its paws to free itself.

So there in the small corner of the universe that he could claim as his own, Eve was. Alone with the only two objects in his life that he needed. Enough to numb himself so the work could go by faster. And maybe in the windows of time in between he could find enough to get a life.

Sometimes the radio picked up stations.

Reliable only every now and then, the radio seemed to catch the echoes of a note, rare enough that it was always the first time in a while. Something original that stuck to the walls of his cage like graffiti. It was music in that way only a voice could be, in the midst of meditations of an infatuated fool. How did it go unnoticed for so long? Embarrassingly so for a Class E individual whose natural inclination for perceptiveness was a baseline and unstated expectation. It was hard to tell within the comfort of his confines that was the driver's seat, but the wind came from the west. Making its way through the branches of trees along the street, only strong enough to send them into a short sway. Cool enough that standing in the shade on such a hot day might be tolerable. With a scent still reminiscent of the salts of the ocean it brought with it scrubbing his brain with sea foam. Dealing in massive extremes a work like his so often demanded diminished the impact and magnitude.

But he could drown in the ocean still.

He was already drowning in a small strip of beach, before having touched water. There was enough energy in Eve's body for one man in his entire, and very long, life. Someone that was his only true necessity. Heart beating against the leather of his own collar. Olive cheeks blushing from the embarrassment of someone as perceptive as he. It wasn't enough to let the sounds graffiti his limo, he needed to paint himself in the shades of voice.

There was love among the yearning, loss, and affection gathered on the radio waves in San Anlos. The familiar voice of Christopher screamed at Eve over the static roar. For Eve, a man who so often thought about the end of things, if he had thought to recount his feelings in that moment he could say it with pride. At that moment he could die happy.

"Get out of the car!" Christopher's voice yelled barely intelligible, but just in time as the explosion of orange engulfed Eve.

CHAPTER 5: ENTER THE HEROES

It was an entanglement of limbs and squeaks from latex suits contorted at angles of all kinds. Obtuse and acute, but not limited to. This, of course, was the precipice of events to occur. Her memory was already a jumbled mess of color palettes. With every new occurrence it seemed to Christina that absurdity was only starting and mounting in size when no end in sight had decided to reveal itself in a readily fashionable fashion. Infancy had yet to divide from maturity for her, so she stumbled around still during the events in which she killed five named individuals.

And just as she would describe in every retelling of the retelling, "It's best to start with the buzzing."

The electric pulsations were constant, like a digital heartbeat within her own skull dampening her entire surroundings with every beat to a worrying degree. Christina might have freaked out rightfully so. However, no signs dictated a need to worry, so she followed accordingly to the lack of instructions. Against her better instincts of course. There she was with an electric pulse in front of the shelves of milk in the near abandoned grocery store. Although she would never risk saying the last part in front of Xiaodan. There she was when the white latex gloves behind the milk reached out, standing still atop the linoleum floor while innocent whites of imaginary lights told her nothing but the letters organized into the single word: ENTER.

Meanwhile, a limousine was inclined to explode, Isabella was stalking the aisles looking for certain groceries of her own, and Marcus was stopped at door with his hand in reach of the handle before something in his chest and not his head told him to go right. More importantly, what could only be described as mysterious appendages lurched forward, pushing the refrigerator door open and heaving Christina inside to the uncanny depth with the clatter of racks of plastic milk gallons disapproval. All in a single swift movement.

Christina let out a yelp before the electric buzz ebbed back into the priority of her focus. Her head hurt more from the pressure swelling within her cranium than from the collision it made with the cold gray floor. Once again her senses weren't her own and she forgot about the world around her, more literally than ever before. It was an icy cubicle of steel, sustained only possible by the microcosm that each grocery store provides within the neat gargantuan sized refrigerated containers. Inside the cold lighting, in communication with everything else about the freezer's aesthetic, offered Christina the chance to view goosebumps sprout vigorously along the surface of her skin. Perhaps it was the drop in temperature in tandem with the tide of wireless headaches that continued to be the prevalent source of her woes, but for the life of her, and throughout the rest of it, she could not place the blame as to why she never bothered to survey neither her left nor right.

For clarity and consistency's sake it was easier to simply admit she was stunned into only complacent observations like always, without the slightest movement from her neck.

All this was to set the stage for the swinging and waiving of not one, but four pairs in total of gloved hands around the peripherals of her vision. Just as Christina began to adjust to the abrupt change in surroundings, enough to realize that she was cold and should certainly be afraid, the dance of her emotions that was morbid curiosity against her better judgment and instinctual fear was short lived. A small buzz now flooded into a river of electricity, running laps between the grooves of her brain and threatened to knock her out, making her question if the possibility of an aneurysm would save her from whatever was about to come. There were no clear directions that made themselves apparent to her where they should have been. The hands continued to wave around the edges of her sight while she struggled to adjust from one shaky knee to the other getting up.

She didn't scream yet. There was no sign in the world that was her script telling her to do so. That's not to say she did not have the urge though. She most certainly wanted to. As the cold refrigerator insides started to fill with the obnoxious rainbow of some kind of chalky colored smoke or gas she fought against the urge to do so. When the distortion in her head reached a climatic level in rise and she fell back down to the support of one knee she did not let out a yelp. When the stupid theme song started to blare she didn't even groan in annoyance.

The crescendo of activity surged with what would normally be the deep rumblings of a drumbeat, but morphed at its core and filtered through the auditory funnel of some kind of torn speaker. The lights began to spasm just like the muscles along her body. Rays pierced through the veil of clouded hues to stab her ocular nerves with the most severity. This is it. She was dead or in the process of. The grim reaper was actually a quartet apparently and in the throes of what she had to assume was death by internal hemorrhaging within her brain there was nothing else but to give into the grace of terror.

The momentum of all these details. The smoke. The sound. The lights. The explosives being set off outside, out of sight but present in the shaking of all buildings along the streetside.

All of it connected to the:

Miraculous.

Superb.

Powerful.

Fantastic.

Wonderful.

Christina was terrified to say the least, as consciousness pulled back out from shore showing the ground underneath it for miles waiting for the tidal wave to come crashing in. But when the waves did not come pounding into the coast of awareness the winds did. Now all that was before her was the grotesque need for attention combined with latex suits, white gloves, matching belts, matching boots, and cheap clunky helmets. Their headpieces were a matching set, like alien twins from another cosmos, but they weren't. They weren't quite identical either, all similar until it was the hue of color.

"Do not fear!" they barked in an upbeat, nearly unified chant, voices reminiscent of a text-to-speech player. The total effect of which was counterproductive to their message. "We are the Suteki Sentai 5."

There were four of them that Christina could count: yellow, pink, blue, and green. All of them stood posed with their arms outstretched in an attempt to create a human star. An attempt only because the bottom left corner point was missing. Their use of appendages with artificial rigidness in addition to their delivery and approach was the exact reason the fight or flight response has remained constant throughout evolution.

"How lame," Christina groaned. Terror subsided and she could finally get up.

To be totally true to vision, they were superheroes of a sort, the kind of Sentai shows she used to obsessively watch as a kid but refused to admit to. You couldn't find these action figures in stores though, let alone their live-action U.S. adaptation on T.V. Their uniforms were true to source material, clunky and seemingly hard to move in with the bends of latex fabric and the lagging justle of their helmets. All of it was colored monochrome except for the whites of gloves, boots, and belts which were all stark in contrast. Even the signature piece of their uniforms wasn't outstanding, the helmets had a generic horizontal strip of visor to see out of, a few flashing lights atop for design, and in place over each mouth was a different cartoonishly drawn on one. They seemed like they were supposed to be child friendly. Their actions said anything but so.

With invasive practices of acoustic, thermal, and standard HD perspectives alike, the members of the rag-tag defense force full of ulterior agendas and so-called justice attempted to ease the angst of emotional hypothermia, as well as the very much possible physical hypothermia, with news and reports of damage.

"Lilac damage total = 53%," Yellow spurted out with misshapen mechanical fuzz through the speakers in its head. "Brent Street damage total = 78%. Peabody Drive damage total = 64%. Total casualties = 0. Total injuries = 1."

Christina might have not recognized the names immediately, but she was aware enough to realize that Suteki Yellow was referring to the roads that made the nearby intersections along the side of the shop. She was especially aware of the last part of the report, but the lights flashing along Suteki Green's helmet interrupted her thoughts before she could dwell for too long.

"Diagnostic Reports," they blurted after a short period. "Suteki Orange Status = offline. Primary: Offensive Measures (EXPLOSIVES) = COMPLETE. Secondary: Evasive efforts = INCOMPLETE. Success rate = 0%. Current target incoming. Repeat. CURRENT TARGET INCOMING." The lines of speech slowly started to fade into a screech-like dial-up that was beyond Christina's years to be accustomed to. So it was uncomfortable to say the least, but the lights flashed along the helmet once again. This time with the voice readjusted in pitch and volume.

"Connection status to Tandem Tantrum Toys and Co. HQ and surveillance systems = down. Current central hub = ROVING TYPE NULL BIOLOGICAL PROCESSING UNIT."

Every string of words that were barely sentences was all, in fact, new information to Christina. She was barely prepared for the one behemoth of a problem that dressed business formal, let alone the leviathan of one that ate cities and poisoned privacy. Only parts of things began to make sense in the familiar words that were rapidly recontextualizing lots of information for her. She recognized the name Isabella Luna, and the brand Tandem Tantrum Toys and Co. It was easy to remember what exactly they sold when the brand logo was in her face and embossed on belts of the Suteki Sentai 5 members that now encircled her and blocked her way out.

"Don't worry," Suteki Pink tried to comfort her, putting their arm on her shoulder which Christina would have shrugged off if given the room. "No one will find us back here. All we need now is an order."

"You're bad at making people stop worrying," she replied.

She couldn't tell if it was possible through the metallic non-expressive form of the cartoon hero's mask, but she thought she made out a pout. All of it was very repulsive to her, and the fact that she knew they were not wrong did not help calm her worries anymore. The only resolve that she had was the deep visceral disgust it brought out from her which was enough to distract from the panic she should have been burdened with.

Refrigerators don't bleed. Yet red was seeping into the floor of the room.

Christina ignored her desire to avoid all contact with these people for long enough to shove her way through the circle and start for the door. The warning signs were apparent again and she had no desire for another outing with calamity like the other night. The name Isabella Luna was enough to tell her to find her grandma and leave. Tandem Tantrum Toys and Co. would just have to be another name she should consider herself lucky enough to know to avoid from now on if she didn't already before. Anything else, she considered herself absolved from the responsibility.

The electrical hum coursing through her body sent trembles that were easily mistaken for bad nerves. Enough to steal her attention for a moment. She forgot about the quartet of heroes standing steps behind her waiting for an order. The other threat she would have forgotten about was nice enough to send a reminder through the walls. The screw eviscerated its way through milk cartons, plexiglass doors, reinforced walls, and all the wiring and wood that went along with it. In an instant, a massive window-sized hole was drilled cleanly behind Christina, the feat letting out a tortured screech of metal along with it as the street exposed itself to her left and the store exposed herself to her right.

Christina was frozen, proper behavior in cold temperatures like refrigerators but not for close calls with death from razor edged projectiles. From inside the store Bella locked her gaze on the single item she came here looking for. The alien invader was yards away, halfway down the aisle, and strutting toward the back wall when she caught sight of colored fumes leaking out and heard muffled theme music. The whole action was a little reckless she had to admit it, but nonetheless, it worked. Bella was reassured enough to wear the self satisfied expression that Christina found far more terrifying than anything else. The terror was most likely amplified when taken into account that the fireballing head of the missing member, Suteki Orange, came falling through the hole.

CHAPTER 6: PARADES AND FESTIVITIES

When gifted with the amputated head of a person, or the impersonation of, it's human nature to recoil in existential dread and terror. This was exactly the crisis in character that Christina would have acted out in all its scenes, sentences, and chapters.

She screamed. Strong enough in those few seconds that the breath wore out in the lungs.

Her only savior in details and evidence was the readily apparent factor that without blood or flesh seeping out the head at her feet was, although certainly humanoid, a mechanical one. The Suteki Sentai 4 quickly rebranded with only Suteki Green, Blue, Yellow, and Pink and commemorated it with their best improvisation to a hat dance. Grossly inappropriate for the occasion as was every other detail in her life at that moment. The onslaught of oddities obscured any prophetic signs of the necessary actions to take.

In short, Christina was lost.

Luckily so were the Suteki Sentai 4, and as advertised on all merchandise boxes for their action figures: '!They speak on their own :)!' Without direction to act, it was up to Suteki Green to offer aid.

"At Central: Should we begin evasive maneuvers?"

It took a moment for Christina to recognize they were addressing her, too preoccupied with the now fire retardant covered head in her hands and thoughts of what possible responsibilities she should now be responsible for. Suteki Orange had enough energy saved up in its shares of batteries within its helmet alone to initiate a fire suppressant action extinguishing the ball of flames that had engulfed it.

"At Central: Leave me. My body is recyclable." Apparently, there was just enough battery power left over to scare Christina as the mangled, but notably chipper, voice cheered. She doubted the validity of that statement but dropped their head instinctively without hesitation. It wasn't her decision that she actually wanted to make, so regardless of her input her feet had already started to bolt in the same direction as the mechanical masked vigilantes. Her priorities had yet to be made, but she knew at the very least that there was no point in looking back through the window of an open hole when she could feel the draft of wind breaking against the titanic presence of Isabella approaching. Christina had yet a reason precisely to be fearful, but more than enough reason to know that she should be.

Isabella watched attentively while she acquainted herself with the rather empty taste of disappointment accumulating at the tip of her tongue. From day to night there was a pleasant smile, in theory at least, that adorned her face. It was stuck on by glue stronger than social convention, masking true intention even now. However, little could truly be done to obscure the compiling hurricane winds underneath as she looked through the window frame of a newly carved hole. Her head sat propped up in her hands, her hair lifted afloat in a weightless manner it tended to do in times like these, all in the same affection as someone would look out the window to view a scene of wilderness before breath is taken away. Only this time Isabella saw no peace, she saw meddling hands of the most artificial variety somewhere between running and prancing away with her intended goal.

Eve pulled up through the fallen aisles and fleeing grocery goers, nearly slumped over the wheel as always, but this time complimenting his depressing aura was the carcass of an automotive beast. Its bones had been stained, charred from ash and burns. Bella could only form a single question between the iron clamped teeth behind her smile.

"Is the puppy dead?"

Eve's heavy sigh was more than enough of an answer. The final gust of wind rolled in required to instigate a storm of tropical categorization.

"Can you drop the humble servant act for a moment."

She talked from a podium comprised of a mountain of forgotten and abandoned school memories obediently in their desk. It was within a monochrome world that only dictated itself between white and the pitch black of shadows. Gray storm clouds circled overhead indistinguishable from the gray sky.

"You, above all else, should know not to discredit me for an idiot," she spat.

"I would be dead otherwise."

She let her eyes size his figure up and down. Now was still too early to do away with that possibility. But regardless, it was not her point. She took away from him, picking her feet among the remnants of an old woman's dream toward the front doors, a step strong enough to send classrooms into havoc within her.

"I don't need your trust."

"But you have it," Eve interrupted pushing open the driver's door only for it to fall off the hinges in a useless heap.

Her breath was drawn sharply with frustration. "What I need is your complacency. And if not that, then the signature apathy."

The sun was still high in the sky beating down on those who were outside the cover of shade like the alien pair. However in the eyes of labor, if she was to waste any more time like this then there was little in her heart of mind that could reasonably say that the rest of the day wouldn't go to waste. Even though the light warmed her skin, it poured color into the leaves of weeds and tree tops, it bounded off from every stone, brick, and wood surface sending the lunchtime world in a glow, hers was of a world regardless. Fixated and focused to a point of contention and peril, she wouldn't turn to her friend because she could not.

"Treat it like a bonus for a job well done Eve," her voice was quiet, making him strain to hear. "You get to finally honeymoon along the coast like you have always wanted. Leave the cultivation of warheads to me." The sounds were effective with the power of floods and mudslides.

Torrential tremors shook the earth, whether within the bleached dream or colors of San Anlos she could not tell.

"Now fetch."

Christina would have felt exhausted, she certainly would have collapsed already, from both the speed and distance covered by her escape among masked comrades. City blocks that she would have recognized as a familiar backdrop to her everyday routines were momentarily immortalized as Death Valleys capable of grounding her to dust from the tremendous force of purely instinctual brute nature. Luckily she was spared from such sentences when she was quick to catch the violent magenta that climbed her legs waiting to rupture her muscles when she tried to keep up with the Suteki Sentai 4, the troop of those who only traveled at constant speeds of an unstoppable caliber. Leaving humanity at the wayside, she chose instead the uncomfortable but smoother ride along the back of Suteki Green, piggyback style. This was the fashion of her evasion until a sudden stop was made at the sight of a certain stranded screw.

Standing propped up by its flat head like a miniature steel monument blocks away from its initial release was a single screw. The only major difference now was that over the course of its aerial pursuit it had expanded in size until it was a minor mountain, roughly the size of a car. Of course, Christina had no discretion of her own as to whether they should have stopped or not. Discretion and discernment had left her to grow up all by herself. No, what the remarkable fact now was that somehow above the electrifying heat slowly vivisecting the lobes of her cerebellum, her occipital lobes still took it upon themselves to view what was not there. The sight of pink hearts and bouquets of roses dressing the group like the entity of Valentines was only a superficial honor before the metal altar of harsh and cruel decisions. More so visible than before, the air itself was stained pink with the smell of hazy Sunday mornings and elementary school dust. Credit went to Suteki Pink who was the source of the only legitimate color present as they dispersed pink smoke from the pellet dispensers along their arms in accordance with Central's fantasies. Among spectral roses she made out the legs of a boy crushed and with Suteki Green's advice in one ear sent out the command to retrieve Marcus from the immense burden.

Once again she had been deaf to her own fears of what bloody sights of the deceased might be buried underneath, even ignoring the signs of danger made apparent to her in metaphysical roses wilting and decaying before her eyes. It was a flash of infantile blue, as the dead corpse of a person lurched forward unaccepted to the fates the laws of nature demanded. Marcus sat upright pale stricken and flesh pulled tightly like he had been dead for ages only to shake it off with beads of thick sweat running down his head. Those were the colors painted in her head of course. Really, Marcus laid there unconscious as a screw had collided with his head.

"Thanks, person." He greeted her more out of social etiquette rather than genuine feelings.

She stayed there in a crouch looking at him. Her eyes focused and intent on his. She knew something important, more so than ever before. There were no signs needed, there were no colors that had to paint out the obvious and hard to perceive for her. She knew she knew something. The only thing was that she didn't know what.

"I know you."

Marcus didn't respond. Idiotic as usual, he sat there waiting for something else to happen until she opened her mouth again.

"Your name. What is it?"

"Errr... it's uh Marcus Alvarado."

"Nope"

"What?" he asked.

"Doesn't ring a bell." She started to get up but kept her eyes focused on him. There was something there though. The pain in her head only worsened and something tugged at her insides when she looked at him. It was only between her legs that Marcus finally caught sight of the vigilante justice that surrounded him, and only in the seconds later that he could actually realize to his best extent what was happening. More importantly, he saw the danger readily available and the exact one he had been chasing, already in an approach. Isabella had set her eyes on them. Blocks away, he could make out the shape of her tall body, and more importantly, he could feel it. The silver reflections of her gaze twisting, distorting, and morphing what was before her.

All of which is to say that it elicited panic. And he liked that for the time being. Christina had blue sneakers, he didn't necessarily like those. However, he did like the fact that when he looked at her he was reminded of tight constrictions choking out his last breaths. Just like now, when the walls were closing in it was harder to breathe. And there was one way to make it worse.

"We need to run."

The joy that Christina held from this man for the mere fact that she did not yet have to listen to herself but to the confidence in another's voice was jubilant.

"That's like a great idea," was all she had to say about it though. The simple words were enough to pierce Marcus in the heart in a way that could only make him fall more in love with the events of today. Never in his life could he imagine such ecstasy.

It was in this manner that Christina would be responsible for more than one death.

CHAPTER 7: SCHEDULED INTERRUPTIONS

"Although I have no white flags I can promise you I come in peace."

It was not quite gun point that Lauren considered herself to be held at, but nonetheless, she decided it best to entertain it as such for the moments sake. A single white glove, bent in the familiar manner of an improvised pistol, was directed right at her face. Point blank really. Far too close for comfort and past the point of personal invasions. That wasn't to say Suteki Green wasn't capable or insistent of violence, but the trace droplets of bloodlust present in their mechanical core was laughable if Lauren had the chance to compare it with the amounts she carried. Truthfully, the roles should have been reversed if anyone knew any better, which they did not. So instead she continued to humor Green, holding her hands above her head in response to the hasty theater stage spotlight of attention that was on her.

Although currently it was scripted for her time to perform, she was more than aware of who the actual stars of the show were if her newly acquired uniform indicated anything at all. Two toned, divided between a blue and purple, her buttoned collar tucked into a black jumper skirt, even her shoes and glasses were newly purchased for a shade of purple that was company suggested and therefore mandated. She had spent all day in the costume beginning the arduous process, much like most things in her life, reinstalling city cameras along traffic lights, rooftops, and more. All this in time to view the theater that was Christina, Marcus, and the business appropriate spacemen. Truly a three ringed circus except for this time the glorious possibility of death wasn't just an option, it was already well recorded with casualties.

Or at least casualties in a loose sense of the word. Technically they were recorded as injuries. Ideas like that of the permanence of consciousness were better tasked to those without hearts to carry out and not her ill-equipped tongue. Lauren felt no joy when she saw the combination of Suteki Pink and the piggybacking Marcus caught at the neck by cold black chains as the pair attempted to escape, but she couldn't manage to pin down any sadness at the spectacle either. Lauren did not smile either. Not even when the infamous Bella, whom she was only hastily briefed on recently, muttered something about not protecting a boyfriend's toys and hurled a football sized screw that reduced the Tandem Tantrum Toys and Co. property into a hail of metal bits and circuitry. Ever since she had donned the inquisitor robes of a corporate experimental storefront retail associate she feared the traces of her personality, and soul for that matter, had slowly been leached out. Having just clocked in for the first time that morning she considered it a fair assessment. It was enough of a viable excuse to ignore any and all responsibility of feelings she should probably have had watching the fatalities through security footage. In truth though, there were always other reasons for apathy and like any functioning individual she did her best to avoid them with her work and worry until she could be buried in the ground, her rotting corpse rendered the only sign she was dying from the inside out at her moment's end.

If Lauren was to be struck down at that moment, possibly from the useless finger gun pointed at her now but more possibly something entirely else, then her venomous mouth that she had so poisoned herself with for years would forever remind people of who she was. Years later it would kill the grass and salt the earth above her grave by proxy. They may not know her name, but they would know to watch their step before her. Luckily, she was spared from such a condition and deserved no easy rest. Instead she stood there taking in her place among the rooftops and was reminded about the blocks and blocks of similar ones that spread for miles. Waiting, freeze framed, for her fellow actor to say their part.

"What are you doing?" Christina asked. She made sure to give ample amount of precautionary room between the two of them to the point she almost had to yell from the opposite side of the roof.

"You're not even going to ask my name first?"

"It's Lauren isn't it."

It was in fact, and the Lauren in question squinted with a keen disapproval in being outdone. The girl must have had good eyes on her to see the nametag from afar. Christina did in fact. Just not the kind Lauren was thinking. The purple brand of identification may as well have been plastered on her forehead for people to read across the street in the eyes of Christina who had such details reiterated to her.

"Stalking," Lauren finally answered.

Tandem Tantrum Toys and Co. required for all employees and store associates to have an adept understanding of lying with at least 10 years of experience. Lauren could never, so instead she had found a work around. Many times she had found her own comfort in not a painless death but in a long, lonely, agonizing, drawn out one. A death that stretched out so far that she was bored of it by the end. So instead of the pins and needles of lies, she chose to fill her sentences with smotherings in frivolity. Empty speech to stall herself and any patient onlookers who didn't have the processing power in each of their heads to realize any better.

"Christina Zheng. Age 18. Height 5 feet 4 inches. Hair color black. Eye color brown." She started on her path toward the girl.

"Hey, you better not mam," Suteki Green shouted. She ignored him.

"You know these reports miss out a lot of details that I would personally like to have. For example, that chin of yours is very pretty and small it makes your jawline sharp but your cheeks puffier don't you think? Would you consider that a positive or a negative? Or take your clothes for example. I think you can tell a lot about a person by the way they dress themselves. You took the time to add layers and even though you have a cropped long sleeve sweater you still have a shirt underneath so that you are more covered than exposed. You don't have any nail polish, nor do you accessorize with jewelry and earrings. I'm guessing you like good clothes but not necessarily anything that would bring attention to you or your body. You have all blue sneakers which aren't easy to come by and nearly match the shade of color in your tee shirt-" she stopped herself sort with a caught breath of fresh realization.

"Is your favorite color blue?"

For the first time she bothered to meet Christina wide eyed gaze only to realize their faces were inches apart.

"Are you angry at me?" Christina whimpered. The domineering woman was glaring down at her, Lauren's eyes were strong enough to break past the constraints of glasses and bore through her opponent. All of which made Christina want to shrivel up into a ball more, but she could not, having been cornered at the rooftop's edge. All she could do in her corner was pray for her heart to not explode from a new kind of panic she had never been gifted the chance to suffer from before.

"My favorite color is blue, that's all. Or at least one of my favorites is blue. I actually have two overall." Lauren looked away and retraced her steps. Suteki Green kept their sight on her, but it was useless in the end. Maybe she was angrier than she thought, she couldn't tell at this point. She wouldn't get the opportunity either.

The roaring spin of helicopter blades broke the moment that would have been awkward silence as none other than Christopher attempted to land the machine.

"You're problematic girl," he yelled over the slowing screech of blades.

The helpless damsel that was Lauren stood there in the distressing position that was far too close to the helicopter and in the targets of Suteki Green, but only for a singular moment more. Christopher walked squarely for his target without the time to entertain antics, giving Suteki Green only enough to raise their arms in defense before the plunger tipped dart stuck to their equal parts helmet, equal parts head, ultimately shutting them down. Frozen in space, all motor functionary units gave up to complete their last movements.

Yet again there was nowhere for Christina to run, so she stood there in gaped mouth shock as Chirstopher showed off his plastic foam dart gun.

"It is microchipped. All it has to do is have the matching identification and be close enough to the local wireless sensors in the Tandem Tantrum Toys and Co. product to verify an override code."

The girl just nodded, open mouth breathing in reasonable exasperation with contemporaries only in goldfish in need of water. The sight of which made Lauren's insides reach a boil to the surprise of herself.

Christina could barely formulate words. "I don't know you," was all she could make although the exact use of this wasn't clear.

"Don't worry we know you," Christopher assured her rather badly. "We are very sorry, but you will have to excuse the lack of formalities today. For the past hours, as you may have guessed, there has been quite the ruckus left in the path of your chase." Christopher stopped and gave him time to drop the customer service act after realizing had just said the word ruckus. He snapped his fingers, which was a small feat with his leather gloves, letting Lauren know to bring out the tablet. When he started up again his voice was more monotone, letting the annoyance of the workload seep in.

"You might be brighter than you look running away from that woman Isabella, more than the other kid at least. In a perfect world, I would have intercepted you en route to reinstalling downed cameras, taken you into company custody, and briefed you on the situation. However, when our perfect null type zero factor reactivated you became a roaming central processing unit. That is to say, your empty cranium took out camera footage and the Suteki Sentai 5 along with you."

"We assumed that they responded to a panicked fight or flight response from the other night and just now escaped to find you." Lauren cut in holding a tablet in her hands that was filled up with the views of street sides, storefronts, and parks all around them. "Recalibrating the Suteki units will have to take more resources, but now that we have you out of Isabella's immediate grasp we can remove you from the equation. The rest should be smooth sailing, especially if we can keep tabs on them like this now."

"What about my grandma?"

"Your grandma will see immediate medical attention if necessary from the local hospital on behalf of company resources," Christopher sputtered out in an automated response.

"No, I mean right now. My grandma is right there," Christina reiterated pointing at the bottom left corner box on the tablet screen.

That's the thing about plans. Contrary to nearly all reports filled out and recorded, plans never go to plan and any hope of a peaceful resolution among the assets they cared about was forsaken with Xiaodan. The two employees turned to look at the reconnected cam footage with incredulous shock, meanwhile Christina watched with a more familiar kind, as Xiaodan hobbled up the grass toward the figure of Isabella in the park. Christina didn't join in the incredulity until she saw the pixels that were her grandma lifting the walker she depended on so much over her head and proceeding to slam into the alien woman.

CHAPTER 8: IN THE DOG PARK

Thunder, lightning, fire, brimstone, gin, tonics, and every other kind of those immediate threats took second priority when in comparison. Although so, it was a pleasant day to enjoy the open bouquets of life that the world had to offer. The sun was still bright enough to melt the poor disposition of any man if he stood under it for too long. Hot enough that the heat could burn through the right of mind senses and one could forget the difference between the equator and the poles. Marcus had begun to comprehend this discovery in thought, although he lacked the luxury of fully comprehending his own comprehension.

As of yet at least.

He sat there at the bottom of a slide that microwaved every cell along his bottom side to the point of fusion with sweat and the plastic playseat. Under the microscope of both sky and attention it was apparent that he was covered in a layer of liquid. The question now was: 'Is Marcus perspiring like sweet tea on a Sunday morning or have his insides been so long forgotten that its condensation of the cold dead is sticking to his skin?' It was a manifestation and dictation as to how his future would occur, and although as much as he would like to insinuate he had full control over his decisions, truthfully he had little input in the process. Marcus' future was, as it had always been, chewed up to a butterlike paste and spat down into his broken beak because he would never grow without so. Still as of yet, he had not reached the point to taste any or all things bitter. Even in the hostage situation of a children's park he managed to have only savored flavorless school halls, sweet afternoon skies, and sour citrus deities in his lifespan.

How he had ended up at the park was a short chapter in its own right. Although like any high energy occasion in life, it was a looming predator one moment and in the next nothing but the outlines of a distant 'once was'. After the brief dehumanizing experience that was saddling up the humanoid Suteki Pink he was ready to escape. As for why he wanted to, he could not really capture that loose reason himself. So when he felt the tight but surprisingly comforting embrace of cool leather against his throat and a familiar clink of alien metal chains like dinner party bondage he really did not mind at all. There was just enough time, although not up to his own discretion, to be pulled away from Suteki Pink as they performed impossible leaps into the air to ultimately watch the humanlike steed explode in a fireless destruction. And with the less comforting embrace of concrete and asphalt he awoke in the most literal play structure that had existed within the proverbial play structure of his life. At the bottom of the slide and possibly by his own volition he sat wrapped up in chains that at one end connected to him and on the other, after all the twist and turns, led up the slide that only rose off the ground a foot or so to the grip of Isabella. But it was not her turn to speak just yet, instead the first voice that came was from Eve who stood more humbled and tired from age not apparent on his face at the bottom of the slide and a step away from the boy. Disappointed as always but this time disappointment had a new tone of voice.

"You should have listened," he grunted out. "First and foremost, you're a stray and I can only let you run away once."

It was his job after all to tie things down, pin them in place, and to bound and gag everyone and everything if need came to be. And need often came to be.

"Hey Marcus," he crouched with his knees popping from exhaustion to reach the boy before him and make sure the specimen could hear well while hoping that his coworker might not. "You know, I get the allure of fireworks. I'm not above the excitement of spectacle and dreams too. But for all my many years of the work and spectacle I have had front row seats to, I never really understood one thing. Why do you want to run to oppressive arms rather than caring ones?"

It's the question he asked when he saw Marcus running back to Isabella's vicinity, and the same one when he caught sight of the duo running with corporate escorts. They never run far enough. No that wasn't quite right. They never know when to give the run up. It's the morning routine of a vial of poison with your breakfast. So when the time comes for you to enter the viper's den your ready to make multiple trips. It's the repetition of a single plotline along your pages to make up the entirety of your story. So that by the end of your years and the culmination of the story it's just a single day. It's not a race towards destruction or perfection, but the race itself that bursts your muscles from exhaustion.

"It's the reason why your heart has been buried and the sole factor as to why that man has become a reservoir of everything that you are not."

Isabella couldn't even find it in herself to glare at the man, no matter how infuriating his stupidity was. Instead, she looked at him with an unfamiliar pity which translated to a condescending glance regardless of her intentions. Eve stood up with a sigh, regretting his decision to speak if it meant she felt compelled to add her input.

"It's the reason we sweat," she continued. Of course her thoughts and words weren't strong enough to bend metal or minds, all it was good for was tired muscles and a fever pitch of

STCKR: platonic panic - 149

hot blood that seared her frontal lobe with harsh reminders as to her existence.

"The sticker is important."

She directed her words at Marcus now as she began to wound the chains with her left hand, bringing her prey closer at such an agonizingly slow pace she could torture slugs. Since their first meeting Isabella finally gave Marcus the long overdue, but not without purpose, courtesy of an explanation. Indeed the sticker was important. With her right hand she pushed her hair aside and framed the backside of her neck. More precisely she directed Marcus' attention to the 3 inch vertical slit in the middle of it. A literal fracture in the monolith that was her character, and with two fingers she procured a thin piece of paper from it.

A sticker to be exact. Depicting three dog heads connected at the neck and all almost identical to any mental images of a famous greek hell beast. Indentical except for the top of their heads that were fused with unaccommodatingly large yellow bells and bows, the fact that the breed looked like a more amiable labrador puppy, and finally the fact that the entire pup was colored strawberry red.

"The sticker is important because upon immediate introduction into foreign bodies it reacts with the makeup of sample organisms for express cultivation of resources. There is a science to it that is far beyond you right now, but just know this: the combination must be right. Consider it like hormones but far, far, far more consequential to your existence. And when the balance is correct a connection is established allowing for communication with the specimen's subconscious mind and the required metamorphosis to occur. Isolated biological creation. For easy and ready weaponization. Marcus, with my specific capabilities my function is to create the cores for warheads through the synthesis of samples. Small orbs with enough energy to open up planets. I go planet to planet and find two samples to synthesize. And if there is collateral damage it's not my job to worry. From you though, I need something more."

She spoke the lines like they were rehearsed and rehashed over countless reitterations. Marcus would never notice it, however. The sweating was not caused from the heat of the day, but from nervousness. Any desperate glances were devoid of the aid of a benevolent god, but he knew better than to expect that. His modern baptism only was instead interrupted by the intrusion of a wildfire that refused to burn out. One that was filled with enough justified anger and resentment that in the course of minutes her body coursed with a strength she forgot she had. Strength enough to lift her walker over her head.

Grandma Xiaodan, with more to lose than to gain but through a brashness that only came from the rightful confidence, breathed her dragon breath in the sense that she used her walker to deck Bella.

CHAPTER 9: TEMPORARY GAZES

"Your grandma is dead," Christopher blurted. A statement that only attracted wide eyed terror from Christina and a swift slap from the hand of Lauren.

"Don't say that you idiot." she hissed. The old woman wasn't dead. Not yet at least, but if she pointed that out now the girl next to her just might fall apart.

There were currently three pairs of eyes watching events unfold through security monitor feeds brought through to the tablet in Lauren's hands. Information translated to pixels and filtered through avenues of means only possible to Tandem Tantrum Toys and Co. Six eyes and one set of high resolution panoramic visual sensors to be exact. However, the mechanically inclined beheaded individual was officially considered dead at this point in official reports as power had been all but terminated with a lack of a sustainable fuel source. The rooftop meeting watched with an intense scrutiny, interpreting the abstract bundles of pixels as multi-dimensional masterpieces as each viewer was imparted with their own personalized and ultimately subjective takeaway. Each of them watched with both satisfaction clouded in guilt and fear that stuck to their skin like prickly thorns. A feeble aged grandma of long past achievements had just achieved a feat that had either been dreamed about or instinctively done so without knowing.

The death of a dangerous red sun, the sentence for the crime of ending peaceful nights, the torture for a long distance relationship that would span galaxies. But more importantly, they wanted to know if they were about to see Ms. Xiaodan achieve the fruits of her labor in bitter tasting consequences, whatever form that may be. Something from beyond the feats of any of their imaginations and dreams happened in place of. In stark contrast to the elusive dreams of the night that escaped the grasp of memory in the subconsciousness of sleep, one such fantasy occurred before them and emblazoned itself into their memories. It started in the swirls and curls of hairs that writhed like a sea of pythons as the figure of Isabella arose from her fall. But instead of the expected world altering calamity, the fire made human that was Xiaodan was greeted with a different kind of execution. The disarmament of a warm embrace that was so tight and strong enough to smother the dragon's breath within her leaving only a homely fire of family left.

As much as Isabella hated the phrase, the stars had truly aligned for her in that moment.

"You are the greatest kind of change in this world," she whispered into the ear of the old lady with unprovoked but earned earnestness. Eve was a man of many reservations. It was a fact molded into the very fabric of his personage as a Class E individual. He made concessions in his life as he was so adamantly instructed to do so. One of these was to pick up after Bella's messes, just as he did now catching the loose sticker fluttering through the air.

"I told you, Marcus. I don't let strays escape twice. Just promise me you can finish a task when it's given to you."

No matter, what they still had a job to do and a product to create. His gamble was a failure, and the end result would have to be the usual kind of product as all the others. He would find a way to finish the task today as he had always done so before, even if it had to go against Isabella's new desire for rebellion. He was a Class E individual with an apathetic predisposition and a responsibility to catch and restrain strays with no master, something Marcus had more than proven to be and something

Isabella was beginning to hint at. If the job required it then he could live up to his name for the day at least. The insides of his suitcase rumbled with eager chains.

"Wait Eve," Isabella called out. "Give me just enough time to give grandma here a seat."

"Where is Christina?" Xiaodan demanded while taking Isabella's hand to lean on as they took careful time stepping off from the low playstructure. Her walker was a yard or two away, too far to reach at the moment giving no other option but to graciously accept the assistance available.

"I'm not sure exactly. Hopefully coming to pick you up, but if she was smart then listening to orders and running away." In truth, all she had was the gamble that Tandem Tantrum Toys and Co. work ethic was as productive as it bragged and touted itself to be. If there was no audience on the other side of camera screens to watch the spectacle before them then the day might as well have been ruined.

"People with good sense don't need to be told what to do," Xiaodan interjected.

"I couldn't agree more mam." Titanic presences truly did encompass all other precedence. Isabella couldn't help but smile and the words and hold onto the lady tighter with care. Perhaps the day wouldn't go to waste in the end. "Are you hot? Can I get you a drink?"

Marcus watched in silence, letting only his eyes follow along as the unfamiliarly kind woman doted on the equally unfamiliar old lady before him. Even he himself had forgotten about the terror and panic of his predicament for a moment or so, and he wasn't alone.

"We have a job to finish," Eve reminded.

"Then finish it Eve," Isabella snapped. "Try to listening to your elders more often."

"I'm older than you."

"Smart people don't need to be told what to do," she repeated over her shoulder before continuing on her way with Xiaodan toward the nearest park bench without looking his way. "Look at how domesticated and docile you have become in nature. If anyone ordered it, you would roll over and expose your belly to let it be opened. Without hesitation you let yourself be gutted." She took her place at the metal picnic table rightfully next to her contemporary in confidence, finally exerting the effort to grimace in agreement with the complex frustration she had for her coworker across the way. "I have no qualms with the choice in how to live and die, but you could at least try to choose who you want to be gutted by."

The chains rampaged in their black suitcase. The leather handle fought hard against the grip of his hands rubbing against his palm until the skin was near raw.

"Don't add another job to my list. Let me finish with this so I don't have to finish with you after." His voice was soft and firm, fighting against everything else bubbling inside him to find a composure in communication. Nonetheless, the emotion seeped in through the cracks dipping the punctuations in love strewn animosity. His heart was beating faster in his chest than the metal links in his case. For a while, extending far beyond this day, he had been stuck in a discolored box where the sound of static drowned out both him and his memories of gray school desks. In truth, his steel coffin was buried far deeper than he had considered.

He bit his bottom lip in frustration. The sound of his pulse bounced off against the leather collar and sent shockwaves through his body.

A thought had occurred to him the other day. Isabella would undoubtedly die for him, but she would most certainly die for herself before that. She was whipped, they all were, but among the hallways and classrooms, she hadn't lost her bite.

"You sweating," Xiaodan pointed out from afar.

"Just whose side are you on?" he asked. His mind was already made, but he didn't like the answer. It was decided enough that it showed up in the corners of his mouth.

"I'm sorry Marcus, but my love might be enough to destroy me."

Bare your fangs. Class E is meant to capture and restrain the unwieldy lest you develop the taste for such.

"I think I would be able to roll over for Isabella, but I would prefer it if Christopher was the one who demanded it." He added the sentence while looking directly into the lens of the obscured cameras surrounding the park.

All this while happened while placing the sticker delicately on Marcus' forehead, who was all but forgotten in the commotion of things, barely visible in the clear atmosphere of the bright and sunny day. Six eyes watched as Marcus' forehead, which was sweating enough ammunition to supply a war of attrition, was filled with the picture of canines and bells. Only a second was needed for a red bubble to engulf him, starting at his head and swelling to a size that rivaled the storefronts across the street. Then in the seconds following the strawberry bubble burst at its apex with an explosive pop.

That was the point Lauren had stopped watching, not for a lack of interest, but because the updraft of wind destroyed all cameras local to the area. Christopher's attention was still hung up on Eve, evident enough from his dreamy eyes and bloody nose. Christina had stopped watching since the start with the impossible sight that was her grandma and Bella embracing. Right now there was a wall being built on the foundation of her forehead for the sole purpose of impeding her thought, and in a manner that she had always done but refused to think about.

There was a silence, but it was cut to pieces by a single tongue lacking all the delicacy and precision of a surgeon, instead unsheathed for the first time and handled in a way only capable of decapitation and dismemberment of its opponents. It was a sharp blade indeed, but not the weapon needed for the current scenario that they found themselves in, or at least not the one needed for any benevolent outcomes. Present moments have made the rooftop party intimately flabbergasted. The group of heads previously bustling in for good view had all but dispersed in strides. Christopher had all but passed out from the possible hemorrhaging indicated by the massive blood loss leaking from his nose, leaving him sprawled out and clutching his heart because he only felt in extremes. Suteki Greens' body was frozen in place and deactivated. The incapable gaze of Christina looked out over the city completely dumbfounded, mostly for a lack of trying. And Lauren had discovered both a rot in her heart credited to the many imbeciles she had surrounded herself with and that there was no more patience for her own patience. It was a time for offensive measures and although it pained her deeply to admit, her words that were strong enough to slay a beast would have no effect on one of the more literal and instinctual kind. Swords needed to be drawn even if not held by her hands, so she used the only saber that they had. Knowing full well she was in no position to call in the order she made the call: "BEGIN THE GOLIATH INITIATIVE."

CHAPTER 10: CRASHES AND HANG UPS

The shrieks of seagulls filled the small city blocks containing the many vibrations of air as each competed with one another for the prestige of being heard. Glimpses of a black helicopter could be made out between the breaks in the amorphous flock of white wings and feathers as the birds made a mass exodus to the far outlands of rooftops to scavenge for another day. It would take what felt like to be agonizingly long minutes before Christopher could successfully steer the helicopter through the avian frenzy although passengers would assume that a route through such rapids was, in part, a fault of its own. Such suspicions were not entirely false as the now drenched and crusted blood along Christopher's lips, chin, and shirt was evidence enough that his frontal lobe and trenches of critical thought were in much need of necessary transfusions. By the time the company of Lauren, Christina, and Suteki Greens' barely functioning head had breached the boundary of birds into midtown San Anlos, brittle petals of dried red blood had begun to flake off from the battering wind and quick erosion. The process sent petals of it aloft in the air trailing behind their procession of black screeching metal. Deconstructed flowers of human nutrients broke apart, caught in the whirlwind of the guillotine that was the helicopter blades only to explode on impact into speckled particles freckling the blue sky behind them. Contrary to popular belief held by the three passengers at the time, Christopher was not inhibited by a lack of blood. In stark contrast to his height, his body was actually built like an ox. Instead, infatuation made him succumb to his wounds. Infatuation of the highest caliber had enveloped his entire processes.

"They are going to crash aren't they?" From his vatange point, Eve wondered if Christopher was purposely interested in coming hurtling towards the Earth in the first place. For the conscience and perspective of everyone else they would have to chalk up the collision course between the ground and the hulking mass of metal as an act of malicious compliance on behalf of Marcus' three hounds. Each of the heads sniffed the airborne vehicle with interest, nearly headbutting it with golden bells attached to their heads.

Eve had both a gift and a crush for the self-destructive man behind the wheel. A flower, laid out in the pattern made up on the chains that spread out from his suitcase like old regrets entangling and entrapping the three passengers screaming for fear. Caught midair across the street from the park and only a few inches from both the empty office space and sidewalk that it was destined to collide with, the helicopter came to a halt in the web of chains. From the view afar it looked like the links intersected in the right order to make out the shape of a flower underneath the machine and its occupants.

Christopher had also been screaming along with his passengers, but for joy in place of fear. His excited figure exited first before they had reached a complete stop, leaping far enough to bridge the divide of asphalt between them and aiming straight for his target within the park. Eve stepped forward with his chest fortunate enough to be greeted by the high velocity of a pale freckled face and the outstretched arms that belonged to it. He was knocked down by force only for his tall lanky body to be held up by the small Christopher.

"Once again I am reminded about how freakishly strong you are short man," he grunted through the rather tight squeeze of the hug.

"Don't act like you could forget about me giant," Christopher teased.

Lauren was the second to exit with a graceful drop and exercising caution not to speak with any glances of mild interest at the inordinate amount of kisses being shared between the two men, already wondering if company policy sanctioned such relationships. Her immediate attention was more transfixed on the parlor-like atmosphere presented before her through the medium of playing cards, wads of cash, piles of coins, and iced tea along the picnic table under an umbrella. Christopher and Eve had already taken to sitting next to each other and Isabella sat across from Ms. Xiaodan whom she was locked in a game of cards with. Xiaodan looked rather disinterested while she drank her iced tea and won, but focused on playing nonetheless. Lauren was taken aback by the sudden armistice and halted by the idea of loving an enemy. The idea someone could be playing games with a despotic invader perturbed her for some reason. Past days and hours behind her had come to a crashing stop, mixing together from their very own momentum. It didn't feel like a sort of progress anymore, but more like her life had fallen out of line from the usual parade of events. Everything was far more distant and vaguely remembered through the dusty haze of nostalgia, scary only because of how easily the framing can shift. Before her was lounging and lethargy by the people that had achieved more than she ever thought a person was capable of achieving. Large beads of sweat came down from people and drinks alike in a familiar surrender.

Tea was bitter and unsweetened, she feared any weaponized words would be soon regretted.

"It's a balancing act," Christopher pointed. "We're really just teetering on the edge with both ends falling towards some kind of destruction. Isabella and Eve over here would just destroy the city if it meant they could finish their work but, on the other hand, if any of my reports were accurate then corporate executives would have nuked the town into an inaccuracy on the maps." Eve only nodded affirmation at the words and continued to let Christopher lean against him and escape the sun.

It wasn't a treaty in the usual sense. Weapons were always drawn at each other's throats, but if they each had the same true intention then it was a treaty in the end. There really wasn't room for much else but love and destruction within the city limits, yet with enough combinations it brought such a vibrance that no one minded the perpetual cycle. San Anlos was, after all, a stomach. One they resided in as it continued to consume the panoply of food that was itself.

Of course, there were those that were not full yet. There were those who wanted to cut open the creature's insides to expose the options and decide for themselves their diet. Before any of that could be achieved Christina had to first overcome her inability to truly perceive. She was the last to leave the helicopter in a tumble. She was the only one to never make it to the picnic and games.

The eager gaze of six puppy eyes that belonged to a cerberus once named Marcus came bounding towards her. In the same moment, the calls of Suteki Yellow and Blue rang forward as they caught up with Central, no doubt straining their sound systems asking for their next orders. The sudden movement and sound of which elicited the monolithic paw of an easily flabbergasted dog to crush the two highly functioning androids into non-functioning tinfoil. Christopher and Lauren both made a note of the future expenditures it would entail.

Two more deaths, weights of which pulled Christina down and condensed along her forehead. She could feel it now. She had felt it ever since the start of the parade that was today. She might have even felt it earlier in life, but ignored the burden of such because no one else had told her to notice.

A mental block.

She couldn't ignore it now. Colors the same as her fleshy body and tone of her skin failed to spell out what was just out of sight, but regardless it persisted.

"Our consciousness is algorithmic and infinite. Use our bodies."

The mechanical voice of Suteki Green fluctuated and echoed as their head fell out of the helicopter and bounced against the cement sidewalk.

She staggered, her mental image of a brick was left for no one else to visualize or discover but herself. It siphoned off the nutrients tugging at her forehead skin while remaining incorporeal and nonexistent.

Three heads with cocked ears waited patiently for a command while five more watched intensively to see. All eyes focused on her single figure.

"Stop it," she gasped

It was unfair.

"Don't look at me like that now. Not here. Not today."

Each gaze was a nail that was absolutely useless. Who were they to look at her when she barely recognized their faces without aid? It was hypocritical to care when all she ever had cared for before was the color she painted over them with.

"It's not fair. It's not fair. It's not fair. It's not fair. It's not fair." Her breaths were frantic, but she stood there completely still, unable to calm herself. Completely incapacitated in her panic.

If they kept glaring like bright lights toward her she just might catch a glimpse of herself. And the thought was enough to penetrate her block.

"Don't..." Her voice quivered at a whisper as she took a step back. "Don't ask me anymore. Don't look at me anymore. Don't wait for me anymore." With every second the frustration rose as it overtook her fear until she was screaming at no one in particular.

"Don't listen to me!"

Her plea was strong enough to snap her body in two letting the strings of her voice break along with it. The responses were many but the first was a hum in her head and the murmur of not quite natural voices.

"At Central: order confirmed."

And the dead rose.

CHAPTER 11: REGULAR PROGRAMMING

Any and every Pacific coast resident could recite on demand, or at least hopefully, the necessary precautions to take place in the event of an earthquake. All of which essentially boiled down to the rather unhelpful idea of 'hold on and get out of the way'. With residency along the eloquently named Ring of Fire, the Pacific plate made sure to remind of the great possibility of quakes that forever hung in the air of possibility. Equipped with this prolonged fear and common sense, for many citizens of San Anlos the idea of the earth breaking open and swallowing the city whole into a chasm of mantle and crust was one to be waited for until fruition. Especially on the late September day that it was.

Indeed the earth had many tremors coursing through its veins, but the resounding state of fear produced had transpired from two sources in particular. The first of which was surprisingly Christina Zheng, or at least it was a response to her actions. Fallen bodies of mechanical beings followed her path throughout the city and, although temporarily categorized as deceased in reports to Tandem Tantrum Toys and Co. they were, in fact, not. Limbs. Heads. Torsos. The Suteki Sentai 5 had once again found a purpose strong enough for reanimation as they slowly blinked to life in a dismembered manner with turbines and thrusters.

City streets and entire blocks of background were mutilated into a distorted blur as the body parts pierced through the air, weaving with harsh turns around buildings, cars, and corners leaving smoke and a burned trail to mark their paths. From every direction extremities were en route to their central location, sending tremors to echo their travel throughout the earth in the process.

Only two employees at the lunch table had the luxury of knowing what exactly was occurring. Christopher was once again astounded by the perfect null type 0 unit of a person that stood far before them all.

"She really does have an empty brain doesn't she?" he noted admiringly.

Ms. Xiaodan unsuccessfully held back her condescending laughter that came with wisdom regardless of age.

"My grandchild might be quiet, but she is not thoughtless. The opposite in fact." Her smile was replaced with concern in her eyes as she looked on at the girl. "There is too much going on in that head of her's that the great feat that is avoiding the world is her second nature."

Christina was water, streaming through the day, reading people. She was, for all intents and purposes, the most successful underachiever. The scientific question of most concern now was: what would happen when the titular underachiever was given no escape route and forced to succeed? The picnic table had become front row seats to the programming of the century.

Christina stumbled her way around the street clawing at her brain that was now in fact heating up like a microwave. She fell forward with an arm outstretched and caught herself 100 feet above the ground with a gigantic robot arm holding herself up in place of her own. All in time to defend her flesh body with a large metal one against the now feral red cerberus launching itself on top of her.

The second source of the tremors had been the stray Marcus. Truthfully, he had originally been very loyal to Christina whether anyone had bothered to notice or not. He was waiting patiently for a command from her like any well trained dog would, but a whipped dog can only stay docile for so long and he had already been hurt by three masters now. The latter happening was only very recently with people he had just come into acquaintance with. Yet their strikes had been enough to compound and tear open scars from his first. It was enough to make his paws thrash and the seismic bells shake the earth in frustration.

The entirety of midtown was now made the backdrop to a Saturday morning cartoon complete with superheroes, their massively irresponsible mecha suit, and an equally enormous foe monster that was waiting to be slain. A take repeated from ancient history and now to children's entertainment. The beast must be slain by the end of the half hour, this was no special feature after all. The heroes in this instance were in no deficit of the necessary theatrics for the scenario. Fireworks and the boastful signature theme music shot and and emmitted from Christina's battle mecha, the decision completely out of her control and against her volition. The suit of armor made up of the unfolded and stretched metal of the Suteki Sentai 5 lurched forward crushing cars, trees, and light poles alike. The right blocky arm was colored orange, the left with a yellow paint job. For its legs, the left was blue and the other one currently squeezing an SUV against the road was colored pink. Finally, there was the green humanoid head with a stern metallic human-like face and star shaped helmet on top to communicate with the rest of the body and distribute orders made by Christina, who was the current white center square chest piece. From deep within she looked out at San Anlos through a panoramic projection encircling her like a bubble, surrounded by holographic sensors, buttons, and levers.

The battle was on.

Although her head was hot she would have to manage if she had fans to impress. The last part might have been more of the robot's ideas than hers, but she didn't bother to waste the time to decide. The gold belled cerberus was already charging towards her with its tail up and its three heads competing against the momentum of the body. Its fangs were bared and looked more than strong enough to pierce metal. Christina wouldn't have to wait to find out. Her blue leg equipped with speakers ready to burst eardrums swung forward with a cartoonish sonic boost intercepting the dog midrun and sending it colliding with a nearby apartment building, crushing the walls underneath its weight and force. She didn't let up. The dog was barely getting up shaking off the confusion and rubble when a high concentration energy beam of light contacted against its ribs. The laser beamed out from the yellow arm pouring a constant hard light concentration from its canon fixture. Even with its claws burrowed deep into the ground tearing the city floor to reveal the dirt underneath the mutt couldn't fend against the onslaught. The red hound lost its footing, slowly at first, but then with such force that it was flung backward and was pinned against a nearby parking structure, a hole melting through its gelatinous ribs and chest.

"Should we be worried about Marcus?" Lauren asked while watching the show with slight horror and amazement.

"If there is anyone you should be worried about it's Christina," Isabella answered.

Eve squinted trying to make out more detail from the creature that was now afar. "With the stellar infusion, even if Marcus' body was somehow struck within the slimy mess his actual flesh is just as virtually indestructible."

Isabella nodded in agreement. "That being said I would prefer if his body sustained the least amount of damage possible." The strawberry colored creature's surface was frosted and opaque this time, but she had to guess Marcus' actual body was somewhere in one of the three disputing heads.

In the midst of the terror, the far left mutt's head seemed to strain its neck in a desire to turn tail and run. Similarly, the opposite end hung its head down at a depressing low and pouted. The only actual aggressor was the middle face, snarled and ready to froth at the mouth with ferocity. Anyone of these massive craniums could be holding the probably unconscious Marcus and Bella desperately wanted to know which one he belonged to.

Against the parking structure, the hell pup had found a way to scale the wall escaping the diminishing energy of the hard light concentration cannon. Once atop, it collided its three heads together with a deafening roar. The soundwaves surged through the metal bells and outwards reverberating off of every surface. Christina's virtual display went into a fritz eliciting profanities as she tried to make out the red hide among the manic pixels. The most she could do was fire missiles from her orange arm projectile launcher as the cerberus ran in large circles around her. Each of the explosive fireworks collided with buildings and surface streets instead, taking up several moments among the impact before she was able to realize its ineffectualness. That single moment of hesitation was opportunity enough. With an abrupt change of pace the monster ran straight toward her.

There was just enough time for a wager.

"I'm all in on Christina not winning this one," Isabella bet, dropping piles of strange alien coins onto the table.

The massive actors collided far above, knocking the robot down and pinning it to the city street. A yellow metallic arm impacted with the park's sidewalk directly before the group, kicking up a storm of dust, concrete, and dirt leaving a crater and the party suspended over it. Isabella's side of the table was singled out as the only remainder located firmly on the earth and not above the pit. However, it also remained leveled with her fingers interlocked with the table's metal wire holes gripping the entire gamble into place with ease regardless of what gravity demanded of the group. Christopher held onto Eve who remained still and unbothered by the sudden change in seating. Lauren gripped her seat for safety. Grandma Xiaodan sat secured by Bella's charity and dropped her entire wallet into the pot.

"Easy money."

CHAPTER 12: RAINDROPS AND RAINBOWS

Laundromat lethargy and depression, like the inclination that there is something in life that is being missed. Even if not major, it's an adventure not ventured. A taste not experienced. A color that is not seen. More missed because of the inattentiveness required to do so rather than the fact that it has been misplaced. The otherwise inability to recognize that something has been forgotten is only a dearly does of laudanum to be mixed in with the memories of a coffee. When all options have ceded it is easiest in nature to fill up one empty space with things that corrode and kill.

Christina had been swung with such force to knock her from the holographic suspension and over to the walls of what she thought was otherwise an empty and expansive space. There wasn't any light in the small pocket of the world that was inside the giant armored robot's chest. The view of San Anlos midtown was gone and encompassing all flanks was an imperceivable depth of blackness. For a moment the very understandable fear of being entrapped inside started to creep up on her, but the splash of water and a newly unfamiliar touch of raindrops was enough to bring her out of the depths.

She didn't have the luxury to blink before her surroundings themselves blinked to life with white color. Standing up she discovered that it was not a horizonless expanse around her but rather the finite spread of a single block that she found herself in. Complete with white walls on every side and illuminated by no discernable light source. There was no doubt in her mind that she had not left the robot. Before her was a portrait that existed only within the deepest innards of her person. Christina was right in her assumption about the condensation.

There was a downpour frozen not by conventional means, but trapped in space from a lack of explanation on behalf of linear time. Within the pale block there were few things to look at and even fewer distractions for her attention to ignore what was in front of her.

Between the suspended drops of water and across the still pond that was the floor, in the center of the room it sat. A white wooden chair. It was a throne in the sense that it was designated only for someone. A person not of the highest honor but it's inverse. Her mother had tainted countless memories of gray mornings in her melancholic bliss from that seat alone in the corner of the kitchen. Derelict. Out of the way, but not out of reach, so every passerby could be reminded of her failings and then be painted with the color of a child's ocean tainted by the crime of a lack of intervention.

Christina knew exactly why it was her place. Her eyelids were tugged by a tired familiarity beholden to years beyond her that was unbeknownst to many. Behind every single memory was a cardinal sin detested by none other than herself, that to sit in that chair was a fate worse than to drown. A child's tale she forgot that stood only to be remembered with the pompous retrospect of an older adolescent, one fault of understanding only in a new form. Crossing the glass water that stood firm under her feet with each step, only soft rolling ripples fluttered along the surface as a sign of the movement. She made it to the seat, paying no heed to the green buds of flowers out of reach beneath the water's surface.

It was a sour fact to accept. That she was a culmination of what came before. In the end, she would take after the woman that made the trees ache and bend with mourning. That left the sky to wrap itself in forgetful grays. Whose house was stuck in a perpetual morning. A particular morning. One where the music had stopped so as not to disturb her. It was a dark outcome of this block and Christina wanted to laugh and cry at the notion that it could have been any different because of her. There was a string inside her neck pulled taught to the point that she was ready for it to snap and the supports of her body to give out, letting her person crumple into herself.

The seat was left for no one to take but her. The downpour would continue. The flowers would bloom blue.

"Our consciousness is infinite, but our bodies are limited."

The room's walls shook from the force of Marcus' onslaught outside.

"A command is still a command." Tones almost familiar, but not quite spoke in the unseen. "Stasis would be rejection."

She had only just sat down in her throne when five particularly monochromatic and metallic bodies rose to the surface of the pond with the proper grandiose theme song interrupting the pitter patter of now falling rain.

"Life measured by what is broken and life measured by what is given." The Suteki Sentai 5 spoke without moving from the spots.

"Don't say what I think you're going to say," she responded.

She knew exactly what it was going to be. No reiteration from unnatural colors was needed for the bright and obvious nature of the group. They were five consciousnesses that would probably follow her to whatever end that she decided on, whether for the better or worst.

"What is your command?"

That was the thing exactly. There was no command she wanted to give. If there was one thing she had decided on it was that she had never in her life wanted to have to order these vigilante heroes around. If there were two things she decided on it was that, plus the addition of never wanting to sit in the chair she now sat in. If there were three things it was all the prior then, as well as never wanting to put Xiaodan in harm's way. But all those wants have failed and were struck down. Her only monuments to agency remained useless and incapacitated, the agents acting as such near dead before her.

But if that was the case, then the answer was obvious.

Christina was a smart girl.

"So it's clear then."

So smart it made her standoffish.

"If there is a fight I am willing to lose then it's not this one."

So standoffish it made her dumb.

"Don't give me responsibility that I won't let myself be held responsible for."

She stood up and glared at the useless bunch before her. There were so many eyes outside watching her, but only the two set ablaze did she care about. There were so many battles she had lost that day, but only one did she feel guilty for. And never again did she want to. It was annoying, tiring, and lethargy inducing, but if it had to be done it had better be done so she could rid herself of this engagement. Approached with the plain blue that she nearly drowned in there was only one conclusion that she could reach.

"Blue is not my color."

Approached with no other option than steak one must turn into a carnivore. Each of Marcus' heads had made an unspoken agreement in ferocity as the influence of the aggressive one infected the outside two like a contagion. Tearing and biting at the metal panel of the giant mecha with fervent desire, its vision had become concise and singular towards ripping the thing apart. More importantly, it had become aware of the tools equipped to achieve such. Fangs and claws were rampant without consideration or hesitation of such.

Ms. Xiaodan watched with a stone faced expression painted on by certainty one could only have identified as a farce from the grip of her closed fist. Isabella watched both grandma and the fight with salacious content, eager to discover if she was correct in her predictions.

"If it's for mama Xiaodan then I care about it," she whispered to herself. "I know that at least."

Christina was already running from across the pond brandishing the white wooden chair she held at its backrest. She ran full force towards the opposite wall only to stop and fling the furniture with all her might, which was just enough to probably overextend her shoulder. She did not know what to expect from it, but it was most definitely not for all sides of the room to crumble under the slightest touch of the chair. In that instant a burden of weight consistently present was disconnected.

The three jaws of the hound had gotten a firm hold on the white chest and were ready to compete for the opportunity of consumption. It was a gust of wind that was the first signal, flinging out from the machine and through the town like an unspiraling twister. Years of exhaust were now physical from the spins of turbines. Then the boisterous theme music and colored fireworks shot into the sky to explode in bouquets of pyrotechnics. Marcus yelped in pain without an inclination as to how fast the movement was. Without time to realize what was happening the red hound was held aloft in the air, cleanly pierced by a rainbow saber.

Christina had reached a complete 100% synch and detached the colored blade from within the machine's back. The air was electric with energy and the echoes of a tired but strong resolve were even felt by the simple braindead beast. The strawberry monster roared and thrashed, sunlight bouncing off its skin, globules of escaping red goo causing itself to slide down the blade, making Christina lower her sword to avoid being crushed. The freed dog quickly found the energy to lunge at its opponent. A move easily dodged by the mecha as it slid under, slicing open the belly of the beast. Before there was time for the animal to recuperate Christina was readying her thrust, building up a sonic pulse at her feet. Trees and cars alike were uprooted and tossed as she zoomed forward bursting through the sound barrier to cleanly slice off the dog's far right head. Strawberry blood sprayed the empty sidewalk painting the nearby brick building in jam.

Turning herself around and preparing for another strike, Christina was ready to see two heads roll next. Instead, she was greeted by a chorus of bells that sent her mechanics into a worry. However, the trick wouldn't work twice. Before the cerberus could turn tail she managed to glide a kick upwards through the air and strike the middle head away from its partner, stopping the onslaught of soundwaves and sending the dog low to the ground, centering its gravity with a crouch. That single chance was enough. Jumping high into the sky and obscuring the sun she plunged her sword with enough force straight into the left head. Before she could finish landing the creature's skull exploded into red paste.

Defeated and now melting into puddles at a rapid pace, there was nothing left to be done but a final execution. A panting dog looked up at the swing of a downward rainbow saber.

The single human hand of Marcus caught it.

Having absorbed all remnants of the massive beast into his normal figure he stood there holding the end of the giant blade.

"I still won," Xiaodan blurted, already pocketing the cash in the pot. "The bet was about beating the monster not slaying it."

Isabella was focused. She put the table down, pulling it to safety absentmindedly. She was more focused on quelling her excitement. Truly San Anlos would never cease to surprise her. There was so much to do now, but the next step was easy. Lauren was already adding the damages to Christopher's reports as Bella turned the metal in her hand with a twist and shot forward a simple screw.

The metal screech was deafening and vomit inducing, but still better than the obnoxious cheering she heard in her head from the robotic group. Even when the walls of her cage tore open and sunlight struck in she could hear the Suteki Sentai 5 whispering praise to each other, but it didn't matter. Once again Christina emerged from a mountain of metallic waste, only this time to see a world that had been waiting for her to notice.

STCKR: *platonic panic*   -   180

<u>STCKR: PLATONIC PANIC</u>
EPISODE 3: RBTTL

CHAPTER 1: SELF IDOLS

Moments of an old oasis within the city that was her family's dragon den were rendered distant and hazy through the passage of time. Only a few days later, Christina stood in place of her grandmother on her own accord, knowing full and well that standing among the ruins of a legacy like this was a surrealism far greater than Xiaodan's fortitude. A black arrow struck at her one and true vitals. Christina had already known the puzzle pieces, but they were now reassembled in a different order. Memories of reminiscing had already become grainy footage of film, rotted over the days, and a file format not properly fitted to known screens.

She stood among the rubble of the grocery store from the days prior. The mess included the wreckage of rocks and brick among the exposed rebar, wiring, and mishappen piles of items that probably weren't going to sell either way. All of which were sun bleached and collected into piles as per the early signs of rapid development, only made possible by a keen multitude of eyes unwavering in a net impatience. Tandem Tantrum Toys and Co. had already begun to act. The roar and pop of engines, the coughing of diesel powered movement, and the horns and beeps of the dance the equipment played, weaving about to clean the area was the only introduction she was offered. Christina made a mental note to herself, letting the information graze over her skin and sear the moment into her memory with the harsh bright beams of a provocative sun.

"I need to get ahold of Lauren."

Christopher would probably work too, but Lauren was the first name that came to her mind and because of that it was the name she focused on. It was a task far easier within the confines of theory and plausibility. As it happened, life had the inclination to come up at her and not the other way around. What was more important though, was the inclination for those around her to be far more elusive than any ordinary breed of turmoil. It's a nice way of putting she was unlucky, wasn't she?

How lucky she was then, that the statue of a man that was Marcus was making his pilgrimage from between home and school to happen upon the site of demolition to pay his respects. He had only the utmost formalities to act out on for the importance of a death of a dream. Indeed, Xiaodan's legacy was attracting many more patrons in its life after death than it had before. For a while now Marcus had found himself at a crossroads of sorts, wracked by the weight and burden, stopping him from moving forward in either direction. It took him ages to realize that when one is to stand still for too long even the way back can appear like a path forward. The only fear now was whether regression of any sort was a mistake or not. Better yet, would that mean the current self that had previously existed could be classified as "previous" if regression was not true regression in the first place? All he could do was attempt to untangle his tongue and meanwhile introduce himself properly.

"I think you attempted to decapitate me." The words stumbled out of his mouth while his own nerves grabbed ahold of him and pulled his eyes down.

"That's one way to say what's up," Christina responded. In truth, it was quite the disarming greeting between the inquisitor and the sentenced. She had seen him in the corner of her vision, painted over but still barely visible, shuffling along towards her. Regardless of how easily avoidable he was in the scenery of the world, the innate drift of her eyes made it impossible, to the point she was frustrated by the time he finally bridged the divide between them and she wore the emotion on her face plainly.

"Marcus?" Christina asked for clarification.

"Alvarado," he finished.

It was getting annoyingly hot standing in the sun so clearly, but she smiled through ignoring it.

"Christina Zheng," she reciprocated .

Regardless of introductions, Marcus proved to be helpful enough. Discerning which of the unsaved strings of digits that filled up his contacts was Lauren's was a feat itself, but one easy enough to accomplish. Contacts without names and meaningful numbers without order was all in character for the manic archetype that was Marcus Alvarado. Someone who Christina had begun to assume dealt with the obscure more than anything grounded or tethered to a sense of reality.

She had to admit, she could relate a little. Maybe a little too much than she would care to admit. Certainly enough that before she was totally aware of the decision process herself, she had begun to spend more days with him. It occurred in vignettes, at the minutes in between events, the empty space of time, along the corners of her memory, filling up the cracks of her life. Before school they would wait along cracked sidewalks and dried weeds. After school they talked as they passed trash strewn chain link fences. Once again under the shade of an old tree. Another time in the corner of a parking lot, sitting on a patch of ignored grass. Cultivated together with metaphors and imagery largely unimportant, but fun nonetheless. Christina was equipped with enough tools at her disposal to articulate the words better and maybe decipher a better meaning in the time spent together, but keeping pace with the slow Marcus was enjoyable in its own right.

It was a particular Friday morning, before class had started and the blue sky was full with a transparent clarity and vitality mostly uncommon to San Anlos residents. Christina had become used to the visuals that harkened to the new presence that Marcus Alvarado maintained ever since recently. The so-called imagery previously described consisted mostly of fractured handles, torn off doors, broken plates, bent silverware, and the general destruction of anything that was unfortunate enough to find itself in the presence of Marcus. Since their prolific lunchtime brawl that had resulted in the evacuation of one third of the city, the two alone had ushered in an army of fake camera crews manned by Tandem Tantrum Toys and Co. temp workers in order to carry out the cover story of a Super Suteki Sentai 5 movie in the works. It may as well have been real with the amount of effort unknowing temp workers and the androids themselves put into the actual practice. San Anlos had been alive with a constant pulse of momentum ever since, mostly from the matador bull that was Marcus. Complete with a chemical makeup to expound its energy in fullness at any point in time. He had far enough power and strength that it escaped out of his skin and pushed against the air around him.

In any case, his new character nature seemed resolved for absent minded chaos as he was never one to pay attention to his surroundings. Once again there was an air of intrigue because of this. It was certainly a site to behold. A lost child in the streets whose presence was covered by a perpetual ring of dust that could not stand the immediate vicinity of his stride. A total and complete rejection from the world.

The absent minded walks and conversations equally lacking in direction both held a retrospective cathartic quality. The two's San Anlos was much larger and smaller in the same manner. Between pile ups and crashed cars reputed in response to the energy within the air of Marcus the pair had come upon an end destination, possibly from coincidence, possibly from an unknown intended drift.

It was towards the west side of San Anlos, where the ocean breeze lost its reach and the sun better enjoyed bearing down on the foothills. A further corner of the city, it was a little dustier and far less traveled than the rest. New apartment buildings were slowly but surely, popping up between old houses, barely opened stores, and marked the edges of fields of oranges stretching far beyond. Faster than weeds or the citrus trees, the concrete skeletons continued to sprout like reanimated ghosts of the lot they now took up each and every time.

"I heard that they were calling it Sea View Apartments," Christina pointed out. "Kinda cruel, considering it's literally the furthest plot from the beach. Whatever works, I guess." Marcus wasn't paying attention, having already gone ahead with an inclination for high places. The construction of the nearest concrete apartment complex was secured with a chain link fence, but against the astral strength of Marcus' personal space it easily bent prostrate for them.

The rest was easy. After climbing up the two flights of stairs, neatly abandoned at the time of hour, there was barely any time for Christina to begin to have second thoughts about trespassing. The touch of air at the height of the rooftop was enough to send their center of gravity reeling, but even at this altitude Marcus had no worries in indulgences with the minor terror of standing three stories up. Short and unfocused, his footsteps mishappenly took him towards the edge of the unsecured rooftop. Christina, on the other hand, made sure to leave several yards of space between herself and it, her eyes focused squarely with concern on Marcus.

With every movement he made he could hear the clink of metal like dinner plates and glass, or a suit of armor rubbing against itself. The sound filled any and all empty space around them, drawing in the vibrations of aristocracy and class. It was an afternoon sky around him. The hallucination was not a looming blue, but a warm orange of a setting sun like always. The clouds hazy, but present under the filtered light even from this distance. Below him was the procession of dung beetles cast in the dark colors and corners of shows, scurrying, squirming, and desperately pushing their embrace with mountains of excrement like false idols of the galaxy's true center. He didn't need to look above for a now familiar face within the afternoon nor search for the source of an orange overcast any longer. There was a lot one man like him could do, but before anything there needed to be a testament. One he carved into the very sky with a snap of his fingers and a part of the clouds An open gate to the beyond that tasted acidic enough in his mouth to melt the flesh off his jaw.

Looking out into the very plain morning sky, ordinary in every way, Christina called out for Marcus to step back even though a fall would do little to harm him at this point. She was not so much enthralled in him as she was invested. A boy like him was useless in nature. Over the course of a few talks she was already making sure of his safety after trespassing on rooftops, exchanging barely more than platitudes. Defenseless and completely exposed, demanding constant protection.

"What an idiot," she whispered to herself.

He was utterly and totally empty.

CHAPTER 2: EMPLOYEE SURVEYS

Tedium and labor had acquired the scent of Lauren in the recent days after San Anlos' midtown had nearly been leveled with helicopters, robots, and feral strays. Rest was no longer a word that felt familiar in the bends of her tongue, or at least it was a word that couldn't help but cut and slice her against its fine edges. Over the course of a single day, she had become more than well versed in the languages of a passive aggressive and covert predatory corporate rhetoric. Enough so, to the point that paperwork, disaster reports, and edits to recent filing were on par with manifestos and death sentences for a betterment of the populace she could not realize. In such a case as hers, it was a blade that had been heated with a forge kept alight by the toils of an internal debate only to be cooked in the shallow, but plentiful, puddles of rhetoric.

Paperwork perpetually engulfed her, trailing behind her steps like a flower girl bringing the end to healthy work practices, local businesses, and a living wage. Teeth clenched and a tongue sheathed between them, she made sure not to speak harshly, careful to not render the continuous onslaught of dead trees to ribbons and shreds thereby starting her assignments all over.

Truly Tandem Tantrum Toys and Co. was nothing if not full of talented, skilled, and conditioned employees. Lauren was a prime example among many, developing the suggested tendency to count down the clock rather than vice versa. Calendars were marked with the names of days that were now deceased. In a short time, she had buried days beneath her construction of a mausoleum empire. These dealings of trades in mortem had proved vital, impressive, and most importantly in line with corporate identity.

All indicative of a promised promotion.

Lauren knew exactly why she had become so impressive with the shining referral from long time employee Christopher and her constant influx of reports, in part to correct the many mistakes made by the recent remodeling to help Christina. Lauren had illustrated what the limits were of a highly dedicated individual. Thereby only ruining the experience and expectations for any other one. Her life's culmination of reports, surmounting to more than all of Christophers, had become reason enough for the arrival of Tandem Tantrum Toys and Co. headquarters alongside the introduction of new funding it brought with it.

You had to enter through the heavily monitored doors. Pass the arcade machines. Wait in the elevator. Rise up the only skyscraper in the entire city built in record speed, as if it had always been there. And exit on the top floor.

In there was the formality of an executive meeting.

Lauren's breath temporarily got caught in the back of her throat making the thin hairs on her arms stand on end. Imagine her surprise when she was greeted with familiar LED faces surrounding the black meeting table like some sort of surrealist game junkies nightmare. Her confusion stemmed from what a face to face interaction really meant to the Tandem Tantrum Toys and Co. executives. All of which were truly present in the high rise.

It was in the blanketed silence of night that it was completed, with a swarm of armored black SUVs and helicopters all awarded with the highest level of security clearance possible. True and authentic founding members and corporate leaders sat before Lauren in their authentic flesh, or at least their closest comparison to it. The six identical purple arcade machines had been synched through a private cable transfer to local, untouched, and relatively current computers that composed their executive consciousness with an ever expanding memory of dial ups and hard drives.

"LOADING PERSONAL DATA: ID FILE NAME LAUREN 903748854"

The words shouted mechanically through speakers unseen, sending a jolt of shock through an unprepared Lauren.

"TAKE A SEAT"

Taking her seat as requested, the realization came rebounding against the back of her head: she had certainly developed a high tolerance for life, hadn't she? She should have been proud. Ordinarily, someone would give up in the absurdist monotony, but she proceeded to live it out. However, if there were an onlooker somehow peering through the top story windows, one could assume that possibly the inability to find the distinction between the organic and the synthetic in the room was heightened. There was an ascension with assimilation and one that was guarded with gate and code, defining exactly everything with absolute and total definition with no need for formal words present. Lauren was highly regarded now. A Co-Senior employee and retail representative with Christopher. The nature defined with terms and language of flesh and blood was a point of confusion still.

'-processing data-reviewing forms-good promise here-looks angry doesn't she-'

Frustrations were typed out literally along the LED screens of the executive machines. Each one sprouted out a similar text bubble usually with a complaint of some sort. Repetition of intimate thoughts made public.

'-CONFIDENTIAL SECURITY BREACH-CONFIDENTIAL SECURITY-CONFIDENTIAL SECURITY-CONFIDENTIAL

SECURITY-CONFIDENTIAL SECURITY-CONFIDENTIAL SECURITY-'

Alarms and sirens immediately went off at full volume echoing past her eardrums and drenching the room in a sudden red.

"LOOK DOWN GIRL. YOU LACK PROPER AUTHORIZED CLEARANCE"

Lauren had never considered herself one to freeze, but nevertheless, she froze in a panic. She also never had never considered herself one to panic, but still, the words in her mouth came out stumbling and crashing into each other.

"I didn't- it was a- there was- I'm not-"

"SHUT UP AND LOOK DOWN"

Her attention was promptly wrangled and punished, shutting emergency procedures off immediately as she prostrated her head in a silent focus on her lap instead of looking forward.

"I'm very sorry for the intrusion of privacy," she said in a whisper, although the words were originally meant to contain a little bit of confidence.

"YOU LACK PROPER AUTHORITY FOR AUDITORY INPUT." All speakers spoke at once in response. Just like anything else she couldn't tell which one in particular was talking. "YOU WILL NOW HAVE PROPER AUTHORITY FOR ACCESS TO EXTENDED SAN ANLOS REGION RESOURCES."

Acute attention to the finer details to what such a statement entailed informed her that she was now offered the responsibility of production lines and patented products that had been halted on the San Anlos plant years ago. A promotion in theory and practice, but not on paper of course. She was no production line manager, after all, it had been left as storage for some time now, but new responsibilities these days had to be flexible although proper credit through pay or bonuses didn't.

"CONGRATULATIONS NEW: SENIOR MEMBER [lauren]. MEETING COMPLETE."

The announcement didn't need a long winded rant nor elongated exposition. Not because of the cold heart and rigid nature of her bosses, for an entity supposedly devoid of platitudes and connations it certainly did not have any scarcity for them. Instead, the problem was Lauren, whose definition had little need for extra words in explanation. Out of stock was the vocabulary that was once hers in place for a more agreeable type that had a value more easily digestible for consumer audiences.

Bewitched, betrothed, and now she had to be wedded. Christening the holy occasion was access to new resources and paperwork confetti for the age old celebration of a masochist holiday. Her lover was a subjugator that refused form but could be defined by the simplest words, and when the newlyweds are enamored there is nothing left but the honeymoon phase for them to embark on. Together. One that involved a survey. Better yet, one that involved surveillance with the web of mechanical eyes that had no fatigue or momentary blinks in their observations. Lauren found every angle of the city readily available from her desktop at home. It was only information in the hands of a phantom, capable of perception and little more. Her shadow may have been cast through her many visitations, but her body was not present to block out the sun. The web of eyes had caught herself within the motions of work, categorizing and putting information into place. Make no mistake though, her sway over its contents was nonexistent. A spider's web in the same way a warehouse stores its contents. There was beautifully organized information purposefully placed in their proper spots with or

without consent. Christina's family and their intuition had a
decerning distaste that protected most intrusive lenses from
breaking past their walls. The Alvarado household opened their
doors and were barely present to question the effects of explicit
invasions. Regardless of the manner of invasion, Lauren
deciphered every detail and sent her report in the perfect, exact,
and concise definition as mandated.

    Lauren was at the point in her work that she no longer
questioned the words anymore. That didn't stop her from
wondering what effect the effect of distant meanings were.

CHAPTER 3: DIFFERENT WAYS TO FALL

Two different worlds of San Anlos existed. The same dreamy scenescape as always, composed of the many small buildings of San Anlos overlooked from their second story high school window. Lauren would have normally needed no questions to decipher what it was that Marcus was looking at, or more often looking for. That was an inaccuracy in this case. Her prior normal disposition would have found those words unnecessary, but interesting nonetheless. Lauren was certainly no longer any prior incarnation of herself, past a point now where all her greetings were updated to the new formalities carved into her persona with paper, ink, and her own signature.

As it stood, the current, or most current Lauren at least, exhibited a need for a line of questioning directed at Marcus. Not out of any interest in particular, but if that's what was easier for people to call it then she would have to as well.

"What color is it?"

Similar to all the other previous excursions into pure fiction, it would begin with an orange sky.

"That's easy enough."

Just a simple correction. An easy change in hue probably within the range of #ffa500 or so. One box could be checked off.

"What is all there?"

They were easier to watch from here, only because he had never had the present podium of a position to look down to see them before. They crawled through city streets, classrooms, and hallways.

"You're not really giving me a lot to go off of."

It was manageable though. It would have to be. This one required more guess work, but she would proceed under the assumption of the Aphodius Gurancurius species of the Aphodu genus hailing from the Scarabaidene family of the Coleoptera order as the determinant of the certain type of dung beetle about them. That would have to do for now at least.

"Normally there's a distinct flavor isn't there?"

From what she could remember they were dipped in one that was syrupy and sweet. Her taste now was severely incapacitated, but from the odor that wafted in through his window there was the development in a palette of a sour citrus scent. Certainly unexpected, but not a detail she would fail to incorporate.

A citrus fantasy among an insect infested world.

The only thing missing now was the immaculate sun of a god that Marcus regularly visited with apparently.

"It's me now," he corrected her.

She waited a moment, letting herself look him over for any signs of a bad joke but found none.

"Congratulations."

The detail itself was not one that could be considered unnatural, especially taking into account recent events. Her rather disinterested tone was fully intentional on her though, masking any shock she had. Nevertheless, the form was a complete one and her signature would be written through the strokes of her actions. The dream that Marcus looked at so dearly was plain for her to see. No longer was there an ordinary San Anlos. Instead, there was a coast that had shifted to a similar orange color pulled in far closer than it would normally have been in view. There was an insect class constantly pushing false suns toward the perpetual setting. Lauren could see the infatuation and escape that had supported Marcus' survival for so long.

Another box could be checked off. Possibly even a stamp of approval for completion. Marcus certainly did not notice, but there was a wall of papers dividing them and their dreams. If she turned her back to him it would almost have been a throne of copies, but she couldn't do that. Not yet at least. She couldn't help but still look forward to him, even if they were looking from two different perspectives at the same angle. There was the same orange sky over San Anlos/There was the same blue sky over San Anlos... as they looked out the window absent mindedly and silently. Certainly two different worlds indeed.

The first thing to fall was feet against pavement. A clashing choir disturbing the otherwise grotesquely serene dreamland of San Anlos. Marcus could only barely catch a flash of blue sneakers in a blur as she burst through door after door. Christina was panting, fighting back an urge to faint with an equal urge to vomit rising in her fluctuating diaphragm bursting at the seams. Through the halls. Rebounding off stairs and walls alike. At a pace that sometimes incorporated four limbs as well as the usual two. The evidence of her effort streamed down her skin against the gasps and heaves of air. All of her came bounding and charging through the halls and stairs until her current broke against the barrier of the study hall doors. Flooding through the open space Christina finally made it.

"You need to come outside," she wheezed while bent over, her hands on her knees to stay upright.

By the time she looked up she was already catching sight of the incoming screw. Lauren shoved Marcus aside, doing the same for herself and just barely avoiding being impaled through the skull by the thinnest margins of errors. Thin enough that it could ensure hair ends were split.

The standard screw kept on going in its path, boring through further walls until it was out of sight with no discernable stop to it.

"What the hell?" Lauren gasped.

Their desk rattled beneath them as the walls started to tremble. Before anyone could get their bearings they witnessed a kind of quaking. The kind that could collapse brick and stone. More precisely, it was the pieces of brick that were part of the school's walls outside, struck loose from the footsteps of Isabella's strides. Her feet jutted deep into the surface of the building's exterior as she walked. Against human expectation the woman strutted up the horizontal surface with ease and a resentful determination.

Marcus could not register the phenomena. Not to give him the credit for even trying though. He could hardly understand it enough to know if he was actually surprised, let alone verbally feign an exclamation to express it. It was before he could speak that she was already before him. Somewhere along the timeline she had pulled him out of class, but the memories were so quick and fleeting compared to now, where he hung dangling by the head. There was no such leniency for himself that others currently exhibited, his legs tugged on him downwards while Isabella still stood there horizontally aligned next to the open window.

"It's time to prove your worth for once." She spat the words at him with a vulgar animosity. "Show me you can fly."

In a scene all too reminiscent of before, Marcus was deftly dropped without the hesitation of doubt. He plummeted in a free fall that came to a crashing halt against the sidewalk along the parking lot. However this time Isabella offered no chemically induced aid of extraterrestrial sticker for protection.

Nevertheless, his present circumstances made such a fall survivable and while it was not a graceful flight, it would suffice. It would have to be. Isabella bent over the window again, her eyes focused and intent striking right through Lauren and seizing Christina.

"Make your choice girl. I'm not waiting for perfection any longer."

Christina was already out the door and down the stairs before anyone had to tell her again or, worst yet, throw her. That left Lauren, flabbergasted and shocked in the classroom, to watch as the new trio veered down the street of an assumably stolen motorcycle.

There was another way still to fall.

Luminescent and white.

Heavenly graceful harbingers.

The stars filled the sky, blackening what was once blue behind them for an early night as they began their descent toward the earth by the masses. Night came crashing down. The words escaped her not because she forgot them, but because she wished she never had the vocabulary to realize them.

I'm always alone in the end, aren't I?

CHAPTER 4: REACHING FOR THE STARS

The steering wheel was obscured behind the flurry of hands operated by the generally fed up and aggravated aura that encompassed Eve within the driver's seat. The limousine swerved around corners, missing near collisions along the way as they maneuvered through a terrified San Anlos traffic of a world's end.

"He is going to kill me," Lauren noted rather dully into the cell phone.

"Stop being ridiculous, he is not going to kill you," Christopher reassured her on the other end, sitting in the limo's passenger seat. He spared a glance at his other half for only a moment. "He probably won't kill you, at least."

"Reassuring." She hung up.

There was no luxury of entering a stopped vehicle for her. Instead, the lift involved a turning of the car with a screech of rubber and a high velocity drift toward her. Her saving grace was the passenger's arms extended through the open door, ready to pull her in before she was completely sideswiped.

All such disastrous decisions for actions that were reckless and totally unnecessary invitations for vehicular manslaughter were understandable. After all, the sky was falling or the stars were at least. A torrent of glowing, white, five pointed stars were plummeting from the sky in a massive wave that overtook the entire city. All of it was done in no manner that evoked a description similar to gentle or comfortable. At first, it seemed perhaps like an oil painting waiting to capture the stars streaming through the sudden night sky. But distance has a way of warping things and the only grace to arise from the onslaught of atmospheric geometrics was the realization that against the momentum of gravity everything was waiting to be destroyed.

Solid stone-like stars impeded themselves into curated idle walls. They dented themselves through car metal and glass windows. Permanent potholes were newly introduced. Light poles were knocked over while the earth was upturned along with damage far worse throughout San Anlos. Of course, the downpour alone was not enough to cause such an uproar from Isabella Luna, Eve, and their compatriots. That responsibility lay very much with the gothic type font delicately printed into a message onto the backs of each interstellar drop.

'Dear Mr. E and Mrs. I,

Please expect a judge, jury, and executioner.

With best regards,

A.'

Malicious greetings, apparent to everyone who was aware of the type of twist that authors had with words. Such tact was used for placing inside the letters within best regards with something more vile, malevolent, and harder to distinguish from its guise. Such a truth was read with clarity by almost everyone within the limousine. Any explanation from Christopher would have to be postponed as he was too busy with his laptop in the passenger seat, remaining surprisingly calm for his character, while reciting the directions for Eve to follow. All of which were based on calculations and company tracking satellites far above. He was too enveloped in his work to notice the dangerous application of his orders happening in real time before him.

Lauren was not a woman without options though, and her options happened to be vocal ones at that. In the back of the limousine were two perfect specimens who the sight of alone weaponized affection from mere proximity. One would have described them as a genuine power couple, but Tandem Tantrum Toys and Co. had only kept them filed under Dream Babes. Two separate babe editions, released simultaneously for friendly relationship consumption. They would have been perfect if not for a major default in their programming which deemed immediate shutdown according to corporate standards. Lauren was quick to pick up on it.

Touma T.T.T. and Tiana T.T.T. sat interlocked with each other, comfortable in the padded seat along the very back where the light diluted to drench them in a promiscuous dark pink. Across the expanse of the limousine inside were piles of white wrapped gifts and bags from what appeared to be a recent shopping spree. Christopher must have had to bribe the two to come along for the job. Amid the mess were two white metal cases that stood out. Lauren made sure to sit most opposite as possible from the couple, afraid of suspected vibrant contaminants. The machine lifeform with sly and curious eyes was likely barely taller than Christopher's stature, yet somehow already demonstrated strength far exceeding his physical limitations, purposefully terrifying Lauren. Extending his arm out the window he caught an incoming falling star in order to read the message all with little struggle.

"Did that scare you?" Touma asked with a snicker. "Where's your confidence in me?"

She did not have a lot of confidence in the robot man she had yet to properly meet outside of product catalogs and spec sheets. Touma was only half of the Dream Babe product set, and Lauren could already tell why the project was hastily shut down. He was annoying. Being a head or two shorter than her, he certainly acted like it. From the start it was obvious he liked to run his mouth that was consistently drawn up in a smirk only because he was consistently right. He was muscular, but it was hidden underneath a white long sleeve shirt and a blue pleated coat which sleeves he rolled up. It must have been a designer brand, but Lauren couldn't place it. His black cuffed jeans were baggy and ended with rather uninteresting black sneakers. Either his temperament or the non-company attire were reason enough to halt the product line at the two. If Lauren remembered right, Touma was supposed to be a cheery trophy husband type personality. But if Lauren had to pick a reason to not like him it was his gaze, a focus that was honed in regardless of the moment or action.

The worry and hurt in his voice was as manufactured as the rest of him, but that didn't stop it from bothering Lauren.

"It's not outside so keep your hands inside," she answered.

"Confidence," he continued. "Thats the difference between a threat and a proclamation."

Apparently, Touma and Tiana were the ones that were going to offer any explanation to Lauren against her pleading to Eve's and Christopher's deaf ears.

"You should know all about Isabella and Eve if you had the time to pour over their redacted files. I doubt purple sharpie would be enough to obscure the facts for you," Tiana spoke up.

"And, if against all the odds, I don't know all there is?" Lauren asked.

"Then in your sted, we would have no other choice than to elaborate on the current facts of the scenario," Touma answered.

Lauren didn't want to admit to what she did know, but at the same time admitting to the little that she did would be revelation enough. So she waited in the safety of a hypothetical for them to act on their own.

"She doesn't know, does she?" Touma stated rather bluntly, looking over at Tiana with a smile. Contrary to what appearances of personal joy that one might assume from his annoying smile this was actually his version of sympathy. He could never deliver the information with sincere compassion like his better half could. Tiana knew as much as well. In fact, she knew everything about him.

She was crazy for him. He was crazy for her.

Tiana loosened her legs from interlocking with Touma's and leaned in towards Lauren, her tall frame and hair making the distance seem lesser than it was.

The space between them that consisted of perfectly wrapped boxes and gift bags was neatly dwarfed by Tiana's looming figure. She was tall. Maybe it was the company specs that weren't exact or maybe it was because her hair that such a number harder to pin down. The middle was parted and clipped down letting her dense curls puff out in a lion's mane around her sides. Tiana had dark black skin that the gold and red glitter of her eyeshadow further enhanced, highlighting the natural curves and natural form of her face. Just like her counterpart, she was designed to be athletically built but her dense muscles were hard to notice under her clothes. Lauren had been take in with a sharp breathe the non-company mandated clothes of a lace undershirt, red armored corset, gray jeans, red and gold acrylic nails, red mma style padded gloves, and knee high red platform boots that consisted of countless straps it was hard to count.

"It's called standard procedures." she started. Her voice was already more sincere and earnest than the prior option. "Class E: Enforcer Eve is to be partnered with Class I: Instigator Isabella in an effort to control her documented unwieldy temperament while they perform designated responsibilities. Here's the thing. The Luna family isn't really a family, but more like creatures from the moon. Not necessarily ours though. All we know is that they are essentially an organization of homunculus from unknown extraterrestrial origins. Each is imparted with a similar foreign energy that reacts to objects in undocumented ways. i.e. those stupid suitcases they carry around."

"Illegal biological weapon manufacturing." Eve interrupted the backseat conversation. "The Luna business is the creation and sales of illegal weapons for intergalactic and trade. Isabella is supposed to find samples, prepare proper conditions for internal disturbances, produce the proper cultivation of latent energy i.e. the stickers, and then use her specific tools to combine and compact the products into a core. Highly dangerous with the amount of energy it holds. And then they sell it to the highest bidder within space."

"See big stuff," Touma nodded in affirmation for only the glare of Tiana.

"You're joking." Lauren stared at their intergalactic chauffeur waiting for some kind of clue to appear that would let her know it was a charade. Something tearing at the seams of a lie before the truth tore the seams at her sanity.

"What's the difference between an alien and a god?" Eve asked for no one in particular to answer. "The ease of transportation."

Lauren looked over to Christopher who only shrugged. Eve looked up from the urban mayhem into the rearview mirror for a moment. Something was seething in a red hot annoyance inside of her that blotted out the edges of her vision.

Touma couldn't help but laugh at the sight of it so apparent on the girl's face.

"You think that's annoying just wait for this. The Luna family has had no direct correspondence with their point of origin for billions of years now. No so-called 'deity' creator to instruct them, so they have just been colonizing moon after moon as they have always been."

"Standard procedure isn't it?" Tiana snarked.

"Business as usual?" Touma howled.

"It's stupid," Tiana giggled.

"It's insanity," Touma snickered.

"Shut up back there," Christopher hollered.

"Your joking? You have to be aren't you?" Lauren asked. The words seared into the flesh of her throat when she spoke. In short, she was incredulous at it all.

"What, that all seems too fantastic but this doesn't?" Touma scolded, gesturing at the impossibility of a star he was holding.

"Responsible people don't ignore reality to support preconceived notions," Tiana stated. "Get used to it if you live in San Anlos."

Christopher leaned over his seat and tossed her one tablet he had been holding.

"You better get over the annoying disbelief fast then girl."

There are a lot of ways that one's expectations can be shattered. It can be swept out from under you taking down all at once your internal support for logic that has been subtly but prominent until now. Better yet it can be a flagrant denail to your face. Lauren sat in a moving car in the ever moving San Anlos within the Dead Spacial Plot 376 which had been empty of Luna bases up until this point. However, even hanging out in dead patches for too long was an invitation for attention. All that information was easily accessible with a few taps on the tablet, but currently irrelevant. Contrary to popular opinion the sky was not falling equally throughout the city. The stars collided in a specific pattern, one in the shape of a Times New Roman font capital A.

"Class A individuals," Touma started.

"Those with only purpose," Tiana finished.

Whereas Eve's face was stuck in a grimace from the disastrous implications of it all, easily captured in the rearview mirror, Lauren was coming to understand how dull constant calamity was.

"It's a worst case scenario. Nice people don't deal solely in total absolutes." He spoke from the front, more so for himself than for others, fighting off gray images of a schoolyard depression.

CHAPTER 5: CATCHING UP

Isabella Luna was panicked and frantic, and not just because of the star shaped potholes and constant heavenly arsenal that nearly collided with her and her two guests holding on with a fresh desire for life. No, she was scared because she had run out of time.

The moon had been watching and there are only so many rotations of the earth they could go through before disciplinary actions needed to take place. She herself had never known the privilege of being schooled in such elite trade secrets of the Luna familial organization. Such was the life of a mid-class individual like herself. However, Isabella had enjoyed the luxury as an unwilling participant in similar remedial lessons during her later years of education. Before the essential contradiction of her class nature had been carved into her approximation to flesh. There was much to do and many options to take for a regenerative homunculus. She did not have enough hubris to think she had experienced the worst yet that they had to offer. Those memories were only a fraction of it, but it was enough to make a reference to estimate what a complete experience could entail.

Once again Isabella Luna was a young girl running through white corridors, hiding from her upperclassmen underneath school desks after she had let on that her lessons in internal societal disruptions and rebellion had struck too deep a cord. Her mind was again reeling far faster than she ever could, finishing her roundabouts of thoughts and reaching the same conclusion: that she should be ashamed, disgusted, and punished, for ever thinking about the idea of relaxing in an open field under a generously caring star.

"Isabella. You know that's not how you're supposed to talk."

They would say it in that same marvelously innocent tone they had, imitating perfectly the nature they were expected to. Whether she liked it or not, the Adamants were chasing her again. The stars were coming for her. Her dreams were spilling out and escaping.

It's fine.

She could not curl up in a ball and tug on her hair for comfort anymore. She couldn't just pray that her tears would dry before anyone saw them. She could only grind her teeth to dust and let her hate burn in the forge within her until her blood was at a boil.

"Is everything okay?" His words caught her off guard.

"Since when have you shown an interest in other people Marcus?"

"Since it's been possible you could turn me into roadkill," he yelled over the roar of the wind in his ears.

Presumptuous words from a man who never considered if the road would have been happy either when tasked with holding his dead body. There was plenty of time to ponder such thoughts as he had little experience in carrying conversations for so long. Or rather, there would have been if not for Christina who was there to pick up where he left off.

"Not to interrupt, but I do want to still know why we are running."

"Because my compatriot in work listens to his feeling and hormones more than he does logic," Isabella answered in a noninformative way.

Christina busied herself with not wanting to touch on the topic anymore while Marcus couldn't pick up on any sort of obtuse information, apparent on his face and to Bella's satisfaction. All of which was for the better, as she was busy maneuvering through oncoming and gridlocked cars while still outpacing the pestering limousine. If there had been any moment for herself Isabella might have truly realized how annoying it all was. What kind of basic villain chose a standard limo as their ride? The motorcycle felt more stylish if not a little unwieldy. Her passengers had contentions with the latter point in matters of security, but the danger presently posed was too much risk for them to voice these thoughts.

Christina tried to swallow down her breaths as she pulled tighter on a mostly silent Marcus, honorable of him in this case as her strength at the moment was strong enough to break ribs. Marcus, however, at this current point in time had no inclination to worry about that sort of physical trauma or any other kind in fact. Instead, he was more occupied with the torrent of hair that engulfed him once again in his short life while he was pulling at Isabella's suit for safety. In short, stomachs lurched with every turn that nearly introduced the group to the road at as plus 100mph pace.

Eve tossed his head in frustration with a trilogy installment trying to shake out feelings of failings as the distance between him and his targets extended. Christopher was quick and preemptive, already calculating for his boyfriend's habit of sulking. A few taps of his fingers on the laptop and the course had enough readjustments along the map now following a straight line for the next few miles to set his head straight.

That was only part of the process though. Christopher shoved his company laptop aside so he could look directly at Eve and then the rest of the group, addressing them with a stern, but calm, confidence most unlike his usual self.

"When I give you the signal I want you to take your chance."

"And what does that mean?" Touma called out from the back.

"Do your job."

Touma's and Tiana's temperament contested harshly with the severity of the situation, cuddling together in the comfort of loved one's arms.

"Do it in our signature lovestruck style and its deal," Touma contested.

"We kind of have a patent romantic vibe that you can't just kill," Tiana added.

Christopher held back vomit at the cringe arrangement of words produced in ways that stuck him from angles he did not expect. There was a long pause in both the conversation and in thought within the passenger seat while he looked over the possibilities.

"Fine," he muttered with a defeated sigh.

Tiana and Touma held down laughter and punched each other softly but excitedly. Lauren looked between the two couples in an uncomfortable party of one confusion. Christopher turned Eve's face by the chin, letting them look into each other's eyes.

"One for good luck seems like a good enough measure."

Isabella and her caravan of followers rounded a sharp corner, ignoring stop lights and honking cars, only to turn onto a road with a limo fast approaching.

He moved in slowly at first, a little hesitant and nervous for what should have been a familiar motion, but as promise increased just as the distance closed he fell completely into it. Christopher and Eve locked lips in a deep kiss, gunning the car and tossing their party back over pink cushioned seats. Tiana was already flicking the white metal cases open and drawing out an elongated white stock of a similarly colored rifle, the barrel closer to the shape of a flattened diamond than the standard cylinder. Little time was spared as she stepped out onto the passenger sunroof, ignoring the wind whipping against her and the blur of a familiar city zooming behind her. Her aim was true and forward. Touma was likewise, always present to support his eternal love, on top of the limousine's roof laying with his feet in the air and looking through the circled sights of his index and thumb.

"Give her some trauma babe."

A concentrated pulse of white energy shot forth, frying through the air at supersonic speed and pushing against the velocity of the vehicle.

It clipped Isabella. Chunks of the very ends of her hair were severed and a small approximation of her left cheek disappeared. The damage was only minimized with adjustments made in the last possible millisecond as Bella caught sight of the energized bullet from the mirrors. It was damaged enough though, sending her wheels into a near tumble as she shifted her weight too quickly and stilled herself the next moment.

Eve, still deep in savoring the lips of a certain other, let his suitcase open with one hand and the other remain on the wheel. A tangle of chains spewed out through the sunroof, the trademark dream couple dodging the rush, and wrapped around Christina's grappling figure. There was little time to process the ensnarement before she was flung back through the air as chains retracted.

"What the hell now!" The words escaped her mouth as she hit the seat next to Lauren with a painful thud.

Christopher's gloved hand pressed against Eve's chest signaling a moment's pause while he whipped his head around, already prepared with a frown.

"Chill, you're not exactly the priority we're trying to reel in."

Eve was still ignoring the road, blindly but accurately swinging the wheel around while he focused on taking in Christopher's features.

"I'm still down to try it again."

"Focus on the road," Lauren chided.

"Don't worry you're in mostly safe hands," Tiana affirmed, plopping from the sunroof into her seat followed unceremoniously by Touma holding her gun.

Christina couldn't focus on any of their words. One single colorful fact sprawled out before her in a terror inducing glaring fashion. The kind she could only watch in wide eyed shock.

"Doesn't this car always end up in a wreck?"

All present passengers caught their breath for a moment. She wasn't wrong.

CHAPTER 6 : FACTORY RESET

Christina had similarly reenacted the same confusion in seating that Lauren had. Sitting rigidly and as far in between the two ends of couples with the added confusion of trying to preserve as much space between her seat partner that sat across.

"Who is the special girl?" Touma called out to the front. He didn't necessarily wait for an answer although he was, in fact, still listening. More important was the task at hand: tearing apart the white wrapped wedding gifts piled up on the floor with little discretion.

"Don't break anything you spent the company card on, idiot," Christopher scolded from over his seat.

Eve was beginning to suspect that perhaps the limousine itself made people naturally destructive and reminded himself to apologize to Isabella for the many lectures when they caught her.

Meanwhile, Tiana had already resorted to hurling the gift boxes against the walls with reckless abandon, exploding the white wrapping and tissue paper apart on impact.

"Is it always this restless with Tandem Tantrum Toys and Co.?" Christina nervously asked Lauren who she seemed to have already decided was the most sane member of the bunch.

Lauren's eyes moved to look up from her tablet but not her head. "When you're forced to work like this you would squeeze any enjoyment or excitement out of it too." She shrugged off her prior annoyance. "As much as I would prefer to not be associated with these delinquents, they probably have life far more figured out than me. Probably why they are so comfortable acting so irresponsibly."

Touma ripped open a box in half against his chest sending its plastic contents across the interior as everyone stood with wide eyed amazement and horror as an estimated $800,000 dollar piece of VR machinery was about to disassemble into bits against the windshield. That would be if not for Lauren's quick intercepting hand, catching it without breaking pace with her words.

"Between you and me. I'm probably responsible to a fault."

She finished talking, more so to herself than to her unwilling guest. Said guest still did not have a proper response to the stream of consciousness in time. Not before Lauren punctuated it by abruptly retrieving her phone and somehow finding more pressing manners than the situation before them. The whole scenery left Christina in awe as she took in the details of Lauren and her complete lack of concern for the figurative matters at hand, that being the violent entourage of store bought danger. Instead she was intent on the literal matter at hand.

"So you guys are all trying to catch Isabella?" Christina asked, shifting her attention to the others in the limo.

"Possibly remove her of her limbs while we are at it," Touma replied matter-of-factly.

"We were told homicide was off the table," Tiana tacked on, as if it changed anything other than ushering a rearview mirror glare from Eve.

Christina stalled, trying to wrap her head around that kind of mental image she failed to understand. What color was it supposed to be when expecting the splatter of a blood fountain? She assumed red, but was only coming up with white. The kind that christens so called holidays.

"So this is what you're resorting to is it?" The question was more accusatory than earnest and directed to the supposedly faithful co-partner.

"It's a complex situation," Eve answered.

"Is it? Cause what it seems like is that your partner is running and all you can seem to offer is her capture."

Steering wheel leather squeaked under the tightening of his grip. "Not to be rude, but please don't talk on topics that are out of your depth. It's because I'm supporting her that I can tell her when to stop. You don't know what is going on."

"I know enough though. Isabella told me a moment ago." It was a lie without signs to permit it, but Christina was listening to her heart instead of her head.

Eve's glare could have bore a whole through the windshield. It was a blow, for sure, to the man not expecting Isabella to be so plain and open. However, none of that mattered at this point in time.

"The Adamants far exceed any of your expectations when they need no reason to act let alone when they do have the perfect reason like right now. You know she was ready to risk your life to make some kind of super weapon ahead of schedule. Did she tell you that? "

Apparently not. Christina was stunned speechless, at a loss for words, and confused by talk of details she was not made aware of.

Tiana, who had been watching the theater of it all, took a moment to explain.

"You and the cute boy have so much good chemistry. Far more than what regular procedure is prepared to handle. Possibly enough for mutually ensured destruction to facilitate a familial separation, but there keeps on being too many anomalies halting the process. Now she is just trying to produce anything and hoping it's enough to stop the Adamants. A reaction without proper preparations is dangerous. She could level the whole west coast in the process. Its bad business."

"We'll be lucky if they stop at leveling the city as punishment," Eve added.

All of it was dipped in hues and muddled together in a barrage of information that gave Christina much to think about. Much to think about and much more to try to mentally digest.

"I don't like Marcus like that." She blurted it out. A flushed red was already waiting on her face for everyone to see clearly through the pink interior light.

Silence.

"No one said that you did," Lauren finally interjected, cutting through the palpable tension. "Only that there was literal chemistry. Lucky for you, we can fix even that."

She gestured towards her with the VR headset that she had caught, acting like its use was obvious for the topic at hand. Christina just stared.

"Tiana if you would do the honors," Lauren continued. "I don't trust Touma."

"I would be honored."

Lauren was quick, donning a purple company backpack from one of the gift boxes thrashed apart. Just as quickly she put her arm around Christina and pulled the girl's body against her own.

"Hold tight now."

Christina's red did not go away.

There was a tugging at their backs and immediately afterward the two were through the sun roof and hurling into the night sky. Christina's breath escaped her lungs as the wind battered her face. Hard enough that it made it a challenge to scream into Lauren's ear, but she certainly tried. Lauren on the other hand, remained focused on not dying and deploying the parachute right as the limo became a quickly shrinking speck and the road became an equally growing one. The terror of possible fatal outcomes bubbled and popped inside of Christina's stomach as realizations finally sunk in, but as the movement stilled in their slow descent she couldn't stop herself. In the warm night air and holding onto Lauren for dear life she started laughing. A breathless laugh that couldn't be suppressed.

Lauren did not have the vocabulary to properly understand what was going on. The girl finally broke, didn't she? Instead of trying to talk she stayed there suspended over the earth with the near stranger laughing into her shoulder until her passenger was able to quell the spell herself.

"You know a warning would have been nice. I thought you said you were the sanest?" The words left Christina a lot more calmly than any of them expected.

"You don't seem scared though?"

She might have not lived up to the sense of the word, but rest assured she was rightfully terrified. Terror induced to the point of exhilaration. A sharp yellow color that was quick and maladaptive, the kind that got all her natural responses mixed up so that she would laugh when she wanted to cry. Or that could make her so calm near a pseudo stranger, she thought. A total mess in short.

Slowly but surely, Lauren directed their descent towards an empty rural road and what looked like a throne constructed out of old TVs. Soon Christina found herself sitting on her seat atop the display of LED screens, buzzing static, and the blue cast of light. The contraption sat centered along highway lines, equally distributed between the arid dried dirt swatches on each side. To the right were phone poles that came from the city and stopped a little ways ahead of them to an abandoned wooden barn.

"Do you need to restrain me?"

Lauren didn't look up from her work adjusting antennas, checking cable connections, and troubleshooting each problem before launch.

"Tying up girls isn't really my thing. Plus this isn't that sort of program. Think of it more as targeted therapy so you're unable to fuse with Marcus."

"Yeah no matter what that still sounds like an aggressive invasion of privacy."

Lauren shrugged, "I might be the only serious one of the group but I am far from actually dangerous."

Christina was looking over the back of her seat, watching Lauren complete the finishing touches. "I think I still prefer this over whatever the rest of the group has going on."

"You ready?"

It was mostly a formality as Lauren was already sliding the headset over Christina's eyes. Connections were sufficient, battery power was still full, and little damage seem to have been suffered to affect processing power. All that was left was to hit the power button, but her finger stopped in the air and hovered. It was the old habit of curiosity, but this time with much less tact than before. Now she had only her armory of the wrong questions.

"Hey. Why did you decide to start spending so much time with Marcus?"

That's not want she wanted to ask.

Christina also hesitated. Her head was once again empty between answers and questions of her own.

"I can't say."

It's what neither wanted to say, but it would have to do.

POWER ON.

CHAPTER 7: RELOADED MEMORY

First there was the fast expanding white dot among the black screen of the headset display. Then a minor yelp of surprise from the flash of light. Finally, there was absolutely nothing.

Empty space assembled in the most accurate way the universe had to offer. Empty space visualized in an almost identical dusty desert road scene, just like the one she was currently seated in outside the realm of pixels. The same massive blue sky was dark enough to be a new shade of black. The same brown shadowy mountains in the distance and a familiar city far behind her. Even the wooden telephone poles and cables lined the left side of the street. Perhaps her brain actually exercised proper critical thought because Christina was actually able to catch the difference in telephone poles aligned to the wrong side of the cracked asphalt road. One of the few details subtracting to the disappointment she found from the familiar setting, thereby subtracting from the sense of complete nothing so that now there was a sense of at least something.

Only somewhat.

The other differences started to pop out, like yellow street lights calling for her attention in the night. Obvious and foremost, Lauren was missing in this digital realm along with the TV shrine Christina should have been sitting in. Instead, she was standing alone in the middle of the street with nothing better to do than scan her expansive dirt surroundings. There was no shabby barn a mile off. Instead, it had been replaced with a suburban house along the left side of the street. To her surprise, the string of coherent thoughts continued and although she realized it would just be playing into the hands of others there was no alternative option but for her to continue forward.

She couldn't help but feel like it would have been easier if she remained braindead. Following the telephone poles along the side of the road just like she did as a child along suburb sidewalks after school Christina made her way to the home. Much like everything else in this digital dimension it was a copy. At this point the true emptiness began to set in.

The lights were off and the driveway was vacant. Although it was night the house seemed completely empty. Approached with no colors to guide her along the intended path, she was reminded of one of the few times a car had been out of the driveway. Her mom had decided to go and get groceries. When she returned, the eight years old Christina was so excited to help her mom that she came running through the front door and skidding across the concrete, tearing lots of skin off her right knee. The scar had all but faded by now, but at the time blood slowly seeped out while she bawled her eyes crying for help. Her mom panicked, not knowing what to do, and froze until Grandma Xiaodan came rushing out to take over. Christina remembered her mom's still expression and how the woman's first instinctual reaction was to collect the oranges rolling into the street.

Christina opened the door with more harsh force than necessary, the hinges squealing from the stress. She stepped into a small box of a room filled with a couch, a shelf for shoes, and a few books littered around that had gone untouched since they had been placed there. Next was the kitchen where she directed her attention away from a particular drab white chair out of habit in favor of looking at the stove to her right. There had been a time which she had counted on herself to have mostly forgotten. The night when she vomited onto the plastic floral panels of the kitchen floor. On a night when mom had found the energy in herself to leave her chair and actually chat with grandma while watching television. Instead of interrupting the two for Xiaodan to prepare dinner, young Christina had promised to treat them with grilled cheese sandwiches only to catch a stray piece of toast on fire. In the process of putting it out a good square foot of the wall had been charred. The terror of having to tell her mom that night was too much for her body. Christina stopped her recollection for a moment to bite her bottom lip and hold back old, but familiar, tears.

She was enjoying this trip down memory lane less and less. There was really no point to continue down the hall to the laundry room or the bath past the living room. She knew where the house wanted to guide her, and its destination resided at the top of the stairs.

There was mom's room at one end. Then grandma's. And finally, her's. Where at thirteen she often lay in bed screaming into her pillow buried over her face because she knew better than to let her mom hear the sound of crying. But she had no need to venture that far down such a branch of thought. Her true destination was actually the closest room to the stairs, situated neatly between grandma's and mom's. It did not necessarily need locks nor did its real life counterpart have any. But the fact remained that locks and chains from every color of the rainbow were strung before the door and connected at the door frame. Part of her imagined a reality where she would push on the door now and it wouldn't budge so that she would have no choice but to walk away and never confirm the contents of its insides. She didn't want to see the room's insides. She didn't want to completely understand the truth for herself. It would have been so much simpler to remain an ignorant and unaware girl. But overwhelmingly, her muscles knew to open the door which chains and locks fell limply into a tangled heap on the floor without argument. There was never anything stopping her. Christina braced herself.

"It's empty." Marcus pointed out, taking notice of the sputtering engine wheezing beneath them.

"Since when have you been one to take notice of your surroundings?" Isabella barked back. As much as she hated to, there was no choice but to concede that the boy did have a point, no matter how obvious it was.

She could just make it to the freeway overpass before the motorcycle keeled over in death and it would be kicked to the side. It would have to do. The only positive here was that a newly indestructible form of Marcus currently made no reason for her to slow down before their vehicle gave out. Just as predicted, it toppled over on itself with its hard and obtuse edges, crushing Marcus into the road while Isabella ejected herself with a jump before the tired vehicle crashed into the overpass' cement railing.

"What's the plan now?" Marcus asked, peeling himself off the ground.

"Right now it's you losing this sudden habit of actually talking that you seem to have developed."

Their entourage of aggressors was already pulling up to a skidding halt. The limousine headlights directly shone onto the two stranded escapees. Isabella held her hand to shield her eyes. Between her fingers was an orange eagle of the paper variety with chains wrapped around its neck and bound to its entire body like bondage. For a moment there was an old glint of a viscous smile that Marcus remembered, already rising to meet it.

"The sticker is important."

The sticker already had a large bullet hole through it. Now made into just a paper flailing from the wind in her hand. The energy beam from the dangerously accurate marksmanship of

Tiana just grazed Isabella's shoulder and tore a strip off from her
suit.

"The sticker is just an excuse Bella," she called from next
to the open car door.

"Stop it."

"What, too afraid to see familiar faces?" Touma jeered
from the other side of the limo.

"Stop it."

The headlights cut off and Isabella met the gaze of Eve, his
eyes exhausted.

"Stop it," she whispered. Whispers so quiet that there was
no chance the words would travel across the stretch of road to her
business partner.

Marcus stared at the half of the orange paper bird that
fluttered to the ground before him. It would be decided atop the
overpass in the warm night breeze where the air was not
particularly crisp nor clear. Maybe it was from the motorcycle
ride with no helmet, or from standing in a place that was
normally only fond of cars, or perhaps he tasted the San Anlos air
for the first time with a clear palette. The moment had already
passed when he caught his first glimpse of panic in Isabella's eyes.
His mouth filled with the flavor of machinery, gasoline, and
rubber. His thoughts were coated in a layer of oil and smoke. His
nose was tainted with the pungent stink of burning tar. His legs
were strong although his spirit was weak. His arms were
reinforced although his emotions ran feral.

"Isabella. If what you said was true. If I really did exceed
your expectations." He pulled at her shoulder, but she would not
turn around to look at him. He couldn't stop the words now. "You
can depend on me now. If you need to give anything up, give it up
to me. I can help."

That wasn't right.

"I want to help," he corrected.

She smothered down laughter the same way someone would hold back vomit. Her eyes stretched wide with incredulity or possibly at the fear of the thought of such a misunderstanding. Or it might have been from violent urges. Or self lamenting. Or an explicit disgust with no bound. Or something entirely else.

Isabella Luna turned to look not at Marcus, but down and through him.

"You want to what?"

Marcus could see her diaphragm convulsing under her suit and the breath straining in her lungs.

"I need nothing from you," she growled. "I should never expect to depend on you." She took one step after another, turning around. With each one tremors shook through her body and out her mouth into the steaming breathes. Her fist clenched and ground approximations of bone with each word. It was all she could do before the words erupted out all at once.

"The actual idiocy you have to do little more than stroke your ego. I have dragged you through the city with consistent reminders and commands. You would not be breathing if someone was not here to remind you and pump your lungs. In fact, I would have had more success if I smothered you in your bed and drained your body of everything imaginable. Even your lifeless flesh would produce better results than you could ever. All you have ever been good for is disappointing others that were moronic enough to invest in you. All you have ever achieved is redefining what the true bare minimum is. You are so self-absorbed and your pull has only dragged all your friends and acquaintances down with you. Were you not comfortable being the most absolutely dreadful? Was it not enough to be the true definition of worthless? Worst of all, you don't even have the coherent thought to comprehend it all. Or is it that you are afraid of the energy needed to recognize the harsh truth of it? You can act like you like it. You can pretend to enjoy honesty. But there is not a retina in this city that your presence does not bore itself into an unholy amalgamation of all things pathetic, disappointing, and worthless. I would carve it into your flesh and skin a thousand times until it would be impossible for you to avert your gaze."

The words hit him in one singular instance so that, much like everything in his life, he could not process it. The one thing he could understand was the enraged face of Isabella, twisted in a feral abhorrence to his presence and bearing down on him.

"And you have the audacity to suggest you are anything else to me," she roared, with echoes sending his eardrums ringing in the way only something primordial could. He tried to whimper out a response, but there was only the harsh echo of a slap without hesitation.

Eve strained his eyes, afraid that she might have snapped the boys neck, as if it posed a problem if she did. Isabella stood atop of the depressed figure.

"Get out of my sight."

His face was red and went through the motions of carrying the pain without experiencing any of it. It was a response that would have felt comfortable in his mouth days prior, but now not so. Not since he had seen a sunset bright enough to remind him that he was alone.

It's antithetical to describe in text, as his speech tended to subtract with every word instead of its intended purpose. The only thing ever left was something unfamiliar.

"Fine."

CHAPTER 8: DEEP PUDDLES

It's empty.

In the sense that it was the closest resemblance possible to pure emptiness that Christina had ever seen.

The room was empty.

Standing in her father's bedroom, the details appeared more exact to her dreams than she had ever envisioned. Absolute pain in all its details. Surfaces were left untouched from the last time a warm hand had offered such intimate nature years ago, the night when items were packed to leave. The window was shut tight across the room. The bed was nude. All the shelves were neatly bare against the walls. If there was any color that was present beforehand for one to perceive it had been drained out from the gray light that continued to drift in and illuminate without concern nor care from the window.

Christina had the impression that she was standing within an old family photo except there was no comfortable distance of time that oculd be offered. There was no graininess or faded details present to obscure the corners within the room from the witness of her eyes. In an instant, she regretted the old wish to once again not be witless, not when she knew it would have muted the impact now. Tones present would have been spared from her understanding and how unfamiliar it truly felt when it should have been anything but. If it had been another her, another brain, one that could not depict the truth, then maybe she could have distracted herself by the platitudes and nostalgic ideas of standing in the same space her father had stood. That there was a tether to him somehow more than her mere existence here. But the current her knew there was no such relationship. Christina's eyes scanned the room and were enthralled by everything that was absent. The photos not on the walls. The clothes not in the dresser. The notes that couldn't be left. The trinkets that couldn't be departed with. Bubbles were bursting inside her chest as she confirmed each of her worst fears.

That her father's departure was slow and methodical. Nothing and absolutely no one had left a pain strong enough in his own chest to try and forget his past. No guilt remained that he could not bear to be reminded of in his absence. There was no memory that was better left in his mind only. No emotion was left to stain the room in color. Not a single connection between her and the man that took part in her creation, but not her growth. Without it, she couldn't use that string tying the two together and wind it around his throat to remind him of the people he gave up nor could she pull on it until he was close enough to finally wrap her arms around in an embrace missing from her earliest memories. All because they were complete strangers.

She had known it already.

Christina had less than before when she had never entered the room. Before she had learned more than she had ever wanted about a lesson she was all too familiar with. There was no need to reassess the topic through virtual occultic means. It had been apparent enough to witness, day after day, every pained movement on Samantha Zheng. Every dinner that sat in absolute gruesome silence. She knew the story all well enough. No one had to tell her again. Physical torture would have been preferred to the option.

Lost in thought, she didn't notice her foot placed into the rising water. Before her, the house had quickly filled with water taking her under while stuck inside. Her mistake of a gasp only allowed all the air within her lungs to escape in the form of bubbles that ascended above her. In only a matter of moments her two lungs had become lakes. In that sole instance the suburban aquarium was still and placid. Another quaint house to populate the street of the same, even if it was not truly situated there now.

But the Xiaodan house was not quiet for long. Nor was it ever. Not when it was the lair of an old deity made human, or vice versa. Steam hissed through the wood cracks and between the tiles along the roof. There was a tired ache within the hearth. One that existed not within the kitchen downstairs nor Samantha Zheng's and abandoned bedrooms alike. Behind Christina was a fireplace of a grandma's room, flames licking out the door and into the hall casting everything nearby in its warm glow. The energy was fueled by a compassionate rage along with all other sorts of emotions. A true orange color filled Christina's vision, more distinct and pure than any faux one she had seen before, combatting the constant blue waters of life.

Complementary colors in opposition. Water had evaporated out the second story of the house in a sizzling vapor. Anytime the liquid level rose to meet the flame's warm vicinity the heat boiled the blue into pressurized droplets. Retreat only existed for the body of water in the sanctity of downstairs. All of which gave Christina just the right amount of time necessary for her to collapse on the floor coughing out with intense pain as water evacuated her lungs and air reclaimed the space it had missed. She didn't think that she could die here, but she also didn't know whether that to be fact or not. The only thing she did truly know was that she was not out of the house yet.

There was no path that could ignore the particular shade of blue anymore. It was a color of her world like all the other ones. Mom's blue. The blue of Lei Zheng that gave way to Samantha Lei Zheng. Just like how she had changed the name from her first to middle when she was old enough and after a certain man promised he liked the sound as much as he liked her. Blue. A dreary color that puddled at the woman's feet. Downstairs, through the still water of a flooded house, was somebody sitting in the same spot as always. Solemnly lost and isolated.

"Why?"

They were the first words that came to Christina's mind as she took her first willful step into the water.

"Why did you do it, mom? You knew it as well, didn't you?

The truth begged to drown in her throat, but she dragged it out. Water rocked against her slamming into her face and pulling her down, but a heat resided in her, drumming through her veins and boiling the lake around her.

"Dad is gone."

The flooded stairs screamed in the escape of vapor.

"He left. He didn't want to be a part of this family. He didn't want to be a part of our lives."

She stopped halfway downstairs. The heat had subsided in favor of a burden cracking the supports of her chest. It was not a pace sustainable in the old waters of the living room. Lily pads and moss grew atop the surface, but she forced herself to move.

"We weren't enough for him. I wasn't the child he wanted. You weren't the wife he could love like he said he could. This house wasn't the one he could live in."

It felt stupid screaming about a man that she had never met. But any tears that rushed towards her eyes and threatened to burst forth only made her feel even more angry for having to feel such a stupid way.

"Cause he isn't here anymore and hasn't been for my entire life. And he isn't coming back. You have sat in that chair mourning for a loss you can't even feel. That room has been ignored for so long because you and I both want to refuse the truth, to hold onto some useless fantasy."

Christina had been holding back crying while she wadded through the rising living room pond, but the cold tears came streaming out now.

"But it won't change the fact that he doesn't love us."

Her weeping left cold streaks along her cheeks leaving her skin cool and vacant.

"I don't have a father and you don't have a husband. Not anymore."

The words didn't want to leave her. They wanted to drown themselves in the silence of the water where no one could hear them.

"So why?" she screamed. 'Why couldn't I have a mom? Why did you have to make me hate you? Goddamit I already lost one parent why did I have to lose you as well?"

She had nearly made it through the living room. Her view rocked with every wave sent through the water's surface, prior tranquility now at a storm. Each step was pushed back with the riptide. Each movement was a struggle. Moss had started to climb along her arms, holding her back if she did not go about tearing it off.

"I just wanted a mom. I wanted you to hold me, to be there for my highs and lows. I wanted to share so much of my life with you. Day after day I came to you ready to be your child. To have that special connection with someone. But you didn't want that, did you? You wanted to envy and lament and pity and suffer and give up and imagine another life. Every single day you would rather waste, mourning this life."

Her chest rocked inside and out. The spray of this virtual watery grave managed to reach her mouth and into her lungs. The process of breathing alone was laborious and stung.

"Did you know? Did you know how much that hurt? How much pain you caused? The damage you gave me?"

Christina made it to the kitchen doorway but the water rising far too fast, engulfing her completely. Her throat was stripped and raspy. Her body still ached and her lungs burned now with a fire inside of them but she could not stop now. She fought to stay above it all.

"I am more Xiaodan than Zheng. I refuse to give up mama. I don't want to live my life in guilt. I can't fear every action I make will break you. I have wasted 17 years of my life because of you and I will never get back. Dictated by a mom who never bothered to meet me halfway. But I will never take that seat of yours."

The crying was done now. It was harder to do so after nearly drying herself out and sore throat. All she could do was struggle against the doorframe and gasp for eventual opportunities of air. The moss was ever present along with its pull and the ceiling came fast approaching as the rocky waters increased. She took her last gulp of air and dove.

The kitchen was completely submerged. Waters were still in contrast to the other room's current, a moment frozen and preserved. The old wooden table and metal utensils were floating all around her. Christina paid it no attention. She was in search of Samantha Zheng, sitting in the corner in her white seat still grounded to the floor.

Beautiful in stasis as always.

Eyes tired and depressed. Titled from the weight of so.

Eyebrows in a permanent state of sorrow.

A plain white dress and long black her brushed over her shoulder to hide her thin figure.

Sitting hands folded in her lap and looking over to a far off distance as she had always done.

Christina shifted through the water towards her. Reaching towards the ugly floral print floor and planting her two feet, until she stood in front of the woman she called mother. Her hands touched the woman's pale soft cheeks. She could feel the pain for a moment. The water had so much pressure from down here it encroached on her chest and wrung out every last breath so that there was no other option than to submit. She let her thumb caress the woman's face, brushing aside stray hairs. Feeling what had been left forgotten and untouched.

"Was I not enough for you?"

Christina slapped the woman before with a force strong enough to send water exploding out of the house, shattering windows and tearing doors off their hinges.

CHAPTER 9: ROAD RAGE AND OTHER EMOTIONS

There was a standoff on the overpass between Isabella, Touma, Tiana, and those within the limo that refused to get in the line of carnage for one reason or the other. The deadly and famous power couple was presently ready to live up to their name and hype by combatting the fearsome monster in mostly human form before them. Tiana had already taken her rifle with her a few feet behind the limo for cover against Eve's protest. Touma produced two weapons of his own, exiting the limousine's interior with a white case similar in style to his partners. However, with his expertise being hand to hand combat the only thing within his smaller luggage was two thick, spiked, and pale titanium knuckles. The perfect compliment to Tiana's, in theory and focus groups at least. Touma was a variable that Tiana assumed would most certainly make every shot she took much harder than it had to be. At this point in their relationship, she was used to the rather common, but nevertheless intrusive, thought of shooting right through him. Alas, her affections proved too much each and every time, even if Touma could technically still be reassembled.

"Look alive Isabella. This should be refreshing," Touma jeered as he approached casually with a smile on his face. Straight towards an Isabella who was experiencing miniature convulsions and twitching all over from a surplus of turmoil. Solid energy ran in the currents under her approximation to skin and escaped as steam between her deliberately concentrated, but nonetheless rough, breaths.

"Make no mistake," he continued. "I fully intend for this to be an exercise in total dissection. But cathartic destruction can be therapeutic in a sense."

There was no response. And there was not going to be one regardless of how long he waited. Only when that fact was readily apparent did he dare turn his back on the target to look out over the edge of the concrete wall and into the sight of the city lit up from disaster.

"If you think about it, you're probably one of the first people to stand exactly where you are on this road. 5pm traffic can be a killer, but people still wait for hours or so because they know it will get them forward. Sitting holed up in their cars, refusing to get out. Just waiting. I know we have to be at each other's throats, but I still genuinely care for you." He said the last part while finally turning back to face her. "Remember that when I am tearing you limb from limb."

"Don't waste words with me."

From a suitcase she had somehow managed to keep on her she extracted two screws the size of decapitated heads. Both capable of exactly such purposes.

"You and I know the next few moments well. Your manufactured making against my faux flesh. Until the other's insides are lying on the ground."

"I would have it no other way."

Tiana, who had been waiting for her other half to stop rambling in the way he liked to, wasted no time in taking her shot set square between Bella's eyes. Her aim was perfect only for the concentrated energy to be deflected at the last minute with interstellar metal screws sending the energized bullet sideways. Not anything enough to inflict damage, but just the right amount of distraction. A mistake that would be paid in full through bruised approximations of skin and broken approximations of ribs. Touma released patented crass and plentiful aggression into Isabella's abdomen, sending shockwaves through the air along with it. Only for Bella to react with enough speed to intercept the attack as it landed, screw in hand. His metal fingers met with her gut along with a whining metal screw that spun with a sickening screech until Touma's ring and middle finger were completely torn off. It was reason more than enough for Tiana to lay down a barrage of suppressing fire while Touma jumped backward to regroup.

Every bullet went scattered in every direction as Bella's screws whirled with imperceptible force. Each swirling into a minor whirlwind in her hands.

"Fair enough," Touma whined. "These things demand a certain pace to them."

Christopher winched in a familiar pain at the sight of expensive repairs that he would have to hand install, knowing full well he was going to get hell in the process and pay deducted. "You should be out there too," he pointed out toward Eve.

"Like it or not I am dedicated to my new commitments."

"That's cute bro. Real cute even. Don't use me as an excuse to escape your problems though"

Eve knew Christopher was right. The sound of his voice journeyed through his ears, into his temporal lobe, and was processed by his auditory cortex. But before then he was already completely overtaken by Christopher's words. He had the truth ringing through his head with the strength of mistake better ignored for the cure of time. Christopher could see the struggle in the way Eve's eyebrows knotted, in the clench of his jaw, and how his eyes were slow to move upward to see before them.

"I don't know what kind of man loves me. But the one I love is the same one who would help his dear partner as well. All paths are leading towards destruction whether we stop it or not. What's the point of taking care of me if it ruins you and everyone else." Christopher grabbed his boyfriend's hand and waited for as long as he needed until they were eye to eye. "Better yet, maybe I don't like being cared for like that in the first place. Whatever happens, promise you won't leave me figuratively or literally."

Eve couldn't ignore his boyfriend's words if he tried. Nor could he ignore Isabella who had resolved to send a screw hurtling towards them to eviscerate Tiana's cover. Clamping down on those very gloved hands with all his strength, Eve dove out the door as the metal screamed in a way only the vocals of a dangerous screw could while it tore through the vehicle like paper. Twisting through the center of the car, a tunneled hole was left while the screw sent the limo flipping to the side of the road.

Christopher laid exasperated on top of Eve's large chest pinning him down underneath.

"This is a bad example, but you know what I mean."

Eve rolled the man aside in the most delicate manner he could, dusting themselves off from each other. He knew full and well. It would have been easy to recite the lesson stating that the best defense was an offense, stopping the danger at its source. But he refused to speak in over encompassing generalizations and platitudes as per his class nature. Sayings like that totally ignored that half the job was defining the problem and what defense and offense looked like. So instead he opted for something a lot more simple and concise.

"Yeah, yeah."

It was good enough for Christopher, who had neither the patience for wordplay nor the right mindset to keep on contesting ideas presented. In truth, he didn't really know what he was doing as well. There was no plan, only immediate remedies that seemed right in the moment. One problem onto another. So while Eve seemed situated in what one could assume was the least self-destructive and most constructive course of action for the moment Christopher retreated, already onto another problem. Phone in hand and numbers dialed.

Isabella came bounding towards Touma only to leap into the air in the last minute and land successive barrages of kicks with her heels. Bearing down from him from above and shooting through the space between the flurry of legs came a screw in hand, ready to tear the robot's head open. Tiana cursed as she struggled to align her shot, propping herself with one knee after rolling from the wrecked limo. The only action capable of putting a stop to mere machinery devastation was the black chains that snapped against Bella's left leg and wrapped themselves before flinging her down against the road with a velocity that would break backs when applied to a normal person. Strong enough the links themselves shattered.

"Let's stop with this farce. This wasn't your plan Isabella." Eve approached with his suitcase in hand, stating the words solemnly like a eulogy.

"Come to resign as my handler?" she replied, already on her feet and running circles around him like a predator beast.

Tiana's bullets trailed after the alien woman, failing to close the gap before Isabella did exactly that between her and Eve. From behind, with a wind up from a twirl, Isabella landed the resounding blow of her foot directly against Eve's approximation of a spine, shooting him forward. Touma was already above her, blocking Tiana's sight as he dove his good fist in a single vicious motion into the side of Isabella's head, sending her cratering into the road with a puff of dust and rubble.

There was a cackling from within the cloud of fine cement particles. One that elicited an innate disgust within everyone's stomach on an instinctual basis and not so much a personal one.

A single pale hand shot out, parting the cloud around it, grasping onto Touma's head with a dangerous strength that held him off the ground. Not strong enough to break him, but enough for Isabella to shield herself from Tiana who was seriously questioning the stain that headshotting her fiancé to hit Isabella would have on their relationship. Eve spared her from the shame, letting loose a net of chains from his suitcase. Black chain links clinked together as one wave after another poured out and engulfed his stray partner in business. Quickly Bella's constricted figure was engulfed in a solid black mass of tightening metal squeezing against her approximation of flesh and ready to grind her approximation of bone into powder. The only thing exposed to freedom was her head in order to speak and listen.

"You get to keep your arms today," Touma snarked, even though Tiana really wished that he wouldn't.

"Isabella," Eve started. "You know just as well as I do that this isn't how you are going to achieve that dream you shared with me. Rushing it now is only going to hurt you as well as everyone around you. Messing up now is just giving the Adamants more reason to act."

He let out an exhausted sigh. One only capable of someone who had experienced troubles and turmoils that far exceeded his years accumulated in his long life, but not enough years to tell him the right actions needed. No lesson, specific line, or question from his decades forced into memorization within classrooms not of this world could have prepared him for the right words to say now. The proper things to speak were never readily at hand nor comfortably formed their shape with the lips. It sits caddywhompus on the tongue and travels in the air like a dull petition. He could only hope his words reached her while he placed his hand to just about where her shoulder would have been.

"I'm sorry Bella. The plan didn't work out like we thought. Things failed tragically and were facing the same worst case scenario somehow worse than normal. I'm sorry that I can't give you the same kind of passion that you give me. I'm sorry that we can't fight for you the way you fight for us. I'm sorry if it hurts sometimes. Because it shouldn't. But if I can't be the kind of person that stands before you I'm going to be the one that stands behind you. Ready push you when you need to be, catch you when you fall, and hold you when you need to be held."

He hesitated with a careful earnestness in his words that Isabella did not bother entertaining. Spending no time to think, she clamped her jaws onto his hand and bit hard enough to completely sever approximated flesh to the scream of a not so imitation of a reaction.

"Do you not have decency?" he yelped, cradling his open gash next to his thumb.

"Not when the end of the world starts with the letter A." She spat out a chunk of homunculus meat.

"No one is ending things but you."

"Don't you get it, Eve? There is no more patience left within the cavities of my heart. To put it bluntly is to put it best. I'm tired of it all."

She shrugged off her words with a pitiful concession. Within her one had deep inside the tangles of chains there was still a screw. One in which that rotated with a ferocity that the air around it pulsated with heat, fast enough to shred the solid astronomical metal encasing into black glitter with ease. Massive amounts of force sent the air rumbling and the entire concrete structure they stood on struggled to stand upright against the tremors.

Isabella spoke every word with a serene calm tranquility only possible through the oppressive guiding forces of confrontation. No doubt, if she had even a modicum of the personage presently set back during her adolescent years her classroom experiences would have unfolded differently. Terror would have been ingrained into her house and she would have not had to stand in San Anlos on a full moon night to savor the experience of a defeat achieving such totality. Before the group stood a caged beast that had succumbed to its wounds but, not one in particular (Chapter 9 Paragraph 34 Line 198).

"As a Class I: Instigator, it's only fitting that I am the one who tells the end of my story. And I will end the world around me if I want."

Touma sent a nod towards Tiana, letting her finally breathe a sigh of relief pent up since the fight had started. He came dashing forwards, past Eve, and ready to lend a decisive blow with his good arm. Isabella greeted the robot boy with a genuine smile that nearly caught him off guard. A falter enough for Isabella to quickly release her screw through his extended arm, contorting the metal before tearings it's way through and out his shoulder. Only by shutting off his electronic nervous receptors did Touma lend himself enough clear mind to speak.

"I don't need a win for victory. I just need to be supported."

Tiana's sight was locked onto at least 1/4th of their intended promise. It would have to be enough to count for retribution.

Isabella's eyes were only able to track the events in the last moments. A solid streak of white hot energy traveled through the air in an instant. Sent right through the space Touma's arm should have been.

White paper-like material fluttered out, escaping from the massive wound, letting loose her insides. Internal paper mache hung in the air around her, littering the road below. Isabella's left arm was completely severed.

It was silent.

Isabella Luna slowly fell to her knees as she cried.

And it was silent.

CHAPTER 10: ENDING HOMES

"We are out of options. Just do what you have to do."

Lauren had just finished Christina's virtual cognitive simulation and was prepared to observe her progress when Christopher interrupted with a phone call. Him ending the said phone call was only redundant as Lauren was already long past the point of discarding the phone and abandoning her work. It would have to solve itself, she decided, because she was needed elsewhere. Desperately was the process, by a necessity that was reiterated with each heavy footstep and labored breath from within her burning lungs in her own sacred sidewalk frantic ritual. Flinging her weight from side to side, she forced herself to move when her feet protested the actions with near failure. A few blocks away, heading towards the same monstrous gallows was an exhausted Marcus. He was experiencing an ache in his muscles that was never truly existent and almost frivolous in his suffocated pain when placed in distinct comparison with Lauren's current state.

It would be false to define his current state of mental awareness as regression or anything of that sort. The details were carved out and solidly placed in the strong factual surface of cleanly cut stone that was used to build escapist fantasies and prisons alike. Ones that could transcend the role of any realism that would have supposedly grounded these thoughts as a prevalent core. Secondly, Marcus was a man built upon impressionism more than anything else. A fate of being interpreted, but not understood. Any palace constructed on such foundations was only fortified in favor of extravagance. It was all a roundabout way of stating, rather sophisticatedly, that it was impossible for someone to regress any further past the point of origin, at least in the linear course of time that humans like Marcus abided by. A sentence reiterated countless times within his head. There was a purpose and decision as to why an infant blue followed him wherever he went, inescapable no matter how hard he dreamt. Sweet sugar was not a taste he had forgotten nor never had the luxury to truly savor the flavor before. Rather, its installments into his daydream made a bland necessity in his mouth, strong enough to morph rancid smells until it was almost citrus. Marcus wandered nearly aimlessly in manner among city streets, slowly drifting toward the pull of his destination in the midst of his fantasized downfall.

      The sky was falling again. Not in the literal sense that anyone else could see.

      Only a select few had the unfortunate privilege to witness the sight as an imaginary god forsake him with mere absence alone. Massive chunks of an orange sunset facade painted onto stone came plummeting down into the earth of San Anlos around him, reshaping his mental landmarks of a fake city with every collision. Dung beetles, rarely remembered, had already completed their mission coated in filth long before sundown had ended. The only last excrement to push into its final resting place was himself.

      Panting on the sidewalk. Hands on her knees. Eyes cast downward and far more solemn than she had intended to priorly.

      Lauren stood there before the Alvarado house waiting for its first ever intruder. Slowly, Marcus continued towards her without care within.

      He could stomach anything if he could ignore the flavor.

      He should have been able to at least.

      For a moment it was just the two of them. Alone again. Within a sleeping city. Only close to each other. His side to hers.

Her side to his. This time facing opposite directions. The many
eyes that populated the block and recognized as neighboring
houses were closed and asleep, oblivious to any sin that would
transpire then. A conversation solely between them: Lauren,
Marcus Alvarado, and the empty house before and behind.

The latter was dark, looming, and haunted. Cast in a
shadow blacker than the night sky backdrop.

"You shouldn't do what you are going to do."

"I shouldn't be doing a lot of things."

"That doesn't justify another mistake."

Marcus tried to laugh.

"A mistake implies that there is something left to preserve
in this scenario. Lauren, when have I ever had a way with words
before? Above anybody else, in that house, you should know that.
Days spent second guessing how shallow I could be as a person. I
don't understand how you could get lost in a cupboard somehow.
Can you fathom how guilty I am?"

"I can't believe that?" She retaliated, finally turning to be
transfixed on the house as well.

"Then my idiocy is transmissible. I know that these
problems shouldn't hurt me. There are countless ways to achieve
a variety of success and make my heart full. I'm sure if there was
an ounce of logic in my body I could have figured it out by now. I
just want to make a new memory, but it's cruel that reality is
impressionism defined by incapabilities. If you're still as smart as
when I first met you then the subtext should be easy to find."

Marcus had never turned to face her. From her view she
couldn't tell but it seemed like tears were swelling, wanting to
escape from his body but it was hard to make out. Of course she
understood the words that were quietly written between the lines
of his dialogue and the information wrapped together in his chest.

At what point was the house haunted? When it was deprived, forgotten, and cursed?

If there was anything she learned from the past days it was that words were an entity far more than solely definitions.

A what point does a house convulse with evil and malice? When it was empty?

Those were far from the right questions. She had to look at it from Marcus' perspective. Down halls and rooms she had seen in person and through the screen. Drawing upon barren interiors with photos of a couple and not a family. A kitchen left spotless and unused with a fridge that couldn't sate the smallest of appetites. A T.V. room with a couch to seat two, a keen eye could catch the casual stuffed animal still lounging around the rooms in preparation for the nursery. Above the stairs Marcus slept surrounded by blues skies, green hills, and happy animals that had gone unattended by their creators after three years as well. Present within the Alvarado household was a family with a missing sun, seemingly still a newborn.

Do you think the house understands the meaning in that? Or is it only annoyed and confused?

Such was the conclusion that Lauren could have formulated days ago, when it was still the familiar faux and fake afternoon sun warming both of their spirits and allowing observation in a like minded way. Too late now was the offer for reconstruction. Geography was damaged and changing. They both had to abide by such results.

It was orange. The teardrop that leaked across Marcus' cheek and then onto his finger when he wiped, it was colored orange. Bright in color that it stood out within the dark night as it mixed with the half of a ripped sticker in his hand before it shot upwards into the clouds.

From the clouds sprouted an orange hand of no god growing in an opposite manner towards the earth. In other words descending. A mass of chained birds writhing but alive, interwoven, and tangled until it made the culmination of many curses.

The sticker was not important now.

Marcus realized it. Not when in incapable hands at least. It should have never been. But he had never been so. Even now he needed it. Lauren had one last means necessary to stop the utter destruction with a gift of parting painted purple and loaded with enough tranquilizer to send an elephant to sleep. Lauren pressed the Tandem Tantrum Toys and Co. dart gun into his neck while realizing a conclusion of her own.

"I despise you." For all her depth of the English language she spoke with an evenness that balanced the words along the air it stood. "I despise the masochist that is guilty of everybody's crimes."

She couldn't tell if that was the right or wrong thing to say but there was an order of importance to the matters. Foremost being her finger on the trigger ready to stop this futility. In came Christina. Faster than sound would permit, she stopped with a cratering impact before her entrance could be heard. She had heard the phone call interrupt her simulation. Her company VR headset was still on and connected to her own wireless biological server that let her hijack the use of the BODYGUREAR ISSUE 04 OFFENSIVE SET MODEL 4452. It was a round blue mecha, propped up on two pegs for legs with a circular chest that attached to circular shoulders that attached to oversized arms and massive metallic mitts for hands. Said mitts held her in one and with the other it delicately crushed the gun Lauren held.

"I don't like him either. But I can excuse his actions just this once." It was a temporary gesture from Christina that was nearly meaningless with no intention for further actions. It was enough for tonight though.

A nearly dead hand with no singular heart to beat out its pain weighed down on the empty house in a punishment, crushing together masses of empty promises, vacant memories, hollow words, photos without families, kitchens with no food, rooms with no people, and all the years wasted that had not been lived.

CHAPTER 11: BASIC FACTS OF THE MATTER

Important facts of note prior to remediation involvement. San Anlos remains residing rightfully within a recently recognized blindspot of the Luna family production practices. This is included along with several other space provincial blocks ranging, but not limited to, provincial code UI7365-VS8378. This information is to remain confidential and communicated solely on a need to know basis. Prior individuals with a recorded history of operations within provincial codes of concern are to be better monitored, recorded, and analyzed according to the Luna expectations for assigned duties. Generated weapon production is to be immediately secured and transported within safer holding facilities after communication is confirmed of ground units.

Class I individuals historically have shown behaviors negative and combative to the Luna expectations for the conduct of family members. Remedial lessons are greatly encouraged for proper recourse and adjustments to select individuals psyches. Class I individual "ISABELLA" illustrates extreme unwillingness to follow standard procedure and demonstrates dangerous behaviors and tendencies when performing assigned duties. Immediate remediation is greatly encouraged. All activities within provincial codes of concern are to be evaluated and observed for analysis. Current expectations have been underperformed and the time frame exceeded. Authorization for immediate handover of responsibilities complete. Termination of Class I individual is pending.

Class E individual "EVE" has been assigned to prioritize Luna expectations and maintain a regular schedule for duties. Information pending from observations on accuracy to goals.

Immediate interruption of current activities authorized. Request for Class A deployment approved. Contact pending. Further suggestions and course of procedures will be decided after field evaluation.

CHAPTER 12: UNINVITED GUEST

"Let's keep this brief shall we?"

"Words are best served minced after all."

Two children spoke with identical voices similar in every aspect of their lines except in duet. The one only dined on forbidden fruit and the other on murdered meat. Today would offer no exception to such distinct palettes. San Anlos was a mere city, not a buffet. The inhabitants only toiling, not devouring one another. Finally, and most importantly, two voices aligned perfectly to create something wholly complete. Whether separate or individual, it was the same. There was much to be corrected and set straight, but of course that was below the bare minimum expectations for the Adamants. As many things were.

Isabella's tears were beginning to dry. There were never any actual scars, but she wished the trails would. She wanted wounds burnt deep into her face to remember, but such blemishes were not befitting for a Luna. Instead, a constant influx of momentary sadness, strong enough to tie her throat quietly with ribbon, would have to compensate for preferred physical reminders.

Christopher had returned next to Eve, scornful at the bittersweet sight he would have made renaissance paintings of days ago which now felt like a past lifetime. The great calamity made women was now lowered and beaten. Posterizing from the weight of it, sullen eyes downwards, all of which was concerning to a world she had fought valiantly against. Her arm was weak and limp in her lap, tired from damage far greater than any amputation. Touma and Tiana hung back unsure of what victory now entails other than being tired from this race toward what had seemed like an unachievable infinity. Most of all, Eve could not ignore it too. The sensation of it was itching at the back of his jaw, sending shivers through his teeth in a manner that exited like electricity at the tips of his fingers. Mourning for a death he would not yet entertain. But a financed mourning nonetheless.

The tranquility of loss was only interrupted by a white glare of a spotlight once again. White bleaching every surface it found in the dead of night. Without time to look up, the overpass shook from the impact of a massive child's letter block 'A' painted red. The force of its impact holed itself into the concrete in a single fast and succinct movement. Best put, the party could feel it before they actually saw any interlopers nor their vehicles from above. Instead, the pulsating gravitational disturbance beamed between the earth and the space metal, sending eardrums popping respectively. Acid reflux was slightly catastrophic and waves of anxiety were complimenting factors to go along with the murmuring atmosphere. Sure enough, above them all was a spacecraft almost comically stereotypical and hilarious if not for the severe threat it positioned itself in all of their lives. The spotlight was nothing of the sort, only escaped light from an opening bay at its bottom surface forming a space far more sterile and white with light than any of them could have imagined possible to perceive and maintain. The sight of which burned retinas and mechanical substitutes as well. Peeking out from the opening were two smiling faces of identical children with the same pale face, skin, and white bowl cut hair.

"You have been so irresponsible we couldn't help but notice."

"Hopefully this one lesson will last."

A bolt of lightning shot out from the port striking the gigantic letter block sending each side toppling down revealing its true nature as a present and the gifted limousine inside. It was a similar electric energy that had spread through the particles of water within the air, almost electrifying the sky itself ever since the interlopers had entered the same stratosphere as San Anlos. Immaculately, the group shared in a quasi reverent silence now manufactured out of their evolving logic for surviving malevolent social structures, the most important of which was to not be the first to speak. Because of this both Adam and Abel had plenty of time to make their prolonged entrances as they floated down delicately within the white light. The one hand of each was holding back their black sailor caps from drifting away, the other of each was secured to similarly black colored suitcases. The pair landed with grace, contacting with the earth and finally the gravity that dictated its happenings. Standing upright each of them only measured the height of the average elementary student, half the size or less of most persons present. From their black sailor uniforms, their matching shorts, high socks, large ties, small hats, pale skin, and white bowl cut hair they were indiscernible from each other. The circle of white light slowly began to shrink while the port closed.

"Eve," addressed either Adam or Abel. "I expect you to speak. I also expect you to speak only when spoken to."

One of them stood in the center of the subtracting spotlight, directly blocking Isabella from the rest of the group, while the other child walked the perimeter around the group.

"It's not an order. It's just a fact of life."

"Just as lungs breath and hearts break," the other one finished walking just in front of Tiana. "It's possible to teach an old dog new tricks, even if the challenge is heightened."

"But every stray can have a tame nature beaten into them," the center one finished. "You know I harbor no ill will, just a plain unbias."

"So when we do things like this its only because its equivalent."

A black cattle prod was extracted from their suitcase and pressed against Tiana's trigger arm. A course of white hot electricity ran across her synthetic skin only for system meltdown and numbness before erupting into a pain too fast to be prepared for. The metal burst into imperceptible shards shooting into the air around her and tearing off at the shoulder. Her following scream was much more of an instinctual reaction than anything else. Pain from having sudden loss and not so much the experience of it. A reaction the twins were used to.

"You're the devil!" Touma spat, ready to lunge. He was only stopped by an interruption of a microchipped dart shot from the hands of Christopher, shutting him down.

"No. We are creatures of Genesis, or named after such at least," the nearest one answered. "Plus, the devil makes no profit."

Eve hunched over and placed his hands deep into his pockets to such a drastic degree that his eyes were nearly level with those of Adam and their short stature. At this point they stood in complete darkness underneath the hum of the spacecraft.

"You're here now. What do you want?"

"Your understanding is wonderful," Adam congratulated. "As a result of your incompetence and defamation of the Luna name we will have to make up the difference in losses. As of present, we are taking over this job. Meanwhile, you will reinstate confidence in your representation of the Luna name by finally living up to your class identification and holding the defunct prior Class I individual until an export can be made for major reconstructive remedial methods to be enacted."

"As usual these are not threats nor suggestions. They are proclamations."

Abel stalled there a ways away, knotting their eyebrows in an honest effort of concentrated thought before closing the distance between their intended targets with methodical speed. The twin's eyes were solid silver disks, non-reflective of any world around them.

"If it helps though, we could do our best at making a threat."

Abel held the electrified ends of the metal prod a micrometer away from Christopher's throat who was careful not to gulp at this distance.

"We are behind schedule so you must understand."

Before Adam could finish black chains had already shot out from a suitcase, ensnaring a catatonic Isabella within the new limousine and placing her in a funeral pose. More chains wrapped around the vehicle's outside, further securing it before bringing the car to a stand on its hood with its back end high in the air. The metal coffin towered behind Adam's small frame, enough to crush them.

"Perfect. Then we can head straight into stage two."

The heavy blanket of white light once again escaped from the opening of the spacecraft's port as Isabella's resting place was levitated upwards and slowly stored within. Adam strutted past Eve to where Abel stood, never once experiencing hesitation, nor wasted actions, nor stray behaviors like a look behind. Eve, on the other hand, was writhing with rage pumping through his veins at the pure unhelpfulness that seemed to course through him at greater concentrations.

The enforcer did not like being enforced. In fact, he often felt in ways that were contrary to it. However, letters do not fall to earth for no reason. And in the same vein-

"There is no action without purpose."

"No thought without reason."

"If the Adamants do so then it was destined because that is the nature of things."

"A net progress."

As words parted so did they do so with their hair, revealing small slits in both of their foreheads. With ease, they each retracted a black sticker of a rabbit with crescent shaped ears from said openings. And with greater ease, they pressed it against the arms of a stunned Christopher. Eve, veins ready to burst in his temples, had only disbelief as his weapon of choice while he watched. Projection without results.

"Don't avert your gaze," Adam pointed out. "Sear this into your memory once over. And understand these arguments are regardless in life when it's a matter of facts and infactuality."

The two twins jutted their cattle prods deep into Christopher's protected insides of his thoracic cavity. Through his muscled sides and in between the defenses of his ribcage they sent volts of electricity into his body stirring every organ into action. With a great pace his flesh contorted and morphed like a gelatinous mass, thrashing at the energy and pulling itself away until two giant black hares leaped from him. The gigantic creatures escaped into the night before he had the chance to crumple against the hard concrete road. The twins swiveled and tilted their heads, letting the sides of each temple touch. Above them each cattle prod raised and met the other sending electricity coursing through them and into the surface, coursing through the flesh of an unconscious man, the metallic bodies of beaten robots, and buzzing within the ear of Eve.

"Our will is fruition because it is expected. We are the adamant truth."

STCKR: platonic panic - 264

STCKR: PLATONIC PANIC
EPISODE 4: TYPHN

CHAPTER 1: BAY CITY BLUES

San Anlos had finally drowned.

The city was submerged in blues that made priorly clear and recognizable landmarks unrecognizable. At some point, the earth gave way to the ocean which soon met its end with that of the cloud packed sky, but all these details were undiscernible. It was a blue hour that refused to end, sending days into a similar hue.

Under natural pretenses, there would have been a contrasting orange glow of activity shining out as warmed orbs against blue sidewalks. However, Sana Anlos was past the point. Streetlamps had long been dry of energy. Houses were boarded up. Windows were shielded.

It was typhoon season after all. Precautions had to be taken. Things and people had to part. Disaster had to break at any moment. How lucky was it then that Tandem Tantrum Toys and Co. had prepared, in correspondence with the local government, disaster shelters for residents to barricade themselves in. Protection was complete with promised supplies, food, and running water. To school gymnasiums, city hall, and any other locations deemed large enough to barely fit the masses and accommodate an accumulation of anxious civilians, they marched with their most precious holdings in tow.

It was most certainly the time for typhoons. However, the palm trees did not bend in stress from overbearing winds. Raindrops did not pelt every available surface. Water did not overwhelm poorly managed drains flooding streets. Homes did not rot. Yet the signs were there with a malicious compliance to certain expectations. The sky was crushingly heavy with clouds above the ocean. A bruised storm blackened the horizon. A crisp air filled the city's lungs, one lacking in the prescribed dose of pollutants and obscurity. Radio slots and TV news segments had drilled home the important notion of public safety to comfort the most mentally draining aspects to make what would have felt like an unwanted guest into an obligatory one. All of this is to say.

"It's convenient isn't it?" Christina asked while running down the empty streets to catch up with a BODYGUREAR ISSUE 04 OFFENSIVE SET MODEL 4452 that she had sent surging forward before her.

On the other end of the phone call Lauren let out a pained breath of air. "Of course it's convenient." At the moment, and against her better judgment and nature as a cynic, she tried to just be grateful that events coalesced in a charitable fashion rather than a combative greeting. The kind of greetings with complications that she had begun to develop a familiarity with. Rampant destruction and collisions of chemical warfare against a similar type of mechanical one reverberated through the air, echoing off the surfaces of empty halls, vacated buildings, and a once lively bay city. To anyone that was in a position such as hers, there was a new form of contemporary worry for shelter. Not an unfounded worry, but a pervader and sign of justified concern. Christina had been preoccupied with leading Xiaodan and Samantha Zheng to safety, although the prior of the two was already more than capable of compensating for her granddaughter's absence. A sentence wasted to explain. Instead, new to a solely heroic position, Christina was generating quite the volume in noise as she rapidly raced down through the avenues of San Anlos, occasionally calling upon her brain synched mecha to carry her and soar through winding paths and rounding corners in a blinding blur. Lauren took it upon herself to authorize the clearance of the bodyguard unit for extermination purposes. In a way, it was fulfilling its initial mission as Christina crushed black rabbits within the confident mechanical grip of the titanium hands the size of tables.

The targeted gelatinous masses of black were easy to spot with their towering crescent contoured ears and their unignorable feat, unlike any rabbit on earth, being their massive size that rivaled a truck at minimum. The equipment was integral, Lauren went as far as to befit the novice with access to top of the line information with blatant displays of all manner of security feeds in the white VR set Christina wore to better view the next possible disasters to exterminate. Together, the average San Anlos resident did not have to ever deal with the self-destructive knowledge of the calamity befalling the city. That and anyone unfortunate enough was sure to be crushed underneath a massive and frantic paw of a prey animal that was given far too much destructive capabilities to handle. Even with all the help and aid present, Christina still struggled to stay upright and run against the tossing and turning of the earth from rabbits bouncing.

"As much as I love to hear your voice I'm going to have to hang up now," she pleaded more that dictated over the phone to her friend.

"No, you won't."

Lauren frowned and hung up first, putting away her phone as a shipment of food from Tandem Tantrum Toys and Co. was rushed in on a cart pushed by nervous delivery men. It only took a glance to size up the cardboard boxes of dry food and the amount of now expectant people within the school gymnasium.

"This isn't enough," she cursed.

Once the sentence left her mouth the delivery men were already jogging out the door. No one in the equation present had the power to change the facts. It was an inequality, she corrected herself. The necessary individuals or mechanical parties capable were all not there. In the warm orange gymnasium waiting for more people to file in, the temporary herd of evacuees readied to realize the situation they were really in.

Across the city, the head of temporary defense measures once again situated himself deep inside the derelict internal organs of a rotted factory, having made the penitence to corporate for all his transgressions with an indignant amount of unpaid overtime which he was still currently working through. He had already made his goodbyes to the world and his own personal one outside in preparation for the temporary void of his workspace. While a naive hero of justice committed a search and destroy policy for vermin abound, Christopher was embattled in a harsh war against the oppressive force of a spacecraft manned by nothing more than adamant children. All manner of anti-aerial artillery were let loose from enough button presses that his fingers would have been raw if not for his gloves as they switched from keyboards, mouses, handheld consoles, gaming controllers, and arcade sets to operate the weaponry. Nonetheless, the entitled glee of the children that he wanted to punt remained and he could feel it emitting off the headache inducing blue light of screens that surrounded him in. In need of water and a break, the most Christopher could do for satisfaction was interrupt the underside of Adam's and Abel's spacecraft to his displeasure. Tugging against the surface of the earth in a defiance to gravity, grace, and great impossibility the alien vehicle continued to fly to the best of its ability.

Under the actual barrage of lasers and missiles exploding against the bottom the twins had found a routine of crashing through ceilings and walls, lodging themselves into the tops floors of houses and buildings. It was nothing more than a fact they continued to work with, as anyone unfortunate enough to be home would only result in a new generation of rabbits and an addition to the hysterical people once they reached shelters later on.

The city of San Anlos was drowning in blues without being able to touch water. The pain was almost natural as people began to file into the gymnasium, huddling together and greeting familiar faces. The causes may be taboo and the damage may be from the fantastical, but the symptoms were most natural. Being a perspective based on reputation and consequences there was no way to distract their gaze anymore.

The city was smothered in blue.

From a tablet, Lauren's heart dropped at the site as a limousine entangled with chains and adorned with funeral bouquets plummeted from the opening of a spacecraft. With the car standing upright she easily recognized the crushing of the center fountain of Trifecta Park that was situated along the foothills towards the city center. There was a purpose for the act of course, but it's not like she was offered the right words for it until everything was too late. Marcus picked up Lauren's call as she kneeled down behind the box of food and hid from the gazes of people.

"Where are you?" she scream whispered into the phone, holding back tears if she wasn't so annoyed at him.

Unfamiliar streets in blue. For everyone else, but more so him. The recognized routes of San Anlos had each become wayward and inverted to some degree or so. Its new colors had drenched it.

"I'm not exactly sure," he answered sheepishly.

By now the other neighbors had made it to some sort of shelter, Lauren even recognized a few milling about nearby. All of which left Marcus with an annoyed and increasingly worried set of parents in tow who had never been good with directions, lost among the city's sidewalks. Addresses seemed jumbled and unrecognizable, partnered with houses that did not match. Marcus may as well have been an infant with infantile eyes in a new city that should have been his home. Lauren didn't want to wait to hear all this communicated, or rather, she didn't have to in order to understand enough.

"You're past the point of hope. Hand me to your mom."

There were pale twins expecting nothing less than reason.

There was an overworked boyfriend once again seething with rage.

There was a business partner contemplating a two front failure.

There was a girl learning how to properly address people.

There was another becoming a part time hero.

There was a single boy, but not the only one, lost in the blue world.

There was a gravestone of a limousine marking the awaiting burial of the city.

There was a seafront typhoon.

And there was Isabella, drowned within her prison without ever choking on lungs filled with water.

CHAPTER 2: ENTITLED DESTRUCTION

The gravity of the scenario that caught San Anlos in its pull was not one that managed to escape Christopher's understanding. Nor was it one that he could find a way to escape even if he tried against the force of nature, unlike many recent invaders that had defied the status' norm and status quo. The canyon of difference that divided the two parties was also a factor that did not go unstated, a break in nature that couldn't be closed but only bridged. However, Christopher was most eloquent in feats of construction and as such, proficient in all means of innovation. He was already familiar with a position of recognized success without a formal adventure into academia to attest to. He was one to feast rather than to think, what was most advantageous was the blood and human emotion that coursed through every piece of work. A factor reciprocated to the many superiors and executives in Tandem Tantrum Toys and Co. daily life that operated within an equivalent to oil and diesel coursing throughout its veins. The eve for construction was long past, with an end that tasted of rubber and gasoline on tongues mere nights ago. Now was the time for lamentation of losses, but in loved ones' lethargy that Christopher was accustomed to.

He reclined in his seat as he once did when he was a temp employee expecting a temp job. Now all he did was take in the subtle forms of his temporary eulogy that he flipped between his fingers, blocking out the view of a computer screen's live footage of an approaching UFO. Today, but definitely not right now, was a time for commiseration. Surveying his room squeezing him within its restrictive size, he stood up to stretch out his kinked muscles, popping bones and synovial joints that hand long held their breaths. The artful eulogy he pocketed and for his nerves he tried to release them with an exhale.

Christopher Abadie was an intelligent man. He could already picture the scene of immature invaders. Within a complete white void of opposition a single holographic screen displayed the view outside, one which Adam peered over and Abel piloted from. Having dropped off their precious cargo as a proceeding action, the end of the procession of Tandem Tantrum Toys and Co. and San Anlos industries' deft defenses was next. Christopher turned off the last of the computers and monitors before exiting the minuscule metal container of a room, saying goodbye to the familiar whirr of noise and oxidizing stench that kept him company. Walking into the shady darkness of the main storage warehouse of the factory, he waited for the entrance of key players within the game of drastics that they existed within. Ahead of him was a black dominance that he waited in, blocking the sight of his own gloved hands before him. Only the sound of his breath was saved from the false night's erasure, still made distant from perspective though.

It was a setting for the villainous, villainy, and villains.

Outside the twins introduced themselves to the repugnant scent of a dying industrial beast that could only aspire to their heights. The sick sea's low tide had risen to a disastrous clash against the gray stained beach and sand dunes, all of which was only fitting. Land to air artillery missiles fired from the automatic defense system trailing streaks of smoke everywhere they went until, ultimately, they were interrupted by the twin's electrified descent. Slowly, just as before, they departed from the ship's opening and drifted weightlessly to the beach floor in the ring of white light around them. They pointed their cattle prods, rerouting explosions to land against the earth to announce the perfunctory entrance.

Writhing in his recollections and anticipation for a collection of minutes he surmised that he would need years to properly forget, Christopher wondered. What kind of villain would prove more persuasive in the deliberation of power? The tyrannized terror dealt in triplets or something more admirable? From across the vast empty space of darkness, a feature that neither party would be foreign to, a box of light pervaded its way through with Adam and Abel standing within, suitcases and weapons in hand. Fortified as ever. Christopher normally would have spat in a diminutive distaste, however today's skirmish demanded something else of him.

"Not many cattle have the privilege of a name for us," Abel called out from across the building.

"Be proud of your achievements," Adam finished, extedning a genuine hand of appraisal.

"What's your purpose?" Christopher asked, partly lost in thought and partly too enticed by an answer to the most arbitrary starts. A single fluorescent bulb blinked to life sending a dim yellow cone of light to stave away the shadows that had enveloped him.

The setting had to be only fitting for such a meeting.

Adam's response to the question came in a chuckle and stride. Christopher had his own laugh well. The diabolical was disparaging and disturbing, as such it was only proper to let out a laughter that was contorted, estranged, and trodded upon to reach higher avenues of venture. Adam and Abel walked in, bombastic in the reserved confidence of their demeanor. Existence purely, through and through. Expectations and satisfaction held onto every clamped hand, energized and sustained by their own bodies themselves, impressed by no one else. That was the nature of a Class A: Adamant.

"Does the wind need a desire to move?"

"Does earth's tectonics have a goal in mind?"

"What is the solar system's justification for its actions?"

"Why are stars born and for what reason do they allow themselves to go supernova?"

"Should a black hole be questioned for its intentions?"

As a Luna, they are only a reflection of brighter light, a proper grace not set before them. It was a mere, unequivocal, overwhelming fact. As Christopher watched the set of children walk through the stuffy interior blackened in a pit of darkness, a part of him dropped into an understandable panic. Moments not for words. These two, much like any Luna member he assumed, could spend hours a day monologuing and spitting rhetorical nonsense. Only a few could make such a selfish trait flattering. There was no such desire within him to try and understand their point. What he did desire was to remember where the titanium bear traps were situated along the hallway. He need not wait for a moment longer, as the satisfying click of a loaded bite aimed at amputation resounded in the silence. A single flash of symmetrical lightning was immediately followed by a white shimmer, reflected several times throughout the hall with the cacophony of many bear traps exploding at their hinges leaving a hiss in the air.

Adam tilted their head in amusement, white hair falling to the side. They were firmly unperturbed by the annoying contradictions that floundered on the beach in resolve before them. It's a shame his procedure was not more rhetorical from a character such as his to the characters before him. But their performance could not be overlooked. Christopher ignored all thoughts of belittlement, unirritable only out of principle, but mainly because he was busy pulling out soundproof earmuffs. They were needed for firing off the recalled Fondly Fried Lazer Beam Cannon that he balanced on his shoulder after frantically searching for it at the edge of his spotlight. The buzzing hum and possible third degree burns on his freckle pale skin along his shoulder and neck would be worth it if he could impart just one of the freakish moon kids with the wisdom of a painful discipline only viable through a needed bully. The light inside the cannon flickered into a highly concentrated stream until it bore itself through the air, melting away the space between it and its target. All of this, only for the current of red hot energy to be swatted away and deflected by a swift arm and electrified stick of space metal.

"Physics isn't even supposed to work like that. How is this supposed to be fair?" he huffed, with a defeated exhale of resentment that he tossed away along with the burned remains of the dangerous toy in a useless tantrum.

As usual for Tandem Tantrum Toys and Co., the facts of a maliciously complicit ingenuity were no use. Corporate operations only pale in comparison to A+ effort granted in feats commonly taken by sales associates to carry them out. Enough effort to allow for the commoner to despise him, a fact Christopher lamented quietly. With a flourish of his hand a large pixelated screen turned on above them, standing suspended somewhere in the darkened void. Displayed among the digital bits was a view of a UFO ship above them through the sights of a satellite targeting system setting into place.

"My last gambit."

The two entertained the effort with mild disinterest in their smiles, apathetically watching the blue beam tear through the clouds, stirring the very air with energy, as they casually continued their own approach. The weapon of destruction struck against the immovable object placed within the sky with little consultation for the scene's theatrics, blue energy being separated and refracted to countless harmless currents throughout the clouds.

"Is that really all of it?"

"How many more do you have before we can officially consider it a final effort?"

Adam and Abel had entered the main warehouse from the long corridor and stood on the bottom floor just below the stairs that were cloaked in the darkness. They stood in just the right place that Christopher only had to pull a lever for the floor underneath them to give out revealing a factory's intestines with a purpose for evisceration. It was a process made up of grinders, rotating blades, circular saws, and filed down gears. An internal compartment that's starvation was evident in sparkling surfaces, whining noises, and mashing metal with nothing but malnutrition. The metal rusted walls of the entire facility vibrated and shook against each other. Christopher's ears were caught in a limbo between popping and not while the contents of his stomach fluctuated like the tide. An antigravitational underside from the UFO above kept the twins aloft just out of reach from the mouth of the mechanical jaws that belonged to a pit full of mechanical blades.

"I hope that is all there is."

"This detour was interesting, but ultimately work cannot be completed until this part is over."

A heat fizzled between their cattle prod's ends. Christopher rushed up the last few steps and turned on the lights eager to watch his final and true gambit take form before the entirety of the facility was uprooted. He felt for the eulogy in his hand and massaged the back of his neck, nervous sweat pouring down and mixing in with a little bit of blood from burned open skin.

With the lights on, his expression could not be counted on any longer. It was at times like this that he was truly grateful to be a being of flesh and blood. His stifled laugh couldn't help but escape as the excitement and anticipation was overwhelming him in a sensation that he could feel in every cavity of his body. In the end, he was a villain but not a corrupt character. He knew what a one sided relationship could feel like. When a relationship for love was one unrequited. And that was no longer a purpose he enjoyed complicity with.

Grabbing at his chest that was not fluttering rapidly, it was time for him to act. Behind him, layering the entire second floor and stacked high along the outer rims of the first floor below was the fruit of his recent hard work. Explosives were readied and rigged to detonate with the click of a button that he extracted from his uniform's chest pocket.

"Malnutrition doesn't mean starvation. A body fed on only things like a diet of boxed snacks and canned food would be a meal, no?"

The Adamants looked around adamantly at the surprises San Anlos had in store for them, still caught weightlessly between the mashing mechanical mouth below and the rusted ceiling above.

"I have been eating this kind of punctuation for this entire chapter of my life," Christopher continued, sweat pouring down his neck and drenching his shirt. "Myself, truly a villain. And this, my desire for destruction. I am an entitled lover, but that is not my purpose. My purpose is to love."

A single click of plastic echoed throughout the room with wide eyes, but the unsettling factor was the words spoken in the temporary silence before a fiery crescendo.

"To have purpose is the evidence to perceive. To perceive is to live. You said you are a force of nature, but tell me."

Does the moon have life?

CHAPTER 3: STUDENT DECAY

    In another lifetime that could be measured in the units of days ago Lauren could have likely envisioned herself with a human colored stain pooling at her feet. Under the blinding glare of the gymnasium fluorescent lights and atop the rarely waxed floor there could have been a serious pool panning out, true to the name of a red sea. A feat like this would have only been possible through the sharpest of blades with one of the most refined edges, honed to the delicate pinnacle of near fragility to be the ultimate tool for the harshest of punishments. Red could have been coming from a guillotine's fountain and the encompassing sentences of terror. In any scenario, the most prized possession in the yellow room of panicked strangers by two or more degrees would have undoubtedly been a well trained tongue. However, a tool of the most esteemed quality is a tool all the same and doomed for every laborious square inch to be hammered out in compliance.

    The Tandem Tantrum Toys and Co. uniform only painted a target marked directly on Lauren's back to reduce her defense to the endless calling of blows, strong enough in frequency to whittle away at the coldest cut of steel. Christina could only watch as one rightfully concerned family after another ungrateful one cornered the teenage girl for necessary answers. Both the serious and needlessly annoying voices stung Lauren's conscience with venom alike, slowly but surely sending a slick trail of paralysis from the bottom up. From the basement of her abdomen, it traveled up until it took over her entire body. Packed tightly up against each other with the warm light that had been hidden from the cold world, outside pressure was pushing on all sides as nervous people clucked about wondering if the future was a mutilated one or not. A corporate dictated response that had been tailored along with much everything else was Lauren's only ready equipment. Her own vocabulary and rhetoric had long since been muzzled and restrained. Her own jaw was forced shut with black bands stringing her mouth dooming it to be torn apart by a restless knife with no release. The shredded remnants only managed to continue to tumble out half answers and worthless reassurances as her own dialogue within her skull refused to be domesticated, barking against the very orders and phrases she uttered.

Aggravated, possibly far more than any other person present if she could have measured such intentions, she resolved to settle her own conscience with a tight silence and eyes lost in motion that communicated far better than any of her words that she was ready to snap. Never had her restraints become so apparent, a sight strong enough to make her want to drill her head through the nearest wall. That would be, if not for the confident Christina swooping in from across the room as the sprouting noxious purple masses of color pulsated with an internal tempest storm.

Unfortunately the novice vigilante was still just that, and if the problem did not require the solution of assault and beating from the hands of loaned weaponry it was a solution very much out of the depth she could dive for.

"I could punch someone if you want me to."

Lauren shot a glare her way toward the girl that was already covering her own gasp with her hands. It was not a thought she had entirely meant to say out loud.

"Pummeling was not exactly the idea I think I'm willing to take right now," she hissed, although if Christina continued to give her an excuse to be so snappy then it might just be the respite she needed.

In the meantime, a similar but stronger set of weaponry filled the room and engulfed the party in rings of orange flames. A band of the strongest shade encircled the room with everyone present inside, of course, the actual extent of which was present to no eyes but Christina's. Anyone else would have their retinas and occipital lobes process the sight of a stern grandmother swatting away hands with the strength of years and cussing with a hot breath that may as well have been a fire. Ms. Xiaodan stood before the palette of supplies, rationing the food in strict bundles against the whines of hungry stomachs and hands. Christina laughed, and Lauren stared in awe. They both continued to forget the ways in which Xiaodan could surprise them.

However the mute girl was not silent, and Lauren immediately jumped at the chance to act with a rapid calculation of the beginning and end quantity for the supplies present. Like them, there could be a reason if they made it so. All they needed now was more entrees. With passing words and threats with a busy Xiaodan the pair of girls prepared to leave, but not before the Alvarado parents left a desperate plea to occupy both their heads.

"Please find our son."

That much should be easy.

It was through a maze of empty hallways that refused to connect and wind the way they were once thought to. The atmosphere, once bright, had since cooled and chilled leaving only real sensations against the eyes and skin. A discomfort that was always present but recently made aware. The air was not freezing, but it was certainly cold enough. The floor was not entirely blue, but with the reflections of a burdened sky outside the windows it was nearly there.

Such a sky as it had ever been. Packed full to the point it was brimming with its contents depressingly so. It was a blue sky. One that had never been so common before. A blue sky of cloudy circumstances that suffocated San Anlos from the real world. Such a place truly did not exist.

Within his chamber doors was Marcus, as alive as ever and uncomfortably so. Face down on his desk, he sat alone. Isolated as much as he could from a world that's grip he could not escape from. There was no light in the classroom save for the influx from the windows casting the room in an eerily transparent quality. In the back, Marcus attempted to call upon a command that was usually so easy for him to achieve.

Eyes closed.

Body still.

Room Silent. Even the clock on the wall had cracked glass and was no longer working after having its constant ticking beaten out.

Every sensory detail was discomforting against his skin, like morning dew to wake you up, or the digestion within the intestines of some larger beast. Smooth muscle squirmed against his every inch. It was supposed to work because it had always done so before. No matter what, he would stay there until a fantasy of greater proportions would heed his call. Maybe this time he could live safe again from dreams of grandeur and his realities alike.

Then why was the clicking of footsteps the only thing he could focus on? Lauren pulled back the classroom door to reveal a very much alive Marcus, against his own best wishes. "Of course, he would be sitting right there," she muttered.

"Where else would you want him to go?" Christina asked back.

Old tactics like these wouldn't work, it was something that the girls reminded Marcus of with their presence alone. The land of the dead was reserved for those who passed the qualifications of being dead and he was still very much alive. It was an idea he genuinely was in dismay over. It was all so much to see, that any previous depiction of his existence was rendered condescending compared to the color stolen reality that only the roughest forms of photography could capture.

"Get up Marcus. I can't accept this fantasy of yours."

First, it was her breaking down the walls to his world, then to his social bubble, then his fortress, and even his protection from aliens. What more could people want from him? He had given them everything. He was a corpse decaying in his very confidence, rotting in a nature with no release.

There was something he was missing. Lauren pressed her finger again to his forehead, only the very end holding up all of his head off the desk. Her words were certainly a knife that was ready to cut apart arguments with reason. But it would never be possible in situations like these. She couldn't expose what was behind his breasts on her own behalf. Only he could tear away at his own skin. The most she could do was beat the facts into him, hammering the truth against his head.

Maybe then he could hear that heartbeat of his in his ears.

"There is nothing left to give until you find it yourself," she declared.

"Have you no mercy?"

Marcus pressed his head against the wooden desk with enough force that the sound only hurt Lauren and Christina. The latter of the two had been spending her time surveying and searching through all of the desks until she came across her prize. Christina had the impression, and rightfully so, that Marcus would move for no one. Above all, not for himself. In fact, he was planning on staying there forever. At least mentally into whatever future San Anlos had left, however sort of prolonged it may be. Alone he was going to sit and stay in his classroom for eternity. She knew full and well that the distraught hold desperately onto adolescent years even when there were so many left to live.

"You can't stay a child forever, and a teenager even less."

From behind Marcus she emptied the contents of a forgotten water bottle onto his head. If he may have not found a reason to leave they could certainly make one.

"Neither of us, your good friends, would want you to die of hypothermia," Christina remarked in partly feigned dismay.

"Statues like him grow moss in these conditions," Lauren snipped.

Marcus only tisked with a sharp inhale. "It's cold."

"Good," Christina answered, grabbing him by the shirt collar and pulling him up. "You're awake then."

Lauren pointed again, poking her finger into the boy's chest with an inordinate force that it might have hurt him a little bit if she stopped to think about it, but she was too focused on her next words.

"When your awake you have no choice but confrontation."

CHAPTER 4: SHOPPING THROUGH MEMORIES

Marcus was very much alive against his most passionate, or rather passion lacking, desires from his heart. Ironic for the fate he deemed necessary for it. However, no matter how zealous someone might be to change it, the facts of his existence within daylight were still sooner to fall and collapse back into a land with no familiarity of doldrums. That is to say, in his generally notorious way of inflated grandeur he refused to move himself from the seat. Yet it was his pride as an absolute moronic adolescent toddler that demanded him to do so, although he obviously saw the inconvenience differently. Confidence was determined unfounded and irresponsible to only the many included, with a source of a distorted self image to their best discernment.

Solely capable from the head on his shoulders, they wondered if a puddle like the thin one spread across the floor was enough that he could drown in. Eventually, the answer was not 'no' but instead 'he could probably attempt to'. However, they were right in concluding that hypothermia would be the first to find a home here before any other possibility. The terms of the agreement were never fully understood nor accepted, but while there was a chattering jaw and the more treacherous flush nose and jumbling of words the actions were clear to take. Marcus made no effort to go out of his way to stop his friends either. He wasn't strong enough to count on himself, but just strong enough to deem when he allowed for helping hands to pick him up. Possibly the instinct for survival had actually kicked in for once. Christina and Lauren would have been utterly confused at this event alone, possibly concerned even in the sudden change in character alignments if they weren't preoccupied with the feat and hassle of general obligations.

Christina haphazardly looked for a solution to the problem she caused herself, tossing open the teacher's drawers until she was sufficiently dissatisfied with her results. In a quick inspection outside the window overlooking the cracked sidewalk, still distinguished from its negative impact of crossing paths with the Alvarado boy days prior, Lauren tried to think of the possible solutions from the tools available.

"It's been through enough," she decided regarding the 'it' that was Marcus. Though the priorly used option was certainly an express one, she decided against it. "You're still indestructible though, right?"

"mmmmmhhh," he muttered out in a confirmation against the underside of a new towel Christina had thrown, herself taking far too much pride in landing the hit.

It was in situations like these that Marcus felt it was not only appropriate, but customary, to scream, kick, flail, and otherwise cause a general nuisance for the perpetuations. However, against all his instinct and intuition he refrained from the possibility, instead deciding to sulk as Lauren and Christina dragged him through the hallways by the collar of his vest and shirt. Around his neck the fabric pulled tight against his throat and his pants left his legs sore from the friction. The struggle was real and evident enough with exasperated breaths and aching muscles, but the determination was ever more tangible with the two girls.

Christina was the first to give up. She was also the first to recognize that such methods were not suitable, not out of a lack of effort but rather the opposite. There needed to be a reallocation of strengths. It was a strong and valued argument and one dialogue that Lauren replied to with full sincerity.

"Don't you think I know that as much as you do?"

The two dropped the alive corpse of a boy's head without consultation.

"Wait right here." Christina didn't want for an answer or agreement before she ran off to the front of the school and outside of view. What was expected to be seconds turned out to be minutes alone with Marcus in awkward silence before the interruption of squeaky metal against metal announced their friend's return.

Christina had managed to find a shopping cart outside, pushed it inside, up a flight of stairs, and rode it with excitement and fervor toward the duo. It must have been displaced in the panics of recent nights they assumed, but given their intended destination it was a vehicle fitting. More importantly it was solution enough, as the two went through the effort of tossing the attempting lifeless boy into the basket with very little regard for safety nor comfort.

"Who is going to push him?" Christina asked, already making the choice in her head by asking the question first. After all, the options were only limited to the sizable pool of two.

"I think whoever has the best navigation to store is best." Lauren wasn't going down without a fight. "You have been to the Bargain Bulk grocery store tons of times with Xiaodan, right? Since they have been rebuilding your old store. I wouldn't know the fastest route."

Christina wanted to hiss. This girl was good. Somewhere in that moment the fluttering heartbeat of Marcus was a little less faint.

"You know Lauren is the biggest one of us here," he mumbled out.

What the idiot meant to say was that she had a few inches in height over both of them and was a build stronger than the rest, nothing necessarily to hurt her or take offense by. What Lauren meant to do was find the nearest cliff and let go of the cart. Instead, she conceded to push the boy, Christina taking the opportunity in her friend's wounded ego to hold onto the hand bar and ride in between Lauren's arms.

Among the many now unfamiliar streets sprawling about a city that none of them could recognize there was an abundance of familiar memories. Collections readily understood were packed into every block. Imagery that brought nothing within them but memories awaited in every glance. The question for each viewer was, exactly what would be taken with them in the shopping cart of theirs? Among suburbs of tightly haphazard and thoughtfully occupied houses alike, the walls had been ignored for many years. From closed and boarded up windows Marcus recognized only the lesson that even houses were strangers that watched and enacted their own judgments. Christina peered through kitchens with peeling plastic floors, burned walls, and a corner she could firmly match gazes with. From crumbling walls and the wreckage of home invaders the pair saw dead pasts that remained buried within memory alone, for better or for worse. With every intersection and street camera Lauren was reminded of the waste that comes from the products of successful and high achieving individuals. The cart rattled over sidewalks speckled with impacted holes and dips in front of an equally ravaged library, unattended before and now pouring out its internal organs of papers in the wind. Littering the world was Lauren's journey that went uncompleted and abandoned. Purple prose ridden starts, takes without direction, and cold, cold sentences that had no remorse for their meaning. The conglomeration of words which caused anguish.

The trio crossed through a park created with the contribution of a corporate friend that gave the impression for many that a city could only flourish if it was allowed to leach. They skated circles around a casket of a limousine, within it a creature beaten and submitted slumbered in all but mortem. From which, they shared a newly nostalgic experience of disaster.

Eventually, the group finally arrived at their destination. Beyond an empty and abandoned parking lot, one that had never been so before, there was a monolith of a Bargain Bulk grocery store. It was here, before they made it to the pulled down sheet metal doors but past the not yet closed first set, within the quasi hall not meant for people but for carts, that Marcus was ready to make his first purchase.

"You can't be serious?" Lauren remarked.

"He most definitely is," Christina noted.

Marcus was already fumbling through his pockets for change.

CHAPTER 5: ENLARGED LIVERS

Marcus was completely, totally, and absolutely enamored, enticed, and memorized by the sight before him. The buttery yellow contents reflected the warmer light of its surface, only further transfixing his attention at the contents of the large glass metal container. It was his will, his desire, his only immediate future, and his decision all his own.

"Do you really want one?" Lauren asked, with a healthy, if not astonished, shock.

The object was vital to further the maturation of Marcus' character into the next chapter of his life. Except the object in question was only any one of the many vibrant sunflower yellow colored baby duck plushies packed tightly together and squeezing for space to sit in the oversized claw machine. Being a gauntlet for children's attention before any actual trek into the store its purpose was obvious, and in so it had succeeded, once again ready to entertain the toddler of the trio. Christina was already taken aback at the sight of such an honest gaze from the boy, herself overtaken with a panic as she fumbled through pockets for the gatekeeping toll of minor cents that was needed to fund the current obsession. Obsession was definitely the correct word and a yellow, fuzzy panic was the perfect hue for the occasion. The nervousness was a continual popping inside his chest at a note that was concerning and dishearteningly earnest, to the point it become a temporary normal. Lauren had all but conceded to not add more substance to Marcus' anticipation, however, she similarly extended a comprehensive review in the one hand, offering up her coffers to complete the change necessary for the mishandled fortune of an archaic claw game.

Time was certainly limited but any investment to get
Marcus to actually act was considered worth it for the personal
return if tentatively offered. Over and over and over and over and
over and over and over and over and over and over and over and
over Marcus fumbled his way putting the quarters in. From all
angles observable within the scene his trembling hands navigated
the unintuitive controls. With their faces pressed up against the
glass sides Lauren and Christina watched in equal, if not more,
anticipation provided by a substantial investment both monetarily
and another. His breath swelled up within him, but Marcus held it
and then let loose a controlled stream of air echoing off the
insides of his lungs. His mind filled with pending obliviousness
trying to focus on the right timing. The corners of his body were
alive with the noise that leaped and howled from every extremity
while he tried to stay perfectly still. The group stared as the
annoyingly feeble metal crane successively failed at maintaining a
grasp on the cheap stuffed animal. With each attempt their sweaty
hands squeezed harder against the machine. Christina and
Lauren especially were obscured by the fogged glass from their
breaths while Marcus tried to blink away teary distractions from
his eyes.

That was until all available currency was a past
expenditure and only useless dollar bills were left within each of
their wallets. Marcus stood ready to fold in on the space that he
took up. The result was depressingly expected. Christina on the
other hand squinted trying to better envision a thought for a
moment.

"It's not like we're going to get in trouble now."

Lauren was a step ahead of her friend, already testing the
density of the glass with a few flicks.

"It doesn't look like it would be that hard either."

When all else fails they could still break into it. Of course, there was a lesson to be learned from the fact, but at the moment the teenagers were preoccupied with getting the stupid plain yellow duck plushies by means of vandalism if necessary. The idea was one Marcus was lenient to, already watching with a desperate yearning like an unspoiled child: blankly, but meaningfully, at the damage ready to unfold.

Something crashed nearby. Something loud but muffled, with enough force to send a rattle through the floor. The dull fluorescent lighting above them slowly went out one by one, leaving only the solemn glow of the caged stuffed idols before them, the strength barely enough to illuminate their faces. All three of the teenagers stopped their preparations for destruction temporarily, the cold air was frozen enough from their hesitations and stood against their skin. The collection of attention present was directed to a strained singular point of interest, nothing like a nest of plushies but instead a sound hard to make out. Something was beating behind walls and dividers nearby, emanating from the metal sheet covered doors that were fully pulled down on the semi-halls other side.

"We were supposed to be getting food and supplies weren't we?" Christina reminded the group rather bluntly.

"I think we might be getting a proper excuse for why it's taking so long," Lauren noted, trying to move past the very real embarrassment she had over forgetting about their intended objective.

The three of them stood there in the small circle of light that the crane machine offered and waited while the beating continued. Then slowly, silently, suspended in the forced night around them, two hands touched the very outer rims of light quickly followed by two more. Marcus stepped backward while a familiar couple did the opposite.

"Dang, it's a party at the grocery store today," Touma teased rather than commented, with his usual smile creeping onto his face. Any guard that Lauren and Christina had drawn completely deflated at the site of the power couple. Marcus was still wary, placing himself behind his two friends just to be comfortable.

"Don't try to act superior idiot, you're lucky we ran into them." Tiana checked her fiancé with a light slap on the head and turned towards the girls. "He wouldn't have been able to finish the one job he had otherwise."

"We both wouldn't," Touma corrected.

Lauren would have questioned them as to why they were here in that exact moment that happened to be so coincidental. Christina might have offered to charge and greet them with a hug. However, Marcus was the only one to succeed in his preparations and plans, giving them a blank stare. Tiana's advice was only dully noted by many.

"From the looks of it, the three of you guys seem to have a very specific appetite," Touma continued on, starting in a monologue. "A select decision is being made by you on what to fill up the space of your bodies with. I mean it's at least select partly because of the environment. After all, in my experience, everyone is simply engorging themselves on life around them. Engorging themselves, especially in San Anlos above all other places."

From someone else the words might have been cloaked in corrupt insinuations that would have rather stuck to the rim of light and in the shade of shadows. However, with a cunning and critical face, or because of it, Touma did not move his words for the benefit of amateur insults of the occasion.

"After all, what is anything but a banquet for you to enjoy to the fullest?"

He placed his hand on the yellowish glass of the game in the center and looked through the diorama of ducks at the group. His eyes were meeting theirs.

"Do you know what foie gras is?" he asked.

It was a term unknown to the majority of the kids. At most Lauren remembered it was cooked with either a duck or goose, she wasn't quite sure.

"No, they aren't going to know what foie gras is," Tiana butted in, interrupting both Lauren's thoughts and Touma's speech. She was tired of waiting or possibly rushed with her more important task or maybe even some kind of mixture of the two and more. However, what she was for sure was dwarfing both the claw machine and Touma too, both physically and verbally as she leaned atop the prior.

"Your questions are a long way off from the point Touma." She didn't bother to look over at his face to see a reaction and instead looked forward still. "What he's trying to ask is, what do you engorge yourself with? Or at least, what do you want to? When your liver enlarges and it's time to dine, what will it be that you had filled yourself with?" It wasn't until she was done cutting to the chase that she snuck a glance to snicker at her pouting fiancé.

Invisible rope bound and constricted his throat tighter than ever before, for some reason Marcus actually feared that he was not able to breathe. A reason was exactly what he was looking to purchase. His body wanted to regurgitate itself with spasming muscles and a scream that was stifled wracked his hollow skull. Thoughts failed to form in his head, however a single sentence was slowly written in black typeface.

Don't you think I know that?

Rigid and frozen, the only actual tether that was left holding onto his escaping focus was the small, but firm, hand of Christina squeezing at his shoulder. No colors were needed to recognize the image of silent hauntings within the abandoned halls of his body. And so she squeezed, possibly a little too tight but he did not let on, while not exactly sure why but sure enough that it was the right course of action. The sight of which stung in a way that might have felt a little good to a beaten tongue held in between teeth, a bite mark now gouged into its fleshy surface.

"While we are on the topic of meals," Tiana interjected into the silence. "We have a date with danger."

Touma took a step back to fumble in the shadows until he returned with three pristine white metallic suitcases, two of which were flipped open while the third was offered in Christina's direction.

"A company welcoming present in these trying times."

Unsure but eager, she took the suitcase and opened it to reveal a new VR headset with her name engraved along the front.

Christina Zheng.

"What am I supposed to do with this?" she asked.

"I guess you do still need to get permission if you want a mech to be dispatched." Touma stalled for a moment trying to think, but Tiana finished the thought before he could.

"Just ask Lauren then."

"No," Christina turned the wireless headset in her hands. The colors were starting to become clearer but she was still nervous. "Why do I need this now?"

Tiana chuckled lightheartedly, or as lightheartedly as someone could when they were brandishing a white energy rifle at their side. In the end, her body language expressed more of a nervous laugh compared to any other. Touma, on the other hand, wasted no action nor effort. He tore the metal sheet protectors off with a large smile to reveal the resounding pulsating music inside the grocery store. The prior fact was only overshadowed by the artillery worth of fireworks set up ready to launch out. There had been a change in entrées. It seems only rabbit was on the menu tonight. They never had a chance in getting supplies, because if it wasn't one thing it was another. Sure enough, a rumbling began in the city of San Anlos and it was only getting louder.

CHAPTER 6: DEAD DREAMS DAYLIGHT

There was something absolutely melancholic about a seaside sunset. The orange catching fire to both ocean's and the sky's blue. There was only to be suffered a quiet death. Among the small strip of land along the beach that was readily available for public use Eve stood, or rather was hunched, in his interpretive performative penance while watching the daily momentous event undergo. He had positioned himself just out of reach of the sand strewn sidewalk and the incoming ebbs of the tide.

From his sea level vantage, the unrelenting blues that drowned San Anlos did, in fact, find it in them to relent, if nothing but by a forceful parting of the sea clouds. Errant rays of orange sunlight, like a truly uninvited enemy, made sure to strike at the visible angles giving the pocket of the coast a wholly generous orange existence in comparison to the rest of the world.

It was a beach of a world itself.

One that Eve promised to put to rest in an attempt to thank its creator that was responsible for the oasis within the dark blue. Slowly and lethargically, in a wholly reluctantly familiar defeated manner, he had made progress towards the wetlands and the cremated corpse that refused to be. He would have loved to have the confidence that his love would be expecting him, but in the end his nerves pleaded for at least some greater evidence than mere hopes. Before him there wasn't much to do, but nonetheless, Eve still found it within himself to be desired for labor. Walking south, along the coast without ever making it to the soft patches of grass or the dunes dotted with curly and sturdy green pants he was stopped. First and most of all, he was stopped by the predation of the old habit.

And for just a moment he listened again for the sound.

Frequencies reverberated along all available surfaces, slicing through the air and finding their way for one to collide atop the other and against his eardrums for him, and only him, to discern sense from the run on congested nonsense of it all. The salt withered ocean brushed again the sky. Its silence, almost sharp and discernibly cruel. The outcropping of large rock buffs were crashed into with water and roared, as was intended. The sand occasionally puffed, shifting every now and then from the rough breeze. Palm trees high above swayed like denial driftwood. Somewhere behind him, a seagull squealed in its distinct hum while wandering about the parking lot. And most emphatically, the sky was empty. Quiet. It was absolutely silent. Ready to be buried for the day.

In that single frame, Eve could have existed for an eternity with a perspective drawn back and perpetually establishing just how barren the picture and picturesque was.

In some of the most unreasonably rigid seconds of his life, he could have instead allowed himself to secede to a tide of relaxation to sweep him up and carry him from this city.

Marcus was screaming.

Much like the negativity of his internal thoughts, Marcus' screams were left to an expanse of black nothingness. The moments of memory prior were filled with a jubilant Christina and equally smug Lauren pointing as to where the first described overly excited companion needed to send Marcus. Transportation was via reduction to a mere speck in the sky. With a quick flash of a robotic arm that belonged to a blue mecha quickly deployed he was sent ascending into the cloudy sky and rather immediately descending into a literal orange bay vision. His landing came in the form of collision and burial, his head and neck were planted vertically deep into the wet sand. The blood drained from his feet and arms that dangled in the air and wet towards his head. Against all his strength, he couldn't pry himself free. The only thing that he could do was feel the water about his stain along the beachside. As much as it had been possible the waves pulled in closer than before and the high tide found its way toward the shore, encompassing him in the process.

Curses assailed his vocabulary. Eve had to give his props to Lauren, she knew how to do a good job. Whatever that job exactly was escaped his understanding, but he was never one to question things like that. Or at least he used to never be.

The message was clear. His serene vacation of a false ocean had been interrupted by the missile of a human, stricken out of the wet sand only a few feet displaced from jagged rocks that would have caught him. The muffled sound of screams found a way to whisper between the space of dirt particles and raced up his body to his ears in the most obnoxious way possible. Eve had crouched low to the earth around the boy and returned the whispered screams with another.

"Would the child rather live the day up than buried?"

Only a muffled yelp of surprise was a response, but it would have to suffice as an affirmation. A moment or two was spent, extended within Marus' mind to an agonizing length due to time's malleable nature, while Eve entertained his own amusements in the dirt.

There was a pause.

And then there was an eruption of sand as Marcus was torn out from the embrace of wet earth by one leg and flopped onto his back with a hefty thud. Pellets of wet sand and crabs showered him, both of which were tossed and coughed about.

"Daring. Dreams. are Dead. by Daylight."

If there was one lesson that Eve knew far too well it was that singular phrase. The value of its understanding oppressed all others.

"No idea can survive both fantasy and reality. No world could have both."

Marcus was in no position to speak, still coughing away the remnants of sand and the side effects that came with a cranial burial. Doing so, he failed to properly consider what exactly were then indentations and, more importantly, preparations that took precedence before freeing him. Perfectly encompassing the boy's sprawled out body was the outline of a coffin etched into the sand, leftover clumps still stuck to the heels of Eve's black leather shoe.

Life in San Anlos, as ever, had a fitting melancholy. Any sort of anger that had long waited in Eve's bones was removed and replaced with another tired sigh among many that kept him full. It was an apathetically pitiful sight to behold, but unlike his pushy partner and friend Eve had no interest in indulging himself in one sided conversations. There was, ahead, so much unpleasant and annoying noise in the world. He refused to contribute to the rancor by delving into the depths of discussion. An assault with words was not his fate nor job priority. It had never been.

"Now that you have seen two perspectives, does the dream still persist?" Eve asked, gesturing outwards to the oasis around them.

Two worlds, belated and lethargic, but the purpose in meaning by no means found an escape for once from Marcus' closed eyes. The tone of voice from Eve came across distanced hills away as an echo over static that separated the inbetweens of everything around him.

"No," he answered weakly.

The dream was dead. Cremated in his self disgust. Better not left a memory at all.

However, it was enough for the appetite of Eve, the man who fasts. For the first time, Marcus truly took into account the looming height of his senior. Against the directions of the setting sunlight Marcus stood in the shadow of a hunched Eve. The details were irrelevant, captured and covered in the darkness of his body.

"What I asked was..." he continued. The words were hardly organic and hardly discernible over their final distortion. "...is the root of desire buried dead? The results are unsatisfactory. The reality is depressing. Then with funeral is it to be given satisfaction?"

Perhaps the distortion had sent the ails of his being away from each other, but for once Marcus was not a body paralyzed with the actual stillness of resignation to his fate. The mangle and dead birds inside his caged chest refused to die without the acknowledgment of death throws. A prickly violence overcame his heart and citrus mixed blood filled that taste in both his mouth and noise.

His head was a dead one.

His fantasies were a slain god.

His escape, a changed vision.

The orange coated beach at sunset was a scene of nothing but purposeless prose and irrelevant details.

He knew that now. But for a moment Eve saw the world warped and reflected in the brown pools of Marcus' eyes. It was a look he had seen before. One that captured what was not there and demanded from it results. It was the sight of a refusal to give into a solemn death, not to be full on a diet of malnutrition. It was a search for a voice among the static.

Was his shadow not dark enough, Eve thought. Was the darkness not deep enough that they could give up on trying to achieve anything? Carefully, towards a past reality, he redirected his mind into the gray scale world that fully existed, one bound in black chains. Within every memory, around each person's throat, with every struggle the restraints only pulled tighter. It was shameful wasn't it?

"The Luna business is not in weapons, but in corpses. My dealings are in dead aspirations, broken hearts, and the bodies left behind." While Eve spoke, his freed hand, not preoccupied with his suitcase, went to work undoing the buckle to his black leather choker.

For the second time within the city of San Anlos, Eve Luna bared his most private details. Centered around his point of origin and being was a complete void. There was a small opening slit along the surface of his throat. Atop his adam's apple. From it, he slowly and lethargically retrieved a slip of paper with his long fingers.

His arm extended for the sticker to be held above him and a little to the right. The world completely focused on the paper alone and all else belonged second.

"Would you believe it if I said within this universe there is far more within San Anlos than you could comprehend? Just as much as there is beyond. The body that remains has the form that only fits solitude. That corpus is tied to Babylon. It doesn't exist exclusively. Every time you have buried anguish of a cruel melancholy to your name you have only feasted on the physical."

Marcus had the impression that such a conversation was beyond the reach of him and the setting of a sundown beach, but whether he liked it or not the daylight of his ignorance and San Anlos' alike was setting. There was no perpetually infinite fantasy to hide in. When the comfort of stasis was revoked all information must be revealed, and so a man of mostly dead dreams expected to find if a boy could kill his own off.

Marcus' mouth salivated in search for a taste to mark as determination.

"What is your essence?" Eve asked, leaning with a tortured figure that denied Marcus' deftly dumb nature.

"What is your meaning?"

His hands clenched with a rage because he could not find a belonging in proverbs.

"Is there life within Marcus Alvarado?"

The San Anlos beach was one of inescapable black and white grays. There was a sterile silence that only rose in crescendo with the blink of fluorescent lights and murmurs of punishment. The job would be finished yet.

With a shaky hand Eve placed the sticker on Marcus' forehead. Marcus was a silent boy who now had beads of sweat pouring out from the sight of an unfamiliarly distraught Eve. Golden rivers ran down his boy, beating away the gray existence. The sticker broke down, drenched. The art of a single golden halo with rings, now unrecognizable.

All of which, to see what Marcus dined on.

Or what dined on Marcus.

CHAPTER 7: CIRCULAR CEREMONIES

The city of San Anlos that belonged to and within Lauren was caught in a spiral that was perpetually 2 degrees off course.

Atop the Bargain Bulk grocery store she saw it for herself. A carousel view of the newly unfamiliar bluescape, only fitting for her clinically diagnosed twirl. It was permissible ballroom bloodshed of her self pride as she was forced to embrace the employee Touma, all from her current situation spurred on by the dream couple's equally dreamy and incoherent line of critical thinking. Apparently, after shooting off rather than throwing down a gauntlet for battle and announcing the excited extermination of either them or enlarged vermin, the only proper preparation was a dance.

Hands together. Arm to hip. Arm to hip, likewise. The indoor speaker volume of the store music was at an indecipherable maximum. Eye to uncomfortable eye. Lauren had successfully managed to catch herself in every kind of rotation that day. Christina, on the other hand, only enjoyed such misadventures and actively took part in the antics. Every few moments intersecting Lauren's and Touma's circular path was Tiana's and her own.

At present, there were countless other pressing actions to take, but according to Touma this was the best action to act on. At the very least, Lauren would have liked to pretend to have had the option to pick the better partner rather than endure the gaze of her ever planning and mischievous dance mate.

"If you think I'm too perceptive for my own good the least you could do is make your face more readable." Touma laughed at the comment on Lauren's thoughts not yet made public.

"Stop complaining about a little hard work." She already knew his words were more for placating her pride to lessen her shock, his skill came easy to him and all to her annoyance. He was too perceptive for his own good. Indeed, she could gather right now that every city street, corner, room, locked door, and hidden secrets were readily apparent to his vantage point. All bets were losing to eyes like his if it was contemptuous.

"Can you shut it up in there?"

Lauren glared at the familiar phrase that left Touma's mouth which did not stop for her to gather her thoughts.

"Your inferiority complex is showing."

"I'm not one to think unfinished thoughts nor mince my words." Even as the words left her mouth she could hear the lack of resolve in them catch like the air stuck was within her lungs. Truly she was entirely factual to a fault. The kind of objective analysis only offered by a mishandled subjective mind. It was without precise detail that Touma would have liked to dance in circles with her hiding assaults and ambushes between the spaces and punctuations of lengthy paragraphs. There was a joy for him to have in watching the feeble fumble about. However, and most importantly, he knew that Tiana would have no pleasure in seeing such from him. Likewise, the city of San Anlos that he saw so clearly would neither give him the venue in time.

"The blues do not stop." Plus there were rumblings about but that much was implied, or at least Touma thought so. Better put, he expected Lauren to think so. "It breeds likes rabbits doesn't it?"

Lauren did not understand. For her many words, she did know she was someone who no longer had concise in her expansive vocabulary. The blunt force trauma of letters and syntax was nearly enough to define herself in recent days past, and it was in scenarios like those that she feared that days dipped in blue would be the end of her. Scenarios where she would have no choice but to be beaten over the head to understand, and worse yet to be understood. Touma put it succinctly. However, in short, Lauren did not understand.

That being said, even in the most tasteless and pitiful word there was an inkling of meaning. The only thing that Touma couldn't quite figure out, and infuriatingly so, was what kind of word Lauren was writing deep inside her within a dark inky pit of meaning.

Christina had happily kept pace with Tiana in their simultaneous dance even if she had to stretch to her tiptoes and make Tiana lean downwards to meet each other. The music was hard to make out, but it was easy enough for the young girl to expect the right moves and follow the rhythm of her gracious partner's lead. Continuing in that mentality she did not need colorful signs to know that there was a needed partner swap, and so the two girls pulled each other close with an extra warm squeeze.

"Between you and me, you're my favorite of the trio," Tiana whispered into her ear. "You've got good childish justifications."

There was only complete sincerity within her syllables that it nested in with long tickles into the back of Christina's head. The young girl beamed with a smile far older than that of hers.

"It's very mature of me isn't it."

The rest of their dance cards needed to be filled. Tiana stepped away and tossed Touma aside and took his place without ever breaking pace with the rhythm. The interchange would have to be made a little more quickly. The dance, a little faster. The rumblings, a little closer.

"Did my fiancé bother you?"

"Far too much," Lauren replied, matter-of-factly.

Their dance was made far easier, that being because of Tiana's strong arms. Strong enough that even though Lauren was taller than her peers present, Tiana had still decided to just let the girl's feet dangle a little above the roof's surface. Upheld with one pair of hands interlocked and another around the other's back, they danced with the robotic dream babe holding the company employee aloft. It was a dance with large sweeping motions as the torrent of their perspectives only continued to spiral into an infinity infinitely descending. Lauren glanced over to catch sight of a Touma talking circles around a Christina that in return looked moderately but mindfully engaged.

Parting from her gaze Lauren focused on the smiling face before her. The whole image was shaded with an aggressive realness that not only offered, but demanded, the revelation of immediate and direct answers. The question that Lauren struggled to put together was if she could handle it. So she wondered about the same questions aloud.

"It's a celebration after all," Tiana replied but did not answer.

Before Lauren could say anything else to contest that sort of retort Tiana was listing off plastic figures, such as information of a factory destruction and a coast completely washed out in grays finally put to a long overdue rest.

The twister of a dance continued still. The sole image of a love struck and infatuated employee run ragged and burned of energy in a hot plastic casket formed in her mind. The words made themselves out slowly. Individually she could understand them, but when all pieces coalesces the pieces were indecipherable.

"Just tell me if he is dead," Lauren demanded.

"Trust me, that man is harder to kill than you think. I doubt it."

It was a straight and honest answer from her, but not quite the assurance she needed. It wasn't necessarily wrong, but Lauren wanted to feel a fact strike cold and harsh against her skull.

The rumbling was deafening and damage echoed with migraines in their heads. It was a slow seething pain with no sharp edges itself. So Tiana worked hard to offer one.

"What's the use of an answer if you can't understand the connotations or meanings? Is it a sad or depressing or melancholic occasion? Was it the blues?"

For the first time, Lauren realized over the distortion that they were dancing to the blues. No wonder she had trouble with the rhythm. Tiana gave her a steep dip, carefully to hold Lauren as her bleach fried braids touched against the surface of the roof.

"What was the point in answers for someone who can't find the answers in a single ceremony?"

The music wasn't over but Tiana and Touma put a rest to the dance and met each other at the rooftop's edge.

Hand to hand. Eye to eye. Hand to titanium knuckle. Hand to rifle.

The entire building rumbled with terror that vibrated through all of San Anlos as the night came.

"You may not have noticed," Tiana pointed out.

"But the dream babes production line had been discontinued," Touma finished

The two kept the warm smile they had always shared with each other. Trembles were coursing through the ground of the city. Blocks yelled with movement and buildings jostled with an inclination to crack and collapse.

"We have said the vows plenty of times before," Touma started.

"But we get to truly test it out tonight," Tiana replied. "No chance in hell though."

"I would never allow it."

But for better or worse. Until death do us part.

San Anlos was trembling. That blue night a couple shared a deep kiss before casting themselves downward into the festivities of a destructive panic. A blow was struck to her head and Lauren was hemorrhaging a pain that knew no definition. The only other sensation was that of Christina's deeply warm hug protecting from the cool ocean breeze.

CHAPTER 8: MARCUS

"I come from a level of far more extremes if you can believe it."

It didn't actually matter if Marcus could believe what Eve said, or anything really now, because the fact of the matter was that times were becoming more extreme.

"A body without a soul is merely corpus. What happens to a person when his name has gone unspoken? When the essence has long been forgotten? When there was no animus within useless memories to remind? When the body is left to fester, the organs left to waste, and the stomach is filled with black tar? When a life has existed far longer than it had actually lived? In that case, it would be business as usual, as it had always been before. The corpus would overtake the internal balance and scale out the animus until the day the individual would be completely lost and waste away."

Marcus, standing before Eve, was the prime example of any lesson that the alien's many previous experiences could have taught. To have given his entire life without living for a single day, there was nothing but the taboo and incorrect within the body named Marcus Alvarado. He was a boy completely made of dreams with no meaning, words not spoken, and memories left forgotten as readily as they were made. He had no such relation to the concepts of life, the balanced, and the natural.

Beads of gold sweat had already become a crown that could be classified in the process of movement as the pools of liquid fortune committed to a mass exodus. Freedom could be forced on the misfortunate, even still, along the often deeply tortured San Anlos coast.

The sticker was important.

After all this time, it turned out that Eve couldn't deny its role of more integral importance.

"The Luna family trade is in more than just biochemical weapons of mass destruction. It was the production of weapons from both body and soul. The sticker is merely a band-aid of sorts. A simple tether of enough animus to give abnormal human corpus purpose and direction. It was only excess that had fantastic results. A fantastic disgust piled up results in only greater fantastical creations and creatures once the inhibitions have been totally perceived."

The sticker was merely a band-aid.

Million dollar sweat and gods blood had completely left Marcus Alvarado creating a conglomerate of the drastically desired within the ocean. Left on the ocean shore was a husk, completely drained and dehydrated of any gusto and being. Marcus had been caught in a perpetual stumble and catching himself.

For once, his physical ailments seemed in correspondence with his mental ones. Such a feat was absolution and heaven.

Divine professions and fortitudes of faith had abstained from any further protections of a heathen and Marcus could feel it, or rather, he could feel the sand sticking to large pores, sticker against his skin, wet earth knotting his damp hair. Most annoyingly, the taste of salt and sand layered his mouth, hidden between each crunch of his teeth with every clench of his jaw. The end result of the last bit sent tingles through the insides of his bones.

Within a gray beach massive golden streams of light from the city of dorado ran through to the ocean and sky, painting select strips of reality with value and divinity. From a familiar ocean there was a regurgitation of a being most accustomed to Marcus Alvarado.

This was his dream the whole time.

"There are always more extremes."

From the ocean of Marcus Alvarado there was an everyday god. Eve steeled his grimace with the help of clenching lungs as realization pierced him with an edged hammer. The thought had never occurred, but it seemed that San Anlos business was one of excess. Marcus was truly of a value most desired.

A worst case scenario of Luna Protocol. Section 0 Article 1 Paragraph 1: 'In the event that individuals fail for speedy procurement of specimen the risk of animus/corpus breach of capabilities is greatened. Business is to be aborted immediately. Specimens are to be executed if possible.'

"There exist such things as a being of complete soul. Pure animus." Eve still found it hard to truly imagine, even when he himself had met plenty. Met was the wrong word. He had experienced plenty. "The one thing they lack is all things physical of life."

Body.

Form.

Flesh.

They have no need, after all. But there are always occasions that can be categorized as rare. When there is enough physicality and taboo in a person's being that one cannot resist the intimacy. Before him, Eve had a set of fireworks that could not have gone unlit any longer before a beast of ravenous proportions. With the garden comes bouquets.

A dream undreamt for daylight prosper. What makes up a person's body and soul? Corpus and animus. The real and the dream. Because dreams need a way to die. That's what he had always known.

The band-aid was pulled off with the last disturbance made whole. Only so many times could they bandage a problem before it became malignant.

A sleepy god awoke.

The massive figure lay atop the ocean surface. The still ocean surface. An ocean devoid of motion and waves. It rose from the water without disturbances to, enormous enough to dwarf blocks of San Anlos alone. The silk button shirt floated in the air, the distance past its chest immeasurable and disappearing past the stage of the horizon. Its head alone was enough to block out swathes of the sun and sky. The bronze metallic halo was melded into its gray bruised stone flesh and disappeared beneath a marble carved face and blue veil. And the veil had been drawn. Its complete and total splendor of idolization was staged for all to consume. With a single sacred breath the celestial brushed away with ocean stench and the smell of San Anlos.

This was never Marcus' dream to begin with. There was a home within the boy, but not for him. Everyone else was merely invaders. Marcus stood there, shaking and thirsty in a dissatisfied awe. Eve stood in tremendous terror. Golden Heaven Reigned Before Them.

And then it was decapitated.

And then it was dismembered.

And then it was dissected.

And then it was gutted.

And then the heavenly being fell apart at non-existent seams, falling deftly into the ocean, crashing against very existent waves for all to see its red fleshy innards.

"There's always bigger extremes." Eve looked to Marcus and Marcus looked to Eve. It took a moment for both of them to realize that the other had not spoken. From within the dens of livers and intestines of the lower abdomen came a voice of a boy in red. Pushing himself through dripping and steaming intestines he appeared. "Essence given form. Dreams given reality. Life given body."

Eve turned to Marcus and looked the familiar boy in the eyes, into his eyes, past reflections of the world to impart with whatever was inside a fraction of fear that resided within his own body.

"There is no such thing as a compact with a god," he repeated the memoriezed phrase, but his oration with far more urgency and terror. Marcus saw the glint of the man's teeth as he spoke. "It's cannibalism."

In a situation like this, certain natural responses would have been the most likely and proper course of immediate action. One's stomach would have spasmed with the most unwelcome discomfort, others would have preferred to have never been disturbed from their early burial moment ago, others would give up from reality altogether in a faint, and even others could take it a step further into a final parting with this world. For Marcus, the blood ran to his face, filled his cheeks and the tops of his ears, and his heart skipped a beat.

It was enough to make him blush.

The insides of Eve's suitcase shook with a violent fervor on the beach until, finally, black chains spewed forth. With a single motion of his hands and a heavy breath held still Eve sent all number of chains out, wrapping around the palm trees, shambling through rocks, and tunneling themselves under sand before resurfacing tethered to the earth below. All to entrap, ensnare, and bind the creature from gardens of realities above. Spider's silk of metal was posted to every corner of the scene that was one orange tinted fantasy with Marcus in the middle of its orbit.

From the ocean, from the corpse, from the boy in red, from his presumably red lungs, was an echoing laughter.

From the edge of San Anlos, from the beach sand, from the tired boy, from his nearly forgotten lungs, there was only the murmur of a thought beginning. Something perverse that slipped between the empty synapse space of his brain until it filled his skull.

It was an unfamiliar taste and texture in his mouth. A lonely part that was not his. Something he knew only in the terms that it must be avoided. Rejection and organ failure.

From somewhere behind him Eve let out a holler for him to stop, but Marcus was already caught up in trance set on taller horizons of his very existence that were set to clash.

The boy in red's hands flickered with movement and a both blessed and bleeding intestine lashed out at the beach, exploding the earth where it crashed and snapping any taught chains with pitiful ease. Through seawater Marcus fumbled about, holding onto said innard after it draped about the coast. He barely managed to stay afloat as the sea floor progressively slipped out of reach until it finally dropped. Against the currents and riptides, fighting to hold on and reach the air above the waves, he struggled. Just as his muscled ached and arms prepared to give out a familiar hand extended from the mass of heavenly flesh to grab hold, pulling him inside the red drenched cavity. His lungs burned with exhaustion, his mind melted from confusion and his eyes were seared from staring at the boy before him.

The body was familiar but unknown, dressed in a loose fitting red sweater and short black pants the same hue as his hair. With his movements more and more skin was revealed and covered along his ankles in the space between red sneakers and cuffed pants, along the baggy sleeves of his arms and upwards, down the low color and onto his chest, through the bends of the sweater end that moved in the draft and onto his torso.

"Who are you?" Marcus asked while gaining as much of a normal intake of air as he could.

"More importantly. Who am I to you?" The boy in red retorted.

But Marcus could not determine the answer. Staples kept in place a large circular sticker of a red X over the entirety of the boy's face. Droplets of blood peaked from the ends of these staining the paper.

However, that was not what made it undesirable. The senses of a mouth of bloodshed overtook his own. Without any smell of reality to ground him in place Marcus was adrift in an iron tinged goo.

"I am no longer me. You are no longer you."

There was something else that snuck up through his nostrils and tugged at an appetite he wished to have been full of years ago.

It was the smell of expiration.

Rotten fruits and dead flesh.

Repugnant and disgusting.

It was rancid. Everything was rancid.

With his movements more and more skin was revealed and
down the low collar and onto his chest, through the bends of the

But Marcus could not determine the answer. Staples kept
smell of reality to ground him in place Marcus was adrift in an

"I am no longer me. You are no longer you."

There was something else that snuck up through his

CHAPTER 8: MARCUS MARCUS

The rope was coarse and itchy, burning as it dragged against Marcus' own skin. The boy in red had stopped walking into the space that was dense and cramped within the in-betweens of guts only to turn around on his back towards a dreary Marcus. The latter of which was beginning to truly experience fatigue, dehydration, and migraines in the humidity of intestines. All of which was far too demanding of his focus that he couldn't expend his little attention to notice that beneath the boy's red shirt there certainly was something squirming. Something moving.

This far in, he could feel the entire structure of meat heave with every exhaust already caught in the movement past the death throes.

"My malignant."

Marcus had finally found the words to answer the boy with no face. It was much less of an answer than he could have thought of, but rather one he tasted in the back of his mouth. If the stranger in red had eyes to stare him down Marcus assumed that he would be doing so as he answered his words for a moment and a moment only.

"Is that so?"

The boy's voice was grainy and coarse, like sandpaper was disjointedly applied to the corner of each syllable so that someone couldn't help themselves but listen to every sound. In that instant the boy bearing the name of Marcus Alvarado, heir to the worthless name, stood on the precipice with a mouth dripping red with blood. A path filled with wonders of the mind and thoughts that would pervade his very being for days to come.

In short, he would be consumed whole for his entirety.

However with an old world of orange idolatry outside and dead to all others, himself included, there was no path left but forward and within. A path into a slimy mucous-like membrane of a pure red nest of innards, hot and convulsing with each of the two's movements. It was one fantasy for a nightmare, one that could survive the harsh glare of the sun. When the dream overtook the body there was nothing left but a resignation of the flesh as it would be his no longer.

The truth was hot steam that burned each time it shot against his skin. There was nothing to do but brunt the coalescing pain as he trudged inwards through the red marsh of organic infrastructure.

The actual particularities of a god were not important. In fact, there were larger creatures in the universe, made of animus alone, titled only for actions and beliefs. They themselves could not tell you the intimate intricacies of the universe better than Marcus, but certainly no worse. Yet when the boy in red first saw the existence of Marcus, the night he left the stratosphere with the ferryman of a choking grip, the sight of such a naturally disturbed wellspring of black tar pain built up inside reminded him about a memory that he failed to fully recollect. Now with the compact through teeth, Marcus Alvarado had expectations to fulfill.

Everything was becoming deeper. There was no other option but to crawl further and further. The space to retreat was cramped. The space to be was limited. Marcus was nearly on top of the boy in red, close enough to see something unnatural squirming below the surface of his shirt and to feel red roped bondage around his body, strung up and tied all the way from his neck to his crotch.

The boy spoke over his shoulder and they crawled without ever looking back. "Have you ever eaten yourself into a slumber?"

Marcus himself did not have a large appetite, especially in the company of others. Additionally, although lying in bed was a specialty, sleep was hardly his sole occupancy. It didn't matter because the strange boy had, rather recently too in actuality. He ate enough to gain a form not his own and sleep for days without disturbance. The thing is, after a serious dream one isn't just the same as before and the food simply stops coming. Animus was without touch, but he could feel things now.

Something felt right, but not completely. Character's traits are defined by the character's actions, so he would put it bluntly.

"You have no purpose. Not enough essence. You're doomed to the diminished, so the choice left it simple. Will you be eaten or I?"

There was no turning back for either of the two, the weight of an old god's decomposing flesh folded in behind them just as fast as they could crawl through. Bent and prostrate on all fours. Marcus followed the course of the strange thing before him, the two covered in a slick layer of sweat, and let the boy pull him closer for an embrace. The last scene he might see, he thought, may be a red one. Not quite what he had imagined.

"How long are you going to stare at that false sun of yours."

Sunflowers crowded the ground of his, fighting against him for space. The supply expanded for miles around him in all directions, firm green stocks lined against each other with solar yellow tips. The odd stood out through the field of flowers enclosed by far off mountains, but Marcus did not notice either. The surface of the earth was in a perpetual infatuation with the sun. Daylight resonated against the petals. They followed the light. It was harsh to look directly at it. So much so that Marcus blocked some of it with his hand. The warmth was so apparent that his leg, caught in the shadows of greenery, felt cold. How long had he been standing there waiting for the days to only continue? The image of the sun he was transfixed at burned past his retinas and seared itself into his occipital lobes. Ripples of wind tumbled through the rows of flowers, light glinting off in the movement. The sudden force sent him backward, his foot barely catching himself.

He almost tripped on the classroom chair behind him. Before him was a scene that he had always been looking at. A false city that was tinted to a citrus hue. One stuck through a window frame and distorted. It was a San Anlos that never existed, with an everlasting sunset and ocean far too close to be considered realistic. The same faux San Anlos he had spent his time walking about and running about when had the energy to do so. The only thing he had learned within that classroom was a lesson in fatigue. He put his hand onto the window sill to get a better view outside only for an intense heat to scorch itself against his palm, burns interlocking with his fingers.

The beetle denizens of his San Anlos lined every side of the sidewalk, pushing into their dung balls toward uphill. His own hands had been pushing into the infernal surface of his own solar burned dung that was only barely convincing as a galaxy's center because of its stinging gaseous exhaust. His own dung enveloped his hand up to the elbow, but he caught himself and pulled himself free at the last minute. His arms retracted with third degree burns that he experienced with a dazed distance instead of actual pain. His brown skin was a singed red and stung against the very particles of the air.

Below the painful arm that his eyes followed along was the sight of the plain white carpeted floor of his bedroom. The same white carpet that ran up to his nursery walls that refused to be painted something different since childhood. Against them sat untouched notebooks filled with old and abandoned children's drawings. Stray books were stacked and left unread. Piles of clothes littered the floor. Only the bed had exhibited evidence and signs of use. All of these were details that he was accustomed to ignoring within his head. What drew his interest was the glass casket placed in the center of the floor over a bed of orange marigolds. Alvarado laid there in peace just and he stood there above it, both without flaws and sin.

Unaged.

Unmatured.

Unaltered for complete perpetuity.

The urge to vomit was overwhelming now, but nothing broke too far past the residence of his stomach and the bottleneck of his esophagus.

There was always something underneath the surface. As the red boy pulled Marcus distastefully closer his shirt was lifted to reveal what his chest and gut truly was. The entire thing constricted with a tight and methodical bondage pattern of red rope that Marcus was sure had a proper name, but like many things, he did not know. It was through red knots and taught rope that dark stained ribs protruded from the creature's lower chest, like crustacean claws unfolding impossibly long and showing ease in the hold around a helpless and beaten Marcus. The red boy's skin was wet and goopy. Slower and slower Marcus was submerged as he was pulled closer.

A decision could only be prolonged for so long before it became a decision in itself.

He knew that already.

"I have form," the boy whispered. "Therefore I have a name."

What would it be?

"Is the life of Marcus Alvarado one that has been lived?"

The words were hot. The breath was heavy. It was all very revolting.

From dawn to dusk sunflowers faced the heat.

It was raining mangled bird corpses in San Anlos.

The burden was a heavy one.

The god's guts were slit open and spilling out.

Even if the sun was too close sunflowers would reach toward the heat.

Dead birds piled in the classroom, falling out the windows and filling desk drawers.

Bondage choked the bedroom strung across every surface

The sunflowers were orange not yellow.

Corpses were easily lit in the heat.

Even marigolds could be stained red with blood.

Buried birds were there in the soil far underneath the flowers.

The city was a ball of gas and fire.

The day left blisters.

The infallible body was bound in a shrimp knot.

Corpses did not sweat in the heat.

Marcus was drowning in the red flesh. Ribs gatekeeped his escape. For a moment it was fine. For a moment he could keep up this pace. For a moment it was totally okay. For a moment he could manage. For a moment he could stay there. For a moment was all that he had to get through. For a moment more. For a moment more. All he had to get through was another moment. For a moment it was perfect.

Then it was not.

Then it was worse.

Then it hurt and he did not want it to hurt. If it hurt then it was wrong. It hurt so much it was hard for him to breathe. The pain was so significant that he wanted his bones to break from the pressure. There had to never be anything because there was never any evidence. He had no justification. Only time was the validation to the pain. If he still was a dumb, useless, inconsiderate kid then at least he would have gone without the ability to know so. But he wasn't and no matter how much he stressed over it he could not go back.

What was he supposed to do about it? If the solutions escaped him then he wanted everything else to as well. He wanted to give it all up. He wanted to release it in a scream into his pillow at night. It existed in the way that he refused to eat until the pounding in his head reminded him everything was wrong.

Because things could only seem to get worse.

It was disgusting. It was abhorrent. It was a lot of things. But what was really important was none of that. What really make his stomach hurt and skin crawl from the rancid stench inside was that he already had his answers to each and every question. He already knew why he was so angry and because of that why he didn't want to feel it all again.

He knew that he was tired, that it was sickening, that even if he wanted to be a kid again it wouldn't fix anything. He knew that the very fact was part of the problem. It did not escape him that he was never the child that he was supposed to be. No one knew it better himself that there was no evidence of a person in that house, to those parents, in that family, to his friends, to himself. Most of all to himself. He knew that he did not know. Then it shouldn't be a problem then. He should be okay with being unpleasant, alright with knowing he was annoying and inconsiderate. But for some reason unknown to him, on hotter days it was a burden too heavy to bear. He just wasn't enough to handle the little bit of pressure pressed onto him, and he decided so. It was a mere failure, but it was always failure.

The nothing of Marcus Alvarado was the nothing of guilt. More than anything else, he knew that problems like his were deserving of reason but not punctuation for his actions. Maybe if it didn't seem fair. Maybe if it didn't seem right. Maybe if he couldn't track the path of his exact grievances to a source that seemed to lead back to one common denominator it would have seemed easier to cry out against.

And that's what made him pathetic.

What else was he after failing, because he was most certainly a failure. It took minimal awareness to know everyone around him was angry. No one in his life had an easy state to be. But when Isabella is giving her all for her hopes, what can he do? When it's Christina who should get any help, what does he take? Lauren is the name that everyone should have on the tips of their tongue, but his is more feebly greedy. Eve deserves the time to love Christopher, but he stole that. Tiana and Touma demand all the peace possible, but they're too busy existing perpetually on call.

Every single fact of life made him want to crumble under the weight that built up inside his lungs. He had spent years not being enough. He only had memories that couldn't be enjoyed. He was dreaming in the taste of regret. Every action he has made had been the wrong one. Every decision he had chosen was a moment wasted.

What was left for there to be dined on? What was there to make himself out of?

"Whos was Marcus Alvarado?"

His lungs filled with red distaste because everything seemed to be red in his last moments. He let himself taste the color and let out a yell that morphed into a scream and ended up as a cry. One that sent shockwaves throughout the constraints of the boy in red.

"I am disgusting."

He pushed himself up with a shaky arm.

"I am abhorrent."

Red fluid coughed out of his mouth.

"I am self-obsessed, narcissistic, and greedy."

His eyes met with the space where the boy in red's would be.

"I lack the proper compassion for others. I hate to be close to people. I have no ties to ground me to others."

His back was against the boy's rough and scratched ribs. Ribs that slowly gave away with ease.

"I am a problem at every level. I am unhelpful, self-destructive, hateful, and filled with contempt and jealousy. I lack maturity. I avoid my problems. I drag people to my level. My pain begets pain."

His face was directly above the creature's own.

"But I realize something, something far too late. But I think I get it now. That if I give up now. Or maybe if give up on giving up now. Or start trying instead of giving up. Or giving up on not trying. Or find the meaning in that kind of action instead of focusing on how it's communicated..."

His own face was inches away, sweat dripping in the hot, insulated, and claustrophobic cavity of organs.

"...then maybe my pain can finally lead to something else."

It was hot in there. There was no option but to notice his sweat.

"I am atrocious. My guts are rotten. My persona is expired. My dreams are dead."

"My taste is rancid and my lungs are red," the boy in red finished.

There was so much pain in his one minuscule life that was already so little at that same time, he felt it impossible to truly deal with the burden of existence. What was a person to do with an entire life wasted and unlived?

"But the band-aid can only stay on for so long can't it?" the boy asked "The sticker is important."

"Because it has to be peeled off," Marcus finished.

Marcus' fingers went under the edges of the circle with a red X, tugging slowly to pull up the staples with it. Blood dripped down the boy's face.

"What am I?" he asked, a smirk spreading along his mouth as it was uncovered.

"You are my days better left forgotten. My memories of hate. My life of failures. A boy wasted."

"What is my name?"

Marcus uncovered one eye then another. The face was revealed.

"My autonomy. Marcus Alvarado."

He closed his eyes looking down on himself, and opened them looking up at Marcus.

In the past days San Anlos was home to many firsts. However, for the first time, Marcus would truly contribute.

For the first time, he embraced someone.

CHAPTER 9: CITY TREMORS

Her vision encompassed a universe of light blue minuscule pixels that stretched out to every observable corner. For Christina there were many hoops to jump through. Ones that arrived in a slow procession of white dots accumulating to amass into pixel shapes. Squares. Circles. Triangles. Rhombi. Octagons. etc. And the process was slow. And the process was tedious. And the process was repetitive, requiring the bare minimum of her focus that she couldn't truly distract herself fully.

Lauren readied for diagnostics to safely finish before she set up a wireless brain sync. Each second she spent scrutinizing graphs, charts of brainwaves, connection statuses, and loading bars on her phone until the desired green colored ones of each displayed. Finally, Christina had slid herself through the tunnels of loading screen rings and into the desired identical screen of blue pixels, the color in between the sky and the ocean. Suddenly, but quietly, there was a shift to a conglomeration of white pixels along every screen. This time they were arranged in the abstract symbol that had a better interpretation in meaning based on context not present.

A checkmark: meant for success and congratulations.

Some kind of movement jolted upwards through Christina and her head lurched forward. Once again, electricity coursed through her brain, running the closest to a natural equivalent to high processing computer power inside her organ, as energy surged through axon tunnels of dendrites at a pace that could have only been described as blinding if either of the two could see it. To supplement this Christina would have to concede for a hefty acidic haze in her head and Lauren for a single efficiency rate distinguished as 100%. Such was a statistic that was simultaneously false and true, false because it defied all prior set expectations set before it, but true because Christina Zheng was most certainly giving up the offer of her complete and all effort that she could muster.

It only needed a second.

Below them, where the parking lot met the pavement and yellow bumps along the sidewalk ramps, Tiana and Touma welcomed the rabbits of exaggerated size with everything but open arms. In actuality, Touma grinned only for a split second before the two forces crashed against each other.

"Just as we agreed," Tiana reminded him.

"Mix it up."

"Switch roles."

It was with a momentous step that Touma placed his right foot into the parking lot asphalt, with such an impact and velocity that it nearly toppled all parties nearby and sent cracks running through all directions. The movement was one only in preparation for momentum. A momentum that culminated in a clap that molded the entire motion of his body into one singular point of condemnation.

Air split in half with the direct force, dissecting the parking lot and blocks sitting behind it into two halves. The hordes of oncoming rabbits were more than included. Blue scenery was stilled. Still only for a moment for it to be followed by an uproarious current of air bursting out and catching up with the destruction Touma had set forth. The shockwaves of the single clap reduced the standing rabbits as stains of thick black gelatinous globules along the pavement and asphalt.

The stampede continued, financed with an unknown but large amount of rabbits pounding against the sidewalk and filling up the nearby intersection in no time. Each step coursed through their own jelly being in a fit of rabid shakes, but the creatures did not care. Not a second was spared to be donated to relaxation or recuperation for any party.

Tiana was already in place at Touma's front, closer to the edge of the parking lot to greet the late arrivals with a quick succession of pinned headshots. A chorus of shrieks went up in the air and prior monstrous bodies were reduced to oil slick on the asphalt. She continued to plow through them, anyone that attempted to storm her was specifically introduced and then parted from with the end of her barrel. The luckiest of the rabbits had the burning end of her gun placed in their mashing mouths and their dark bodied liquid splattered into a rain around her. When three more tried to go for her sides she was already prepared, setting her sights on the closest one in the front. When the last two found the energy to leap and attempt to dogpile rather than charge she slid underneath their bellies on the slick floor made from the corpse of the prior. With the concentrated beam of linear firepower she filed cleanly through them. There were more and more and more and more and more and more and more coming through. Tiana let the momentum carry her along the slippery floor and channeled it into a bullet filled ballet twirl, spinning and letting loose all manner of precise and imprecise shots alike, keeping the rabbits at bay.

Christina's brain was singular and set with intent, shaking while bolts of lighting flickered within. She was across the city looking at different colored tiny dots. Sun rays cast shades of gold along the water. Water that erupted with a tsunami, like a fountain of glittering ocean water. Sand weight and something unidentifiable was slated to pose a threat but Christina shrugged it off and kicked out the remnants before much could pile up as her perspective grew more and more and more and more encompassing. First streets. Then blocks. Then the whole city's districts until the entirety of San Anlos was plain to see from her point of view. Movement was slow and theatrical. Actions were lagging but with precise outcomes. Each and every decision she made was not only recorded in Tandem Tantrum Toys and Co. servers but throughout the echoes that reverberated through the steel, cement, wood, and most importantly plastic makeup of the city.

With only a few stunted movements of the lower extremity functions she had come upon a fleet of nighttime pest inland and the face identification of barely recognizable specks of very recognizable people. It was at that instant that Christina took off her headset to shudder at the enormity of her decisions that toppled rooftops and sent violent shakes through highway systems. The sea was dearly disturbed, so it was really no surprise that it would offer a solution such as this one. Looking at the weight of prevalent decisions in person always made it seem a bit excessive, but even Christina had to admit to the absurdity of this kind of executive employee privilege.

The Kaiju Destroyer 0010 was exactly that. A city reducer.

It was a purple painted terror constructed out of titanium and the exaggerated fuel of 1970s nostalgia from senior designers with a fresh salty rinse and a new coat of a gleaming, starlight, metallic shine. The titanic head and sensory component appeared more akin to an alligator while its tail was far too elongated to be considered so. All of this was, in fact, purposeful to avoid possible copyright infringement. Furthering the divide was its ginormous haunches, or at least what would have been haunches. It seemed that its legs and arms were reversed so that its hind was smaller in comparison to its massive arms, shoulders, and claws. When it walked it really crawled and when it stood up it really looked like it sat in the same manner a dog would. Complete and total, the beast's nature was to destroy all and it was exactly that which Christina had failed to consider. There were no signs that provided a path like this. No color encompassed its meaning. Standing face to face with consequence sent a chill down her spine and reminded her of the fact that the biggest likely blind spot always seemed to be directly between her own eyes.

The idea of a hero is a juvenile and adolescent one at best, and at least an integral complex for a child. A lot of Lauren's words seemed to have missed, but if there was going to be at least one she demanded that it would be these ones. If her words were blunt then she would have to beat them into Christina's head if she had to because the truth of the matter was simple.

"Heroes are public enemy number one." At least reasonably speaking anyway.

There was a trail of crushed buildings like soda cans underfoot leading all the way up to the parked Kaiju. Situations were beyond repair and for each one there was a specific solution each equally unobtainable to reach. Someone that inserts themselves into other's lives and associate themselves with every possible trouble is not someone liked. Christina was caught up in screens too close to ignore, delicately crushing neighboring department stores boarded up as she needed. She clawed and stomped her way through annoying animal crowds. The clouds heaved and rumbled, in that instant light struck several times at once. Across the city a school gymnasium roof was ripped off and a new generation of rabbits was formed.

"You can't save everyone," Lauren said as she caught the sight just as Christina did. "So a hero's job is a martyr's profession."

When the eyes of others are your judges there is no true good and no true right. Lauren was a woman of artillery and knew better than anyone the worst that people could damage in place of violence. So the question racked her being and depressed her lungs.

Why does the free pig teach the others to butcher?

"You decide to pick your own win conditions and terms." Lauren stood back and waited as Christina stayed at the edge of the roof right above the festive carnage rampant below.

Silent. Eyes awake. Screen to face. Mouth closed. Eventually, she had torn through a whole new onslaught of rabbits, ones that she found to be particularly familiar. Avoiding only and all damage possible to her few allies in extermination. A ringing and distinct three beeps came from the kaiju head giving Tiana and Touma just enough seconds to dive out of a line of the inferno that shot out the mechas jaws and engulfed the street. Carefully and slowly Christina turned herself around with unblocked eyes. Lauren could clearly see the brown irises of the girl's eyes.

A deep and cool breath was wound up inside her for a reason that had waited patiently to be spoken and could not wait a moment longer. With their release it sent a waft over every inch of San Anlos like a stray breeze. Eyes of her's snapped back into place and waited. She didn't like how things like this happened. She didn't like how she didn't know the words to describe it.

There are lots of things a person can control in their life. More exactly, there are a lot of larger concepts in life that someone can't properly catch. From inside the kaiju chest a white fire was brewing. Christina looked right back at Lauren, not turning away.

"For each and every small thing I come across in life it is easy to decide how to act. It's just for the larger things in life I'm helpless. Just like I had always been."

Her throat burned, but it was necessary as a pure pale name flickered behind her eyes.

"The Zheng name is one of melancholy, sadness, depression, and loss." Just as she said her name the air was wet with condensation, droplets forming against her skin. The name was a bouquet of flowers drowned in the floral pattern of a peeling kitchen floor wrap. It was a reservoir that was ready to burst at any moment within Christina, the bearer of the title, and it would be no surprise that she was tired. In all honesty, she abhorred even the sight of it but by now she was tired of rejecting things. "Has it ever occurred to you that I am a selfish person? Helping other people is a one sided action and little about it is for the stranger. So the Zheng name is the one I own and I can't stay caught in the rain forever. A name is important, but its definition is the one I make so I'm going to change it. Through a lot of little actions. All together. That add up to something big. Something larger than me. Something I can be proud of."

A white hot mature fire, hotter than which came before, seared the parking lot and road singing cars to their bones and popping the fragile glass windows. Any rabbits caught in the scorch had burst and disintegrated without a trace. Lauren watched in awe, studying it inadvertently and firmly. It was a fiery declaration and solution. Her own brash words had missed so completely and now by her most trusted tool of trade she had been executed.

It was a beheading.

From behind her, without looking, she caught her second shipment that was long overdue. The clean titanium behemoth of a kaiju was dirtied with climbing rabbits. The creatures were adept enough to climb the layered metal panels stacked along the figure. They would have to stain it too, as Lauren wasted no time opening her packaged rifle and exploding the creatures with electrically charged bullets bursting inside them.

Christina would have turned around to look on in surprise but Lauren had grabbed her hand and pulled her close.

So close.

Until she could hold the girl softly. Her face reminded her of something important. Something maybe she had forgotten to say but wanted to. Or maybe something she had wanted to say but forgot the words how to. It didn't matter though, because she could say it now so she was going to.

"If you're going to let everyone count on you then the least you can do is count on me."

Even Lauren wasn't impervious to a fool. Christina let out a giggle that translated into laughter buried in the other girl's arms, because when someone reassured so intimately in your life decisions sometimes there wasn't a proper response. So she went with the natural one.

CHAPTER 10: CAUGHT IN THE MOONLIGHT

The city was stuck in its blue era, but that point was more than already made. Rabbits ran rampant, but this has already been explained. Marcus and Eve were out of sight, but the reason was priorly stated. A Tandem Tantrum Toys and Co. facility was finally laid to rest, but such a matter was already addressed. Isabella slept, but no more could be said on it. A couple had christened their marriage with mortality and each other with harm, but the details were already explained. Christina and Lauren were closer than ever before, but that information was rather recently described.

Just as before, Touma and Tiana tore their way through onslaughts and ramparts of both San Anlos overall, but in particular the parking lot and streets along blocks surrounding it. If they could ache or lose their breath they would have surely and recently been out of it. Instead they conceded to work regardless of the possibility of the dark void posed by rabbits goo that stained their clothes, cuts, and gashes in synthetic bodies from the stumps of overgrown teeth and enlarged jaws respectively. Christina and Lauren had taken to focusing on the right side of the shopping center, rendering giant rabbits into massive toys between claws and the exacerbated machine force of a robot kaiju maw. All around them were the ruins of the smaller department, dollar, and bargain priced stores along with the reduced fee movie theater. Buildings, regardless of occupation, were caught in the swipes of a tail and the underside of claws as Christina attempted to alleviate Lauren's workload to little avail. At the current rate the many surprisingly agile rabbits would bury the kaiju in numbers alone. Lauren made the mental note to report the design flaw in the armor plating layout to management as soon as the ordeal was over.

Fire breath was cool and all, Christina had to admit, but looks could only go so far and the other immediate and permanently present alternative was not one she was inclined to pick just yet.

"Maybe. Probably not," she muttered to herself. Slowly, the initial idea ran through her head in time to be considered less of a ludicrous one. All signs told her it was a stupid one, obviously so. "Hey Lauren, could you call your friends for a moment?"

Lauren would prefer to specify them as friends from work, but that didn't really matter at the moment. Either way, she put the call on speakerphone while Christina let out a nervous laugh as a greeting.

"You're going to want to start booking it in the opposite direction."

"We never run from a fight. That would be embarrassing," Touma yelled over the commotion.

Lauren had already rolled her eyes and Christina shrugged off the stupid claim.

"It would probably be more embarrassing to go out in a ball of flames?"

"What are you talking about? That sounds like the coolest way to go."

The call cut off for a second and two voices could be heard bickering for a moment before Tiana picked up.

"Don't worry," she replied sweetly and nonchalantly as if it was a Sunday morning call and not in the middle of an extermination war. "I just picked up the idiot and now we're running."

Christina let out a sigh of relief. "Good, now double that distance." And she hung up.

"What are you planning?" Lauren asked.

Christina lifted up her VR headset for a moment and took the moment to walk over to Lauren and rest her hand on her shoulder. Her eyes looked deeply into the girl's before her.

"I know you're going to go insane because of me," she stressed. "I want you to try to keep those thoughts to yourself." With that, she slid her headset on again with a mischievous smile and immediately tackled Lauren down for cover below the rooftop's concrete excuse of a railing.

Three distinct beeps could be made out over the still titanium beast and the clutter of rabbits pounding against metal. Lauren's heart dropped and she did, in fact, let out a loud scream however, it was actually forced out by the explosive shockwaves from kaiju flames. The kaijus's mouth never opened. The fire never had an escape for this attack sequence so emergency systems were engaged as they were intended to do so, but never with such dark intention. Through gaps in the metal panels and escape vents fire protruded from the seams of the metallic kaiju. Enough fire escaped to engulf it in a sudden and swift blast of white, incinerating all foreign bodies on it. The flames shot out in all directions leaving a scorch mark on the face of the earth itself, burning its signature along the city buildings in char and ash. Pure unadulterated heat started to burn at the ends of hairs all over the two girls' bodies as they lost liters of water in sweat from the high level of temperature and nerves from being nearly burned alive in the process. Part of Lauren wanted to hurl Christina off the roof right then and there, but she ended up getting caught in the infectious laughing fit of the reckless girl.

Christina brought it on and it was hard to make it stop. Stop, it did though.

There was a color most pale. Sterile. Enough and whole. Her ears were already popping and her chest tightened as she felt weightless for a moment and the pull of gravity lessened. A spaceship loomed in the air above them and it would have been cartoonish if it wasn't so terrifying. Lightning struck against the kaiju unit. All observable rabbits followed the signal of a white light in the sky. These were the facts of the scenario.

The Adamants had arrived.

For a moment it was a concentrated lighting storm zapping against the metal kaiju in electric strikes, sending energy vibrating through its outermost layer and temporarily putting intricate computer systems on the fritz. Christina's VR headset blinked and flickered uselessly for a moment before the broken image of city blocks fell into place for a proper scene of pixels. Lauren's phone vibrated against the rough and sweaty rooftop, sending both girls jumping for a moment.

"We don't do this often, but we kind of love your vibes and me and Touma are in the honeymoon phase. If you are interested in joining us, feel free."

The venue was set and fixed: Trifecta Park. Lauren looked up to see a faint white dot over there and barely had the time to let out the remark, "Gross," before Christina was running to jump onto the back of the Kaiju.

The center square of the donated park was a swirling mass of creatures painted in the colors of a quiet night sky. It was this such stampede that the kaiju crushed underfoot chasing after the Luna UFO. Not Christina though. She and Lauren stood at a respectable safe distance away, hidden in the grass and sparse trees along the furthest corner edge of the park that stretched

long in one direction but not large overall. Enough space was
between them and their target that Christina could really get into
her role as a prehistoric predatory threat to the hare's concerned
dismay. But the results spoke for themselves. Her view was slow
and sometimes distorted with a lag, but it was no matter. What
mattered was making sure the Adamants couldn't steer out from
her 1832 x 1920 pixels per eye view. Her claws tangled with the
vehicle's trail in the air. White fire breath only raised the city's
temperature. Clamping jaws dined on empty space and blue
clouds that were only getting larger and darker. It was only with a
final twist and lash from the feeble weight of her tail that the slow
moving metallic monstrosity could outmaneuver the spaceship
that was too caught up in prior bouts of evasion. The strike was
slow and burdensome, but the aloft spacecraft shot towards the
earth. The process was an explosion of white, sending both the
metal ship and beast falling with a mighty boom, burying
themselves into the grass.

      Dirt exploded, grass erupted, and concrete paths cracked
and burst where they sat. The sky rained pellets of earth for only
an extended moment. A flood of white light pooled on the ground
from that UFO hatch. Light bounced off the dirt and concrete. A
two dimensional full moon illuminated the space at their feet and
then grew. In the time between seconds the full moon projected
onto the ground encompassed all participants at the park making
everyone in the air lungs rise for a second. Contents of people's
stomachs went weightless. The two teenage girls, almost adults,
along with a honeymooning couple and residual rabbit stampede
were slowly made free of the ground by a distance of inches and
then feet. The only body not affected was deep within the
dimensions of a casket at the epicenter of San Anlos' burial and
Trifecta park alike.

And, of course, the Adamants.

The two children had slid rather unceremoniously out of their vehicle and onto an earth flush with colorless light. Each of them bore a stern apathetic, almost despairingly so, countenance as they walked towards the groups suspended in the air.

"Is there life within San Anlos?" they asked in unison. "Most certainly."

"Because it must comply," Adam added.

It was Abel who acted, eyes cast downward with an expression of purity that was devoid of such as they held an already extracted cattle prod into the air. The air was electrified. Even the rabbits shrieked just as the earthlings did. Lauren could taste her tongue burn a little. The earth was caught in the orbit of the sun. The sun sat in the center of the galaxy. The galaxy was one of the many that occupied the very empty room of the universe. The universe was nothing more than a garden of order. The Adamants were adamant in all ways. The venue of San Anlos was set to produce a product that it must. There was no alternative possible. However, the two were starting to come around to understanding the means to such ends. If a city must be wiped out then it must. That was neither fallout nor accident, merely the facts that were and always had been. These were the facts of life and reality. The Adamant combination was perfection. It did not need to go stated, but in this instance it was.

They stood with the grace of age and youth. They spoke with complex clarity. They were a fusion of space and soul. No balance necessitated. No falter within. Look to the sun for power and life, but to the moon goes order. There was a hierarchy to this universe out there, and it was one they reigned supreme over.

"The Adamant existence validates each other and thereby validates itself and thereby validates our own."

Even the small sea breeze lacked the compassion to move. The chill of nightfall lacked the energy to touch the suspended city.

"But that's a tortured logic isn't it?" It was only Christina who had it within her to speak. She was speaking from the arms of Lauren who caught onto her as she floated a little bit too high too fast. However, for all she cared she was speaking to herself, putting her thoughts into words. "It's seeking validation elsewhere before finding your own within." If she had followed that standard in her life she would have drowned in a kitchen. It was the process of putting a price on yourself measured in the determination of expectations, making it cheap at that. To give yourself away in exchange for an impervious simple mind. The thought alone made her shudder without a temperature change. She looked onward past the influx of sticker products to Adam and Abel with a look of true pity. "There is no life within those confines."

Each and everyone said the same words together. Under their breaths, through silent struggles, within horrored gasp, they whispered it, and when it couldn't be said aloud, then in their heads. The same question as always.

"Is there life on the moon?"

The twins' eyes widened. In them was a sterile world ready to shatter. "How do you all come to that conclusion?" Abel wondered.

"Because there is a difference between simplicity and simple." Lauren spoke up. It was a difference that escaped her understanding, but this much at least did not evade her. "The truth has a simplicity to it but your perception, or lack, of does not."

For example, Christina snuck a peek into her headset and, more importantly, selected an option that had always been present. All manners of guided missiles and rockets left twirls of smoke as they shot from the body of a felled kaiju. Nighttime rabbits were struck, still in the air, and exploded into multiple messes until gravity accepted their drop to the earth. All of this was, in fact, easy to understand alone, but to process all in such a short period of time with all manner of lights, sounds, and sensations clamoring to overtake one another ultimately made it only a bundle of minor details difficult to be understood.

If the Adamants were one to yell they certainly would have, but instead they did exactly what they were meant to, as they had always done so before. They went to work as usual. Tight smiles, fake laughs, and false cheers were total restraints that kept them choked. Directions for action were clear, they needed to consolidate their damages at this point before the attack. Adam kept movements minimal as they electrocuted all rabbits caught in their path into a formless sphere that only grew in the air as it accumulated more. And on the other side, Abel occupied themselves with the few remnants of an explosive surprise charging the very air above them to create a protective dome of a barrier. The last of the missiles collided with the electric field exploding in the air before their target, breaking against the field but never through.

Tiana was the first to collect herself from the fall and contest these actions. Quickly, she sent a barrage of energy pulses in the twin's direction only for Abel to dispel them with ease, meeting each and every one of them with a simple tool and simple movement of the arm. "Are you the type that comes back for payback?" they asked. From afar Tiana laughed at the question. Certainly not her. But her other half was a different story.

Touma was already in the air behind Abel and slamming his white titanium knuckle against the back of the kid's skull, sending them skidding far against the grass to the right. Adam spun around ready to retaliate for such acts but Lauren had finished running to the kaiju corpses and popping open a faculty hatch and calling out to Christina. From inside, countless red eyes lit up and out poured a small army worth of robot raptor units. Each unit contained a set of claws and teeth strong enough to tear through far more than each other. Christina set her sights on the twin.

Adams left foot instinctively stepped back and they wanted to tear it off. Their weapon, high in the air above, split the suspended ball of slime into infinite small ones and charged them each with enough power to send the infuriating human machinations to the closest thing to oblivion. And if not that, then they would desperately see to it that their metal was warped beyond use and repair. Metallic raptors swarmed the center, masses of them were pelted with erasure, completely losing chunks and space of their being. For the few survivors, the machines were caught in the electrified grasps and Adam saw to it that their promise was not false.

Following their sibling's lead, Abel readied themselves and halted the latest barrage of energy bullets from Tiana mid air and reorganized them around themselves over and over again. The white beams of energy blinked in and out of place as Touma weaved in and out until he barely found it within him to dodge at close range let alone strike. Given that, he jumped backward and retreated for a moment. At that point, Abel extended an electrified touch to the farthest layer of beams and set them into a spin until there was a circling halo of erasure around them. Abel was ready to return each and every bullet shot towards them in kind, if not slightly altered.

Adam reduced each raptor that approached them into contorted scrap metal and Abel returned each white beam back to Tiana and Touma one by one. These were the facts of the fight.

Also a fact was two separate foam darts with suction cupped ends that somehow managed to strike the heads of the two unassuming children. Binoculars sat atop the head of a figure of an ex-company employee, as fit as he was angry and as angry as he was small, while he peered over the top of the nearest rooftop of the surrounding houses. Christopher Abadie in the flesh and soul had yet to make his own impact, even if he was just trying to match the energy present. Afterall all, he was only a distraction for now. Keeping the focus away from a fleet of birds.

Red birds.

Mangled birds.

Gelatinous birds.

Those of which descended onto the field to welcome the guest.

CHAPTER 11: INSOMNIACS

The murder of red flocks first found their misshapen flight path through the streets surrounding the park, wings battering up against the side of the houses and townhomes on all fronts before closing in on the crushed stone center. They became a red whirlwind contained around the limousine tribute. The process itself was completely pummeling in all senses of the word. Bones and feathers flapped against all mourners present. With their strike they lodged themselves against ears, into open mouths, and found a way into the folds of clothes. Occasionally the unlucky bird collided head on with the people's very own head or socked them in the gut.

The couple waited through the bombardment, shielding each other. The Adamants attempted to defend themselves. Lauren blocked the brunt of it from Christina, using her body as a shield while clamping a hand over her own mouth.

Worst of all was the sensation. A wet and sticky sensation. One that made them wonder just what kind of red substance was being spread across their skin. In all senses of the word, the convergence was disconcerting. So much so that fighting was put to a halt. All temporarily paused beams of energy in Abel's possession were let loose as they lost their concentration.

Then, as quickly as the cyclone came, it disappeared. Each and every one of the priorly distraught heard the bodies fall into useless heaps on the ground before they opened their eyes to see them. Dead birds. Mangled birds. Red birds. They littered the park floor. In their place was anticipation and the figure of a red boy sitting atop the vertical limousine, looking rather gleeful and pleased at his own disgusting entrance. It was not just anyone either. The face was familiar and recognizable. Something that should have been easy to identify if not for the outrageous events that ruined participants' focus.

Marcus Marcus Alvarado Alvarado.

Christina and Lauren both shared a look of shock from far away, still concerned if they saw it correctly. A wave of relief washed over them soon after seeing their long absent friend in these unusual circumstances. Neither of them wanted to admit it, but both worried that they shared a large responsibility for what might have transpired to the boy to end up like this. However, worries would have to be postponed. The sound of clanking metal drew everyone's attention to the base of the limo and the sight of a rather plain looking boy in comparison, one easily overlooked as he picked his way through the twisted raptor metal toward his friends.

Marcus Alvarado.

More relief washed over the girls now, but the idea of two Marcus' may have actually been worse. Once again they postponed their consciences for tonight. Meanwhile, Christopher Abadie had been watching it all unfold, having seen the flock coming in miles away. From over the rooftop's edge he peered with tension concentrated in his eyes, examining every detail and searching for his own wellspring of relief to show up with the rest of them. The answer was right before him, but against his expectations. That being, he stood right behind him poking at the space between Christopher's shoulder blades.

"You're going to tear your back up like that if you don't calm down."

Before Christopher could turn around he was twirled and interlocking lips with Eve Luna, each second savored. And then Eve put his hand on Christopher's chest and gave them space because he still wanted to slap the man.

"You're an idiot."

"My plan worked didn't it?" Christopher retorted. He didn't know how many times he would have to say it and in how many different ways, but he would repeat it to the end of time if he had to. He didn't want Eve to use him as an escape. He didn't want the paralysis of fear for a moment that could be stolen at any moment to ruin the moment itself. He didn't want the threat of losing a boyfriend to ruin the process of actually having one. And he didn't want Eve to be essentially a functional corpse if it meant he himself would live comfortably. That's what he wanted to say at least, but the words that came out of his mouth were a little different. "Just because I think it's hot when you look tired and depressed doesn't mean you always have to be."

Eve pulled him close so that their chests were against each other and he could feel his breath against his own cheeks. Eve would also repeat it to the end of time. "I said I am going to choose you from now on."

"Choosing me doesn't mean giving up on Isabella."

"She was going to destroy the city."

"No," Christopher stopped him. If Eve wasn't so handsome he might have strangled him from the frustration. "These twins are going to destroy this city. When are you going to just admit that." He fixated squarely on Eve's dark green eyes and pulled tightly against his back, giving the man no option but to stand straight and tall. Eve looked into Christopher's brown eyes and realized that this wasn't the type of choice he couldn't reluctantly stumble into.

How despairingly tiresome it all was.

He looked to the park and sighed at it. "I'm glad my sticker worked."

Christopher returned the extra folded and crushed stickers of a pink heart pierced by an arrow. "Honestly I'm a little disappointed that I didn't get turned into a big monster. I guess I'm too healthy."

Eve let go of his boyfriend and picked up his suitcase. "You're armed right?" To which the answer was a show of a company handgun strapped to his thigh. "Good. Give me a minute and then give it your best shot."

Touma and Tiana didn't have time to shout greetings to Marcus as Abel was already sending wave after wave of writhing electricity out through the air in a circle around them. For Touma, the question was how he could get close while not being fried. For Tiana, she asked herself if her long distance energy rifle was good enough to dish out pistol whips for the personal pleasure of it. Marcus never actually made it to his friends, now lively behind the trees and bushes near the sidewalk.

Adam was experiencing something unusual, they had to assume it was anger, and sent sighs of electricity through the metal heaps and organized them carefully. For Marcus, there was an open path in which he picked up the pace into an awkward run to finish. For Adam, there was a direct line to Marcus. They let the energy course from the cattle prod in their hand and writhe across their skin and around their eyes which glittered with intent and focus on their mistake of a target. Then they let the energy run down their body to the ends of their feet and let it pool. And let it grow. And let it expand. And let it release. When Adam took a single step it carried them yards in an instant. In one moment they were gripping their weapon in a restrained rage and the next they were before Marcus, releasing the entirety of their animosity into the boy, intending to fry his brain and reduce the nuisance to a puddle. The cattle prod was forced deep into the boy's gut and alive with electricity, but then it went deeper. Marcus did not yell, or he did but not in pain necessarily. Adams' arm went even deeper. Their arm was engulfed in a red gushy body.

"How did you get here?" they asked rather calmly towards Marcus Marcus.

The boy in red smiled as the alien twin was slowly pulled into his gelatinous gut. "My name is Marcus Alvarado. Why shouldn't I be here?"

It finally clicked within Adam's head that this was going to be much more of an annoyance than they originally thought. The realization was too late as stained ribs clamped down on their back and pulled them in.

Abel was beginning to take what they thought was pleasure from watching the two robotic lovers helplessly avoid their presence. Their slow walk was matched by the robots scurried run in an effort to distance themselves. Perhaps too much enjoyment, as they failed to notice an average bullet coming towards them until it was a hair's width away from their eyes before they deflected it with a return to sender swipe. Somewhere on a rooftop Christopher rolled to dodge the incoming bullet and felt the heat of roof tiles bursting against his skin, too close for comfort. He cursed at the sight of such a good shot getting deflected. It didn't matter though, the shot was a distraction enough. All around the park, a slew of black chains strung themselves up ensnaring, entrapping, and attaching themselves to houses across the street, the few thickets of trees and bushes, the light poles that dotted the light poles, the center fixture of a limousine coffin, and each other. From every angle they wound themselves until the entire park was a hard to navigate web of binds.

Eve's suit battered in the wind and tried to unbutton itself as he ziplined down a set of chains, holding onto his suitcase with both hands as it carried him straight towards the limo. Abel, who had not anticipated actions from another Luna family member like this, looked up to see. Touma, who very much could anticipate the actions of people within San Anlos, took his opportunity by uppercutting the alien child's chest so hard that every particle vacated their lungs as they were sent flying upwards. However, the flight was not for long and Tiana was above them, slamming the heel of her boot into their occipital lobe, bringing the child face first deep into the now torn up grass.

From within Marcus Marcus, Adam was smothered in red and losing the air necessary to stay conscious. With every amount of energy left within their body they demanded it be charged within the cattle prod's ends and released its contents into the monster before them. A flash of white noise and light temporarily blinded everyone. When they finally blinked the distraction back there was Adam weaving through chains as they ran from two opposing spirals of red birds released from the cages of Marcus Marcus' ribs.

Marcus, in the mundane and normal flesh, watched on without any possibility to help the people in front of him. Sitting atop the limousine, having swapped positions with his counterpart, there was only one person present he had any chance of aiding. So with his feet dangling and both hands resting against the bumper where he sat, he spoke. He spoke absentmindedly as he had always done before.

"How long are you going to stay in that sleep of yours? Alone in a bed with all your inadequacies. With your failed dreams dead, now superstitions. Not yet buried, but comfortably not alive."

Isabella would have definitely not appreciated the fact that he could relate to her properly now. In fact, she would probably find it detestable. But above anyone else, he knew the danger there was to hold something so close but refuse to set eyes on it. He wondered aloud, but this time finally speaking to someone in particular.

"Does it hurt less to never have to open those eyes now? Is it truly comfortable now?" Ahead of him, Marcus saw Adam run to save and prop up Abel. He had to give up the act. No more purple prose, words with loose meanings, thoughts unfinished, and useless proverbials just to fill up time.

He had to be honest.

"I'm sorry that these things happen to you. That your life was dealt a hand as one like this. That you had to do it alone for so long. That you kept it to yourself while meeting so many people." He realized just how many faces she must have known over just how many years she must have lived this life. Each one creating something far more impactful than they ever desired within the deepest parts of her. Every time it must have stung more than the last, digging deeper into her heart, tearing chunks out of it. Reminding her something. No bondage could fix it as it was no longer what it had once been. Isabella doesn't get to rest because there is still work to be done. Forever. Until her end.

He was sorry, but there was nothing he could do. "These feelings that hurt, that sorrow, that pain, that regret, it's something only you can decide to deal with. So after all these years, if you want to rest then you deserve to rest. If you want to sleep until the sun burns itself out then you can do exactly that. You deserve a break. You deserve so much more." Once again he struggled. Words escaped him because he couldn't decide on the right ones, but he wanted her to know this. "It must make you sick, but I want you to know that I will be here to worry for you."

Indeed it was sickening. All of it. The entire moment.

All of her. Disturbed. In all senses of the word.

A heartbeat beholden to no one beated against the walls of her fully furnished confines. The limousine shook in the cement it stood in. The metal vibrated with ferocity. The chains binding it shut resisted with impatience. There was no rest for the sleepless. No sleep for the insomniac. Siestas did not quell her worries and dreams did not soothe her woes. Marcus could feel the limo beat faster and faster in his hands until the continuous pounding began to make them sting. How she had wanted so little and so much. A freedom denied to her. A life not permitted to have. A denial of an investigation for a solution. The world gave her no such space. The moon would have no persuasion. And so she wished on the daylight sun, but there was no answer for her.

Isabella was reduced and humble. She had been fed on a diet of malnutrition without thought of what her appetite needed. There was no correction from such. It made her ravenous. For this dinner and for the others far out before her current present, she didn't quite know what she desired for. But for now, she knew that she had to eat at least. Eat whatever was before her. Digest all that was in her way. Chew through that which stood in front of her. She wanted this moment to be clamorous, to create an assumption of spectacular, a glittering sight of carnal catastrophic cravings. She wanted a bouquet of the most grievous, a buffet of satisfaction, a cathartic end to this diet, and a beginning to one reveling in a self-sufficient filth.

There was no feast to be had in the colorless world that occupied her mind. There only was domestication and subjugation. Inside her was a heartbeat that sent trembles and quakes.

Adam pulled at Abel and Abel pulled at Adam.

"Do we need to remind you?"

"We don't play." They each talked separately but they were indistinguishable. "There is nothing if not results."

And then together.

"So it's results we shall get."

Both ends of their cattle prods got closer and closer within a minutia of space between, but never surpassing the gap to touch. Above them, the space itself went white with a dangerous kind of energy. One that was volatile because it was controlled.

From the rumblings of the limousine nearly forgotten Marcus felt an identity that refused to go forgotten. Reminding others in the way it cracked stone and tore through metal and ripped its way through the car's black ceilings.

Throwing Marcus from his perch was the Class I: Instigator. Product and bearer of the Luna name. Red eyes cast. Positioned on all fours. Volatile because of her refusal of control.

Isabella Luna.

CHAPTER 12: SITUATIONS SCREWED

In a world that was completely cleansed in light Isabella stood out, objecting to the stark colored reality. In a pale cast light filtering into the harsh moonlight Isabella was a stark shadow. Defiant to the state of matter around her, light diverted and bent around her silhouette which was beholden to no one but her. The eyes of hers glowed with a serious tint of red, obfuscating the sight presented before her. The sight of famously recurring faces, like the two in front of her, meant memories running for cover and many more infamous ones.

Looking at her with apparent aggravation, Adam and Abel both forced their cattle prods into the others as an ill defined ball of pale deletion formed. Around them and growing was a hum that seared the world into a definitionless plane of existence cleansing San Anlos of all its details.

Marcus was gathering himself at the base of the limo when Eve suddenly held a finger to his face to shut him up. "Not quite yet," Eve said, answering both questions Marcus had yet to think much less ask. At the height of the newly torn up limousine Isabella did not so much stand, but crouched on all fours ready like a rabid animal. Her claws dug into the metal end, tearing at the bumper and crushing the car around her fingertips. The mass of her long hair stood in the air above her, each strand agitated and at attention. From her mouth came out a smoke of breath that burned and stung, changing the air around her. Her canines flashed with a snarl almost as if to point at where and how the damned will rest. And the growl was a deep guttural growl that slunk over the earth like mudslides and avalanches against the mountains. It was a low decibel of inhuman sound that found its way navigating the sands of time to end up here. Always just being heard for the first time. Always agitating. It was the type of sound that piled up against each person's skin and stuck to them like sweat, but never properly made it to their ears. It was for their bodies to hear and their being to understand.

The Adamant response to that was an exchange of nervous laughter quickly cut off and a pace for world end quickened. Such was a pace that would not be successful, as the predator mashed her jaw and for an instant disappeared. With a flash of commotion, only the merest suggestion of movement, the chains that entangled the park snapped together at once into useless chunks of metal falling against grass and concrete in helpless thuds. Before either Eve and Marcus had time to process the events unfolding, the casket that had held her for so long was ripped from its place and hurled into the air as if weight was a factor that did not apply to such an animal. Claw marks, crushed ends, and a torn roof were all sent plummeting toward Adam and Abel caught stuck in a pale drained commitment. In the last moment they dispelled such an easy end to them, instead sending the oblivion they worked so hard for together into the underside of the limo. The limo was there for one moment, a ball of erasure touched it the next, and then all at once it was totally consumed and gone as if it had never been. Without themselves funding an unreasonable justice the white light unfolded itself onto the world and disappeared, leaving only the now darkened shades of San Anlos behind.

Hungry and carnivorous, appetite not sated, Isabella bounded towards the two like an animal. Within milliseconds she was atop of Adam, clawing and swinging her body as they flailed in a panic. Her two feet were planted on their shoulders and her fingers interlocked under their chin so that she could pull with all her strength. She was prepared to perform a beheading through brute force alone.

Adam yelled from a new panic and made the executive decision to electrocute them both in their last attempt to melt Bella from the inside out. She shrieked atop them and from all fronts the glass to houses and cars shattered into lacerated dust. The pain was strong, but it was no pain enough to stop her.

From behind, Abel pushed a cattle prod deep between her shoulder blades and set their blast to full strength. Energy erupted and torched a hole through her clothes and the approximation to skin and flesh along her back, exposing delicately fake insides that fell out with few movements. Isabella roared again and finally let loose of her hands on Adam only to kick back off the kid's body, sending them tumbling forward and catching herself in a crouch behind Abel, ready to pounce on her prey. Her fingers dug deep into the approximation of human flesh until her knuckles were buried into the base of Abel's neck. The twin let out a tortured yell just as fountains of an approximation of blood began to squirt.

Isabella's stomach began to bubble. Her mouth salivated.

She placed a foot squarely on their back and pushed, fingers still clutched and tearing away at the base of Abel's neck. Colorless paper fluttered out as fluid sprayed. Abel let out a pained cry, eyes rolling back, before falling over from the force of it all.

Isabella gathered herself for a moment and stood in a stance similar to that a human would have. Leaning back, she licked her hand and exhaled a tired and partly satisfied breath of calm air. Against her cheek, she brushed off a droplet of blood with her filthy hand, only painting the bottom of her face and mouth with more infernal colors. Her arms fell with exhaustion behind her, dangling deftly along with her heaps of hair. For a moment she waited, looking up at the night sky of clouds and not stars.

Then she set her sights on her target. Adam was already prepared for her aggressive approach. From twisted metallic corpses of scrap metal, they exploded the raptors into millions of metal shivs and held them in the air above. Suspended by a current of electricity was a palace of misshapen blades. They assailed the earth, slicing through the air with high pitch wails erupting from the ground where they clung. The earth was stabbed countless times as the dangerous descent of roving blades left a trail after Isabella's pace. Her arms ache with exhaustion. Under her nails dirt stung and rocks dug themselves further up. Her hands and feet slapped against the earth, blistering with a newly scathing sensation for touch.

But she did not stop.

Truly and evidently to all present, the child itself included, Adam faltered as she neared. Weaving in and out of near death, each breath of Isabella's that came in was labored and struggled. Millions became millions more, and so on, and so on until Adam finally halted the onslaught only for a moment. A new armory of razor blades filling the sky. A prelude to their finale. That of which was above her aloft, waiting. All of which began to plunge in the exact same second.

When in the face of all encompassing doom there was only one way to go and that was forward to face. With every ounce of energy, every moment she had loathed up until that point, every memory she hid from, every sensation she tried to forget, every detail of Isabella Luna, she tossed it into her furnace and bounded towards them.

Her approximation to bones cracked from exertion.

Her jaw clamped shut on itself and ground an approximation to teeth.

Her approximation to blood boiled and poured from her ears.

Her fingers began to split at their ends exposing approximation to raw flesh.

Her joints began to rip, tearing at an approximation to skin.

Behind her, the assailing house of knives plunged into the ground. The sound of metal plunging through skin rang in the back of her head as a few strays lined along her back and interrupted the clamor of her torso, but she barely acknowledged them. The attack had missed its mark.

Hand flat and fixed, aimed for the pale child's throat only to be blocked by an electrified strike. In the same vein, a repetition of blows followed. Isabella was ready to shove her fish and feet through the child. Kicks were attempted to be brought down on them while each and everyone was interrupted in their final moments. She went for his throat again and Adam blocked. The two stopped there for a moment in the battle of wills.

"You of all people should know your place," Adam scolded, but they were not talking to a poor relative or classmate. Their words reached a beast of their own production.

Hairs spasming unnaturally in the air behind her. Eyes enraged and not obligated to this world. Animosity frothing at her mouth. The only response she cared to give was a spit of her approximation to blood mixed with the pits of her cheeks worn thin and the tip of an approximation of a tongue.

The two combatants released each other and stepped a few paces back.

Adam drew their weapon of absolute anything to their side, ready to force it through Isabella's own skull and release her of position in this life.

Isabella roared with a ferocity not capable of a human mind.

They lunged for her head.

She charged, breath burning like a fire in her lungs that was burning from the heat inside her. Muscles popping and ripping from such a force. Boiling blood bursting from her skin, completely refused to a violent loss. Eyes stabbing with agency from an unnecessary gaze. Feet breaking from her power. Bones ground to dust from her effort.

Adam let out a final yell as they charged, releasing every particle that composed the entirety of their being feeling the atoms that made them loosen and drift.

Their cattle prod had first touched her hand, grabbing onto it as it was backed up against and into her chest.

Her other hand touched only the cool fresh air. The night was still. The storm hadn't come yet, but it would. The clouds in the sky isolated them. Left for company was only each other.

She brushed the useless toy aside and slowly she drew her arm back through Adam's chest, watching without a single clear thought in her head as the body collapsed.

She stood there, sweating from the heat. Burning against the night. Immolating herself.

Eve was the first person to come across her path, one that she set out on with only two feet against the earth and finally clear eyes. He held onto her suitcase but stopped just short of offering it up. After such a display hesitancy was not only natural but encouraged. Isabella, on the other hand, ignored such fundamentals of human intuition and pulled her business partner closer into an embrace. Holding his head in one bloodied hand and his ear against her bloodied mouth she let out in deep and tired sighs her whispers.

"You know if those two weren't there it would have been you."

He shrugged it off. "Fair enough." Her suitcase was shoved into her chest giving, Eve an excuse to separate himself from her. "You are back to your combative usual now?"

Bella opened up her case and peered inside with a smile. "You are far too correct." With a single large phillips screw in one hand she met his gaze. "Business as usual isn't it?"

It was not. In fact, Eve did not know what usual business would look like now, let alone how to go about it. But he did know that he was not going to become too much of any sort of obstacle for Bella in that moment, so he resolved to stay out of her way.

With slow and decisive strides she had already stared down a helpless and average Marcus only a few steps along the concrete path. He fell with ease, only the slightest of pushes needed. She sat herself on top of her, legs on both sides of his body. Leaning over, stray hairs toppled over her shoulders covering the two as they failed to meet each other's gaze.

"Where just a couple of disappointments aren't we?" she asked, with the slightest bit of a losing smile.

"It's always been like that hasn't it?" Marcus answered, with a smile of his own.

Bella looked down past his face, trying to shield her own as tears began to slide down. She couldn't help herself from laughing. When did her young boy Marcus get so mature? "You know it's not like you to actually say something kind of cool."

The two let out awkward chuckles amid pained coughs as she leaned over more. She rested against his chest until she was laying, exhausted, completely on top of him. With the tip of the screw she pulled up the shirt over his chest.

"The mixture is not perfect."

"I wouldn't dream of it."

The screw plunged deep into his chest and he began to slowly churn just as his entire being was changing red. Marcus Marcus Alvarado Alvarado hugged Isabella Luna as she finally sated her appetite and consumed him.

His body began to lose form caught in the mixture of it all. Underneath them all the ground itself started to warp and twist as if it were one massive gelatinous smoothie. Jagged metal scraps firmly buried were liquified and incorporated with Marcus' red form as it shrank and compacted into a red slime. Slowly but surely, it all diminished away until there was only left one standard completely average red screw. Marcus, Eve, Touma, Tiana, Lauren, and Christina were gathered behind Isabella as she held the object close to her own heart.

From afar were those that abhorred it adamantly. In slow panged and sullen struggles, with ripped insides flying out from torn open gaps, they stood. A power instilled inside shone bright through their eyes.

"The Adamants do not commit failure, we do not allow it." The voices were malformed and warped, echoes where there should not have been and overlapping pitches that could not have been possible. "We cannot allow it."

The two struck their cattle prods into the sky. "You do not understand the extent to which the extremes are."

"There is no fate."

"There is no forgiveness."

"There is no room for mistakes."

Lighting shot through the clouds.

"There is only us."

Thunder rumbled.

"You."

From under their white bangs were two small slits in their foreheads. From each, a massive stream of black and white stickers spewed forth, reaching up into the night. All the black inky fluids accumulated from Luna work and fantastical rabbit corpses throughout the city shot upwards.

"And the moon."

Rain began to fall as the typhoon finally landed. Lighting struck the scene, drawing back the curtains of the clouds over them. From behind poured a completely white light. The pale surface of an astronomical sphere engulfed the horizon, drawn far too close to the earth than possible. Above them was the radiance of a false moon. As moonlight escaped through the parting clouds it touched the twins, erasing them into refractions and reflections until they were completely gone and the curtains could close.

"We are nothing, if not Adamant."

STCKR: PLATONIC PANIC
EPISODE 5: RNFLL

CHAPTER 1: RAIN INVESTIGATION

The relationship between the concepts, that of rainfall and the South Western city of San Anlos, was certainly a specific one. It was peculiar. As the usually dried and almost lifeless hills of dried brush were sprouting with a vibrant green, water drops painted the entire earth in a color two hues darker and rich. It was peculiar, how the usually ignored storm drains clogged with the accumulation of the year's debris failed in their hour of need. It was peculiar, how normal roads became near rivers and how the natural curves and dips of the city pooled with water flooding sidewalks, businesses, and houses alike. Every surface of San Anlos was soaked, drenched, and wet from the total downpour.

As the people hibernated with a sigh of relief Isabella and Eve did dissimilarly, sitting on a patio that was ignored in this weather while being drenched and completely wet. The actual name of such a small cafe was not relevant, as it is for most unimportant things. The hole in the wall lacking the bare minimum signage had survived off of the continuing charity of local regulars and now interstellar customers too. That fact, along with her current state and so much more, was not something Isabella ruminated about. She didn't waste time thinking about such things nor did she waste time thinking about the rain. It was while she was sitting under the onslaught of water that she watched as her tea was quickly displaced and replaced with raindrops. The droplets were heavy and battered against her skin at every angle. Within the gated little seating area it was a scene of a small unimportant pond.

How peculiar it was that the frustration came not from the fall, but the collisions. How interesting it was that rain was defined not by the action, but by the location. The hold that the

mere momentum of the droplet had over the citizens only came
with the idea of a collision. The relationship between San Anlos
and rain was a peculiar one. A phenomenon that lasted rampant
among sparse weeks in the early starts of spring, at least for the
last few decades or so. There was a time and place that no longer
existed within San Anlos where rain was something to ignore
among common days. Now the idea of rainy days and wet seasons
was a fantasized, forgotten, and coveted one.

A San Anlos rain was a gray expanse of a single morning
stretched over countless hours regardless of the proper
formalities. It was a veil to a new faux moon that now crowded the
sky. It was a peculiar rain that reigned upon every surface it
touched. It was an important rain, a mixture of cloud, water, and
all manner of pollutant chemicals available. It was a passive
aggressive rain that struck at an angle and pounded against car
roofs, walls, windows, and doors. It was a destructive rain that
would mold walls, send street lights sliding within mudslides, and
halt all manner of transportation functionality. It was peculiar
how fast a San Anlos city was not a city of rubble, quickly cleaned
but not forgotten with unfinished and empty office skyscrapers
jutting out of the earth. Like titanic metal skeletons of glass and
steel beams that rose and waited. It was now a city of screens and
LED advertisements on every available surface of not yet available
industrial monoliths. A city breached. A city of a plastic
foundation. How peculiar it was that San Anlos rain almost
stained the patio concrete, how it filled teacups, and struck skin in
an unfamiliar way.

Across from Isabella sat Eve and between the two were
their respective porcelain cups that had at one point been filled
with black coffee from a matching basic white kettle. However,
much like anything else, the rain was anecdotal and her drinks

were anecdotal and the contents of her drink were the same contents of the rain at this point. How peculiar it was to be in an unimportant cafe with unfamiliar drinks next to an unfamiliar crime scene. How peculiar it was that the rain, that would have just as well have stained, somehow washed away all the blood of a freshly made victim.

Beyond the lines of caution tape Isabella peered from her seat at the unfamiliar body. One torn apart with abusive blows, evidence of an aggressive beating as an end. It was a body without blood, but enough metal and plastic to make up for it. It was a victim dressed in a now soaked black and white made uniform. It was a corpse missing a tongue. For a moment she almost recognized it all, but Eve reminded her that such a thought would be only insulting.

Truly how peculiar San Anlos was in the rain. Truly and utterly.

Marcus could feel the particles of dust line his nasal cavity and feared for the rather intrusive idea of what breed of foreign particles he breathed in. Although the hallways of the hospital building were only recently emptied his mental picture of a world now abandoned painted over his surroundings in the colors of connotations to his dismay. The Seaview Community Core Hospital facility had only recently been vacated, gutted like a fish, of everything long established as available for removal. Items were pulled out and moved to an up to date hospital building a block away in the form of one of the latest gifts from Tandem Tantrum Toys and Co.'s charitable city reconstruction efforts. The old building was now stuck in the limbo of promise, waiting for the clamor of wrecking balls or a retirement into an aftercare therapy facility.

Even with all this very practical thought process and discussions, Christina couldn't help but shake at a cold sensation. She kept seeing a sickly shade of green at the edges of the dim fluorescent light where the last of the illuminated mixture met with the shadows along the corners. If the hospital was to be anything, it was most definitely eerie.

Lauren, on the other hand, only saw a group of new adults more excited in pointing out shadows than they were at actually jumping them. If they could do anything better it would be to shut up. The basement was cold, colder than it would have normally been for the sterile environment. Their trek was lengthy to the opposite end of the building before Marcus could actually be seated for the real occasion.

The examination would be a simple one. Another act of charity to make sure that nothing in the creature that is the final Marcus Alvarado before them had been unfortunately damaged in the absurdist events of the prior days. The squeamishly yellow light of the examination lamp blinded retinas as it burled through all the layers of its tinted glass. However, Marcus was far too polite to complain, only just impolite enough to let out a disgusted groan to his friends.

"Grow up, this is important science," Christina chided, already in the process of poking and pinching him all over.

"What your doing in fact is not actual science." Lauren, occupied with an actual list for physical diagnostic checks, was marking off boxes and was similarly quick in her response.

"Come on he's dumb, he doesn't know that." Christina was now stretching out his mouth.

Marcus actually attempted to compensate for the last time he didn't complain. That is to say, he actually squirmed in his seat and eventually caught Christina's hand before she was about to poke his belly like a baby. If the examination was for something as menial as this then he was going to question why he had to ever leave the comfort of his bed.

Lauren finished hammering on his knee and scribbling notes away in time to look up at him over her clipboard. A flash of a smile was accompanied with the last of surgical light as she swung it forward.

"Just because the truth is just out of reach and sight doesn't mean that it's not there," she said.

"Chill with the mantras," he grunted.

Uncovered from the shadows was a massive MRI scanner to the surprise of the two as it took up most of the space of the room. Marcus made no quick movements which was admirable. The inside of the machine wasn't necessarily scary. Maybe that was because with such poor lighting inside it was harder to notice how cramped it was. What he did notice was that he didn't know what to expect.

"Has it started?" Christina asked.

"You will notice."

They were leaps ahead of the boy who was just preparing to ask the same question when a loud jolt of electricity shot through the inside of his head sending his eyes rolling back. Christina yelped, but from Lauren's fixation on her tablet she couldn't tell if it was planned.

It was a museum of sensation, a parade of imagination, a crowd of consciousness, festivities of the most rancorous kind. Everything of his being was thoughts, smell, touch, and taste. Each and every facet becoming its own different set of experiences until it was indistinguishable from each other. Slowly the world around him came to focus on a dense green one. Multicolored shades faded into the usual ones and Marcus realized that he was actually caught in a tumble set in a downward motion stumbling through the foliage.

Palm tree fronds, blades of tall grass, leaves of brush, and the thickets of bushes smacked against his face like punches. He climbed through pomegranate and avocado trees. Things began to feel familiar as he chose his path through the orchards of oranges, lemons, and limes. Of course, he stopped along the way to admire each and every succulent and the nopales that always found a way to touch him. Their tunas were radiant in the sunlight. Through the field of sunflowers and rows of corn he progressed on until ,unknowingly, he burst through a final tree line out of the dense greens of foliage, entering into the territory of light rays. Rays that hung outside of windows, climbed walls, sprinted along paths, sauntered beside the river, and jumped about in the gardens. Before him and below him was the vast valley and cradle of life, a city along a river between land and sea, surrounded by the guardians of mountains on all sides but one.

He fell down.

He fell from the goliath of earth he had been standing on and crashed against the dirt road into the open lot of a pueblo completely made of adobe buildings. Coughing out dirt and dust while simultaneously gasping for air, Marcus got his achy head up to see a figure of white before him.

Gleaming and luminous, body draped in intricate vestal garments and shining chains, rings, and pendants of gold that matched the glow of a crown of light, it stood there. Every detail was absurd as a single hand of light with rings attached to chains that draped from finger to finger reached out to him. Without a second's hesitation Marcus spat at the dirt before him in an instinctual and guttural response.

The apparition burst into a shower of white. Factitious features were replaced with a singular figure of Marcus' own features, but slightly adjusted. Skin richer. Hair darker. Wrinkles around the corner of his eyes and mouth from smiling. He had a body with signs of far more activity than Marcus' own. His blank pants were thin and worn out around the knees, and his boots were scuffed. Against his dark skin the green striped shirt stood out. Weaving in and out of the green vertical bars was the embroidery of vines. Inconsistent and wild. Alive by the second.

It was Marcus that had to wait for a moment as the stranger caught his breath and, if not for the dreamlike state of it all, he might have gotten annoyed by the man's laughter. His head was fresh and open, but caught in a spin so that everything seemed to be a nature more familiar and agreeable. Even now with the man's introduction, his name offered no surprises.

"¡Bienvenido a la vida Marcus!" he cheered. "Indeed that is not the kind of saint your Saint Alvarado would want to be."

"And what kind of saint is that?" Marcus wondered, counting the vines along his clothes. Underneath the shadow of an old tree beyond the echoes of the boy's young years, Marcus stood while Saint Alvarado sat atop an old wooden crate leaning forward with his chin propped in one hand. Marcus hadn't had the time to take it in fully, nor was he capable of it either, but from what he could make out there was the hot dirt of the open courtyard surrounded by the walls of adobe homes all around. And in the center rose the tree.

A smile like his would have been an infestation if not for the product of descendants before him. In the midday, it was apparent that heatstroke would get them before a reply would.

"Are you not surprised?" Saint Alvarado asked instead.

Marcus' fortitude to be unbothered was impressive. "I don't even know what completely goes on most of the time."

Saint Alvarado sighed, letting his shoulder drop. Among the adobe walls were murals of people Marcus didn't recognize because he couldn't, all dressed in clothes that belonged either in family records or history books. He couldn't decide yet. There was something vaguely familiar to all of it.

In truth, Saint Alvarado was no saint after all. More rather, the purpose of such visions was not a purpose at all. Something was moving underneath.

"What's the meaning of a meeting like this?" Marcus finally asked, his eyes distracted by moving embroidery.

"Nothing really." There was an answer finally. "Before you is nothing more than your own subconscious at this point. Probably. You have no way of knowing for sure."

The heat bore down on the two of them even in the shade. "Something as bothersome as this is pointless?" Marcus complained, although asking alone remained a bother itself.

Leaves of green along twisting vines writhed through the green stripes as if alive. Saint Alvarado stood up and walked towards Marcus who took a few steps of his own backing out of the shade. Still in view of the murals surrounding them though. Sun soaked into each other's skin.

"Possibly," he replied. "But what's the matter with a little celebration.?"

"Congratulations from my own ego seems hardly worth it."

Heavy and calloused hands fell onto his shoulders. "Ah, but that's it right there. The proper connotations. Congratulations from an ego none other than yours. It's a feat itself."

Marcus started to suspect that the implications of this meeting were greater than a mere subconscious, but the intentions seemed proper enough so he went along with it.

Saint Alvarado took a step back. Embroidered vines had taken over his shirt, now blooming with pink flowers.

"Your growing. Revel in it." A quick motion of his hands and the world erupted with life from behind him. Flowers burst out from the ground. Confetti threw itself upward along with petals. Dogs chased each other and their own tails. Cats ran along roof tiles. Macaws, parrots, and avians of every color sang and dove throughout the sky. Laughter and shouts were heard above the clamor of guitars, horns, violins, drums, pianos, and more inside the buildings. Bells rang. Dishes clattered. Lizards scurried. Fish swam. The sun beamed down on them.

"Growth and Revelry. That's all there really is to it."

Christina peaked over Lauren's shoulder at the many charts and reports intermixed with brain scan images. "It looks like a butterfly."

"Thank you for being quiet," she jabbed passive aggressively. She really didn't have the time to waste when she was preoccupied with fearing all the possible results from a situation like this and worse, how it might reflect on her. Her minor panic was interrupted by the sound of sputtering and smoke.

At that moment the hospital room was alight with all colors. Marcus shot a color from his eyes and mouth that tore a whole through the imaging equipment and the floor above and the floor above and the floor above and the floor above and all the other ones until it reached the sky above.

Lauren saved the data.

"Punctual. Extravagant, but punctual," she noted.

Christina just gave a thumbs up. After all, Marus was still alive even under the smoldering wreckage. "Don't forget to make a note about the obvious phenomenon right now."

Lauren almost slapped herself from her own stupidity. Marcus opened his eyes to see the two girls standing over him with concern, but also mixed with a neutral apathy for these types of things by now.

"Everything all right bombshell?" Christina didn't quite ask.

"Technically it was more of a laser beam," Lauren corrected, even if Christina was not going to acknowledge that she was right.

Marcus' only answer came in the form of laughter as the raindrops began to land on his face.

CHAPTER 2: PARTINGS

Among raindrops that only came in the groupings of many and purposefully made sodden the mud in planters and slick the surfaces of sidewalk pavement, it was impossible to decipher from it the minuscule shards of glass. Both of which glittered with faint reflections and within each of these were illusions of the fake one again. As with many aspects of human nature, one would have to look upward to understand the happenings of that below.

The sound of rain rattled with thunderous volume against any and all blockades before it. Against the roof of the limousine was such a pleasant sound that she failed to remember how she had ever forgotten it. Pleasant enough that it made her desire for a moment to immerse herself to let the details sink into a mental image she could hold onto in years to come.

Rain among the San Anlos rooftops. It was an experience far worse than she had remembered before, driving up a wall in the limo. The disastrous ascent was far more exhaustively devastating than priorly, rife with pollutants of the auditory kind as the equipment did its best to not fail. Behind them, they produced explosions from a force of wind and pressure that shattered windows and propelled the shards in hundreds of directions from underneath the rubber tires and mishandled nature of Eve's chauffeuring. Left in their trail was only a track of torn open rooms with a closer grasp of the cold outside, to the astonishment of no one the skyscraper was left unfinished and gutted so soon after the building's construction. The other contributor to exhausting destruction was what waited before, maybe not directly though. Eve stood before her, holding open the car door and waiting, prepared with an umbrella to protect both of them from the rain this time.

Raindrops. Rainfall. Rainstorm. Rain weather. Rain. Rain. Rain. It could not go understated nor overstated just how encompassing the effect of rain had on the psyche of a San Anlos individual.

Isabella stepped out onto the gray rooftop in a matching world of wetness that, at the moment, knew no other state. A state so much so, that each step was a numerical temptation with the fate of disaster and falling. So much rain that the grip of Eve's hand buckled under the constant force exerted over his umbrella. So much water that painted murals washed off the walls of the most important buildings below. So many droplets that the homes and stores long established rotted away with mold and mildew. So much rain that only the steel and glass would be left.

"And the sky compliments it all," Eve noted, for the two of them.

"Disgustingly so," Isabella agreed.

A cast of gray capable of creating a washed out city by its presence alone. A blanket of clouds unanimously uniformed in tone and actions. An expanse of gray obscurities holding back the true presence of a false light already known.

Looking up Isabella made sure to stay underneath the shade of the umbrella and willed herself to see through the clouds to no avail. San Anlos was unsettling, deeply within the furthest reaches of her gut. She could only imagine, clearly at that, a sky swallowed up by a false white waiting for the utter destruction of a manufactured city. The gradient of white to gray had escaped her imagination and the earth wept for it. Deeply it unsettled her, making her fingers tense and her hair twitch ever so slightly. Because it was the emotion of anger, disgust, and probably even anticipation at the idea that her work had only just begun. So the world's end for one, defined by bleach, was already one she was ready to part ways with. Turning back to Eve, she smiled her signature sinister smile where the corner of her lips curled like a carnivore's and eyes fell upon a victim like daggers bashing up against the skin.

"Our letters of resignation are due."

He smiled back at her with his signature grimace only he was capable of. "An exchange of break up texts." From his free hand he held out her suitcase.

"A formally addressed farewell." Taking it, she delicately flipped the straps up to search for her object of desire.

"Our very own obituary entry," Eve chuckled.

"Whatever it is, it's words of parting."

All these feelings made her certain of one thing. That rain in San Anlos was exciting. As it struck against her skin, cool water colder than the air and hiding the only actual avenue of warmth she had present within her cheeks, she relinquished her safety with a step. All in an exchange to be in fingertips reach of the elements. She completed it with a step that could make canyons in the earth and send cracks through mountains. For now, it had to make do with the singular rooftop that gave way under the force of her sole. Isabella set one foot deeply into its concrete existence sending quakes through the skyscraper's foundations as she lurched forward hurling a standard screw toward the sky.

Air was cut.

Rain adjusted its course.

From the reflections along it, the two became faint silhouettes in an equally shrinking gaze of the metal object as it ascended to separate the clouds. The sky parted. At first, it was a single faint string of delicate white light that escaped the veil.

Followed by another.

And another.

And a single other.

And a single other.

And a single other. And a single other and a single other and a single other and a single other, until a heavenly arm of innocence extended from upwards to touch the once top floor, but now rooftop, of an empty corporate building. More importantly, it was a white purity of want made into light that touched the business clad people in all the same manner as the rain had. It wanted to at least, in actuality Isabella once again retreated into the shadowed umbrella interior as Eve looked around to make sure he was doing likewise.

Within the second that took a few moments of time for the single movement, she made walking back inwards there was an absolution. A conquered one. A cone of ascension. An adamant erasure. The evidence was in the missing tips in her strands of hair that shifted around her. The space itself had disappeared and just as she did before, fingertips towards the edges of light, she outstretched her arm. Millimeter by millimeter she moved until the inches of her fingertips were gone, leaving the level edge of raw exposed insides stinging in the cold. Eve tugged at her collar, dragging her towards himself and feeling the shame she should have for her own stupidity. Around them, they were trapped in a prison. An easily escapable prison, but a prison nonetheless. And all around them they allowed for the notion to be entertained because, and with their full complete honesty, the idea of Adamants acting as their name entailed for once was hilarious enough to ignore the impending crisis purposefully on track to crush them.

Limbs twisted and bent around them on all sides. Incandescent hands pressed against the furthest reaches of light like palms against frosted glass, and far too many of them. Pairs upon pairs. All trying to enter under the shade. Elbows interlocking and bending to avoid each other as they reached closer until it was a complete and total entanglement of limbs. Isabella squinted among the appendages to make out faces, ones with opened mouths that began to stretch. Elongated and contorted in a pain far more unnatural than the bends of flesh would allow. Eve placed a hand on her shoulder that she quickly held onto as a tremor was shared between the two. From it all came the chorus of whispers. Each a different speech of the same words, all coming together into a crescendo's collection of hums and hushed words. The sounds tiptoed across her skin, wandered aimlessly through her hair, avoided her eyes, left her legs light, and tickled on the backs of her teeth while finally arriving along the rings of her eardrums but never fully committing to being heard. Even the acutely sensitive ears of Eve strained to hear the words. And words they certainly were, full and stark in absurdity that was most unaccustomed from the speaker's mouth. Bella suspected such of course, if only she could pick out exactly which mouth before her were those.

"Struggle and violence. It's through consumption we are better."

The choir stopped, leaving a long almost agitating pause filled with only the chatter of rain on cement.

"Reflection and passion," they started again. With each word, their many arms snapped into a different position. "Great does not ignore complexity."

The same incomprehensible form of the mass of appendages stopped flailing but still drew closer. Close enough that Bella was tempted to lash out, if only in words alone.

"And what is impressive of passion and light reflected off a false moon?" It was lies upon lies, absurdities interweaving.

The arms clamored towards the two, each face drew close, the features indistinguishable. The movement began in the space between one another, a flurry now beyond the first wall of limbs pressing up against the light's limits.

"It's in that kind of existence that we will become more of again."

Handprints clamored against the glass-like barrier. "Do you understand..." The limbs were fast. "...what ascension is?"

Bella and Eve held their breath for themselves and each other. A dance began with the flails of limbs made of light along the entire false rooftop in a false city filled with false buildings and false bodies where there was false light under a false moon. The dance of the damned continued.

"Falsehood through truth."

Hands and faces squeezed.

"Life through death."

The climate was ready to erupt from the mess that enveloped the two. The rain never stops.

"That is what we offer. Only the most esteemed. Only the adamant. Ascended and all."

Infinite hands and faces squeezed the abstract enclosure around them. Eve's grip tightened around the umbrella, fingertips creaking. Meanwhile, Isabella remembered her first night back in San Anlos. Just like then she was in a shower of glass, but unlike then it never touched the ground. The shards of light only slowed down and stayed suspended in the air afraid to breach the shadows.

Violent tremors passed between the two partners. Animalistic heaves and breaths ravaged the insides of themselves no longer. Against empty buildings, bare walls, and unfinished floors the sound reverberated without care or abandon. Bella fell onto her knees gasping for air and Eve's chest ached from the pain. The laughter was too much. It breached past the definition and achieved hysterics. The comedy was too great for the two. Bella willed herself to look up, wiping tears from her eyes and conjuring enough air to let some words out. Already the hole in the sky was closing up and the visions surrounding them were dissipating. The only thing left was ghostly apparations of certain bodies, tethered but descending from the clouds. Still, she knew they could hear them.

"You wouldn't think it's funny, but for once your name is fitting," she stammered.

Eve leaned on her with a genuine smile. "What would an adamant person be if not absolutely desperate?"

Together in voices completely inhuman, they finished. "Adamant denial. It hurts to see us so alike after all."

CHAPTER 3: ABOVE WATER BREATHING

There was not a lot that Christina would have considered beyond her help. Marcus, however, very much straddled the boundary into such territory. Repeatedly. Lauren had promised to lead and navigate the trio through the mostly devoid, yet not totally flooded, San Anlos streets as fast as possible, but as every turn started to look a shade less familiar than the last she worried that a pneumonia ridden Marcus was both A) one Lauren found disturbingly funny and B) one she could not quite give up on.

Two umbrellas bobbed up and down under the constant onslaught as they searched for the nearest bus stop. The third member of such a trio continued to break pace ahead of them deep into the rainfall with purpose. Clothes drenched and arms outstretched with every movement. He ventured from flowerbeds, splashed into puddles, slid along flooded street sides, and generally was a juvenile nuisance. Most of all, and to Christina's worry but Lauren's delight if the supposedly covert smiles that could she caught every now and then meant anything, Marcus ran about with his tongue outstretched and mouth agape. Marcus freely welcomed any and all raindrops into the confines of his body.

The rain in San Anlos was no usual business. Unusual of the most usual means.

There was so much steel, concrete, and plastic in the area where it wasn't before. Even with a morning fog permanently in place and more than on schedule life had found a way to compensate far more than needed. New pollutants that lay on the skin gathered in the cracks and stuck to the walls. In one way or another they penetrated like a toxin, salting the soil of everything relevant. Although she couldn't really be bothered to worry about that exactly, instead it was only the reason for which she wanted nothing more than to throttle Marcus and brush his teeth until they were ground to dust. None of which would happen because she was far too focused on the all important task of keeping pace with Lauren.

Side by side.

She had purposefully switched the hand that held her umbrella so that it could bump into her friends with every few steps and send a rose cloud into her vision to obscure a gray washed out world. Somehow in an empty street, crowded only by raindrops and one idiot, they seemed to be colliding and nothing else remained in focus. Her focus was falsely fixated on a fact not totally there and entirely present between the two, so intently that she had to be pummeled to wake up from rose bathed dreams. She missed the obvious information, like how for a moment the weight of her umbrella was light, or that the latest step didn't squish with flooded sneaker soles like the last one. If not for Lauren catching up to her oblivious toddler ahead she would have probably been just like the boy, but then again Lauren was her blindspot so who really was to blame? Any excuse to distance herself from Marcus was absolutely necessary, even if together the three of them stood huddled underneath the decrepit bus stop covering.

"How oblivious you must all be."

Her voice entangled them like silk.

"Has your good sense washed away with all this weather?"

Her teeth flashed with bright whites, a stark contrast against the darkest corners she resided in. Encroaching purples hung in the corners and crept through the shadows like cobwebs in dusty basements. Christina turned around just in time to catch the realization with a sudden jolt of shock to accompany it. Marcus failed to respond entirely.

Every hair on Lauren's body tensed and her mind let out a frightened yelp. Once again her mouth was paralyzed and fought against the very words of such ideas. She stood there still and frozen as the web of Isabella's hair and den of strands tied around every corner, bend of the bench, and angle of the covering. Locks of hair circled around her waist and tightened around her throat, trapping her wholly and entirely.

Only because she had welcomed it so wholly.

Christina was already sitting next to their feared business associate. Either way, she was comfortable enough to lean on the shoulder that was Isabella's happily. Marcus sat down similarly while taking ample space for the moat that now accompanied him, only because he had no idea what else to do. Lauren stood there in total shock that she had completely missed such obvious theatrics of Bella. There was a lot that every one of the three had tossed up to nature in such unusual circumstances. For example, the bus stop was no ordinary bus stop, if only because the churchgoers made a point to wait a little extra and treat it with more care because of the prior reason.

Behind them was a small, almost unnoticeable small church. El Corazón Divino lacked basic expectations like a parking lot. Instead the rundown building was stripped of paint and missing roof tiles as it had decided to put its pride in the small lot sized park in front. The space was barely enough to fit a handful of people let alone the poppies, irises, dandelions, and roses that bloomed for all to see only during a few days of the year before mass. However, most notable were the statues.

Lauren made a point to refuse to sit after such startling interruptions, although she never actually explained so. Instead, she pondered aloud about Bella.

"What now makes you gift us with threats and stalking like your old normal business schedule?"

"Oh but it's anything but, if only because it's back to the unusual usual business in such weather."

Much like her web of hair protruding from the corner where she sat, her words had a way of entrapment in either ways Lauren did not understand or in pure nonsense alone. It didn't matter though, because Bella had a hunger in the pit of her stomach. One that rumbled each day and guaranteed to her that eventually the feast would taste far more divine each time. In a storm like this everything was easy to mistake for another so she wanted the answers plain and simple, although Lauren was far too ignorant to ask the right questions.

"You three seem relaxed for the world's end, don't you?"

Within the park there were several statues. The normal ones for such a location: Mary, Joseph, St. Francis Assisi, Arch Angel Rafael. Normal ones. Cut from ordinary stones. But important enough to be protected from poor weather. As a result, each and every one of them had heads bagged.

Marcus let out a groan that resonated spiritually with the rest of the group. Christina started with explaining the day's events and asking if there was anything that they needed to do in some kind of attempt of a preemptive excuse when there wasn't any kind of trouble yet. Lauren, on the other hand, experienced a slip of the tongue only for a second. Short, quick, and innocently honest but for the better nonetheless.

She complained.

"We have been dealing with mortal peril almost every day. Of course we would be a little tired."

The statues were important so the straps were tied tight.

Christina was stuck looking between Lauren's embarrassment and Bella's reaction, caught in a mixture of surprise and tension. Even the inattentive Marcus started paying attention.

Bella crossed her legs and leaned forward, head propped up with one hand, elbow placed on her knee, and pulling her web taught with tension. Lauren could feel something inhuman tremor throughout the mass for a second alone.

"And when do you think you will have the time to solve these problems that multiply into new ones?" It was a threat more than it was a question.

Once again Lauren failed at the assignment given. This time without an answer of any kind and only capable of remembering the bus schedule. Bella waited in the long silence only to decide to continue because when it rains it pours.

"Your mistake is because the rain is never what it seems. Rain in San Anlos these days without spring cleaning is invasion and burglary."

The bags were so tight around the throats.

"Were you just going to wait for the rain to stop?"

Bella seemed to temper herself for a bit, in part because of Christina who grabbed her shoulder with a stern grip and was ready to see red even if it was futile. They didn't know yet, but they really wanted the rain to stop.

"But the only way to stop it is to stop it yourself."

Tight enough there was no room to breathe.

"12:15 pm."

Their eyes turned towards one Marcus who sat silently still. Lauren, in fact, was the one who accidentally spurted the information. Bella either laughed or growled at the mess before her, depriving the insights of other's perspectives, but it was all the same.

"Unimportant," she determined. "Your ride is twenty minutes early."

Sure enough it was, as well as accompanied with handcuffs and chains. Ones that burst through a black door and enchained the three before flinging them inside without a moment's notice nor time to express shock. Bella closed the door behind them and was unfortunate enough to take a seat next to the sopping wet Marcus. Christina tumbled and partly huddled into Lauren's arms, but that wasn't the reason for such seating arrangements.

This time everyone's vision was a red one.

To one side of the limousine's cabin was a row of comfortable seats lining the cabin. On the other half were clips, strings, and sinks that could be secured shut. To their side were developing plates in place of cushions. The next question was more for anyone, but Christina, adept at interpreting nonsense, had a far more unfair advantage. So when Bella asked them all what was in said developing photos she barely needed time to examine the many angles of a crime scene.

"That's not a person is it?" she answered, far more confident in her words as a statement rather than a question.

Bella smiled. "Not human yet. At least not now. It is undetermined."

"What is it then?" Marcus asked clearly lost.

Once again Lauren failed. Once again Bella's white fangs stood out from the darkness. "What else?"

Home. Appliance. Homicide.

CHAPTER 4: INTERIOR INTENSIVE IMAGING

The scene within was both the interior and simultaneously exterior of a headache. The interior because if there ever was a physical manifestation of such a slight against human existence it would be in the neighborhood of what Christopher was experiencing around him. The exterior aspect was also true because all the stimulating sensory overload that encapsulated the bound and gagged Christopher in the center of the room did likewise within the mental headspace of his cranium.

Every flash of color was a sharp explosion of razor blades behind his eyes. The freezing heat of television screens left his skin reeling like melted wax. His guts were dusty with dry air and a drastic need for moisture. The continuous collision of pale skin with the folded tips of paper planes was reminiscent of rockslides to him and the hum of machinery that, up until that point he had successfully managed to tune out, now bludgeoned and hollered in the forefront of his throbbing brain.

Underneath the cover of a constant rate of rain, rain that splattered and ricocheted off the concrete sides of newly erected buildings, was a city emerging within San Anlos. A city with concrete blocks like these. With minuscule rooms for normal sized people. Cuboidal and rusty air conditioners dangled recklessly out of small rows of windows along the otherwise unimaginably flat walls of gray concrete. Someone reasonable might begin to wonder about the processes as to how a behemoth of construction could be set and finished so quickly, however, the sheer volume of such construction present deterred any rational line of thoughts like these. Instead, many things went unnoticed, or noticed, but as a fact with little care about debate. For example:

Christopher Abadie's headache, or the fact he was bound and gagged in a plastic chair, or the small maintenance door carved along the outside of the cement blocks like this sitting subtly and extending into the deep cramped halls with pipework protrusion like interwoven vines of industrial forests. All these were facts with far too much volume to do anything but accept them. Eve Luna trekked through the dense metal foliage to reach a smaller unmemorable door similarly labeled for maintenance.

Barrage.

Inside was only what could be described as a barrage.

Of sensation.

Of information.

Vision.

And sound.

Take for example: Eve blushed. And Eve blushed. And Eve blushed. And Eve blushed. And Eve blushed. And Eve blushed. And Eve blushed. And Eve blushed. And Eve blushed. And Eve blushed. And Eve blushed. And Eve blushed. And Eve blushed. And Eve blushed. And Eve blushed. And Eve blushed.

Over and over, among nearly infinitesimal screens if not for the fact that there was in fact a certain finite amount. It was an amount dictated by the surface space present on the four sides of the standard, if not larger than needed, maintenance room. The surface space was the same save for the metal door Eve, Isabella, and the unfortunate teenage trio entered through. Indeed they were completely devoured by the open maw of technology. Old TV screens crammed against themselves and fuzzy to look at images packed all available space making up the walls, floors, and ceilings. As below so was it above and to their left, right, front, and back as well.

"That's adorable," Isabella remarked, halfway caught in a mocking tone and her own accidental sincerity.

What it was really was annoying, mainly because Marcus, who was nervous and awkward among affection, hovered around the doorway which was now a blockade by his presence. The act of which elicited a shove from Christina and Lauren to send him on his way.

Tiana and Touma enjoyed the torment while it lasted and agreed to pout as Bella dragged them by their collars to sit them down in the neatly arranged foldable chairs a few steps away.

"Kittens on their ninth lives should know not to play so much," she scolded the two.

Christopher, a newly freed man surrounded with only more headaches, reevaluated his entire life with every massage of his joints and tense neck. That is until Eve pulled him close, heavy arms cradled around his boyfriend and burying the man's head into his chest. Christopher did not mind resting eternally in him.

"I'm sure it would have been a great presentation," Eve reassured, taking a glance at paper planes lying around. "But you might have to wing it for now."

Fireworks combusted among pixels. Blues streaks collided against purple, but as Lauren was far too focused on the present paperwork she did not notice the body language of Christina. Over the course of a few days the overachieving girl had acquired a certain set of skills from employment in corporate culture. Of those was to be well versed in the jargon of the inquisitorial elite language of business formal corporate speak nonsense. Among the bundles of loose pages and reprints along the illuminated display floor in front of her softly lit by a similar fireworks display were graphs, data points, tables, paragraphs, and notes crammed into the poorly functioning margins. All of which made the bags under her eyes deepen. Certainly, it was one of her many current worst fears now present.

Marcus, drenched now in his own sweat from the insulation, fanned himself in an attempt of serene self-centered ventilation for his chest. With a final breath full of Eve, Christopher shoved him likewise into the front row of chairs and preemptively blocked mockery from the back row of instigators at the public display of affection. Everyone had taken their seats.

Incredulous.

"San Anlos is an incredulous city. The people here are all incredibly stupid. On the topic of the geography and all participants present within the city limits, they are all inarguably screwed." Christopher wanted to laugh but every exhale of air was hot and bitter with a fanatic disapproval. "Do you not understand this is a world's end event? A final calamity. A perfect doomsday." There was no time to control himself. Every fiber of his small body was pissed. His skin was flushed and red hot to the touch, making his freckles harder to spot and his glasses fog. Even the dream couple had gone to great lengths not to cuddle in the back row in such temperatures.

Black leather gloves on hands clenching with rage stretched across the four planes of the room, magnified to a magnificent scale that Christopher could grasp everyone by squeezing the entire room in his grasp.

"So about the papers?" Eve redirected motioning down, unfazed by his boyfriend's theatrics.

Hard reset.

Science and reports came first.

"Perpetually suspended above us is a white orb of energy completely erasing any and all things that enter its vicinity. Approximately at 11:43 pm four nights ago the object had been

placed within the lower atmosphere above San Anlos."
Christopher turned his back away from the group letting Bella
catch his side glance at her. "My congratulations to our guest of
honor who didn't finish them off when she had the chance." All it
took was a single finger snap and a single row of television around
the room switched to photos of the sky at different points in time.
"Currently all air traffic within 100 miles has been grounded or
rerouted. Personal experience had already informed us well.
There aren't many seagulls, crows, or birds in general out and
about these days, but let's hope it's in part because of the rain too."
Different but similar footage repeated over and over on the
screen. As confident as Christopher was it was unsettling, to say
the least, to see one flock of panic after another erased from
existence from mere vicinity.

"And what do you expect to succeed with your weird
voyeur hobby?" Isabella asked.

He forced out the most contemptuous smile while the
corner of his glasses lens cracked.

"First of all, it's called surveillance. Secondly, true to the
Luna name that deals in intimate details for replication, the faux
moon behaves almost like the genuine creation. The only
difference of course is its weaponry."

Just as all his prior properly prepared paperwork would
have presented poignantly and with accuracy, there was a present
cycle that the creation revolved around.

"It certainly seems that the faux moon is more of a
fantastical structure of some sort as there is a rhythm of energy
coming from it. The output is greatest during the day when it is at
a full moon and the power is consolidated during the night when
it reverts to a new moon."

"But that's not what you are worried about is it?" Bella instigated, stretching her legs in her seat. Lauren's face dropped to a pale cold bottom, only noticed because all cameras focused on her for a second and her alone. But only for a second. Christina poked the face that she liked so much and leaned over bringing with her waves of amiable and affable affection that this time Lauren actually noticed. Christopher hesitated, caught off guard. All eyes and screens once again focused on him.

"Correct," he affirmed nervously. "I was just about to get to the other part."

Tiana and Touma were fanning each other. Christina and Lauren were both worried about sweat forming at their brow and made sure to not worry too much or else they might end up like the wet sticky precipitation mess that was Marcus. Said Marcus was now drenched in both precipitations from the outside and himself as well.

"It's getting hotter isn't it?"

Bella let the phrase slip through curling lips. The last thing anyone saw was the glint of the light from her gray eyes and white teeth, and then.

Darkness.

Black.

Indescernerable darkness.

Every TV expended its use at the same time with a voltage filled flourish leaving the group in a void devoid of any sensations except for the most immediate devastation of abusive heat. All that could be made out was her pale face and hands. Hands full of applause.

"Yes. Yes. Congratulations on your report."

Indeed he was right about much. Truly it was growing bigger and increasing its radius of destruction each cycle just as his papers described. That much was fairly obvious for someone's observation.

"Luckily you don't need to worry about familial affairs you are not beholden to."

Christopher refused to respond to that, leaving Bella to sigh and resort to plan B which was initially Plan A but Eve whined about it in the car. One movement was all it took to sweep Christopher off his feet and into Eve's lap even in the darkened space.

"It's not a problem really. It's an invitation only."

In front of them, where a wall had once clearly been, was a single still functioning TV showing fuzzy but legible video footage of a rooftop with business suits under umbrella shade. More importantly, it showed an astronaut of light, tethered and connecting back to the moon. An adamant invitation to finish things. Christopher almost tore the inside of his cheek with his clamped teeth.

"How is this supposed to calm me? There is still the looming problem."

"It's supposed to tell you that it's handled."

"The only thing you have handled so far has led us to this exact issue."

"An issue that is about to be resolved, unlike your own."

"What is that supposed to mean?" This time it was Christina who asked totally within the shadows too.

"San Anlos has always had regular armageddons in one way or another. As above so below," Eve responded. Christopher shifted in his lap, uncomfortable with the direction the conversation was turning.

Eve and Bella captured the chance.

"The problem with home appliance homicide was never the homicide" Bella pointed out.

"Know your audience," Tiana called out.

"You guys have company birth certificates, you're practically people," Isabella shot back.

"Very glad the authority on this topic is the other non-human in the room," Lauren spat, entering the fray with crossed arms and staring daggers if she couldn't speak them.

"What do you think you mean by that girl?" Isabella asked.

"I think it is more of a discussion on defining human nature," Touma suggested.

"Yeah, or maybe a slight jab testing the waters for friendly argumentative humor."

"I don't think any of that is right, but please just excuse Lauren, she has been high wrung all day."

"It's because employee of the month here and his overachieving sidekick can't say no, even if it meant jumping off a cliff."

"That's rich coming from the one with a literal handler."

"Pick your own fights love."

"Listen to your boyfriend."

"Don't leverage me like that."

"Excuse me."

Silence took over the room as all eyes looked at where the sound came from. Emergency lights burst into the room and onto Marcus who was sitting with his hands raised.

"I'm a little behind and can't follow along with everyone, but what exactly should I be doing to help?"

Silence.

The heat that bubbled in Bella and Christopher immediately extinguished with the sound of the boy drenched in rain. Isabella walked over and took a seat next to Christopher reluctantly.

"The plan is a little bit of a mess right now. I guess it's up to you in the end."

"Oh. Okay."

CHAPTER 5 : HOMEBREW

"I don't like this."

Lauren truly did not, in fact, like it. However, Christina and Marcus were too overjoyed at the prospect of further annoying her to stop. That, and they were already well past the point for remaking plans. Christina was smiling from her kitchen, standing partway in front of Marcus on the off chance that an enraged or possibly envious Lauren lunged at their designated idiot. However, Lauren knew full and well two things. One Marcus would be too slow to realize what was happening if she decided to attack and she could probably get a knockout punch in or at least strangle him. Two, that right now she stood at Christina's front door, only a few inches out of the rain and between terror, annoyance, and a hateful apprehension at being the closest she had ever been at a step away from the kitchen. Especially being with the dumb human sponge and savant material, the experience would be too much to handle.

And lastly, she had almost forgotten, point three being that they were all friends.

"Isn't her house in the other direction?" Marcus asked, crouching through the doorway and blocking the already dimly faint yellow kitchen light. Already at the edge of where the sidewalk and the city met Lauren was reduced to a diminishing black umbrella.

"You know where she lives?" Christina replied in surprise.

"I mean, she knows where I do. I felt like I should return the favor," Marcus stammered, embarrassed from either the conscious effort he applied or for even bothering with the task at all. He couldn't decide which was more appropriate. "I mean she told me, but I just recently actually kind of realized it I guess."

Adorable Christina thought. He's like a lost puppy. Marcus definitely walked a fine line between total creep and clueless friend, but she was willing to give him the benefit of the doubt.

With a smile, she faced her friendly idiot and shoved him all the way into the kitchen. And with a disconcertingly frown, she gave one last look at the space that had been Lauren. Really, in some fantasy she would have liked Lauren to stay over as well, even if for just a little bit. After all, in weather like this it's harder to keep going forward. It's far too muddy to find the next right step.

Beige. Brown. Tan. Unsaturated types of oranges.

In short, or maybe in a further detailed elaboration, Christina's living room wasn't something intensely interesting to the average eye to feast on. Marcus somehow had no problem being impressed. The whole area was less of a room to look at but a home to be in. Every corner was evidence of life. Coaster stands, coffee stains, and crumbles on the floor. Everything from cushions, pillows, sofa covers, and an outdated TV with a thick layer of dust on the backside peeking out ,save for the handprints from a time someone had carelessly touched it, was intimate. Nothing could be more alive nor could it be more perfect for the human. Every detail, otherwise ignored by the Xiaodan family, he wanted to integrate into his being. The finite everything to the end of the time down to the faint hum of a heater that was rarely used and the bowl of squishy fruit left on the coffee table.

"Grandma must have left it out to apologize for going to bed so early." For the better, Christina shrugged. She didn't see Xiaodan as someone with the patience for Marcus' nonsensical idiotic insolence.

While Christina worried about last night's leftovers Marcus was occupied with the horror that he wasn't comfortable enough.

That wasn't exactly it. He couldn't quite understand it, only that he was so uncomfortable in the very homely room. Windows to his left and right let in the soft rattle of the cold rain's onslaught like a blanket of noise. Like old clothes in the closet, or your favorite blanket you let get covered in dust. There was nothing to be fearful of.

Then why was he not able to understand the feeling rising from his gut in his throat? It was not a lingering taste that he could passively come to understand. There was no flavor that presented itself pathetically upon the altar of his taste buds, but still, he felt a sensation in his bones. In his flesh. It was intertwined within his teeth. It droned just underneath the skin on the side of his face. It couldn't be covered up and buried no matter how many crocheted blankets he buried himself in. Perhaps his body was taking its revenge after years of improper handling and care. Refrigerated spaghetti exploded with little pops in the microwave and an intangible yellow burst flickered before Christina's eyes. Like lemons in summer to wake the energy in you during the heat. Yellow, like a warm patch of sunlight through an open window. Yellow, like a lightbulb making a room seem a little less empty. Colors warm and fuzzy that make up a home. The spaghetti finally all but combusted, painting the inside of the microwave a murder scene of marinara if she wanted to bother to clean. However, her focus was on the cocoon in the room before her not behind.

In the lesser than average square footage of her house it already felt like two strangers drifting apart in shifting sands. Something was odd about it and what bothered her more was that she couldn't pick out the exact reason why. His lump of a figure had more aggressive weight than just the absurd amounts of blankets on him. A small hand tunneled into the dark murky depths of the bundle and dragged Marcus by the face pulling him upwards.

"It's only 7pm. Please tell me you don't have the same circadian rhythm as my grandma."

"I don't know what one of those words means."

It hurt. It definitely hurt a little to hear him talk, but Christina wasn't quite ready nor truly comfortable letting him sleep in her father's room just yet and instead lied to herself about remediation through procrastination.

"So what do you like to do in your free time?" It was a demand more than a question. Her only answers were the splatter of rainfall on all four sides of the room.

The two of them, suspended in the finite space of that brown box, secure from the storm outside.

And Marcus was still lost.

The same kind of lost as a kid suddenly aware of the size and scale of life. Like a wallflower in high school filled with more terror and apprehension for socializing than death.

"I don't know?" Marcus stared at his hands sitting loosely on the blankets.

"What do you feel like doing?"

Beige. Blank. Basic. Boring. A brown that had been for every day of his life a neutral color without any contrast.

If Christina was quick to anger she might have grimaced and furrowed her brow the way she liked to see when getting a rise out of Lauren, but curiosity had a way of making patience and, foremost, it wasn't like she was facing an adversary. Something bad, but not quite the worst. After all-

"No one likes having homework dumped on them."

Marcus stared, confused. School had just started and he was never one to do his own homework on time, let alone ask for help. Christina shook her head, realizing her mistake. He flinched as she collapsed into the cushion next to him, already a little tired.

"No one is going to go the extra mile to figure out your personality for you. You know that right? It's kind of the price someone had to pay to be interesting."

Marcus' mouth twitched behind blankets he had pulled up, but she caught it before it could be hidden. A grimace. Adorable only because it didn't belong on him.

And there was the delightful hint of green, like treasures in the fruit bowl.

Of course there were things he liked, or rather, things that he would have liked to like. There were countless missed opportunities to have a full life up until now, but his life was measured in wasted minutes, hours, days, months, years, etc. for a reason.

The taste of green was a bitter one, like the apples he had no affinity towards.

He turned around to look at the home setting like this, to see the side doors unopened, the windows closed, the house almost empty, and then he could only hear the rainfall.

"It shouldn't take an unavoidable act of nature to find enjoyment though." Christina lectured while pacing between the TV and the bookcase, passing a shelf filled with board games and drawing utensils during her route. The options were plentiful and time was ready to waste.

Of course he would have given anything to enjoy each and every one of the moments offered a thousand times over. No one dreamt more of being seven and staying up late in front of a TV screen, completely captivated by the world presented before like he did. He would have loved to know what it was like to be lost in the creations of another on a regular basis, or to lose grip of himself and be flung into the expanses, forgetting the taste of coffee from Christina. The idea of playing games with his friends on weekdays and weekends was one he would have sacrificed himself for. His aspiration and excitement only rose along with the tower of wooden blocks and eventually above as he continually made it fall. He could have fallen in love with betting on himself to enjoy tomorrow even as Christina called every one of his bluffs over cards. Boards and game pieces built a kingdom of construction as if his very own creation was expanding the space of the small brown box he had found himself in.

It was through lines of words not phrased, half unfinished like his own, and paragraphs completed that he was enveloped in a thicket of paper. Paper castles, mountains, oceans, empires, lakes, forests, heroes, villains, and more crashed onto him and brought with it the weight of waves. Every emotion was painted through the typeface of black ink and, although Christina's voice and his own found each other, every few moments he could barely hear her. Stories closed and pressed him between their pages, his body crushed in splendor, and his mouth began to salivate. He could taste his world and see it in colors. Christina could see it in colors too.

He was kind of like a toddler only just finding enrichment, quickly locating an object and moving on after only a moment's play, but he seemed enraptured by the process. More than anything, he was being very open. Very Marcus. If she had a San Anlos for a hero then Marcus had found a San Anlos of his own. One without orange beaches and old gods to be slain. It was one with green hills instead of dry barren ones. It was filled with celebration and revelry.

Pale empty schools. A multitude of bugs. Lime babies. Strawberry dogs. Red insides. A fantasy of his own. A dream in service of himself and not the other way around. Translated between scribbled notes and excited ramblings between friends. A San Anlos with a brown box that was warm between his hands and felt like home.

Christina hesitated on pouring a fresh pot of coffee out for him, but she really had never seen the idiot so lively. Her living room looked like someone had invited the storm inside. It seemed to subside for now as she directed the oversized toddler to more constructive tools like the art box that she had not touched for several years. A muffled gasp escaped Marcus as he lifted up the paper to see the marker bleeding through directly onto the coffee table. He could have his coffee black. If he was going to stay up late she might as well make sure it would be late enough to help clean.

CHAPTER 6: DIAL-UP REMEDIATION

"Disgusting. Revolting." Really it was absolutely atrocious in Lauren's professional opinion. Really, it was not a problem in reality. However, being left with the knowledge that those two were going to be staying the night together without her to keep an eye on them had to place in her top echelon of worst fears. Only second or third she thought. It paled in comparison when held up to the infamous number one threat to peace of mind.

If she was going to have any luck today it could come in the form of an out of control car hood or sudden mudslides or a very pathetic way to drown in puddles. And if she was going to be unlucky then she would be able to make it to her appointment on time, if not a little early. The latter of which no one would have liked. It was nearly 6pm, even as she avoided all buses and walked the length of her trek to stall in comfortably uncomfortable dread. Her tired eyes were the only indicators of the time under perpetual grays. That and the clock on her smartphone. Even as she kept her eyes in a constant 360 degree swivel under the dome of her umbrella it became apparent with each puddle soaked step that the glass front doors of the Tandem Tantrum Toys and Co. headquarters would reach her before the most available danger could.

"Disgusting."

Security cameras recorded her say the words in a scowl at the front from all angles possible. Disgusting wasn't the actual word she wanted, but she had given up on finding those a long time ago. The handle was wet to the touch and wouldn't let her hand dry even after she wiped it profusely. Wet, sticky, and unequivocally necessary in her clear sight.

"Revolting."

She entered.

Her first sight led her to an arcade massacre. Digital bodies piled up and spare change was lost. Every source of light in the dimly lit arcade shined the same message for players that were no longer there.

GAME OVER. YOU'RE DEAD. TRY AGAIN. YOU LOSE. LOSER. DEFEAT. X.

The room drowned in perpetual boos to the loser and was nearly impossible to stand in for any amount of time between the harsh flashing screen and the varied, but equally obnoxious, message each machine decided to employ. If she could have broken out into a run Lauren probably would have, but she didn't like what such an action would say about her nor would corporate rules would have permitted it. She didn't know for sure actually, but suspected such and that was fear enough, even if it was the fear that she wouldn't be a proper fit for her role. So instead she compromised for no compromise at all and shielded her eyes with her hand as she bumped her knees against useless game consoles trying to find the elevator that was stuck in the back.

Down a long hall.

"A hall?"

A hall. One that hadn't been there before. Deep enough it must have gone into the neighboring building meaning that the company must have bought it out. There was no sense in making sense of out of corporate capital nonsense, so she didn't. She hadn't for a while. So there was a hall that she walked down, basic and plain with a carpet that was patterned gray and surrounded by office's glass walls on either side. Tinted of course, nearly black so she couldn't look in but they could look out. If she stopped to look past her reflection into the rooms figures could barely be made out. Figures all the same height and build, familiar enough that it could have made her break out into a run. However, that would only ever be an 'if'. The only thing Lauren decided to do was continue down without a second glance. She had been getting good at that skill, she could put it on her resume.

She wondered if it would be impressive on job applications. It didn't matter, she could find a way to brag about it one way or another. It's not like she ever really had a choice. Go to school. Get good grades. Take AP. Do extracurriculars. Get a scholarship. Get accepted to a good college. Be poor. Get into community college. Get a job. Save money. Transfer schools. Find an internship. Get applicable work experience. Build up a resume. Get a career. Work the career. Work. Work. Work. Retire. Enjoy life. Somewhere along the very empty way life had amounted to a struggle to survive, but maybe that's what it always truly meant.

She was convinced that she really knew the proper words after all.

That was the plan after all. One sure to make present bosses, relatives, administrators, and peers happy. If she did it right, when she dropped dead in her old age she would smile knowing her life was a comfortably average one and that the single statistic she made was perfectly along the trend line if not a little above proving a point to someone somewhere about girls, daughters, kids, students, and people like her.

When did it get so loud? Why was the hallway closing in all around her? She was running out of answers and evidence as she started to break a sweat from body aches, panic, or a combination of the two.

There was a sound. A dial-up screech. Thousands of them, crying simultaneously. Digital disillusionment in the office around her and only getting louder.

Louder.

Harsher.

Sharper.

Grating.

Agonizingly.

Suffocatingly.

Seeping into her gut like poison. Cutting into her ears like knives. Tightening around her being like strangulation. She wanted to ask for help but she shouldn't, she reminded herself. So in the end, she didn't actually want to. What she wanted was to finish her remediation, or something like that. Silent measures were replaced with the tortured scream of confirmation. Moments of rest were replaced with periods of anxiety. There was nowhere to take a seat. That was one thing she noticed ever since she started working. There were fewer places to take a seat. Her left foot had developed a blister from standing all day long these past weeks, but she had been smart to balance on her right and avoid excessive pressure.

In the end, everything was working out. She had a habit of working things out. Things ended up being fine. It's when things didn't work out that she was upset. Like today. She was upset, she finally decided. It was already evident from her shaky and languished breaths as the small cold box of an elevator seemed smaller each second. She didn't like it when she messed up like this. The worst part was knowing exactly why. Marus had it lucky being an idiot. He didn't have to sit in his mistakes like stew and let it boil him alive. She was not offered such luxury.

She stood there and boiled in that small elevator box of screams and collapsed into a totally worthless pile of sweat, panic, frustration, resentment, headaches, rising vomit, spasming muscles, and heartache. She racked her brain for a reason why, as if she would find it somewhere there on the cold metal floor. If only she could actually find a question worth answering, then she might have found her 'why'. In the end, she couldn't even find it in her to scream a good final scream. She couldn't even find a reason why to.

So she laid there. And she laid there. There were so many levels to this and for her. She was crumpled for all of them. Until finally the noise stopped far more instantaneously than it had started, on time for the elevator's ding of doors opening.

Doors opened to a composed Lauren standing attentively and properly, with proper uniform and a well placed smile. She was late. There was never a chance for her to be on time.

Before her sat a board room in a single shade of black. Outside gray clouds turned dark as night set in leaving only the sound of rain to clue one into the actual state of the world. The only light that came in was from closing elevator doors and the noxious purple tints of board members' glass screens shining in the darkness, barely illuminating the room.

Lauren waited at the edges of the long black wooden table refraining from sitting until she was given permission.

"SIT DOWN," one of them ordered in a voice indistinguishable from any others. A soundboard perfectly calibrated. "YOUR REMEDIATION WILL BEGIN."

Player two had joined the game.

She already knew that they already knew that she already knew why she was here. Across every screen were the same images that just about everyone close to her had seen. Chalk outlines on cement being washed away.

"DO YOU RECOGNIZE THESE PHOTOS?" A voice asked her over speaker. She couldn't quite pick out which one.

"No." She smiled pitifully and regretted being born.

Across each and every screen was the same word in red.

LIAR.

"DO WE HAVE TO REMIND THAT YOU LACK PROPER AUTHORIZATION-" one board member started to say but was cut by a proper and actual identical approximation to human speech.

"Actually, for today's meeting, it may be necessary for temporary access to high class privileges."

The machines hummed amongst themselves in conversation unwelcome for human ears. Lauren realized just how cold it was in the room, pinching at her skin and trying to carve into her bone. The humming stopped. The rain continued. The girl forgot about the cold for a moment. The chair opposite to her at the other end of the table was suddenly thrust into the spotlight with Lauren sitting in it. Not Lauren exactly. One made out of metal and plastic with artificial hair and skin.

Only an approximation.

But recently Lauren had been forgetting basic definitions like her very own, so she excused herself when the opposite her opened her mouth to speak with her voice and she lost herself for a moment. The Lauren that was not Lauren sat up straight, cross legged, hand on her lap, with a perfect smile. She opened her mouth that was not Lauren's and spoke with her voice that was no longer hers, or at least not hers alone. It was Lauren's voice. The concept. The product.

"The company is willing to see past your product destruction and corporate vandalism from these past days, seeing as your recent contributions have proven to be invaluable."

Another light. This Lauren sat in the seat to her right dressed as a maid and slid over images not seen before. Images of a Lauren of flesh and a Lauren of metal at a cafe patio. One with a bat and another in pieces.

"There is no point in denying. Please just confirm that we spoke with you and we won't hold you accountable for the cost and damages."

Cost and damages, she thought. How much would it take before she lost track of how her life would go? How easy could it be for her to drop from an above average statistic to the kind she feared for? Another stack of papers slid her way from a Lauren dressed in a suit on her left. The actual Lauren that was no longer the only Lauren struggled for words caught in the back of her throat. Words bound and trapped, all since long past their funeral date and buried. If she was going to scream it was going to be now. But she couldn't find one in her so she picked up her pen with one struggling steady hand and fumbled through her signature.

"And what exactly is my greatest contribution?"

SHUT UP. SHUT UP. SHUT UP. SHUT UP. SHUT UP. SHUT UP.

For once the board members and Lauren were on the same page.

"Haven't you heard?" Lauren asked.

Rainfall and silence.

"With the cancellation of work on the Dream Babe line that was stuck in testing we are opening a new and more viable product."

Six board members sat at the table along with eighteen Laurens. Lauren. Lauren. Lauren. Lauren. Lauren. Lauren. Lauren. Lauren. Lauren. Lauren. Lauren. Lauren. Lauren. Lauren. Lauren. Lauren. Lauren.

CHAPTER 7: INVITATIONS AND INVASIONS

"That's definitely not normal," Christina whispered under her breath as she looked out the small window in the corner of the washing room tucked behind the living room. "That's most definitely not normal for this hour of night." She checked the time on her phone again. 9pm. It was late and raining at that, so why would anyone have a good reason to go outside and wait? That of course was ignoring the better question. Why were they waiting outside there and looking in?

"THE OVERACHIEVER," one of the board members answered. Lauren could never really tell which one and stopped trying anyways. "TEST MARKETS HAVE ALREADY SHOWN OUTSTANDING REVIEWS. WE ARE PROJECTED TO MAKE A 33% PROFIT INCREASE THIS NEXT QUARTER WITH THIS NEW ROLLOUT ALONE." Lauren didn't even bother to clench her teeth or bite her tongue or battle down deep rooted disgust. Any previous heat inside her had been extinguished in the unusual weather. She was disarmed and relieved of care. She should have been happy. She had a habit of caring too much. It made her smitten and bitter easily, not good for sales. "I'm so flattered that I will prove to be essential to the corporation."

"Have we waited long enough?" Eve asked, reclining his seat back, hand behind his head and aware of all the horrible possibilities before him, but pausing the thoughts for a moment. Bella stood outside with an umbrella in one hand and the other leaning on the open window. "I think we have been waiting long enough for a moment like this," she answered smugly. A response to which Eve only glared with the silence of rainfall to accompany them on the damaged skyscraper rooftop that they had already visited once before. "A moment more please."

Christina returned from the washroom with a fresh roll of paper towels to clean a now crashing Marcus mess. She already knew to expect a mess from the boy, but to her horror he not only managed to ravage through the fruit bowl but expand the sweet sticky juices to every surface including himself. "Don't look out the windows," Christina told him, encouraging him to do the exact opposite. To Marcus' horror, he did exactly that and found a line of men along the sidewalk. All the same height and build.

HAHAHA. XD. IDIOT. STUPID. SRSLY. LOL. Lauren addressed Lauren in the most annoying fashion possible, barely moving from her pose and without hesitation. "Did you really think that you were the only new product we are rolling out?" No. "Toys come in tandem." Stop. "All that is left is for the tantrum."

Slowly and with the grace of ghosts the spectral corpse of an astronaut descended down to the earth. The clouds parted for a view of a faux black void of night in the presence of a new moon. The pale deceased being was only a skeleton inside a suit, all nearly translucent and made of pure unadulterated white light that was now dimmed. Slowly and delicately, almost fragile but not so, its feet stopped at the open top floor never touching. Its arm reached out. Its fingers outstretched like an old god to man. Its tether clipped to its back extended all the way home. And on the skull inside the helmet was engraved. 'Here Lies Isabella.'

It wasn't a line of men but a box of them, with the small townhome in the middle. They stood on the sidewalk out in front, on rooftops to their side, and on asphalt in the back. All looking. All waiting. And it wasn't a box of men, but a box of boys. And it wasn't just a box of boys, but a box of Marcus. Marcus in different sweaters. Blue. Green. Black. Red. Yellow. Orange. Brown. Tan.

Purple. Marcus with brown hair. Yellow hair. Orange hair. White hair. Green hair. Purple hair. Etc.

"Outlook is actually questionable for the himbo model," Lauren shrugged. "We assume it can be used for physical labor and other expendable feats, seeing as its specialization is rather little. As for the other one..."

Bella let her fingers dance across those inviting her, waving them around and between but never touching the immaterial hand outstretched. Tempting, she thought. But she was in her rebellious phase after all. And if she was going to be fashionably late then she may as well make sure that she made an entrance. Chains shot out of the open windows of the limousine and she wrapped them tightly around her wrist.

The Marcus outside knocked on the front door and waited for the Marcus on the inside to hesitantly open up. Christina and her friend were completely in shock and apprehension, but those were both emotions they were getting adept at. Wet soggy papers from the imbecile in a brown sweater that refused umbrellas were all they were offered for a greeting. "Tandem Tantrum Toys and Co. is seeking rights to use your likeness." "And what if we aren't seeking to share?" Purple like a toxin in the bloodstream. Deep, dark, rich, and consuming. A royal color of white shined like floodlights from where the eyes had once been of the boys on the sidewalk casting the Marcus before them in a silhouette. "We have ways of taking things."

"What if they don't agree to this?" Lauren asked. The actual Lauren asked. The Lauren that was important, or at least the one she would have liked to consider important. In reality, she couldn't muster enough to say 'I' instead of 'they'.

Her reflection was stretched and distorted in numerous ways, but such was the effect on those in her grasp. Bella was not immune either. Nor was the back bumper of the limousine as it warped and crushed between her fingers.

The distinct cock of guns and jingle of bullets readied to fire was the only answer for Christina who had begun to feel hot and stuffy. Marcus said something, but she couldn't hear it over a sound within her ears.

"Who in their right mind wouldn't agree to such an opportunity to represent the Tandem Tantrum Toys and Co. brand?" Lauren asked Lauren. That wasn't the right question though. Neither of them knew it. Who would be stupid enough to say no? That was the correct one.

Bella could feel her body ache and her muscles burn. Her hands and feet throbbed from the pressure as she forced the entirety of herself into the motion.

Marcus called out to Christina, afraid that coffee, spaghetti, fruit, and popcorn along with all the other junk was a bad combination for his stomach.

Silent, Lauren noticed the papers slipped in front of her.

Bella laughed uproariously with the tectonic force while hurling a projectile from the rooftop a second time. Balancing the weight on her one foot she spun around and tossed the whole limo like how a track athlete would a shot put. She released the vehicle like a glorious comet defiant to gravity. And where there was no glass of skyscrapers to shatter there were skeletal steel beams to tumble into the streets. And when there were no more chains around her wrist to give there was a ride to be had.

There was rain in San Anlos. There was so so so much rain in San Anlos. Far too much for the end of summer. Far too much for the start of fall. It fell on black metal and tinted windows en route to leave the atmosphere. It collided against the outstretched arms of 100 unusual robots with machine guns installed and ready, barrels coming out their palms. It fell against glass windows that protected forgetful girls from forgotten problems. The rain didn't stop when robots started the processes to fire on all fronts or when Christina's head buzzed to life instinctively, short circuiting computers as she released the contents of her sudden digital migraines in a three block radius. Raindrops continued to fall as Marcus emptied the contents of his poor diet in a red stream of birds that never touched the peeling kitchen floor, but instead curved to target the imbeciles, one after another. Raindrops poured out onto the fireworks of combustion until there was none left. It was rain that filled the silence while possibly the most Lauren Lauren was possibly at a loss for words. Good thing she only needed two letters and the date. 'L'. Her hand stalled and shook with the pen locked in. "M." the closest overachiever bent over and put her finger on the line she was looking at. "Here and here for your consent to use your likeness and another to confirm that we talked to you about your behaviors." 'Lauren M.'

The rain was needed to see things clearly. The people of San Anlos were just never prepared.

Rain fell around three holes in the perpetual clouds to usher in three astronauts on a faux endeavor. The skeletal explorers waited in their slow descent like false angels. Their hands, outstretched. Their bodies, tethered above. Before an aging kitchen, 'Here Lies Christina.' In the remains of something not quite a home, 'Here Lies Marcus.' On the other side of the glass within the rain, so that with every droplet that collided she could see the details more clearly. Lauren hesitated at the table. Her body froze in place. All of it was in arms reach just beyond the thin glass. Thin enough that each raindrop rattled it. Thin enough that a fist or chair could do much more. Words so clear. Actions so defined. A future so close. 'Here Lies Lauren.'

XXXXXX

"LAUREN YOU HAVE BEEN EXCUSED."

CHAPTER 8: MOON LANDING

Pale. White. Colorless. Sterile. Bright. Clean. Imperceptible, at least nearly so.

Eve remembered how much he hated the inside of these places and once again blinked away temporary aches and tears as his eyes adjusted to the always unnatural well lit interior of the moon. By the time he could see clearly he could see a sight that made him smile, because the mere fact of a crumpled limousine hood burrowing into the otherwise perfect floor of the room was nearly catharsis enough. Nearly, but not so. The back end stuck into the space above them protruding, from the ground the way things tended to do after crashing in the way they did.

He clambered out and unfurled his lengthy body to search for any gaping hole he created only to be instantly disappointed as it closed upon entry, a fact he noted and notably frowned at. All there was presently was a half destroyed car burrowed into the ground, a thing of black smoke coming from where the hood should be, and from that came two black suits.

Black amid countless rolling hills of bleached grass far too itchy and stiff to be considered anything natural. The blades of it crunched too loudly underfoot. They didn't catch the rays of warmth from the fluorescent lights somewhere above and out of sight. The ceiling here rose to a height too far out for their eyes to discern. He didn't bother taking in the scene here. He already knew it well, or at least knew what this approximation was approximating well enough. He never bothered to, but his classmates had spent many recesses out here, in fact, one particular girl made it a routine to skip class to visit. The colorless memory dusted itself off. He knew what came after such action and his grip on the suitcase tightened.

Isabella was already hills ahead of her compatriot, displaying no damage or bother with crashing into another solid object without protection. Her eyes were wide awake and alight. She knew her surroundings well. It was a nightmare veiling minor subconscious closets of trauma. It was just outside her dreams, at the very ends of her life's goals. It was not a place for good girls to enjoy. It was a place for delinquents to cry. Her silent eyes took in their entire distorted world without moving. Her long hair hung limp. Her hands were outstretched, trying to reach something not totally there. Her breath barely filled her body and resonated with a violent emergency held at bay.

She giggled.

Somewhere a little girl screamed in terror.

Bella and Eve whipped their heads around to see a pale colorless child running in a panic, tears streaking down her face. Along her arms was charred flesh and her feet nearly tripped over each other with each stride. Bella recognized the girl well enough, or at least the approximation they were approximating. All it took was a look of her eyes and Eve flung her suitcase over so that the two were ready in a matter of seconds.

The terrified girl stopped in a loose and clumsy halt. Her face contorted in shock and terror.

"Here is a place to die."

Young Isabella smiled.

Bella hissed.

A crowd of hands erupted from the ground and grabbed at the child pulling her under. The moon itself writhed with limbs.

The surface of the faux new moon gave away like a solid mass of clouds, escaping every attempt to touch it that Marcus made. The deceased astronauts had been the journey's ferryman to the astral object up until that point. As the background of a San

Anlos night gave way to the inside of the spacial rock the spectral beings dissipated, sending both Christina and Marcus into a free fall to their surprisingly silent dismay. The space of the lunar cavity they had entered was far larger within than either of the two could have imagined. And it was bright with a pure unadulterated kind of bright that made it hard to look at where they were falling. Nevertheless, the duo somersaulting in the air made sure to see the ground come crashing towards them.

The pale ground.

The white ground.

The San Anlos ground. Or at least an approximation to a sizable chunk of San Anlos. Once completely scrubbed of color and lifelessly still.

Christina let out a gasp, which was a mistake as the air was ripped from her lungs. Marcus back bent against the edge of a stone rooftop before his face smashed into the sidewalk while Christina directed herself towards the empty street lanes expecting the worst. In both cases, the collisions were soft ones against cushioning and gentle moon rock, giving little depressions under the weight of their impact. Such a fall was no way for them to die. That right was reserved for a lonely figure slowly approaching like ominous incoming traffic.

Christina cussed herself out for being so hasty while frantically wrecking her mind for a plan. Marcus watched in silence. Contrary to popular belief, this instinct was not because of an empty head. He was the first to notice the black pigtails of a familiar round face with a slight aquiline nose, heavy bottom lip, and small eyes. However, hairy eyebrows which were normally raised smugly were now contorted and bent. Her eyes that so often glared at him with love, hate, pity, and scorn were instead cast downward in grief. Her brown skin was now pale. Her blonde hair, now black and covered in a white lace veil. Her company uniform was traded in for a flowing white dress that started with ruffles just past her shoulders and went into sleeves, blouse, and a long draping ruffled skirt. Around her long sleeves and covering his waist were black ribbons tied into bows.

"Here is a good place to cry."

From eyes, tears.

Black.

Christina gasped. In this oasis of white the black plunged through like swords cutting straight through the space before she could notice. Black tears came streaming down her face painting the city streets, or staining rather.

"My Llorona. Lauren," Marcus worded aloud. "I never would have gotten that impression from her."

Christina's sneakers flopped loudly against the sidewalk by accident as she scrambled getting up from the ground and dragging Marcus with her as she ran in lieu of an actual idea of what to do. She wished Marcus would have shut up, but instead his words kickflipped her head into a spin and she quit running for a moment and spun around to catch the sight of the familiar face that she missed. Her foot slipped off the false sidewalk edge and once again she was falling on moonrock.

The Llorona had already closed the distance, weeping on brand during her entire approach. A Marcus that lacked the gumption to keep on running let his hand go. In an action against his survival instincts, if he had them, he let his curiosity take over. With a step filled with debilitating fear he walked towards the weeping woman for a closer look. The two stood face to face, silent and still. Only for a moment before the false Lauren's hands grabbed his face and squeezed his cheeks. Christina wanted to scream and cry this time. Frustration overtook any panic.

A bloodshot red rage.

The Lauren made of tears did not stop the rain as black droplets did not fall from her face to the ground, instead rising into the air and pooling against all logic.

Why did she never change? Christina asked herself. What was she always reacting to and never acting? She broke into a sprint and heard her knees pop as muscles were probably pulled. Marcus had not quite reached a pain, but started to struggle in the uncomfortable grip. Black knives were refined from tears in the air, their ends sharped. Christina wanted to save someone, so why couldn't she do that one feat? Marcus hiccupped red flocks and broke free in time to dodge an influx of cruel cutlery, accidentally saving a late Christina by knocking her over as he fell back.

She wanted to cry.

"That's not enough!" Bella cackled. Wave after wave of screams pierced through as an ever present scene of arms was ready to remove her of limbs. She was mad in a twirl, her mass of hair twisting around her like a serpent as each strike of her arms offered whirling screws and ultimate destruction, eviscerating every surface into scraps of paper. This was nowhere near enough to stop her now. Ravenous hands and hungry metal machinations continued to tear through all before her, burrowing into the mountain of approximate flesh.

Eve had to improvise, wrapping the remnants of the now burning limousine in many bands of chains before swinging the weight of the fire ball around him, crushing any outstretched arms in its path. When the wave of limbs rose in ramparts as a response catching the vehicle he pulled it back and stood on it, smothering the fire in chains for the moment. From his suitcase metal whipped out and attached to every continuously approaching hand and pulled them backward, weaving the flesh in and out of its contemporaries, sewing together a patchwork of an appendage bound divide between him and the inside of the moon.

The white San Anlos echoed with thunderous rumblings as a black armada of kitchen knives filled the empty space above, waiting in formation. The Llorona had begun weeping in a fit, letting out wails and screams as she swung side to side in an unholy woe. Christina had froze. She didn't know what to do. Her mind was a white blank aimless canvas of ideas. Her face lost all color as she couldn't even begin to exhaust all possible options. They were going to die. They were going to die and she couldn't even do anything about it. So instead it was Marcus who decided to act, shoving them onto the nearest empty porch and shielding them with a brick pillar from the first hailstorm of blades. They stabbed front doors, concrete slabs of sidewalk, wooden benches, false grass, and rooftops alike. He didn't have time to panic as he was preoccupied trying to learn to multitask, coming up with the best route to take and how exactly he could vomit enough batches of dead birds to distract their pursuer.

Silently, black blades were already falling into position mere inches from his face like an unwanted house guest without his attention.

The thunderous downpour of sound was gone. Instead, to fill the silence between cries was a cracking noise as a now apparent and recognizable black limo came crashing through the makeup of the sky wall along with an annoyed man and a trail of paper shreds from amputated arms. The legions of knives at attention went in with a single wave of Lauren's head as she turned to notice the noise. Christina's heart sank along with the countless knives directly into Marcus' back. A single glance at his expression and he let go of shielding her with his body, nearly collapsing before she caught him.

"Are you still indestructible? She asked in a whisper, afraid of the words that came from her lips because she felt like she already knew the answer. She looked at his back, trying to differentiate between syrupy red and fresh blood.

"Still mostly I think." He laughed nervously as red liquid trickled out the corners of his mouth to his chin.

She wanted to do something to help but she could think of nothing, only letting her hands hover anxiously in the space above his already bloody back. That idiot. "Why would you do that?" she cried with tears clouding her vision.

He frowned at the sight. In fact, with those precious few moments of life he had decided that he did not enjoy the sight of his best friends crying. With them, life was sweet and even the worst dreams were cozy. They tricked him into enjoying moments and called him stupid with an earnestness that made him feel looked after. He liked rainy nights and lazy afternoons with them because he found himself actually living in those moments where he hadn't before. People like them didn't deserve to cry so much. He brushed the hair out of her face so she could see him clearly as his vision blurred. "I don't think you have to try so hard to be a hero or anything like that," he coughed. "You're a good person and that has an impact. I can't help but return the favor this once." He flicked her forehead with a delicate touch, totally weak and distant from any strength. "Don't make me do your homework for you. Maybe being a good person could be enough."

And then he collapsed, his chest barely rising with shallow breaths.

The updraft of black chains whipping past her tossed her head to the side as a lone knife heading her way was struck from the air into the ground next to her. More crashing echoed from the crumbling San Anlos sky as Bella descended with the grace of an angel of war, hair trailing softly behind her, arms cradling the remains of a torn apart girl while she erupted with laughter.

Christina picked up the single knife as the shadow of a busted limo covered her for a second, sailing ahead of her and shielding her from the newest onslaught of blades. She ran without purpose and on instinct alone, without looking back. She ignored the many blades as black chains and large screws struck them from their course. She pushed on without color or direction, compelling her body to move with every stride.

My Llorona is loud. My Llorona is pained. My Llorona can't be silenced. My Llorona can't be quelled.

So she didn't.

She screamed with the force of everything in her body and leaped. And with that empty mind of her's she directed her hands to plunge the knife deep into the forehead of her Llorona.

CHAPTER 9: DEATH ON THE MOON

Stars.

Stars in the black pool of night. At first there was black. Then there were stars. That was how it was and that was how it goes.

Llorona shrieked. Christina screamed. Llorona's head split. The crumpled Marcus was the first to be engulfed in the black liquid pouring out. Christina was the next to drown. Eve was the next to drown. Bella was the next to drown. Like a fountain of an imperceptible depth of black the liquid poured from Llorona's head and drowned the false San Anlos in an instant dragging down its inhabitants along with it. Any initial panic was immediately lost when each and every one of the party's members gasped for air and found it readily available.

It was black but not dark. They drifted downward into a star speckled void further into the moon. And within the faux moon, they found another faux moon. A place that should not exist, but existed it did anyways. They landed on a white surface with gently muted thuds, kicking up small clouds of color bleached dust. A moon that was fake. A moon that was a graveyard. The size was so small that anyone, no matter the height, could see the curvature of the rock in plain sight. More importantly, all along the rock, in a neat grid evenly spaced among craters and impacts, were the flat, square, smooth, shining grave markers.

Even Isabella unconsciously had the reverence to not stand on the small plaques, the only outlier of the group being the unconscious Marcus who laid there, unaware of his surroundings. Christina was similarly reverent only after taking a quick survey and gasp of wonder at the strange moon. Then she was immediately crouching down along her fallen friend. Bella poked at his body with the tip of her shoe only slightly interested.

"You drained him of all that strawberry dipped anger he had left."

Christina looked up with a flushed face and tears swelling at her bottom eyelashes. "What's going to happen to him?" A question filled with such sincerity that even Bella had to look away to best ignore her own emotions, letting out a huff with a quick movement of her hands. From behind her neck she produced a handful of colorless band-aid themed stickers and tossed them to Christina.

"There's nothing special about these considering the state that the boy is currently in, but it is enough to render him a gooey mess that can go back to his normal self afterward."

Christina didn't wait to finish listening. Her hands were frantic, tearing through his shirt to delicately slap stickers over any open wound she could find. Her hands were careful but fast in a flight of movement through the air.

The pale hands were rigid but faster. And there were many. So many. All coming out from the space before each gravemarker, the arms sprung from a place they were not before. With a blur they locked into a different position after every few seconds, at odd angles, reaching out in different ways. The intervals quickened. The hands moved faster. And the spell of silence in space was broken. Not by a heartbeat, but something more hollow. Something industrial without life, like an echo in an empty warehouse. That kind of pounding quickened. The white arms were now swinging rapidly, so much that Bella and Eve stepped back to block their more fragile and human companions in case. The group's attention was drawn elsewhere in their surroundings for a moment's glance, but a moment enough for the space before them to completely alter when they looked back. At what any one of them would assume to be the top of the moon, there was no point of reference to guide them, there were two enormously large, slender, and smooth hands. Those of which reached upwards past their elbows holding a single mausoleum, minimal and sleek with no segments or pause in its surface, as if it had been carved out of a single piece of moon rock. The heavy doors remained shut as light escaped through its corners and edges, waiting to burst forth in a flood. Bella took a few calm and cool breaths and a few steps forward, ready to greet the party's hosts, while Christina failed at picking up the pile of Marcus and tried to cover the boy with herself, returning the favor.

Doors opened. Beams speared through darkness like a spotlight. Like a searchlight. Like moonlight onto the moon itself. And from the minimal mausoleum moved two twins weightlessly in the air. Head to toe, every inch of their being matched in commitment to white like the false structure they created in that just as everything else, there was a complete scarcity of color in their being. No pupil irises of black, nor black school suits, suitcases, ties, hats, shorts, or shoes. All of these were now empty of pigment as pure diving canvases of white. Such was a holy sight and they knew it. Their sailor uniform's collar now floated in the air behind them just as their short hair did, giving it the same effect as biblical halos. Their clothes had changed fundamentally, where there were once buttons and cufflinks there were now zippers. Instead of a tie there was a large bow with its long tail ends curled to busy their fronts. Around their wrist orbited two interlocking bracelets without ever resting against the surface of their skin. And finally, just as they rightfully should have always been, a ring of stars floated around their heads and hats. The Adamants had advanced.

"Is there death on the moon?" Adam asked.

"There was," Abel answered. "In exchange for something beyond such limitations."

"It's because of such," their voices mingled without dissonance. "Mother is not gone."

"Mother?" Christina asked, lost at the sudden familial terms among alien life that alphabetized its roles.

Bella smiled over her shoulder and fought against the desire to erupt into laughter and applause. Instead, Eve burdened himself with the task to answer, letting his voice be even and clear for no one else to hear. "Soul. Complete animus. Essence without form. What you can call a god from your perspective the Luna homunculus family calls a mother," he paused "of sorts."

"Of sorts indeed," Bella snickered. "Most parents don't have their existence overwritten and erased in exchange for children." She turned towards Christina in a crouch and looked into her eyes so that when Christina looked back she could get a glimpse of the pure intimate nothing that made up the aliens' insides. "Unlike you, we have no sin. A marriage between soul and rock. And when our purpose is up they will burn me to ash and make a new child from my parts, just as they have done before."

Christina sucked in a breath and realized there were no colors to guide her in here. There was no warmth on her skin or person to connect to. Bella smiled in acknowledgment.

"I'm nothing without my anger and hate."

"Perhaps in your next iteration we can make a class A individual out of you." Their slow and saintly descent began.

"Still worshiping dead gods I see," Bella scoffed.

"The Luna name is absolute. We have no need for such mortal terms."

"Ah, but I am not absolute. I want to grow old and decrepit. I want to be more than vile and bitter. I want to know that beyond my numbered days is a black abyss that I can't refute from. And when my body feels that fear for survival and thirst for life I could forget this anger and love the way love is meant to be." Isabella grasped at the place over her chest and held onto something red and trembling.

The twins took turns speaking.

"Your fanatic obsessions with the reduction of use is futile and self-destructive."

"Function without necessity, a reality that exceeds your perspective."

"You confuse organization with subjugation."

"The presence of constant defiance demands no other presence."

Bella readied herself. "Death will be my final proof of annulling the Luna name."

The twins' shoes were only the most minimal distance from the rock. "When the day is over, night. Do well and remember that."

Moon Landing.

Bright lights filled the space with a flash as everyone's vision folded in on itself as they adjusted to the bright, white, definitionless hall they now stood in. It was a clash of black and white. Christina didn't have the time to notice that within the twin's artificial hands were two white pronged spears made solid out of condensed electricity and seemingly too long to handle. Handled they were still. Eve processed such information only slightly faster. However, Bella was the first to take note, the soles of her shoes squeaking against the floor as she slid backward, hands clasped on the pure electric prongs of the spear that was hurled straight toward her chest. Without hesitation, Abel compounded the attack, launching their own spear so that the space between its prongs collided with the end of their sibling's handle and sent a whole other wave of force through the weapons. The energy pulsated and dug forward, burning the skin of Bella's hands clean off, revealing white paper insides, and ready to plunge through her chest. Eve did not wait for a cry of help. He was already in front of her with an arm and a snap of his fingers sending a web of chains out of his suitcase stringing the spears in place, tied up in links tethered into the ceiling and floor. Adam was quick and with the single touch of their finger sent a wave of energy through both weapons shattering the chains with a silent explosion and tossing both twin's spears aloft in the air.

Bella only had enough time to reach into her suitcase and send out a line of screws. Ones that Adam easily swept away in one fell swoop after catching their weapon. One fell swoop that during the process of, they extended the handle so that the weapons circumference covered the entire room forcing Bella and Eve to bend backward at painful angles to dodge the swipe of electrified prongs. Somewhere within a corner, Christina dropped down keeping a limp Marcus tucked underneath her. Bella hissed at the maneuver. Eve grunted. Both of them looked up with their eyes in time to see Abel catching their weapon in the air and coming down ready to skewer them.

Marcus was a wet mess, sticking against Christina's clothes where they touched like slime and catching her terrified tears in the goo that still vaguely resembled skin color. He was healing, but in the process looked like melting sludge with the only indicators of improvements being pained groans of his barely present consciousness.

"I'm sorry Marcus," she cried. "I'm sorry that I brought you here. I'm sorry that I got you hurt. It's my fault. It's all my fault."

Her hands trembled when she tried to hold him as he fell between her fingertips. She loathed the idea that she couldn't remotely help in these situations. She was a stupid girl. That was the one thing she knew well enough for herself. It was a repeated failure in thinking of anything else. Another wave of anguish washed over her and she wanted to collapse, but no solemnity was offered. Instead, a messy brown form of what once was a hand fell onto hers. Her face froze and her mind went blank in a weary anticipation. The touch was near familiar and pulled her back to nights ago when the air was warm and she saw catastrophic red. But there was no such red now.

Bella had just enough instinct to twist as she caught herself falling back to dodge the dive from Abel. It was the surge of electricity afterward that caught her and sent her and Eve flying in opposite directions. Their bodies flopped harshly against the hard floor with resounding smacks that echoed. Her breath was uneven and her head was reeling. Every sensation against her skin annoyed her, but she tried to calm herself as she stood up. Adam and Abel were already upon her from both the front and back, ready to spear her and tear her body in two. Two chains wrapped around each electric end at the last minute and Eve grabbed at the metal links himself, flinging the twins backward past him and across the room. Isabella didn't even notice. She was too absorbed in the touch of warm metal against her fingers. Her right hand reached into her breast pocket.

"Are you sure about this?" Eve asked, getting behind her.

She didn't have an answer. Just a smile while she held a red screw with the loosest of grips between her fingers as it rattled

STCKR: platonic panic - 447

trying to escape. Adam and Abel stood there, watching intently as
Bella let go.

The red projectile flew through the air with a scream
encircling the group and tearing up a trail in the floor. Its spiral
grew shorter and shorter until it was closing the distance on the
twins, but they did not falter. Together, each of them held out
their spears. Invisible energy crackled between the two as the red
screw rounded them slower and slower and slower and slower
and slower. That short distance to its target took longer and longer
to cover until Bella's important combination nearly completely
stopped.

Eve's reflexes were lightning fast, just as his decision
making, whipping the red screw back to the safety of Bella's
dumbfounded hands with a chain before anything else
unimaginable could transpire.

There was no red on the moon.

CHAPTER 10: WHAT COLOR WHAT NAME

Christina's mind had fallen asleep under the night. The electricity that she had now prided herself on had stopped buzzing between her synapse space. All that was left was total slumber and perfect null.

"What color?"

The surface over what was Marcus' mouth bubbled, interrupting her crying.

"What color is it?"

The words bubbled and popped, echoing inside her head. Marcus only had the loosest comprehension of the events currently happening and unfolding, but that still didn't stop him from formulating that something was wrong with his dearest friends or at least the one right before him. Isabella was right about Christina and him from day one. They had far too much in common. They were far too much alike. Lived lives far too similar. It was an existential crisis to be in the vicinity of the other, so of course the combination would have been perfect. No amount of remedial lessons, harsh lectures, or forced realizations were going to change them if they weren't willing to change themselves. But if they were so similar then maybe, some part of him thought, then maybe he could bend the rules slightly. So he asked again.

"What color is it?"

His hand started to melt into hers and her head was empty enough that she could hear her heartbeat and his reverberate from their chest, bouncing off the back of their skulls and through to each other.

The red had run out, but he still had much to give. He loved his friends. He loved Christina. He loved Isabella. He loved

Lauren. He loved Eve. He loved Christopher and the famous power couple who were always ready. He loved Ms. Xiaodan and her hospitality. He loved this city. He loved San Anlos so much that it made him love himself. His affection was sincere and so infectious that it could melt in the last of the summer's heat like ice cream on the sidewalk. It was too strong and innocent that it pained Christina's heart to know she still didn't have a way to help.

The clash of metal and lightning could be heard somewhere else, but she was far too focused on the now here in front of her. Something small but dangerous zipped by their side, tearing at the ground.

"What color is it?"

She wiped away the last of trailing tears and tried to focus where no answers naturally came.

"Lovebirds truly don't fly, but if that's the case I'm still not afraid to do so."

Where there are no answers she would just have to make one for him.

"Tonight," she finally started with a shaky breath and hoarse voice. "Marcus Alvarado is completely smitten and awash in pink."

Somewhere in the mix there was now a pink coloration. Slowly but surely, his form came back to him with a pink head of hair and pink drenched eyes. He stood up stretching his back. Where there were once wounds was now a multitude of pink ice cream wings. "I am no cupid, but a seraphim of affection." He dripped puddles of dessert onto the floor.

Isabella was ready to fall to her knees in shock. Her legs felt light and her attention went frozen in disbelief. All she could do was cradle her most precious achievement in her hand against her chest and wonder why.

There was no time for such loss. Adam and Abel were already upon the two Luna members. Eve had managed to stop the first of their onslaught, wrapping Abel in chains as they lunged towards them and flinging the twin to the side. It was the second twin's shots of lightning from just out of reach that he couldn't avoid in time, his right hand exploded and did away with his pinky and ring finger. Adam was ready at the front of his neck with their spear. Movement before death. Eve smiled at least grateful that he could have spent his last few days before repurposement in San Anlos with the people that he cared about.

The whole room had a pink tint to it.

The three of them were knocked off their feet with a large sticky slap. Marcus stood there with melting wings growing longer and filling the room as they perpetually melted into a conglomeration of adhesive puddles. Adam and Abel recovered, hovering in the air and both flashed a face of disgust at the atrocious measures of defenses. Ice cream sticking to one cheek of each of them. More concerning was, rather than evaporate or explode when loaded with energy the surface of the syrupy treat only rather disappointedly rippled with harmless currents. The two wiped their faces and looked around the room.

"You attempt far too much for someone we expect so little from."

"Know your limitations."

They pointed their spears at him.

"That's kind of the thing," Marcus replied. "I mess up a lot. I flap and flounder on the ground without ever taking flight."

The two already had him punctured clean through from both ends and pumped enough white hot cleansing energy through his body it could have exploded the entire fake natural satellite.

For Marcus however, his skin tingled with goosebumps.

Bella and Eve watched in confusion. The twins sliced, stabbed, and speared him to no avail. When they tried to give up and attack their brother and sister again Marcus had slipped and slid his way over with a forest of wings on his back engulfing them, largely by accident. Regardless, he succeeded in battering them side to side within,lathering them in a sizable amount of lovely resistant and stubborn melted dairy product. Bella and Eve would have laughed if they weren't also being hit left and right. Marcus' wings flapped with embarrassment but didn't stop, at least until two screams rang out. Then everyone froze as Adam and Abel shoved their way out, enraged from annoyance.

The air crackled with ferocious energy. Their eyes glowed with a destructive light and muscles strained at attention along their necks looking like tendons might snap from the tension.

"This is a waste."

"This is useless."

They each spat at once.

"One act of abomination after another won't save you."

"Your date with annihilation has been set and there is no avoidance possible."

Behind them, on a wall not seen before, white panels slide apart revealing a massive glass window and a fast approaching city below.

"Witness," they said at once. "As you and your San Anlos destroy each other."

Lauren's feet hurt, her clothes were soaking, her mouth was dry and her legs were aching from climbing stair after stair of the barely finished skyscraper with loose tarps in place of windows. You know, she thought, if you're lucky then later on in life you could get a nice cubicle in a place like this. That's not something she wanted to say to herself, but these days her voice had been saying a lot of things she hadn't wanted. Rather recently in fact. It made her hate herself.

She didn't cry though.

She wanted to, but she didn't.

She was going to cry though.

Step after step she trudged forward and she had forgotten to take her umbrella. She had forgotten many things. She forgot that she had never learned enough things to forget in the first place. She had forgotten there was so much rain.

And there was so much rain. There was so much rain on her chest she was ready to cave in on herself under the weight of emotions.

She still had yet to reach the top. She didn't know why though. Someone powerful to her liked high places, so maybe she wanted to be like that. Someone happy enjoyed the rain, so maybe she wanted to be like that. Someone she loved always knew what to do, so maybe she wanted to know that. Maybe she just did not want to be a vile, disgusting creature of annoyance and wrath like she was.

The fire escape door was heavy and stubborn against her tired breathless and oxygen deprived body, but still, she fell through into a night sky of rain. She tumbled forward to see the veil of clouds temporarily lifted through clumped strands of hair. The end came crashing down like never before. It was one problem after another. Life was a struggle. Life never seemed to rest, did it? The rumbling began, but there was no escape this time. She could feel it in her bones and it was unbelievably uncomfortable. Her chest heaved with a heavy breathless panic and anxiety among waves and waves of depression. This was right, she thought, she had secretly been waiting for it. The thought she liked, and perhaps it was right, but as one world came crashing into another it was apparent that the moon filled her wide and terrified eyes. Oblivion approached its reflections in her glasses and she knew the difference between self-destruction and plain destruction. She had already been cursed so much, perhaps dying in such a fashion wouldn't be so bad.

But she was a vile and angry woman. And she was pissed. Her body was tired, unkempt, and uncared for. Was there ever a word she had truly wanted to say? Was there ever a definition for success she had defined for herself? She had murdered, slaughtered, and killed so many definitions in her life. She had carefully dissected and discarded the worth of words before laying them to rest without ever knowing she was no different. The definition of Lauren was unimportant, irrelevant, and unnecessary. She had achieved everything she had ever wanted. Everyone was so proud of her prospects, she should have been proud.

"Why then?" she whispered, having fallen forward onto her knees. "Why do they not even know my name?"

The air echoed with destructive action. The atmosphere shook. Lauren had experienced self-destruction for some time now, a long time, but just now realized it. She held herself from the wet cement with her arms and looked up to the dangers over her glasses and through her hair.

"Do they even know who I am?" she asked, to no one in particular.

She did not know who she was, but she knew certainly what kind of girl she had become. She was an overachiever after all. A golden student. A star pupil. An employee of the month whose only tarnish was the last stain of a personality she had kept with a sharp wit. She was a grim reaper for dreams, meanings, and ideas. She was the pride of her high school. She was the most capable friend. She was the one going to do things to help everyone in this town. She was emotionally ignorant. She loved far too much. It made hating things far too easy for her. She was the unimpressed youth for tomorrow. She was the unappreciated labor of now. She was the miserable generation of the past. She was the blood of her family, grandchild of ranches, daughter to orchards, and the aunt of juveniles and carved desks.

"I am heritage. I am life. I am in pain. I am not the daydream of enforcers. I am the words of confrontations and the voice of revolutions far too loud to be hushed." She stood up on a shaky leg and looked at her hair and company uniform with disgust. "I am the disturbed sea. I am the personal earth. I am the wretched little girl that you made me to be." She bellowed from the rooftop to the future, past, and present San Anlos she had once loved so much that it made her angry.

From her pocket, her hand slipped out with a phone. It was a mistake that she was the one entrusted with the tools of destruction. Lightning struck against the earth and all around the moon closed in. Short circuiting electronics sprung to life the newly installed massive TVs placed on skyscrapers and buildings of all sorts for advertisements, shaking from the force of the end. The ocean rumbled with movements.

"Know my name."

She screamed amid falling tears. All around her cameras focused on her. Throughout the city, she was repeated hundreds of times over and over along the large LED displays.

"Know my face!"

Something gargantuan and metallic rose from the ocean.

"Know my body!"

Lightning struck building after building.

"Know my heart!"

The storm screeched.

"Know my voice!"

Above the city was a leviathan of metal suspended in the air by a massive turbine howling, an empire of steel and ingenuity.

"Know my step!"

All around the city, countless screens displayed her part by part. Hairs, eyes, nose, mouth, legs, arms, face, ears, fingers, shoes, shirt, and shoulders. Piece by piece. Part by part. Screen by screen. She was up against the rooftop's edge. She knew what she wanted. Maybe not past this night, but at least for now. She wanted to carve the next words, syllable by syllable, into the very flesh of San Anlos itself so that when the land had wasted away and the world was forgotten altogether hers would be the only sound it could form. Lighting struck once again, strong enough that darkness fell on the city and every LED depiction of her fell to the ground destroyed.

The city was an ofrenda for a girl.

"Know my name," she screamed, tearing her voice from her throat.

"¡Lauren Mendez!"

CHAPTER 11: MIDNIGHT IN SAN ANLOS

It was midnight in San Anlos for a city that was never going to experience another midnight again. Marcus, Bella, Christina, and Eve all stood and watched as an unfamiliar San Anlos was fast approaching the faux moon.

Then the city disappeared as they saw what the Adamants wished they wouldn't. And the Adamants watched in silence as the faux moon no longer came crashing down onto a fast approaching San Anlos.

The steel empire was massive and loud. The current of air generated from its block sized turbines was powerful enough to induce maelstroms on the streets below. It was slow moving but immense, lethargic in brushing off the final remnants of seawater from the ocean of its origin. With the last of the waves falling off it was clear to see the white letters on the beast's side. LEVIATHAN. The feat of industrialization looked like the products of several destroyer ships stacked together, lined with all manner of military essentials so that it became a self-sufficient empire of its own, emitting a drone with every movement in the air just above the tops of the highest empty skyscrapers. Its size blocked out the sky for several neighborhoods. Its movement over the city was slow but set in stone. And as the end of San Anlos came crashing down, the rain stopped in a flash of purple that pulsated through. The screech of boilers and generators reached a fever pitch, raising the temperature of the air within the proximity of the ship.

The faux moon of oblivion did not reach San Anlos. It reached a dome of purple impenetrable hexagons of plasma protecting the city and more importantly the LEVIATHAN from the destruction above.

Adam watched in rigid frozen silence.

Abel watched in rigid frozen silence.

The very air inside was cold and contemptuous, refusing to move into lungs without force. Each of the respective halos of stars moved slightly. Each of their set of feet were planted firmly on the floor. Each of them grabbed at their heads with a blood curdling frustration. Their heads were spinning with the wrath of constant annoyances throughout their existence. Their halos cycloned around their heads ferociously, erasing the view of their faces in a blur of starlight as they stumbled side to side.

And just as quickly as their breakdown started, it ended in a homicidal composure. There was not even time for a breath of respite. They stood there still one moment and in the next Adam and Abel shot through the glass window without a single word, ready to erase every last annoyance of the abominable city themselves. Bella and Eve's eyes followed their lunar sibling with total surprise at such unkempt actions. The twins arrived with a fury of lightning striking against the purpled tiled floor of protection where they landed. Where there was electrical contact with strikes of white hot volts there were small temporary openings through the forcefield. An opening enough for the Adamants to set forth an end. With great pleasure they conducted, like maestros, a skyline removal. Those new and not so prized skyscrapers twisted and groaned in refusal as the tops were torn from bottoms and lifted into the air outside of the forcefield. Empty office insides were tossed into the air without effort following the course of lightning, energy, and updraft as both maestros Adam and Abel sent them hurling into a collision course with fellow Tandem Tantrum Toys and Co. product.

"Lauren is there." Christina's heart stopped in time with the realization. Those empty buildings were only mostly empty after all. Sure enough, through torn walls and missing windows, the face of a lost Lauren Mendez could be found in a weightless set of top floors waiting to be shot around.

"What are you going to do about it?" Bella asked, looking from one lost girl to another. But Christina had already decided she wasn't going to be left alone, grabbing Marcus and Bella's hand before sending a glance over to Eve.

"Don't ditch. I would grab you too if I could"

He nodded. She jumped. The rest fell with her. Marcus squished and squelched between airborne obstacles and an entire crew riding on his back until he tumbled his way through the windows that were now doors of Lauren's temporary room.

"You're late to the party," Eve, the last to arrive, chided to the lost and confused girl.

"Shut up," Lauren shot back, wet and tired.

"This is your doing then?" Bella asked, pointing at the LEVIATHAN beneath them.

"Is the falling moon yours?"

"Genuine question, but the tone is noted."

Lauren paused and reevaluated herself for a second. Marcus didn't, nor did they have time to before the room would be sent hurtling into another and reduced to metallic splinters.

"What's the plan then?" he asked. He was on topic for once. It made Lauren chew at the bottom of her lip in discomfort before she looked up to realize that they were all looking up at her. A stupid decision because she didn't have one either.

"Don't you have a secret weapon or something now?" she asked, desperate for a solution. "Use that."

Isabella was ready to start a long winded and defensive explanation but Eve cut her off. "It's not strong enough. They could stop it."

Lauren groaned, not surprised but very disappointed. At least for now it seemed the LEVIATHAN was enough to keep the twins occupied. She liked to think that, but a single glance over would tell otherwise. Adam and Abel had begun spinning, drawing a large circle with their spears directly over the defensive airborne machine, increasing their speed and directing unimaginable concentrations of lightning into one spot. Enough concentrations to tear a giant hole through the plasma field and rip off panels from the construction beneath the dome. So much for the LEVIATHAN. It wouldn't be able to handle such attacks for much longer. That would definitely create a problem.

The room lurched to the side. No longer a projectile aimed at the airship, the room was left in the momentum upwards before it would come plummeting back down. The force field only had a one directional output, meaning that the group could go flying out of it just fine. The lack of Adamant attention meant it was in a free fall, ready to crash into scrap metal against the very hard light plasma dome meant to protect them. Time was running out along with their options. The stakes had been raised exponentially and she didn't think that they had a way to survive.

"What about the cannon?" Marcus asked, nervously pointing at the heavy artillery mounted atop the fast approaching LEVIATHAN currently being destroyed. Bella rustled through her pocket for the red screw.

A massive gun for an even larger bullet sent straight through the heart of the moon. It was certainly a viable solution, Lauren thought.

"Would it work?" Eve asked, holding onto the door frame ready to abandon ship. The room lurched again, tossing them aside.

"The force field is at a 0 degree rotation with maximum output. It's immaterial going out but material coming in. I have a biometric pass through it to access the ship for now. If I could get in there I could manually load it, but the aiming system is automated right now." Lauren struggled to let out the words. "I wouldn't have time to override it and input new coordinates for-"

"I can do it." Christina grabbed Lauren's hands.

"I don't know what the AI defense system is like," Lauren warned but Christina was firm in her decision, looking the girl in the eyes.

"Doesn't matter." She squeezed Lauren's hands. "Just promise you will be right by me."

Lauren squeezed her hand back.

Marcus tasted the flavor of fruit overpowering his ice cream mouth.

Eve jumped out leaping from building to building as they exploded into fragments against the purple dome of security until he landed in a spot close enough to Adam and Abel but out of reach. In his arms was a chain with the other end in Bella's violent grip of her one hand, her other gouged into the nearest wall. The group went hurtling inside the little makeshift room. Adam and Abel looked up from their work tearing the ship apart to see a rooftop come swinging toward them and two figures leap out.

Lauren and Christina both plummeted toward the force field while only the prior fumbled with her fingerprint and her phone for a second. A single person sized opening appeared and she pulled the two of them inside.

Adam instantly went to work, ready to obliterate the mass of steel framework coming towards them. Their spear charged with a bolt of energy at the end, exactly enough to reduce a room into shrapnel on contact. What they were not expecting were two hands to reach out and pull at the spear handle's furthest edge sweeping them in. From the outside, a light of white hot energy exploded inside the crashing room while the sound of metal and screams poured out. The block of construction was on course to flatten Abel who finished what their twin could not. The mass of skyscraper exploded in a shower of microsized metal. Bella landed on her knees in a slide with Marcus' face palming and quickly running after her. Adam had cuts on their face and shrapnel sticking to their skin, only managing to catch themselves in the last moments before deftly hitting the plasma field.

Eve let go of the chain just in time to see two prongs sticking out from his chest and let out a pained groan. Abel had wasted no time, sending a current through their spear so that it seared the pink gelatin soaked clothes and left two gaping holes in Eve's chest. The burst of pain lit up every nerve in his body and set them on fire so that the inside of him felt like it was cutting a way to get out, his mind had almost gone blank. The injury was bad, but not bad enough. He caught a short length of chains from his suitcase and let it wrap around the spear, pulling it forwards further through him before the twin had the sense to pull away or let go, bringing them close to his back. And when Abel was near and in reach Eve pulled the spear all the way through and tossed it away, his chains letting go of it. Instead, he flung his chains behind him, wrapping them around Abel's throat and pulling tight, not to only choke them but attempt to remove them of a head as well. Eve twisted to face the twin directly and pulled a length of chains between their teeth before kneeing their mouth shut on the metal links immediately after. The sound was that of the snap of molars and canines as Abel fell back screaming and grabbing at their face.

Bella didn't punch, but instead dropped to the ground and pushed with her hands, kicking up into the air so that the one foot connected with a surprised Adam in the jaw. In the process of reeling back they swung wildly, letting the inescapable length of their spear compensate and slicing a gash of paper flesh free from Bella's right thigh. She hissed out in pain through clenched teeth and grabbed a willing Marcus to the front by the collar. He didn't need an order, unfurling his wings and letting Bella shield herself behind their cover. Over uneven intervals she swung over and under him to throw out a series of kicks and punches. Before any of them could land Adam spun their spear floating in the space before their palm, blocking the blows as they came. Suddenly, and without warning, Adam's spear pierced through Marcus, its prongs coming out his back with little effort. Marcus only looked confused at the decision while Bella realized it all too late. Shocks of twisted metal flung flakes her back before she could turn to see falling rooftops shrapnel torn apart and pulled forward and into her back. All along her backside and deep into their chest they protruded.

Without thought, Marcus pulled at the spear further through and rolled holding it close. He let himself slide far enough along a melted ice cream slick until he realized that the burning hot weapon was barbecuing his chest he held it against. It was then that panic descended, realizing the stickers were wearing off. All in time to see Bella's throat in the clenched grip of Adam and Eve's own chains and burning his hands and skin off with Abel's touch.

Lauren and Christina stood on the LEVIATHAN'S deck underneath the forcefield and fighting above. However, their attention was not on the brawl, but on the cannon's central terminal before them. Lauren plugged in earbuds to her phone for an easier wireless connection and handed them to Christina.

"This should be enough to establish a connection to realign the targeting system manually."

"How are you going to load the screw?" Christina asked.

"A maintenance panel," she answered, pointing to a small locked hatch with one hand and holding the red object with the other. "Loading it is the easy part."

"What's the hard part?" The words were nervous leaving Christina's mouth, barely wanting to be heard as she twisted the earbuds in her sweaty hands.

Lauren cast her eyes down. "I would do it if I could. I don't know what defense system the AI has or if you will be able to handle it. Worst case scenario your brain gets deep fried."

"Appealing way to put it."

"I'm serious." Lauren grabbed Christina's shoulders and looked her in the eyes that she loved looking at before and the mouth she loved listening to and the face she couldn't stop caring about. And she started feeling the tears rise up again. "Christina, I don't know what to do. I... I don't... I don't know what to say."

Christina let a tear roll down her cheek too and pulled the girl close against herself, letting her head fall against Lauren's chest. She smiled a bittersweet smile because she did know. "Say you're going to be here when I wake up. Say you're going to blow this moon the hell up." She stepped back taking a long look at Lauren Mendez who blushed from the girl's attention.

"I can do that."

"Good."

Her feet were wet. The space was an empty mass of black pixels. The chatter was deafening. The space was an empty mass of black pixels and one infinite puddle of blue pixels. There was a single white door. The space was a crowded mass of multicolored pixels. Millions of them. Each color making up a version of Christina milling about and talking to each other. Christina in the pixelated flesh took a step forward. The puddle rippled. The chatter stopped. All eyes turned to attention. A blue Christina blinked to life in the space in front of her.

"Welcome to the LEVIATHAN automated system version 4.3! Unfortunately, authorization is required for access." The blue Christina gave an exaggerated pout that made the actual Christina's gut twist.

"This is a cruel joke," she spat under her breath. As far as the eye could see Christinas waited and watched. Each and every one of them watched as the actual Christina raised her hand and crushed the blue Christina's head into a pile of pixels and binary.

"I'm going to get access."

Less than a yard away all Christinas spoke at once.

"You can try."

Lauren frantically placed the screw in the base of the barrel and turned around to witness her friend's convulsions. She panicked and ran towards her, holding her head still to stop her from slamming it back.

"Nononononononononono," she cried.

Christina forced herself to move forward. Each and every other Christina forced themselves to grab and pull at her. She could feel their arms burn against her digital skin.

Christina's head was hot between Lauren's hands. "Come on Christina. I can't lose you like this. Not like this, please!" she begged.

Every moment was a struggle of pain and will. Christina was burning up from the inside out. The door was within reach,

but so far away. The hands. So many hands. So much pressure it
was agony. She let out a scream.

Christina's head was alive with electricity between
Lauren's grasp. She could feel the heat in her palms and then a
wave of electricity engulfed the two, rippling through them and
lighting on fire every nerve along her body, cremating her brain
in the torture. Lauren screamed from it all. Her body was unable
to function properly, only releasing a wail as she sat there.

Constant and without failure. The air was hot to breathe
and stabbed at her inside. But still, she screamed out with enough
force it slashed at the muscles in her body and pulled them all
extremely taught like rope ready to snap. The door was in reach,
but the pain was unbearable.

The cannon blinked to life. Christina's body jerked forward
and her mouth gaped open harmonizing with Lauren in suffering.

Everyone above turned in time to see a barrel align
upwards and for two girls pain pierce through the chaos. Adam
and Abel turned their sight on the cannon, but Eve wrapped the
latter in chains and bound the twin against his very own failing
body. Bella opened her arms and legs, forcing the prior towards
her and pinning them, finger diggings into their head while Abels
tore at her throat.

Christina's eyes glowed and she grabbed at Lauren's flush
face in a desperate gesture. The two embraced in electrocution.

"Lauren," she gasped. "I'm falling. I've always been falling.
But I think I'm okay if I'm falling with you."

Abel electrocuted themself and Eve, letting the volts tear
apart the top layer of papery skin and loosen their insides now
near ready to fall apart. Adam dug their electrified hands into
Bella's body and back scratching, tearing away, and carving out

chunks of her neck, chest, arms, and legs trying to break free. Eve and Bella only tightened their grip.

"Not tonight," Eve screamed.

"You don't get to escape the person you've made," Bella roared.

The pain was unbearable, but it was not enough. Lauren choked on her words, but still managed to get them out. "I've been falling, Christina." She leaned in. "But at least I'm falling in love with you."

Something red and trembling shot upwards in a beam of light to reach the moon. And Lauren Mendez's lips locked with Christina Zheng's. And they held each other close and they screamed and they cried and they hurt and the moon exploded and they kissed.

CHAPTER 12: DEPARTURE

Adam watched as the rocket landed. Abel watched as the missile struck. Eve watched as the moon was pierced. Marcus watched as the moon was pierced. Isabella watched as the moon was pierced.

Bella had seen the lift off as she had always seen so many times before. Seen enough through old film from every angel that she knew it exactly frame by frame, memorized down to the millisecond. Slowly the exhaust let out. Tumbling down the sides of the carrier's deck filling the streets of San Anlos. But surely it would lurch into the air. Higher and higher. From the outside of San Anlos it would rise like a red string of fate. Slowly but surely her fireworks would take flight.

San Anlos was silent in the wake of a transcendent breathtaking spectacle. But no sound was needed for the occasion. Isabella did not have to feel the remorse of power that shook the air. Nor the gush of hot air that suddenly released. Not even the screech of raw energy cutting its way through the space or the taste of the burnt night air mixed with approximated blood.

All Isabella could do was take in the beautiful sight. All of it was enough.

Adam saw as the moon tore. Abel saw as the moon split. Bella saw more.

The white hallway floors shined no matter how many times she had walked down them. Past classrooms and lockers. Mindless chatting with her friends at a pace that was not quite slow enough to be walking so as to be on time for class. Running from her terror.

She touched the edges of her desk, placed near the front because she had a habit of not paying attention more than the rest. Next to her were seat partners and friends she struggled to remember the faces of clearly, but the rampant laughter was a byproduct of not shutting up to her teacher's ailment. She looked around the classroom. Her eyes took in the desk and the underside she hid under and only hopefully out of sight.

The artificial grass had always been too stiff for comfort. The heat from the light, too cold. The taste of the water, too mechanical. Nonetheless, in the room was once again the most freedom she had ever experienced. She stood where she once chased classmates, tussled recklessly, and enjoyed imaginary escapes. The grass made her itchy when she lay against it, but it would always be the most comfortable sensation she could remember. To be away. Enough liberation her head felt light and could reach her dreams among breaths of wind.

She was in the doorway of a room with a single drain on the floor that she knew was better at draining tears than sticky blood. She ignored the table and shelves and their fine edged contents she had decided to never mention years ago that surrounded the single drain.

Isabella was sitting in the same seat that she had always sat in, behind the same desk she always had. Eve was to her left. Adam and Abel were to her right. She did not have to look to know so. They did not have to turn to know so.

"It doesn't help for you to know, but we never enjoyed our actions."

"That's just the way things ended up."

"I know. We have all made our decisions. Now we have to sit with the results."

They turned to face her. She did not turn to face them. They sat together in the classroom.

Slowly and surely papers were tossed into the air. The podium exploded into splinters. One desk after another was upturned and flipped. The chalkboard's surface was gouged through. Over walls, across the floor, against the ceiling, its path was carved through.

Together they walked down the hall as glass window after glass window shattered. One classroom, then another. Then another. Walls tore down. Floors cracked.

They passed the open doorway of a certain room falling in on itself. They continued on without looking at the wreckage left.

Together they laid there in the hills, their backsides pushing against stiff grass. Itchy and stubborn, it left red depressions against their skin. One hill after another, ripped from its place. Rocks and dirt showered the room. Light fixtures fell. Rivers were lost and buried.

Slowly but surely, something red and trembling neared them. Slowly but surely, something small and unimportant carved its way through the moon. Slowly but surely, something ugly and useless and imperfect left nothing standing.

Marcus watched as paper fell like folded snowflakes.

Christina watched as the rare origami weather coalesced with her skin.

Lauren watched them take in the beauty in silence.

The rain had stopped falling.

The night sky was clear.

Eve watched as there were no clouds.

Bella watched as there was no moon.

STCKR: PLATONIC PANIC
EPISODE 6: JNOL

CHAPTER 1: LUNCH PREP

Summer heat was aggressively oppressive and on its way out, just as it was last year and the year before. Except worse. Each year. Worse than the last. The rise in temperature was unprecedented just like before. Uncalled for. Unappreciated. Underrated. Unavoidable. Unexpected. Unprecedented. And extreme.

Heat waves and unbearable nights had not only become a San Anlos staple these last few days of September, but also a pseudo event and quasi holiday. School may have started but summer did not end until summer days burnt themselves out. Needless to say, summer heat was enjoyed to its fullest and then past that as well. Classes had long since been postponed for what seemed like ages ago. Summer breaks demanded an extension for salutations and celebrations. In capable hands, the days were successfully mind melting, energy draining, and lethargy inducing. The constant torrential rains of yesterday would have been dearly missed by all weary minds of San Anlos quick to forget the mist of cozy autumn nostalgia. After all, it was still summer and so much had happened over the course of a few days that no one had the spare mental capacity to reminisce.

Wreckage and rubble were left impacted into the gaping cracks of San Anlos' city surface. Damage found its way along, on top, and inside of houses, stores, cars, and all manner of infrastructure. Luckily, the unforeseen downpour on the last night of rain had proved remedy enough in aid when none else was offered. No forecast could have recalled origami snowflakes, wet and sticky with the moisture of the air, nor did forecasts predict the way they coalesced with the people on earth. When contact was made there were puddles of rain and puddles of people, and when sundown passed there was only fresh air and activity of people unaware of their many experiences in the close proximity of death. Instead of health, the people could fret about property and expenses to no fault of their own.

The latest disaster was Tandem Tantrum Toys and Co.'s disbandment of all businesses along with community responsibilities. No company subsidiary store received clearance to open, their locks had been replaced and contact numbers changed. Corporate immediately froze all funds. Without money to pay, people were without work. Construction equipment was without hands to move it and left scattered to rust. When precedence had suggested a sponsored emergency relief effort, there was none. Only individual solutions which had a limited chance to meet the call, like the rare struggling business that had managed to stay open, but only for a few hours or so while their supplies lasted until they too had no choice but to close. The only remains of Tandem Tantrum Toys and Co.'s presence was the still, but very much active, headquarters. There was the proof of the building along with the many logos on products throughout the city, businesses, homes, schools, trash, etc. But more than both of those, there was the construction of plasma.

Purple plasma shined only when the daylight struck at the right time in the morning and turned the city a noxious shade at night. The LEVIATHAN was now only the smallest impression of a black dot in the cloudless blue sky above so that even the best cameras had a hard time making it out when the energy dome was shining to obscure it. Not that there was a point in photography, videography, or documentary. San Anlos was without ways to the world wide net for communication. All that could be played was a private securely hosted domain and the Tandem Tantrum Toys and Co. app for helpful corporate promos from company mascots themselves with tips like: "If you're injured and need help please wait."

So San Anlos once again had nothing else to do but enjoy the heat in whatever manner possible. Moms and dads took a break in the house and company of all direct fans at full blast while aunts, uncles, or godparents held garden hoses up and their thumbs over the mouths, fountaining the water to spray kids. Others relaxed in the shade with cool drinks and a cooler waiting for when the kids finally expend more energy than the heat should have permitted. Summer breaks like these were for the siestas. In the days past, even before the heat or rainwater ran rampant, on a boring morning with a slow to wake fog, San Anlos had started to eat San Anlos. Tangible memories were now only old impressions on the earth where there was nothing else to cherish. Between the cracks, climbing on the walls, and overgrowing in the gaps were weeds. And there was grass. And there were bushes. And there were vines. And there were palm trees. And there were wildflowers.

Between the leaves of stray grass, you could catch a glimpse of her.

Along the crumbling chunks of what was left of walls, you could catch a sense of where she had sat.

Black strands of hair were just out of sight.

The cold of the umbrella's shade just out of touch.

Eyes never met.

Smile quickly forgotten.

She was strolling along the sidewalk until she wasn't.

She was admiring the tallest tree until you could see it.

She was picking her way along green and brown ruins until you could remember.

And then she vanished.

Marcus' hand always landed hard against the glass door of a once family owned grocery store as he continued to draw. Also as he continued to wait. He stretched his one arm reaching high above. He failed to muster up the effort to do so since he had started and when he brought it back to his side she was already there where she wasn't before.

"It's a lot of green. Do you expect it to last a while?" she remarked without turning towards him. Isabella stood there in a black suit, black skirt, and black knee high sneakers embellished with green laces just like she always had before. She stood there next to him, cradling delicately the antique green parasol that obscured all of her face but a peaceful smile that she had never had before.

Marcus stood there in front of one of the few stores not destroyed from recent havoc, underneath the similarly spared sidewalk cover. Today, even in the heat, he was painting onto the glass a jungle's foliage and a yellow jaguar that stalked between the leaves.

"Not really," he finally answered. "Natural things don't really last long like that." It was Southern California after all. Give it a few more weeks without rain and all the now prosperous green hills will be dried back to the yellow and brown brush. "Really," he added, showing his hand with the gel sticks of greens. "Nothing natural should withstand unnatural circumstances like these unless you actively fight for it. Most things aren't permanent."

He frowned.

"For now I will save you the struggle of loss," Bella replied, tapping against the glass window of the storefront and sending enough force through it to shower them in specks of glass. The air sparkled with sharp particles as they held their breaths together and she covered both their eyes with the parasol.

"Ladies first," Marcus reminded Bella while still walking right in before her.

The objective of their mission was sole in purpose and clearly defined, sitting somewhere in the store. It was something that Marcus was not exactly aware of, but his feet had already carried him halfway down aisle five and he couldn't just turn back now. The meat section seemed like the right place if only because it had open coolers to stick his head into. Bella was already there, having been successful in bringing a cart and clearing out the racks of sunflower seeds, spice covered nuts, and banana chips. Marcus, on the other hand, was severely behind. Unless he was planning on bringing a barbecue set and grill with the latter, which he was not. Any prime slab of meat that they picked would have already been considered bad.

The left wheel of her cart squeaked at irregular intervals, refusing to budge. Marcus laughed to himself, less because he found it funny and more so because he didn't quite know the proper reaction, but he was genuinely interested. Either way, his hands were preoccupied with a realization.

For all this talk about appetite and feasts, Isabella had not once eaten meat, had she? Even when she was exhausted from reality and chewing on all before her it was nectar and approximations. Sweets and stickers.

"Are you vegetarian?"

The cart stopped in the produce section, but only because she wanted to. Her umbrella was sitting closed in the basket. The building's electricity was surprisingly still on, but even so, her eyes were hard to make out. She turned and tilted her head, looking away toward the wall of lettuce. Somehow along the way he got lost and could never meet her gaze.

"What does it matter?" she asked before a wall of greens.

Marcus frowned and busied himself with inspecting the bags of grapes. "Don't you want to get some food you like too?" The question had an intended target but was asked to no one in particular.

Indeed Isabella stood there next to a wall's length of vegetables stacked on the lit up refrigerated shelves, but she was also lost in a dense forest. Hidden between tropical leaves, her body was visible through their openings but her face was obscured.

"It doesn't really matter," she answered softly.

His hands pulled back the leaves from the forest world temporarily.

"This lunch is a gift for you. For everything that I kind of put you through. Remember?" she told him.

"You've been through a lot too."

He was there as well. In the jungle standing in her way, reaching out for her shoulder. She shrugged off his words and pushed the cart a little forward.

"It's really because I have to finish getting rid of any extra corpus and angst that you seem to always have in surplus so that I can say I actually completed my job. But I thought the first thing sounded better."

Marcus didn't follow. He was still in that jungle standing tall because the deaf Marcus never learned when people told him to disappear. Her words did not reach him. He strolled over, meeting her through the tangled trees. "Let's just enjoy the festivities while we have them."

She was lost in his sights. "That's the mature thing to do isn't it?" she asked. A voice disembodied. Words for a voice of a person not entirely there. Her arms floated through a vast gray. She was addressing him from a being that disappeared through his body. Her mass, nonexistent. Her touch, like a ghost. Her body, not permanent. She was fog in the jungle.

"You've grown haven't you?" Isabella was already strides ahead of him, overlooking the rest of the aforementioned produce section. Her umbrella was unfurled and blocking out her face so just her mouth was visible.

Just so her smile was visible.

Bittersweet. Marcus grabbed at the umbrella's edge closing the distance between the two as the lights flickered along with his steps, uneven with sneakers soles squeaking against the linoleum floor. "Bittersweet," he said, with a cracking voice and a twitching in his eyes that failed to look at her but not the floor before her.

"Huh?" Bella's mouth was stuck open in surprise at the clear suddenness of his forced action, letting her umbrella fall to the floor.

"Bittersweet," he repeated, grabbing at her arm. "Like chocolate for breakfast on a Monday morning. Or cheap coffee with donuts. Or a sick day that gets you out of school."

Isabella's one foot stepped back reactively, her eyes focused on his hand at her wrist in front of her. The lights blinked one time before someone somewhere made the decision to cut off the power. Their shopping cart went rolling down an aisle in the dark.

"I try to remind myself to think about my feelings. And I think better aloud so I might as well say what I think." He hesitated, still stuck there looking at the ground. Still holding onto her hand. He had, at one point, considered himself good at goodbyes but was now realizing that he may have never understood himself well enough to ever truly experience or express one. Regardless, he wasn't good at this goodbye.

Isabella Luna had dreamed with this goodbye meant. A job well done, deserving of her rewards for achieving everything she had ever dreamed of. She would leave San Anlos behind and find a warm field of green grass and clear blue skies and a bright yellow sun. And she would lay there, free and relaxed. And she would be content.

"That kind of hurts a little, doesn't it? Marcus refuted the thought. It hurt him at least. Isabella took another step back into the dark, her feet unbalanced and soles squeaking too. Breathe still.

"Dead dreams die in daylight, don't they? That's what they are supposed to do anyways. It's why they are dreams, because once you reach them they change and you get another. You can make another. Or another one can find you."

"Get to your point," Isabella whispered rather than spat.

Marcus was no longer a lonely child sitting all by himself in the back of class.

Isabella was no longer a school child hiding in panic underneath her desk.

"Do you think that maybe you could wait for a little before you find your field, and maybe then we could relax together? And then after that, we could do other stuff together?" Marcus' own hand slid down from her wrist and held onto hers. "I have a lot of people that I care a lot about and I think part of me wants you to also feel that way as well."

"Marcus." She held onto his sweaty hand and gave a light squeeze.

"I think I found a friend and I hope you found a place closer to a home." He had given up on holding back the tears and let them fall onto the floor.

"Marcus," Bella whispered.

He looked up to meet her gaze. His own image was caught within a clearly loved reflection of the world inside her irises. But that was not what he noticed.

"Don't cry," he whispered back, wiping tears away.

In the dark and the heat of the abandoned and forgotten the two friends cried. And amid their crying and shaking they finally found each other and hugged.

CHAPTER 2: CCC

"Looks like today is going to be another scorcher with highs reaching record peaks for September at around noon to a staggering 106 degrees Fahrenheit. Reminders go out to cities like San Anlos and San Anlos alone about excessive heat. Tips for escaping temperatures include staying indoors, drinking lots of water, refraining from too much physical activity, and cooling off. Tandem Tantrum Toys and Co. are excited to announce the summer's latest blaster edition water guns. Perfect for staying cool at any age. It's in moments like these that we want to remind everyone to take steps to conserve energy and secure the power grid. At times like these Tandem Tantrum Toys and Co. wants to remind you about our ongoing efforts through the Urban Remodel Fund to contribute to a better city infrastructure such as power grid security. It's through donations like yours that we are able to help in times like these and we appreciate and encourage it. A reminder: Tandem Tantrum Toys and Co. Committee Cooperation Lead determines the applications of tax exempt funds in all circumstances at their discretion. Rolling blackouts are to be expected all week and citizens are encouraged to plan accordingly. Renovations are surely coming and in the works. A reminder for Tandem Tantrum Toys and Co. vandalism: the company takes the destruction of property seriously and will proceed with punishment within the fullest extent of the law. Tandem Tantrum Toys and Co. remains the largest contributor to the city's renovations and recent urban development projects, committing to relocating company headquarters to San Anlos. Please remember that the plasma fortified dome is operated at a 180 degree rotational output. No object inside city limits can leave. Escape attempts are strongly discouraged at this time and will be seen as destruction of company property and resources. San Anlos is in the process of evaluating special grade contaminant matter exposure to the city at large. Please stand by while proper safety precautions are taken. This has been CCC providing you with the current news, the latest updates, and the fastest information. Can I Count you in to C you there?"

"Grandma, for uh the love of god your phone."

Xiaodan tossed over a quizzical expression to the girl before she could realize a dull but distinct sound was emanating from her chest pocket, bubbly, at perfect pitch,$ and with complete auditory clarity. Christina hated the voice, but she didn't want to waste the effort on forming words to express that. Instead, she was focused on avoiding where the calluses were starting to form as she grabbed at her wheels.

"It's annoying," Christina huffed about both her wheelchair and the girl.

"You don't have to tell me. I already know," Xiaodan responded, only about the prior. True to her word, she really did know. So much that she forgot why she even bothered to take her phone with her. She doubted they would need it once they reached the food bank, even less now that all it played was that annoying blue toned girl. "What was she called again?" she asked, shuffling forwards with her walker.

"CCC is uh what they, what they go by. I think," Christina answered, with a grunt at the end as her chair went over the cracked upturned sidewalk slabs from tree roots and she jostled in her seat. There was always something being announced about funds to improve the city, but for some reason Christina was always in a battle to move forward. Grandma inhaled, drawing a hot breath of fire but it was the last thing the girl needed under a heat wave and clear blue sky like this. Even as they tried to pick a path underneath the shade their sweat poured out and stuck their clothes to their skin like paste.

"You should be getting paid if they use your likeness."

That sentence was enough to tire out her wheelchair bound granddaughter next to her more than the actual trip. CCC was the latest product of Tandem Tantrum Toys and Co. ready for market consumption. Ever since they decided that nearly shutting down and locking San Anlos inside a terrarium without a key was a bad look she had been here. If you wanted to complain about a manufactured heatwave from the exhaust of a LEVIATHAN or about rolling blackouts from headquarters energy consumption or the blatant human rights abuse, CCC was right there to give three reasons or more for why you shouldn't. Her skin, perfect. Body, shiny and toned. Her hair, sleek. Teeth, straight. Sailor uniform, without stain or tear. On every screen you walked or rolled by you could catch a glimpse of CCC. Past a derelict storefront with windows packed with TV screens, the lights inside were off but the screens still showed that monochromatic blue virtual villain pointing at a graphic about the temperature and smiling.

Her hands stung as the flesh along her hands blistered from the hot wheels, but she was happy. If anything, Christina was largely saved from the embarrassment some worried she might have felt about her life now. For some reason, seeing her old image dragged through the mud had been a cathartic experience and she felt a little less sad about losing her strength and sensation that was needed to carry her most of the time or the fact that it was harder for her to speak. CCC. Blood rushed to her ears at the sight of the blue girl but the heat bleached it yellow and she could only endure the sweat with lethargy and reluctance.

"Hold my purse," Xiaodan said, only after tossing her bag onto Christina's lap.

"I'm not your uh... your wagon."

"You're right, a wagon wouldn't be using my wheelchair and still find a way to complain."

She sat in shock. It really was too hot for this. Xiaodan had not stopped letting her orange flames lick her words. She had hardly even noticed anything different with Christina, or at least wasn't bothered enough to treat her any differently let alone nicer. It wasn't perfect, but Christina could like it because of what it was. The sidewalk wasn't even and hard to roll over, but the trees were something she couldn't bring herself to hate. The heat was unimaginably oppressive, but she hadn't felt this way in a long time. Like green tea on a Saturday morning. She could hardly imagine anything better on a day like this.

Something crunched underneath her.

There was a sea of green that had taken over San Anlos, like leafy soldiers with a soft occupation if only out of coincidence. They were comfortable without a crisp crackle of age. Not like oranges, browns, and reds. Not like the brown fragments that crumbled with delight caught underneath her wheel as a signal of autumn. It was a single leaf falling apart from the pressure.

"Huh."

Everything led to a dull end. Zero. Nothingness.

Then it came flooding back to her. Colors of all varieties, in every shade of a complete and available tone around her. It swept her up and filled in the empty space of her brain. It stained her skin and dyed her hair. It poured onto the irises of her eyes and waterfalled down the chasm of her pupils. Her breath skipped in shock.

But it's hot. It's summer. She stumbled over her words and kept reorienting herself in the middle of her sentences now because there was no other way forward.

"Autumn still uh autumn uh... autumn still comes, doesn't it?" The air felt colder for a second, like the shallow grays of a natural fog for the time of year, but she might have been hallucinating from heat exhaustion. Regardless, she didn't have the luxury to afford the time to ponder that thought.

Where Xiaodan was Christina wasn't, and where the grandma was supposed to respond she didn't. She was steps behind, studying with distraught eyes transfixed and her finger nearly resting against her lips.

"Now that's something isn't it?" What was the point for such things, to burn up into char and smoke? Christina wheeled back to the wall with Xiaodan, whom she had passed earlier. Not that the wall was special, there were countless other ones that made up the sides of streets, along corners, and through alleys. So much so, that most people forgot about or ignored every number of art haphazardly splashed or sprayed on. The medium depended on whatever supplies such vandals had available. And just like any other work of art there was a message, simple and repeated over and over and over.

No matter how busy its coils were, the build of its body, how long the fangs were, or how fearsome the eyes of the three headed serpent were, shooting stars shot through each. Such images were not subtle, but what made it easier to read was the literal messages along with. With letters so large you had to step back to see it.

'Grow where they build! SUPER SUTEKI SENTAI SYSTEM DELINQUENTS!!!!!!'

Xiaodan didn't take her eyes off of the painting, letting something inside her form in an unrestful twitch in the corner of her mouth. Christina rolled her eyes a little although she couldn't say that she didn't disapprove of the message. It was a little hamfisted and positive where she would have preferred something more pessimistic and cathartic, but this did seem like a more constructive route to go down.

"What's the point of this Christina?"

Something green started forwards.

Christina turned towards her grandma.

Something yellow and excited flashed the lights.

"I thought uh... I thought you would have uh liked something like this."

Something blue boosted the bass.

"It's not like I don't like it."

Something pink left a spiraling trail of colored clouds.

"But you don't uhh... look like you like it."

Something orange readied for explosion.

Xiaodan frowned, more sweat going down her forehead.

"What's wrong grandma?"

Something purple plotted above them.

The answer was something within her. It was written out in the way that the roots of trees made it harder for her granddaughter to go outside, upturning the concrete along the sidewalk. It was how wooden skeletons of newborn houses failed to sprout in place of steel beams. It was in how the temperature set her blood into a boil greater than the days before. Xiaodan realized the answer herself, but she couldn't admit it now. It was easier to say that she was the problem. There was less work in dealing with one person than the rest of them, and as memories and details started to break apart in the heat present it all felt unbearable.

But what was she supposed to think? What could she say? What was there to do? Fire was the last thing they needed now.

She had wanted business. She had wanted a house. She wanted a good school in a nice neighborhood and a family. But everything ended up charred.

"I do like it," she finally added. "I just feel like maybe I wasted my time."

Christina gasped. "Grandma."

The van barreled towards them but managed to not crash into the two, only the very wall they were looking at. Delinquents walked out, unfazed at the nearly missed manslaughter charge.

"We need your assistance," Suteki Green declared as the black van door slid open.

Even though Christina opened her mouth to speak, Xiaodan was the first to answer. "Do we get a free ride?"

CHAPTER 3: DIGITAL SURFACES

Christopher laid there sprawled out, trying to generate the most distance between each leg and arm from one another. The red plastic seat covers from the 50's inspired diner's waiting area were doing no charitable favors as he stayed there, stuck between heat exhaustion and his usual lethargy during breaks. One of the many intrusive thoughts of a frantically paced mind like his stuck to him just like much of anything else these days. Just like plastic seat covers on his sweaty skin. If she stayed for just a moment longer they might fuse to his person permanently and he would be left with no option but to peel it all off or become an unholy creation.

The building was more of a full restaurant and less of a diner, with a complete seating area in the front while customers waited for a table. It was a diner crammed between a smoothie shop and something older and faded that couldn't quite be made out after years of abandon. The front doors were left open because, as much as Christopher cursed and swore, there were no windows that opened. The only ventilation that existed would have to be crafted and Christopher was nothing if not crafty.

"This is stupid," he muttered, peeling his one side from the small couch and rolling onto his belly. Without using his filthy gloved hands, he couldn't be bothered to undress, he finagled the end of a straw into his dry mouth.

He certainly was crafty. A craftsman one could say. A mechanic, if they were being specific, but not limited to. The least Christopher could be grateful for was construction. Like how the building was situated at an angle so that the sun cast the front in shadow even if it was unaccounted for, or how the diner had been built with a milkshake bar so he could carefully create the mint chocolate masterpiece he so delicately engineered. A yawn creaked out of his mouth by something other than his own volition. The heat tended to make the mind melt and the body creak. He didn't pay it any attention, although he couldn't even if he wanted to. His puddle of a brain was too intently focused on something else. He needed the proper signals to stimulate the proper muscles to move his tongue and mount properly around the straw he had resting on the space of cushion right in front of his face. The other end of which was deep within the chilly recesses of his milkshake below. If he wanted it enough he could get it. The problem with that thought is that you never know if you wanted what you wanted more than you wanted to pass out in the moment during this brand of heat. He could have screamed for joy or cried when he finally managed to secure the plastic into his mouth, however that was an expenditure of energy he couldn't care to afford.

"What exactly have I walked in on?" Eve stood there under the doorway where a bell should have jingled to let Christopher know if he hadn't left it propped open.

"It sucks," Christopher answered without actually answering. Indeed his construction was pretty to look at but absolutely useless to use, being a hindrance to reaching the drink in the end. Red striped straws that could bend at one end interlocked from one mouth to another like tubule pipework throughout the room. They were held up by each other and weaved in and out creating a cloud of condensation as droplets sweated from the strange creation. A single massive makeshift bendy straw. A creation that never allowed for the creamy delicious milkshake to reach its intended audience.

"Can I come in?" In Eve's other hand was the handle to a red and banged up wagon with everything a boyfriend could ask for inside.

"How are you still in a suit during this weather? No need to be modest. Strip it off. It's good for your health."

"The invitation is noted but off topic," Eve replied, brushing off the statement. Even so, Christopher's appeal had been so matter-of-factly that he had to reassess whether the man was actually joking or not.

The clatter of straws against the linoleum floor brought him back to his sense to see Christopher with a green frog shirt, black cuffed jeans, old sneakers, green rimmed glasses, and his usual black leather gloves stand up. All of which were still a shock to the eye of a boyfriend not familiar with an intimate shock like this. He didn't not like it though. The opposite in fact. Christopher didn't not like it either, but he was still getting used to having some sort of outward personality himself. He was also getting used to his milkshake by partly chugging, partly scarfing down, partly choking it down.

"You're going to get a brain freeze." Eve saw his boyfriend already wincing in pain.

"Good."

Something was burning somewhere. The indistinct smell of possibly melting plastic or rubber wafted through the air cutting their words short. A minor apocalypse for sensations like the sputtering of miniature explosions or a stinging of the eyes with specks of black smoke to tie it together was present. Their table was ready.

"Right this way Eve." Christopher pulled at his boyfriend's long white tie and led him through the black smoke pouring out from the small hallway before the dining room. A single little generator amid many others was smoking at a rapid rate completely unnoticed in the room by a hard at work dream couple. Or maybe it wasn't that it went unnoticed but rather they didn't care enough to act, or maybe that cared too much and betted on someone else acting so they acted like they weren't acting about how much they didn't care. Regardless, the dream couple had become a couple of dream coders working at two makeshift computer stations in the booths across from each other. Wires protruded from the improvised and stolen machinery, lining the floors and duct taped every which way to stay in place. The couple didn't even acknowledge the other one entering the room.

The handle to the wagon started to feel fuzzy against Eve's palm. Just as black smoke rose to meet the ceiling and what would have to be assumed were now broken fire safety sprinklers Christopher ran for the fire extinguisher. White foam filled a corner of the room. Elastic and wet, like a depressed can of whip cream or a weeping meringue, the contents of the can engulfed the red coughing box of portable electricity.

"I like your gross little nest."

"Actually it's a pond," Christopher corrected, dropping the empty can against the floor with a loud thud before turning back around and pointing at his shirt. There on it was a lilypad with a green frog. "Or a tidepool. I like ponds but we don't have many here so a tidepool would suffice too. I always wanted to be near them. I love watching them so much."

"Is it always lively in here?" Eve asked.

Christopher shrugged, keeping a few steps ahead of his guest. Tiana and Touma didn't answer either. He could only stare at Christopher's back as he followed him toward the end of the room, but he would have liked to assume that the answer was no.

Now that his boyfriend wasn't on company time he didn't need to work himself to death and that was exactly the thing now. Things like breaks. They were something Christopher did now. He took them, just lying down and relaxing. It felt good. Christopher had forgotten what type of good felt like this. Usually work was something that coiled its way around you, fortifying itself into your chest, deep enough to be just beyond your touch. The inside of a nest could look like a cage if you didn't know how to fly. It was all about functionality.

Machines clinked against each other in the wagon that Eve pulled behind him. There were car parts, broken computers, scrap metal, and an assortment of wires. All of which looked more at home in a landfill than here. Eve was a good man, he listened but more than that, he trusted Christopher enough to listen to even if it meant rummaging through garbage.

"Are you ever going to tell me what they are for?"

A warm breath of energy burst through Christopher as he turned around. He smiled and eyes locked onto the man in the suit. Or rather they would have if his glasses didn't fog up and shine with a brilliant glint to his vision. He couldn't really see at all through it, but it was a heatwave and he couldn't be bothered with these stupid games. So he smiled. Surprise and anticipation snaked their way through the air, under the kitchen door, to the back past the milkshake bar, over countertops, along the electric highway of cables, over Christopher's shoulder, to the back of Eve's skull. And it hung right there. The rumbling was loud, creating a sensation in his ears that made him want to scratch an itch inside if people weren't watching. But it was not uncontrollable. And if it was, he wouldn't have to worry about it for too long because he was shocked out of it from the surprise of confetti Christopher had thrown into the air.

"A cocktail of danger," Tiana thought aloud, pausing from her work. Her hands were left frozen above the keyboard.

"Pretty theatrical, but you're allowed to be when the end is worth it," Touma snickered, taking a mental polaroid of the exact moment.

Eve wanted a literal answer.

"It's a surprise worth the wait," Christopher obliged.

"When is it not?" He responded.

It was apparent now that the deaf couple was listening the whole time, but their chatter now was only in the obnoxious typing. Nevertheless, it was a surprise worth the wait for a few more scenes. A few more steps. A few more tremors. A few more rumblings.

"She's a beauty. She's a beast." The words exited Christopher's mouth and hung there between him and Eve while he pushed the kitchen door open with a flourish. His eyes focused in on Eve's face, documenting and categorizing every minuscule and minute movement of muscle. Eve was standing in what could have been the kitchen, being as they should have walked through the kitchen door. However, the insides didn't match the theme of the rest of the building. Not the 50's theme, but more so the whole restaurant aspect of it. Every appliance that should have been was removed leaving an empty space before him. His face was gawking, which is to say that it appeared more like an unimpressed concentration mostly present around his eyes. He couldn't even remember to drop the wagon handle in astonishment like Christopher had hoped.

"You're just going to blow up my new car?"

There, in its infinite black glory, was his limo parked in the gutted room as if there was no other place it should have been. And its passengers were packed in all the space possible within the cabin. They were none other than a dangerous amount of fireworks and pyrotechnics in the most capable hands of Christopher alone. The door rattled within the little space it had between its hinges and the wall as generators hummed at a frightening pace.

"We are the rumblings baby," Christopher whispered, with a smile so strong it had an effect on his voice while he reached up to put his arm around Eve. "You can't just store good fireworks forever."

Eve was an old man that had never known peace. He was a fresh newborn with an eye for passion. He had a cynical gaze and a generous ear.

"Someone has gotta set them off eventually," he replied to Christopher.

Eve was a lighter.

CHAPTER 4: RESIGNATION

The day was already well underway. The sun was well above its precipice. The people were already well exhausted from the sweltering state of things. And above all the LEVIATHAN sailed high, already enshrouded in the construction of scaffolding if anyone could make it out. Its turbines were only getting hotter, shooting downwards the inflamed air as boiler rooms reached a fever pitch in steam. Each and every pair of eyes and ears within San Anlos were preoccupied with their own combinations of worries and woes. Of course, they couldn't have taken notice of her. Even so, it was best not to forget the girl Lauren Mendez.

Noontime had barely come to greet the city, but Lauren was already having a busy and accomplished day. Much to do. Much to enjoy. Second by second. Minute by minute. The day ticked away, but she was not counting. The plan of attack was simple. It was barely even a plan at all, at least not by her standards. It was far too lacking by means of meticulous and finger aching hard work carving out the minute details like a skilled carpenter with the material that was a single day. That of which is refreshing, she caught herself thinking such a thought and incorporated it into her mental library so she could look back on it later. For the past day no thought had been so clear and fresh like the ones made in this kind of heat. Water was so cool when the world was on fire.

Regardless, the start of her day was a simple one. She could wake up calmly without ever checking her work emails or getting ready for school. She could ignore the purple and faded blue uniform now in the shadows of her closets for the moths to feed on until she could find the proper moment to dissect the monstrosity for eyes with scissors and make something new out of it. Yellow had always been her favorite color. Yellow like a clear day's sun, the kind that was present and on time to a fiesta, bringing the heat to dance in and the energy to languish with exhaustion so one could properly enjoy the food. But yellow didn't look good on her, she thought. She didn't think so actually, she knew so. Yellow didn't look good on her by itself, she decided. The right color combination for the ensemble required some proper brainstorming with color theory. She grabbed her favorite shirt, two toned like her work shirt, but different altogether with a bright yellow side and another a vibrant and rich blue. The right color combination for some proper disassembling.

She admired herself in the mirror as much as she could. The gradual movement of her attention drifted from the bags under her eyes present behind her blue framed glasses and upwards towards the roots of her hair. She had been a platinum blonde, bleaching her black hair to a failed perfection until each strand was wiry and too thin. The ends of her braids were fried and stray strands were making a run at all angles throughout the process. Her roots were already showing like a fresh row of brown crops. She gave it a quizzical stare. Every poor box dye set had now become a point of perplexion for her. The reason, in fact, was already more than apparent to her and she knew the exact words for the answer, but the answer was nowhere near interesting or satisfactory enough. Instead, she would rather look back and laugh with a confident perspective and wonder.

After that came her roller skates, yellow and bright like lemonade on her feet leaving a trail of positively bright sparks behind her in the streets. The streets weren't ready for her but San Anlos certainly was. Lauren glided over cracks, avoided rubble, and forgot about worrying how long it would take to enjoy the day like she used to. The heat bore down. It purported itself onto her skin and resonated with warmth along her arms and face. The hairs along her arms and legs were like chloroplast sucking in the energy as crystal beads of sweat collected at her hairline and brows, streaking down her chin when left to their own devices. Sweat migrated down her back and soaked into her clothes, leaving marks between her shoulder blades, along her chest, and under her armpits.

There was a velocity in her body today. She loved every moment of it. Every sensation and stance was a photograph she would hold close to her chest, but first she had to hold her bat. Metal burned against her fingers and palms if she wasn't careful to block the surface of it from sunlight. She cared about nothing more in life than that moment.

Actually, no. There was one thing she cared for more. That being her load of paperwork capable of broken backs and an arthritis diagnosis from its mere presence. There was nothing more she cared about than her paperwork. Scattered and dispersed in the few stray winds offered from the heat exhausted turbines screeching far above, she let it go. Black and white labor was now tossed with all the lack of care she so desperately worked to achieve, like anarchist confetti. Every few yards, with a single throw of her final work packet, she launched them into the air and swung, setting them into a course to explode like dandelions set free into the streets. They were let loose to go all the places that she was told she couldn't but should have. Her swing was fast. The bat was a blur so that even the yellow lettering couldn't be made out along its blue exterior while it bludgeoned any and all paper. And when Lauren Mendez was all done with the destruction of vastial paperwork, the clouds of inactivity, and the expenditures for a janitorial crew to hopefully not clean up because they didn't deserve to work at the ungodly hours they did, she stood there at the front.

All the door needed was a long string of identification numbers and a bar code. All that the record keeping would maintain was that some low class employee performed an unnecessary visit and had two more infractions before disciplinary actions should be taken as remediation in the best of the company's interest. Lauren just considered it more efficient rather than busting through the glass. It was the least she could do so that she could still enjoy the cool air of the AC.

Temperature controlled insides circulated the perpetually dark arcade building. The clamor of noise was now shut off even though the building was still certainly alive with the hum of electricity. Even better, the water cooler was unattended like usual. Lauren all but collapsed on the machine, resting her now festering migraine holed up deep within her temporal lobes against the cool plastic of the jug as direct AC and ungodly amounts of liquid came towards her at a massive influx. She chugged as much as one human body could handle before her stomach cells lysed and the pH of her blood was diluted. A quick survey of the room came with disappointing results as the empty arcade produced a few more memories of distaste, but she shrugged them off. Lauren was not here to play, after all, this was a place of work.

Just as with everything else within Tandem Tantrum Toys and Co. headquarters, it was important business. So she started with a shaky step, her head slightly in disarray, and her chest aflutter as she could feel the edges of her body cool down. Once she got her bearings the onslaught was ready to begin. That's why she got roller skates in the first place. She had remembered how long the hallways were the first time.

The trek indeed took no time during her second go. It was short and she had felt the natural timing of it so well that she could catch her breath as the elevator ascended alongside her spirits. There was, quite literally, no better this day could have gone. She swelled with joy and squeezed her bat in a hug against her chest with love strong enough it could cripple.

"You're not smitten Lauren," she whispered to herself. "You're enraged."

Her heart skipped a beat and beamed with pride as her tongue sliced it in half. That wasn't right, but if she couldn't cut it up with the right words she could bludgeon it without halt. Emotion trickled into the ends of her teeth like someone had managed to tickle her bones, but professionalism ingrained over the years reminded her not to let emotion bubble out and get the better of her.

'X' x6.

All screens were alive and waiting for her as the elevator doors opened up to see the expectations defying woman focused on her phone in one hand. Static sound rippled along the spotless oak table. It rattled against the glass like an auditory trail and leaped along the vomit of grays that made the carpet before running along the beige walls. It was in a sound more like dial-up screeches and less like a finely tuned voice that they spoke to her.

"IS THERE A REASON FOR THIS INTRUSION?"

Lauren held up one finger telling them to wait without looking up from her phone.

They waited.

"I sent it in on my company email so you better download the file before it gets deleted or something." She slid onto the carpeted floor making it look easy with roller blades.

"WHAT FILE?"

Her stomach bubbled with a vile bitterness like a poisonous rotten stew ready to burn and devour the rest of her. A good girl like her, obedient and domesticated into a docile employee, should find the courage to bite her tongue in half and renounce such misdeeds if she valued her place within the company. They would probably package the part and try to sell it if they could.

"WHAT FILE WAS IT?"

She keeled over laughing. Her side hurt like someone punctured it with a lance, but the process was truly painless. It was painless not in the sense that it did not hurt her, it very much did as she took in full account every burst of pain that escaped, but it was rather painless in the fact that she bathed herself in the enjoyment to be had with every strike of ache. Lauren Mendez was a calaca, dancing on an altar that stood above the bodies of countless other near identical calacas below.

"What else could it be? Consider it the heat making me act out."

She skated laps around the office just like she did in the offices that were now destruction derbies downstairs. Inside them were broken cubicles filled with mangled limbs and broken electronics. Loss prevention would have a field day with all the wasted product.

"!!!!!!"

"KEEP IN MIND THAT WE RETAIN FULL AUTHORITY TO PURSUE PROPER PUNISHMENT AND WILL SEEK OUT REIMBURSEMENT AND PRISON TIME WHEN APPLICABLE THROUGH THE FULLEST EXTENT OF THE LAW."

Lauren rolled to the head of the table with apparent disinterest. It was nothing that she hadn't heard before. The building itself screamed through all available speakers. The voices were distorted, twisted, and mangled.

"WASTED POTENTIAL LIKE YOU DESERVES TO ROT WITH THE REST OF THE FILTH YOU PEOPLE LOVE."

They were bright bold letters. Happy and energetic in a playful cursive font easy to read over the painted blue metal.

"Cállate."

CHAPTER 5: BACK TO YOUR REGULAR BROADCASTS

Smiles covered San Anlos. CCC was perceptibly just about anywhere at just about anytime with the same unfazed cheery hot blue dispositions.

"I have it," Suteki Orange notified while scrolling through their phone. "You know she has her own social media account"

"And way more followers than we could ever," Suteki Blue added somewhere behind her.

"Obviously," Orange responded. This grievance was a community held point. Sure enough, CCC social media somehow managed to amass followers in the hundreds of thousands during her short time live on air. Suteki Orange's phone was shoved close enough to Christina's eyes it started to sting.

"Oh wow. I uh I didn't uh... I didn't know they updated follow counts uh live."

"No." Orange pulled their phone back to give it an inspection. "No, they didn't use to do that. They must have added it recently." They didn't actually frown, their head being a plastic sentai style helmet and all, but Christina was smart enough to notice it in their voice so they might as well have been. "You think we could get that many followers?"

"Yeah," Christina answered, a little too quickly and a little too high pitched to be believable. For a moment she wished she had the same kind of fake and synthetic vocal cords as Suteki Orange as they walked off mumbling to themselves and their phone.

"Don't mind them."

Suteki Green's head plopped into her lap. Christina was so desensitized to surprise at this point that she didn't even think of screaming. Compared to everything else a headless or bodiless Suteki Green's head was the least remarkable thing to happen to the famous kaiju fighting Saturday morning superheroes. Suteki Pink had black flames painted onto the edges at just about every side of the plastic parts that were their armored being, giving their presence an overall 180 degrees to what they tended to garner. Suteki Yellow, checkered with white paint, was shifting through the van full of heavy metal equipment while Suteki Blue, who had light blue waves across their body and chest, waited to the side with a boom mic. Orange was already off somewhere else preoccupied no doubt, but Christina had more than enough time to see the floral design all over them. The only odd one out was actually Suteki green or rather, the body of that which belonged to the head of Suteki Green. The only change in their visuals was what looked like to be a backpack holding a satellite dish, but Christina couldn't make it out clearly as the green torso and limbs stood off on the nearest rooftop of a house yards away.

More importantly, and more remarkable, was the astounding state of the community garden she found herself sitting in. After one car ride that was full of turns, bruises, and abundant disagreements on the proper directions to take to get here, she could not have imagined for the destination to be so-

"Well. Abundant I uh... would guess"

"Huh?" Green asked, the mechanisms in the base of their head trying to turn to look at her but there was no neck to do so.

"The garden," she clarified. Beforehand it was mostly empty beds of dirt and dead leaves about, save from the most dedicated attendants sole crop, or that's what she gathered from the sparse looks through the gated chain link fence as she passed by occasionally. Xiaodan once told her no one wanted to hang out so close to the massive obelisk of electricity that was the cell phone tower the city gave permission to perch over this lot since she could remember memories of this pocket of San Anlos in a meaningful way. But now the crops were abundant.

"People like to eat don't they?" Green asked rhetorically, partly to make a point, but also sincerely because their understanding of the concept of food was such a significantly abstract one it would be considered contemporary art. "Even when no one else has an interest in feeding them."

Sure enough, people would be able to eat. There was a chicken coop somewhere off to the side with a cacophony of clucking hens emanating from it but the view was obscured from the middle lots of corn. Rows and rows of corn stood tall, so much it was unfeasible yet tangible in easy reach of her hands. Perhaps it was because of the monumental size of the telephone tower that it added a sense of gravitas to the scene but, ignoring the fact that she struggled and tripped over them, she was at a loss for words.

"We're going to be live in one minute."

In a straight line from Christina's eyes there was Yellow with what was salvageable of a wireless camera they could find, so large the terror could be seen in her reflection along the lens.

"Sound checks out." Blue's boom mic leaned into view of Christina's perspective.

"I found Orange," cried Pink, holding the teammate by the nape of their neck where spandex fabric was reachable.

"Connection is full bars," Green affirmed, their body giving a thumbs up in the distance. "Just like we practiced, remember."

Panic was jumping through Christina's body like crickets chirping at a maxed out volume that told every corner in her body to run but with no intended direction.

"We didn't practice," she hissed.

"Good, be spontaneous. People like authenticity."

"Action!"

"Quiet on set and all that!"

All the background characters were accounted for, but the star was nowhere to be found.

The sweat poured out from Christina more than ever as she panicked trying to be as stealthy as she could while running away in her wheelchair. She could only roll a few yards so quickly before her arms started to burn from the fumbling because of lactic acid. The burning was less of a worry compared to the other terrors present, but all she could do with an empty head and no thoughts was listen to her body and stop.

"What do you think you're doing?" A small hand pushed out from between the corn stalk with a grip not possible of the size squeezing her shoulder.

"What are you uhh doing?" Christina asked back incredulously at Xiaodan with her walker, somehow standing between the rows of corn.

"It's cool and there was corn. But I asked first. What are you doing?"

"Don't forget about me too," Green spoke up, once again with an emotion tangible in their voice. She could see the hurt as their head was still sitting squarely in her lap. She was so stupid she decided. She just about jumped out of her seat with a yelp as the crickets inside her won. All she could do was not meet her grandma's gaze. A few days ago she would have never thought that someday Xiaodan could understand a problem like hers. Not the woman who could command water to boil if she needed to. Not the one who raised a family, business, and better part of a community from nothing. She was a woman of fire and dust from the many halls of history that echoed throughout her. No, that grandma Xiaodan would never understand what it was like for her right now. To sit and watch only, silently, ordinarily. To steep in her sincerity as she witnessed her so called life go by, cemented to a seat by faces she considered too unimportant to have commentary brought from her. All she had ever been doing was barely watching whatever was brought into her forefront. She couldn't run, she couldn't catch up to her friends or even her past self at this point. She couldn't even formulate her worries and pain to explain it to herself and better understand her woes.

That grandma couldn't understand her. But maybe the grandma from this morning could understand. The regret filled cathartic woman of Xiaodan.

"Rise up before I slap you, child."

Christina's eyes dropped crystal tears to water the ground as Xiaodan watched. She was incapable of astonishment at the sight because it wasn't astonishment at all. It was something she wished she had burned away long ago, but that wasn't the right thing. She didn't really want to burn it away. She just wanted to keep the girl warm so her tears wouldn't be so cold in the end.

"It's your mother that raised you to steep in sadness like this, not me. So manage your expectations and don't think for once you deserve my sympathy." Xiaodan was no taller than the cornstalk, but still, in this way hunched over her walker and with freshly combed hair she had little less than a had over Christina. Yet she did not look down on the girl. For a moment the heat felt a little less hot in comparison to the figurative literal fire. Christina stammered out a sentence or at least tried to, but Xiaodan did not stop. "You will not find such charity here."

"I'm an idiot." Christina yielded in submission. Xiaodan loomed over and was just about ready to slap the girl. She lifted her hand setting it on the girl's head and kissed her granddaughter's shriveled forehead. The girl was crushed by blues just like her mother, so it might as well be a plentiful blue, one that waters the crops and prepares for sunny days.

"You will not find such charity from me," she whispered, with a grainy and rough emotion for only those supplied with age and time. "Do you think that I have confidence or that I know what I am doing? You think that I somehow have this power that others don't. My baby. You. Are. Stupid." She held her granddaughter's face in her hands, partly balancing on her, partly looking her in the eyes and feeling her brain whirring with the worry that Christina had always had inside her. "I am an old woman. I say harsh things like old bitter women tend to do. But I love harsher, because life and years have not been generous to me just like they have not been for anyone else."

Orange spewed from her mouth. Christina could see it like always. She could feel the ash sting her face.

"I don't have this power in my words nor do I have a plan in my actions. You act like I burn scorch and charr. For some reason, you love an old, mean, haggard, and tired woman. I don't speak in flames, but you let my words blaze like a fire that warms the house. Christina I don't want you to stop deciding what things are meant to be important to you. But I also don't want you to not let yourself be important to yourself. If I breathe fire, then let it warm the house and boil the tea kettle. Christina..."

Oh. There hadn't really been a color there at all, had there? There was only Xiaodan speaking to her. And there was only Christina Zheng listening. And there was only a color orange that she seemed to like because it was grandma's favorite so she deserved to be painted in it.

"...make good tea."

Christina reached behind her into that space grandma was looking at, demanding a fire to no avail.

"Make good tea because you can."

In the end only she could light it herself, couldn't she? How bothersome, Christina thought to herself while cornstalks brushed past her and parted like stage curtains. The words would not come easy. She would have to pull them out herself. The Suteki Sentai 5, not counting Green, were currently stalling with breakdance and music from torn speakers.

Christina shot Blue a look that told them to play something powerful and punk. Orange nodded to Green's head and improvised the clockworked pyrotechnics. Colored clouds shot out from somewhere far in the back painting the sky in rainbows. Christina took a deep breath that was shaky and nervous and terrified and scared and wanted to hole up inside her lungs and cry to herself. And she forced it out with a not so even exhale.

She looked head on into the camera.

Brief blunt and brash.

"Uh Hi San Anlos. I'm uhh... I'm uhh... going to knock the uh stupid piece of metal out of uhh... of the sky. But before that..."

CHAPTER 6: LUNCH

The hills wouldn't stay green for much longer. Such lush luxuries never lasted in the same line of longitude as San Anlos. Soon enough, that aesthetic of vitality would be replaced with the sad encampment of drying bushes, drought stricken trees, dead patches of grass, and loose rolling hills of dirt looking dry. San Anlos was not a green city after all, or at least not anymore. Not for a long time. It had been coated in dust and dirt dried in the rubble of what might have been and what once was.

And that was not enough for vitality. Leaves would dry, the ground would crack, moss would turn to black rot and a home for termites.

Even now, one could feel it in the moment. The perspiration of the city. It was within your arms and in how heavy the air was. In how your breath could stand upright and a heat managed to crawl and scuttle between the bone. It was in the ache of the back and the pins and needles along the feet. Thirst went unquenched when the sweat was so much.

Isabella hated it.

She was never someone to break in such a way, even in the most drastic and dangerous circumstances. Her signature personality trait was to withstand the annoyance of environmental extremes like a pesky heat. She was supposed to be the annoyance after all. But even now, she had to admit that the solar oppression was reaching a point to be unbearable for even her. Hopefully not a breaking point though. Her body was already in the throes of exhaustion. It was supposed to handle such elevations in temperature, but if it was to be over at this point she wouldn't be surprised. The approximation of flesh on her approximation of bones felt like it was being cooked and prepared to fall into an approximation of meat.

You couldn't think in this heat.

You couldn't act in this heat.

You couldn't stand in this heat.

Isabella laid there on the park table admiring her handiwork with object dissatisfaction. The park was nothing like Trifecta Park. That crop of grass had been closed due to renovations that were never going to be carried out in any amount of time to be considered soon or recent. Where Isabella rested was in a small lot between a thrift store and a smoke shop. Too small to be considered an actual park with a proper name and was more or less a plot of land left undeveloped save for the tireless construction of workers that were stubborn grass and weeds. A few years ago the city decided to drop off a table and bench and promptly forgot about the small pocket of life much like everybody else had. The table was rough concrete and resonated in the heat so much it was prepared to burn her belly through her suit if she didn't have the good sense to bring a blanket out first. Even with her long hair draped over the backside of her body like curtains it was hot upon the lunchtime sun.

"How twisted is it that there is so much water between the sweat and the ocean, but we're stuck in a perpetual thirst?" She closed her hand feeling her finger stick together lightly. "We are cursed aren't we?"

Marcus laughed at her pitifully from his seat, too battered and distracted from the weather to even begin to ponder that kind of question. "When do we actually get to eat lunch?" he coughed from parched thought. She might be right about her point or whatever, he thought. He wasn't exactly listening to her. His poor attention was focused on the school's supply of stickers plastered all over his face and stuck to him like glue and the chemical properties of the banquet of food that piled up on the table before him. Food arranged so that it shielded Bella and framed her as if the main course of such a feast. Cantaloupes were arranged cut open, ready and next to collections of oranges, grapes, honeydews, kiwis, and watermelon. All of which were similarly prepared to eat being cleanly diced, sliced, and displayed. The amount of all piled high and gathered in unfeasibly mountainous peaks around Bella, who was looking to the side and taking small bites of a green apple

"What does it look like?" she asked. "We have already started haven't we?"

There were nuts strewn all over and falling onto the ground. Sunflower seeds, peanuts, pistachios, cashews, almonds, and most importantly the assortments covered, dipped, and coated in all sorts of habanero flavors. Marcus wanted to eat the spicy ones but knew he would regret it without water first. He swiped his finger along the small amount of table surface not used and carefully observed the amount of sweet nectar outpouring from fresh produce which was enough to collect and drink if he had a cup. He didn't pay it much thought though. His mind was elsewhere.

"You have always been one for theatrics so you might as well just tell me what you're planning is going to happen."

Bella huffed, perhaps she didn't want friends after all. If the ordeal of being known truly was this terrifying then she didn't want it. Towers of citrus and melons quaked and toppled as she tossed the apple to the side and stood up.

"I thought all that sin called divinity was wrung out of you a while ago, but as you have always seemed to prove again and again, you have exceeded my expectations. In a way I would never prefer."

She stood there in a freeze frame on the table, one hand drawn up blocking the sun before her face while the other was reaching for Marcus to come towards her as he did not move.

"There is so much food you have to eat it before it rots."

"I think I might be getting full," Marcus replied, peeling an orange. In an instant and a blur she was steps forward in a new pose. Tossing food in the process. This time her hair was frozen aloft in the air behind her and her knees were slightly bent. Her tie was stuck perpetually in the air against her chest and both hands had their fingers burrowing into orange held against her heart.

"Then make sure you get your fill. It's a feast after all. To dine well is the expectation. The goal is to enjoy it."

Her figure quivered with movement and for a moment yellow rays of sunlight strayed. Many blocked out Marcus' vision, erasing the green scene until Isabella was before him, a breaths away abruptly and instantaneously. This time her hair had fallen to her back and she stood tall and towered over him.

"A good guest must always remember to save room for the main course. Did you forget Marcus?"

"And what would that be?"

"Only the finest food as always. It will be rich in vitamins and antioxidants, but don't worry it's still sweet. It's an important reminder to always save space for a portion of greens regularly for a balanced diet. For example, a tree bush adorned with draping leaves and a vine covered tree house among its branches housing a pacing jaguar." She had already retracted the sticker from behind her neck. "The jaguar, as always, can have a little treat. As a reward".

Marcus bit the sticker without hesitation, startling Bella and her outstretched hand. At this point, he was fully invested in Bella's surprises but also deemed her trustworthy which was partially irresponsible. He knew better but he never, in fact, knew better than he knew now.

Bella stood there and Marcus sat there. Bella stood there. Marcus sat there. Bella stood the. Marcus sat there.

"Weird," she pouted. "I would have expected something by now. Maybe you are all dried out."

Bella stood there while Marcus sat there. Bella stood there. Green leaves moved in the wind. Marcus sat there. Bella stood there. The green forest blocked out the sun. Marcus sat there. Marcus stood there. Marcus stood there. Marcus stood there. Marcus stood there. Marcus stood there. Marcus was also leaning, hanging, laying, and criss-crossed applesauced there.

"All you had to do was wait for the roots to grow."

At his feet sprung the entanglement of green gelatinous roots that ran throughout the earth of San Anlos. Around them spouted greenery, massive rainforest leaves and vines filling up all available space. Large stems jutted from the earth and swelled upwards, filling up the limited space of sky under the purple translucent dome. And from the thicket came a Marcus and a Marcus and a Marcus and a Marcus and a Marcus and a Marcus and a Marcus and a Marcus and a Marcus and a Marcus and a Marcus and a Marcus etc. All of which were green and melting, taking a seat at the table and relaxing.

Isabella took a step backward while looking around her in amazement.

"It's green," one of the similarly colored Marcus stated matter-of-factly.

"It's a garden," said another.

"It's a forest," said another.

"It's a zoo," another.

"It's a jungle," another.

"It's wild," another.

"It's an adventure," another.

"It's dense," another.

"It's open," another.

"It's platonic," another.

"It's panic," another.

"It's growing," another.

"It's plentiful," another

"It's home."

CHAPTER 7: VACATION DAYS

The gigantic tropical green leaves pushed up against the glass engulfing the building, just like all the others within the San Anlos city limits, in its massive foliage. Lauren glanced over out the top floor window that now displayed what San Anlos had of a skyline as the massive sticky plants squelched and squirmed against the glass.

All throughout the small strip of coast and inland the earth was cultivated. City blocks became garden plots of immense green bases as street after street exploded with vibrant greens. Trees and brush tore out of the cracked and pothole ridden roads, tossing loose and lifting cement slabs off the sidewalk. They crushed cell towers, telephone poles, and street lights as tree branches and the green stems of foliage weaved in and out, reaching higher into the sky. Emptied parks, destroyed buildings, and abandoned construction sites all excelled with growth as the roots sent ripples through the earth, tossing equipment and dirt aside in the waves and lifting the earth itself. San Anlos burst at the seams with a jungle.

And in the center of it all, a few blocks over, between a thrift store and smoke shop, down an almost retired street no one willingly ventured to drive, was a tree.

The tree.

With a trunk, rich and green, it pushed against the walls of the buildings next to it and its roots weaved in and out of the earth like pythons burrowing. The limbs, draped in vines, pressed against the very top of the plasma dome with such force one could feel the resistance in the air. And in the center of it was not just a rundown tree house exposed to the elements but adobe walls, wooden panel doors, clay ornaments, and open windows around the base and only growing upwards. Clinging along the trunk, built into the tree itself, the building bubbled and burst with new rooms each second, filling up the space between branches. There were bedrooms, kitchens, hallways, temples, altars, attics, balconies, and stairs. The house built the jungle.

The jungle built the house.

Lauren jolted as the air sparked with the energy and the temperature rose to the point even the Tandem Tantrum Toys and Co. AC couldn't compensate for. At the same time, she assumed the hard plasma projections at a 180 degree dimensional rotation reached their maximum output. Her chest rose and fell with heavy breaths that she was still trying to catch. Her clothes were already drenched even in the air conditioned room atop the tower the CEOs liked. She couldn't keep her cool.

Luckily it would only be a few moments longer. Her fingers slipped against the buttons, dialing Marcus' number with a string of soft but rampant clicks. Above the dead dial-up corpses of has-beens and tyrants Lauren stood there with the phone to her ear, head lifted, and chin up. Giving herself a moment to relax. Her left hand was limp and dangled at her side while holding her dented but lovely bat, she had possibly pulled a muscle. The very end of her bat just missed the mangled remnants of archaic arcade machines. Strewn about the room, across the table, and along the floor. She stood on them. Fractured screens, gouged hardware, lacerated cables, and metal panels busted open and torn apart littered the office space.

"Give it a minute for the order to go through."

"Great boss," the voice replied.

Another ripple began, heat wave hostility courtesy of Tandem Tantrum Toys and Co. shot through the air. The glass hissed for a second like a nest of serpents. The leaves pressed further against the glass. Many seething voices of tension were made singular for a second, unified in the verbal assault for a moment before shattering the glass in a dazzling rain of finally sharp particles. Lauren didn't bother to gasp or flinch in surprise, in fact, she knew better and held her breath. All that she could provide was a tired and cold gaze as the call went dead.

"Works for me," she muttered.

She had to make an exit somewhere. She was a freed girl but she still was in a company building and she had to make an exit. There was a newfound anxiety to the decision itself. One that she didn't think would have been there. A kind that was familiar with a panic that festered at the bottom of her stomach and sat on the top of her tongue. It made her want to act out, it made her want to do something reckless, and it made her be conscious of the fact that she probably shouldn't do anything of the sort. She needed an exit, it didn't matter if it was at ground level or the 13th. There was an anxiety that she had yet to escape.

"I have to get out of this building," she muttered to herself. It must have been in the walls or the very air that she breathed. There must have been asbestos in the construction, arsenic in the paneling, or maybe even cyanide on her palette. There shouldn't have been any worry after she quit her job after all. Those weren't the right descriptive words though. She was exhausted, tired, and worn out from all the days of work that had come crashing down in one collection of moments and she didn't know what would come after that. She looked out what had once been the window next to her as the green leaves reached inwards. She must have been a nervous girl after all. There was nothing else she could be, was there? Well there was probably, but she hadn't found the words to describe that sort of answer. That didn't matter for now because it wasn't going to stop her.

There was a clear route out. A defined path forward. A way she wanted to proceed.

And she knew every single word to describe it.

It starts at the wheels with a violent velocity that cuts and dices the ground that it slices through. It goes up the legs with knees that quaked under the force and pocket of gas that popped under the bend. It works up to the open air. It glides in the freedom of a freefall and then with hair caught in the wind. It comes crashing down with explosions at the shins. It gathers at the hands and works its way upwards.

Adobe walls rose from the bark and a single brown wooden door propagated itself into the girl's field of view as she leaped into the air. It opened up without ever having to creak with the sound of ages as the adobe wall itself extended forward making a fresh hall. The building was reaching towards the girl itself. A single pale hand reached from beyond and caught the purple phone that Lauren had let go of.

"My door is always open," Bella said, swinging the said door open to comply in time for Lauren to crash against the tree and keep her going inside.

"And what if it isn't?" Lauren asked, catching her breath in the pristine shade of the buildings.

Bella laughed, her sharp fingers were now caught in the wooden makeup of the doorway as she turned back with a ferocious glint in her smile.

"Then you tear the walls down."

The moment in time was a shared occasion. Both of them agreed it to be a little underwhelming. It was far above them. It was out of sight. It was not directly witnessed. It was a moment to be ingrained in the very walls and to be carved into the bones. But for Lauren, who tore down walls and disassembled bosses, and

Isabella, who tore apart moons, there was nothing else more important than such an event's meaning.

Somewhere above them, a LEVIATHAN boiler room management system had a weight lighted from its virtual AI shoulders as a single order went through a very suspicious looking means of communication. But it was communicant nonetheless and otherwise considered secure so it was to be followed. The plasma shield generators went down. Purple hexagons that were faint in the right glow of sunlight disappeared without a trace and the outside was allowed to come into San Anlos. And San Anlos was allowed to go outside.

The abode walls and wooden planked floors lurched as tree branches were no longer beholden and bondaged to the finite space of limits and free to reach altitudes higher. The rest of San Anlos exploded forth with a massive forest dipping its hands into the sea, hugging the mountains, and brushing the blue skies.

"All it ever seems to do is grow," Isabella stated.

Lauren looked up after rolling back into a wall. "What else is there to do?"

CHAPTER 8: TRUE BLUE

It was hot, like childhood memories of watching VHS tapes in the living room with all the windows open. Because no one could quite make out if they were enjoying themselves until the moment was too late and the temperature was beyond the point they could remember anything that happened. Nothing to show for an entire evening getting over the heat stuck inside the house except for the sound of soft clicks and whirring that were so satisfying they become memories brown and caked in dirt to be unearthed later. Christopher wondered how accurate the scorching memories were after having so much time to bathe in a cooler nostalgic aroma. Compared to VHS tapes, the growing blots of color that was his vision of all the scenery of San Anlos was far more concerning and less relaxing. The smacking clicks and clacks of haphazard squirms in a furious string of percussion was anything but a soothing source of asmr. But the work had to be done.

More importantly, Tiana, Touma, and Christopher had no qualms with such tasks. The twostared at separate screens filled up with rows of little boxes of live footage. Their ocular reticles were trained at a total focus, squinting with fierce force side to side as their attention switched by the millisecond.

"908."

"1120."

"1445."

"1697."

Each of them manually tagged targets for the automated firing turret defense system situated throughout the city because it was faster this way than for the actual targeting program the firearms originally used.

"2234."

"2789."

The sailor uniforms came out in droves. Almost less than infinite surely, but Christopher had an intimate knowledge of Tadem Tantrum Toys and Co. resources to know it was only moderately less than such a number. The far distance between the LEVIATHAN and the closest camera lens resulted in them appearing only like a small block of a few pixels conglomerated in a grayish square, not even enough pixels for a proper shape to be displayed. Far above the green in the canvas of the blue, the skeletal scaffolding shuddered under the force of deployment. Tarps and covers shot upwards as hangar doors opened for the descent of the new Super Star Sailor Girls with blue, mechanical, steel, monochromatically colored, sleek robotic bodies that were cosplaying as humans.

Stainless steel in place of skin. Jet propulsion in place of palms. Solid blue reticles in place of eyes. A metal helmet installation formed like a short bob haircut in place of the real thing. No mouth, no nose, no ears. In the likeness of, but nowhere near the real blue it was emulating.

"Such poor quality isn't it? They must have been rushed." Eve's reflection scrutinized the footage on the computer leaning over Christopher's shoulder.

"Easier to blow up too," Christopher affirmed, watching exactly what happened countless times in the short span Tiana and Touma had started to work. The fleet of militarized high school impersonations didn't have the chance to touch ground.

"3333."

Cheap construction and poor design made them fall like birds. Eve let his eyes bounce back between the computer screens, Christopher, and the reflection of the computer screens in Christopher's glasses. The man's eyes were focused and still, but with every explosion and dropping metallic body there was a twitch in a different part of his face. A movement barely noticeable unless you were familiar with it like Eve was. "You look happy."

"I am."

"3755."

"I'm angry more than anything still".

"3849."

"But this time I could be angry at the right thing."

"4065."

The camera feeds turned to cold frames of digital snow as offline status was confirmed all throughout the city.

"Land ho," Touma called out.

"We're losing firepower," Tiana yelled.

Their fingers' pace was running their synthetic tips raw. Across the feeds, each sight was the flight of energy beams from an endless amount of sailor robots. There were too many, it made Christopher grind his teeth immediately with enough pressure to crush granite. "We can't clear a path for the missile. Not at this rate."

Eve looked over through the doorway to the limo and the special construction in the alley lying on the other side of the wall. He could think of one way they could. He didn't like the thought, but he could think of it nonetheless. More importantly, he could do it regardless of whether he wanted to or not.

Amid the growl of generators and screeches of armed aerial warfare there was the sound of an explosion unlike the rest. Truly booming in response. The sailors did not scream when they were shot through, the sound of screeching metal was enough to unnerve the psyche of pilots and rebels ready to make a dead snake. Green like leaves. Organe like fruit. Pink link gemstones. Blue like frogs. Yellow like bulbs. Xiaodan was screaming with excitement with each turn Christina made in Suteki Green. It wasn't Suteki Green like anyone would have imagined, nor was the rest of the group. They had one more trick up their sleeve and a series finale spectacle to show off, that being their attack jet forms. Each and everyone folded in on themselves and let their metal expand like origami into a different shape until five monochromatic jets remained in their place. It was Suteki Green that offered Christina the honors of piloting even when she refused and now she was stuck in a dogfight upwards. Behind them were the deftly falling remains of robot girls as they burned holes through packs of Christina's cold counterparts. Meanwhile, those said counterparts shielded her field of view from the front, making her flight far more perilous. With their metal grips, they grabbed onto her jet and began to tear when all else failed. The jet lurched along without focus as Christina failed to remain in her seat. She didn't know who exactly was flying, her brain as alight with the buzz of electricity as Green and her own consciousness melded together in turns left and right that they decided unanimously. Too much of her brain power was intent on not returning to the earth in a fireball. It was a dilemma only exaggerated by the whooping cries of both Green and grandma with every successful shot she made along the way.

Across the sky, between massive branches and leaves, monochromatic jets of the Suteki Sentai weaved in and out of packs of mechanical girls in a mad dash. The jet tumbled and twirled until, amid the assault of robot girls and leafy greens, Christina caught a glimpse of her San Anlos horizon. It was a landmark enough to tell her to shove the wheel forward and even out the plane. Once she had her bearings while avoiding near misses with large foliage she could focus on her first goal, slaying the LEVIATHAN. It was a goal getting harder and harder by the moment if the rate of robot girls continued. She took a look at the view outside. Every few seconds she flew right into a robot girl and let them explode against the windshield. There was no real point in keeping track, but as she made it out of the greenery between them and into the sky above there were more swarms of blue robots.

"We are not uh... we're not going to make uh... to make it past," she realized with her gut dropping. For all her good deeds and well intended talk she wasn't going to be able to make it through. It was embarrassing at first, she had just addressed San Anlos at large and couldn't follow through. It made her want to crawl into a hole. But in addition to that, she didn't know what was going to happen to her or worse, what would happen to Xiaodan. Her back sweated and stuck to her seat. Over and over the robot girls flew to meet her and all the other jets. The energy beams could only tear through so many as they swarmed and the girls had energy beams of their own shooting out from the jet propulsion from their hands. One by one, and at an increasingly frantic pace, they piled onto the hood. The panels at the surface rattled and shook as more girls pinned to push the jet back and tear it apart in the process.

"I can't do it," she whimpered, arms hanging as she collapsed against the steering wheel.

"No, you still can," Xiaodan corrected her. Hot fire licked her ear and seared the surface at her brow. As she looked over to acknowledge the sentiment she noticed her grandma's hand on her shoulder. More importantly, she caught sight of the other hand around the ejector button. "Where did you get that?"

Suteki Green did not answer.

"You can't expect me to leave you alone here, you're my grandma"

A true blue shined through her brain with enough color and power of its own that it didn't need electricity to induce a heat. Xiaodan laughed with a burning hearth of her own. "Christina I refuse to rest this late in life. I can do it when I'm dead".

"One, don't uh say that. Two, okay but uh... that doesn't uh mean uhh you have the ability to fly this."

"We have a big family now. How are you going to look after everyone my hero?"

Christina and Suteki Green thought the words unanimously. "Grandma?" they cried hesitantly with pure monochromatic excitement.

"Yes," Xiaodan sighed, maybe a little defeated. "It turns out I'm a grandma of many."

The fire wasn't hot in fact. Nor was it orange. She realized it just as suddenly as Xiaodan was a slowly disappearing figure along with everything else except the horde of robots.

It hits you with raindrops of blue. It flies through the blue sky. Over a blue ocean. It's lost in the air and suddenly weightless. It comes with outstretched arms reaching forward. It's over the reach of factors trying to pull her down, but missing just out of reach. What type of blue was it? She wondered. Of course, the answer would come to her.

CHAPTER 9: CASA DE ALVARADO

It was a garden with grand tree branches swelling and creaking in the atmosphere under growth spurts. Vines tangled in drooping loops all throughout and the brush was ever expanding. It was a garden. With flora of all kinds. Green hedges piled out of windows and clung along adobe walls bursting with pink petals. Trees adorned with purple only found in the spring were suddenly taking root along roofs and petals shadowed the houses in their fall. Similar but yellow ones made themselves seen, now taking hold all throughout the expanding brush. Read tufts that were fuzzy and short. Yellow sunflowers, blue irises, white magnolias, orange marigolds, all kinds of wildflowers, cactus tunas, pale dandelions, and the rainbow of infinite flowers pushed its way outwards of homes, spilling out of doors, bursting from windows, and climbing on walls. And when the right wind struck, it let loose its grip and caught them all in the surge of movement. Masses of petals sailed around the central tree, caught in the updraft ready to bury San Anlos in floral amenities.

It was a zoo. One with yellow butterflies only multiplying in number by the second. Following the path made by the flowers, they chased sweet nectar and the freedom of the winds. Within the branches, black bears climbed and waved to great egrets that passed with grace. Stray cats and packs of dogs paraded the old wood floors while chasing its path up through the adobe construction. Parrots, macaws, scrub jays, crows, and pelicans alike filled the air with calls and movement, tucking into the pockets of small space between massive tree limbs. Mountain lions and coyotes dodged the hot sun and slinked through the cool interior's shadows in their ascent forward through the house. It was a jungle. One where jaguars paced the halls.

"It's a house."

The words left Marcus' lips with the most simple ease, holding no weight to be burdened or struggled with. "Because we're all here," he finished, smiling while the herd of wildlife roamed around them in the halls of an ever constructing adobe house.

Isabella and Lauren tried to stand upright against the surge of movement. The animals passed close by Lauren, close enough to brush against her shirt. Bella was the one to break the stupid silence giving the girl and boy a push forward, walking as creatures parted from their path.

"Don't just stand there. The best children climb trees and slay a beast at least once in their life." They did indeed stand there together amid the chaos of animals. The sound of the floors and tree creaked while it ever expanded and the shrieks and calls of nature went unimpeded. Marcus and Lauren both looked at each other in surprise for a moment only because they couldn't quite place what was different, but something was most definitely different. There was something deeply altered with them, something great that had shifted like tectonics over the course of days that they had just now noticed and they stood there and watched. Lauren looked over at Marcus and Marcus looked at Lauren.

The house shook and tossed them forward. Lauren didn't want to bother fighting it. She stopped where she stood for a moment and let Bella force a hand onto her back again, ready to shove her forward. "A house with many rooms, but one path." She turned and gave her friend a nod before crouching down in a ready position for a sprint.

This girl has tenacity, Bella thought with a smile. She did in fact like her, she decided. She liked her a lot. Her long black hair shot backward from the force concentrated all at once into her arm. Torrential waves rocketed through her own arm and out like lightning exiting through the rod that was her fingers, hurling the girl forward with enough strength to sever spines.

"Do you want to know what makes a home a home?" Marcus asked. But Lauren was an overachiever with heads to sever and backs to break. Instead of waiting she shot forward in a dash. She already knew the answer well enough, she didn't have to wait and listen. Isabella wasn't interested in simple conversations like these. At least not for now. So instead the words echoed through the halls for everyone to hear instead because the nature of it deemed so. They bounced off the adobe walls first and then the ceiling and the walls again until they broke free of the tree line. They were whispered under wooden floorboards and then secluded off into groups within each of the rooms.

"It's when the halls are worn down with the age of life."

Lauren raced upwards, wheels shaking hard with every strike against the floorboards.

"It's when the rooms have been dismantled and built again".

All around her, doorways swung open and shut with enemies inside. Teenage robots in sailor uniforms banged on the walls for a way out.

"It's the stench and wreckage from a familiar source that you just can't get rid of."

San Anlos' family.

She passed a door where metal shrieked from being cut in two.

"With the child that speaks in blades."

Vines writhed out from under another door where the whining of machines slowly stopped.

"Or the cousin that can't help but connect to the color of the earth."

Searing heat and billowing smoke poured out under another.

"The grandma that scorches all she touches."

The distinct buzz of bees deafened the halls of another.

"The aunt and uncle whose love is unnaturally sweet."

The walls rocked back and forth suddenly as Lauren caught herself just as bull horns shot through the door to her right.

"The unstoppable pair of uncles."

She could her eating somehow. The sound came softly, setting up home in the back of her skull. Chewing.

"And the mother who is rightfully never full."

The noise finished. The trespassers were devoured.

Bella watched Marcus, amused as she came over her astonishment at the words that had just left his mouth. "If you keep talking like that I'm going to see you capable of complex thought boy."

"How unexpected of you."

"I know," she smiled. "No good for business."

"Finally," Lauren gasped. The wind beat into her face, air cleaning her eyes dry. The breeze rocked through her, clearing her head of thoughts. It was the moment the dream was directly ahead. Breaking just past the tops of the uppermost tree leaves, soaring with momentum to her goal.

Finally, she had reached the top.

CHAPTER 10: SAN ANLOS SAN ANLOS

"You know that person?" Suteki Orange asked, reading her brain waves in real time to know perfectly well that she did, in fact, know that person. She knew Lauren Mendez very well. She didn't know a lot about the happenings that occurred in the last few moments, but she did know the shape, the name, the smell, the touch, and the girl Lauren Mendez. It was one of the few things she recognized. What she didn't recognize was her own space she had taken up seconds prior as the ejector seat went off in Suteki Green. Nor did she recognize the seconds after when she shot through the air, avoiding the reaching arms and hands of robotic girls piled up and climbing all over the jet. She barely had time to recognize a plan to not die afterward, but luckily that's where Suteki Orange came in. Just in time, actually, to catch her.

"If you uhhh... can uh waste time talking then uh then you uhh... you can land more of the shouts," she grunted, zooming further toward the right flank of the LEVIATHAN towards the similarly zooming figure of Lauren.

The rickety scaffolding shook with every movement of her's as it very well could be considered nowhere within the vicinity of safe. At this height the city was a small collection of blocks that could fit in her hand. The turbulence from even the slightest gust of wind was giving its fullest efforts to knock her off and return her in the most extravagantly horrifying way to that handful sized city. Luckily on this side of elevation there was no heat, a feat potent enough in the absolutely noxious taste of bitter rage on her tongue that she refused any other result at this point but destruction. So she kept low and stayed fast. The odd schematics of the LEVIATHAN's blueprints were freshly emblazoned in her brain as she danced around the shots of incoming mechanized soldiers and knocked the ones that landed in front of her to the side with her bat. Each time with a louder grunt that reminded her time was running out.

"She's probably doing to die like that," Orange pointed out while a group of sailors shot toward the girl

"Then shoot better," Christina repeated again through clenched teeth, a bad habit she thought she might have picked up from Christopher. Condensed energy beams fired in-between the sailor's eyes and left a sizzling hole in the wall right before Lauren's face, in the space hers would have been. Lauren's wide open eyes meet Christina's gaze. The wide eyes of Christina's met Lauren's.

"Idiot girl," Lauren gasped.

"Idiot girl," Cristina hissed through her teeth.

"You're both smiling," Orange noted, perplexed at the discrepancy.

Blue like Lauren's shirt and glasses, Christina realized. The kind that makes her skin glow and compliments her eyes. She could feel her head filling up with a blaze that was warm like a fire. Filling her empty synapse space with a headache of ideas she couldn't quite make out. Suteki Orange's processing systems stalled for a moment, unable to connect to Christina's null thoughts. Null no more. It was a perfect connection after all. Not the type she could see so clearly like the colors in the day, but equally strong. Suteki Orange couldn't make heads or tails of it, but they knew one thing.

"You can't help her from here."

Lauren found a person sized door in the wall and a few moments later a hangar door that was flush with the LEVIATHAN's surface started to open slowly. Christina looked out to the uniform nervousness creeping into her vision as soldiers started to slip in through the momentary crevices of space before she could.

"Yeah, uh... I uhh know." She did in fact know. She just didn't want to think about such a reality. Ejector button in one hand. Concentrating her energy packed into the action, she pressed it. She waited a moment and patted the dash of the cockpit. "You know uh Orange, you guys uhh... you guys are uhh good superheroes." She smiled, letting the words collide with them like warm bed sheets against the dash.

"Made to be Saturday Morning's finest. That's gotta mean something."

"Yeah, uhh... no doubt." This time Christina forced herself out, cutting through the air with determination not surprising but necessary, angling herself in the air to fit through the slowly expanding opening along with the influx of mechanical bodies.

Lauren stood in front of the personal access security door fumbling through the digits she thought were right, but was not sure of the order they needed to be in for the keypad. The clink of mechanical bodies echoed through the hangar bay, colliding against the hard metal spotless floor. "Idiot," she seethed while cursing at herself for not thinking things through. The keypad beeped cheerfully and the doors opened, but it wouldn't be fast enough. An arm grabbed at her back and turned her around. Her one hand with the bat was over her head ready to land a decisive blow, but Christina's arm was already around Lauren's waist and lips interlocked.

"I told uh... I uh told you I uhh... would catch you," she whispered, her breath rough against Lauren's face as she lowered her weapon. Behind Christina were the remains of machines with holes in their pristine smoldering chest, or in their heads, or a combination of the two. She dropped a small orange colored laser pistol that clanged against the metal floor.

"Now you can uh... can catch me," she yelped, as her legs began to shake and give out.

"Your helpless," Lauren huffed exasperated. "Coming here without your wheelchair." Meanwhile, she was already giving the girl a piggy payback ride into the next room.

A city leveler and grand sentence stealer. Lauren didn't quite know what exactly the inside would entail as it was a censored detail even for her old employee privilege. Whatever it was, it had to be important enough that its specs and purpose were confidential. Lauren was hoping it was the main central station for all communication to dispatched robot units. Christina was looking ahead and already surprised to see her stupid perfect face flashed on every available surface, smiling back at her.

"It is CCC back at you again with a new report. This just in, the SAN ANLOS V2.0 update is fresh and ready." The lights far above turned on row by row. Bright, cold, and harsh, shining off every surface like new diamonds. The insides weren't what either of them had expected. There was no communication station or weapon of destruction inside. The LEVIATHAN was a city leveler for a reason. Because afterward, there would have to be a new city to put in place. All throughout the massive expanse of its industrial insides, for at least what they could see, there were pristine gray buildings with the company logo. They were rows and rows of houses probably waiting for the moment that they could drop down and fill up the space of San Anlos until it wasn't San Anlos anymore. The two were walking on a rubber floor that was a makeshift sidewalk throughout the grid-like infrastructure inside. It was suffocating, or at least trying to be if Lauren hadn't forced herself to gasp and breathe from the shock of it all. It was terrifying.

"It's better than that," CCC snarked from everywhere. "It's dangerous."

Plastered all inside of the beast were screens. On the corner of houses, next to the doors where they would have displayed a home address, on street signs, and in the insides of homes with TVs was CCC smiling and looking back at them.

Christina noticed it a few seconds before, but the rooms were not empty. "It's worse," Lauren corrected. The room coursed with an invisible energy of movement that couldn't be made out. Something was in that version of San Anlos' rows of buildings packed side by side, each neatly outlined with the Tandem Tantrum Toys and Co. logo. Lauren peered into the closest window and touched the wall. Her heat dropped. Suddenly the subject line to the LEVIATHAN's schematics made sense. Rapid urban development for product distribution and brand loyalty. She looked inside the nearest window. The insides of the houses were no better. Company toys with company furniture with company food inside company walls. But more importantly, inside the company walls was something that looked back.

CHAPTER 11: TRIPLETS

"To think it would have such a stupid ending," Christopher wondered aloud. He could feel the warm touch of the frenzy high up in the air, all it would need is a minute or two to see how it goes.

Tiana and Touma were still working through the seismic proportions of force that shook through them and the rest of San Anlos. They were not typing anymore though. Most turrets had been offline by now. Instead, they were working together on holding down the long barreled sentry turret with added pressure propulsion, customized to give the lift needed to reach the higher altitude necessary outside of normal range. In layman's terms, the barrel was a lot longer than it should have been and its firepower was restricted enough that it would either fire far off into the distance or blow up here and now.

"What is really remarkable about this, is that you really sure are fine with shooting your boyfriend," Touma remarked.

"Your fiancé would do the same to you in a situation like this," Christopher shot back. He gulped, sweat running down his back and not totally confident in his own confident words. Touma just stood with wide eyes, not sure how to answer. Tiana shook her head, focusing on her breathing and instead trying to finish the task at hand. If and when the cannon successfully fired it would be enough to level the street if they didn't keep it in place. Perhaps it was too hot to stay outside, Christopher thought.

Lauren jumped out of the hangar door with Christina literally right behind her into the open air. "When uhh... did they get so loud?" Christina cried, more annoyed and less concerned for her life than she should have been. But then again, what was there to be alarmed about when Lauren was right there?

Behind the falling two was a literal horde of sailor girls glued together into a singular flock pouring out from the mouth and every building inside the LEVIATHAN in a desperate chase after the couple. Each and every one of the robot girls was cackling monotone and soulless laughs as if cement had suddenly had a voice. The odd inflections of each overlapped with each other and cut themselves off. A mess in sound just as much as they were in person.

The wind whipped against the two girl's faces as they plummeted toward the earth. Lauren's braids blew backward and tugged at her scalp as she attempted to wrestle ahold of her glasses. Christina buried her face into Lauren's shoulder, shielding it, and held on tighter.

"Blue," she screamed. "The type uh... the type of blue that makes uh yellow look better. The kind that uhh... the kind that uh brings out the uh best in you. That's the kind I uh want to be."

Lauren would have rolled her eyes if she was able to at the moment. She would have also laughed if the air wasn't being ripped from her mouth every time she exhaled.

"You're an idiot," she gasped. Her stomach was empty and aflutter nervously with the vocabulary. "But there was something about idiots that I can't seem to overcome. I'm glad you make me talk about such nice and stupid things though."

Neither of them had a plan.

Neither did Christopher as the blocks of San Anlos shook. The force of the shot sent cracks through the streets and whipped up the loose fragments into the air like dust while glass shattered. Tiana and Touma struggled to keep the machine in place and in the last moment it sent them flying backward into the air filled with foliage along with much else in the area. They didn't plan for these types of things.

Neither did Eve, but that did not stop the car from passing on, rotating forward at not nearly the speed of light but still something fiercely related. The couple of girls falling caught sight of him standing atop his limousine and pulling at the chains warped around the car so that it curved and dodged tree branches, massive leaves, vines, and the occasional horde of mechanical sailor girls. Even the flock of girls laughing behind them did not interfere as they dispersed into the air, giving up on the chase as they were engulfed and by changing greenery when in reach of the city.

His work wasn't over. Not at least until it was too late and he was alive and beyond the crowd of metal and greens. This last job had to be the most bothersome yet. He grimaced, his tie slapped against his face and there was nothing that he could do about it. Chains spun around Lauren and Christina's abdomen as they were just about to plummet back into the jungle and hurled them upward. It was so much more troublesome to work when there were people to care about. For a moment he was really scared about what would happen today, being that he willfully stood atop a bundle of explosives and shot out of a cannon, but then again he was the one that decided to trust Christopher and it paid off. From all his journeys throughout the galaxies he had developed a good head on his shoulders, but San Anlos had a way of decapitating good heads and putting on ones that did things like stand on fireworks. Regardless, he sailed higher into the air than he thought he would, but nowhere near enough high enough to reach the LEVIATHAN. The tree line was just out of reach underneath him, but the metal was even further above.

"Isabella," he yelled at the top of his lungs while steering the black missile downward so that his voice could reach above the pitch of the wind and roar of turbines. Eve shot a glance to the business casual figure standing from the tops of the tree and sent swift chains her way which she graciously accepted with a smile. Her feet were planted firmly on the enormous width of the one branch. From where she stood she reached her arm out and caught onto a band of chains that connected to the volatile car. Careful not to break the chains, she spun on one heel and pulled the vehicle towards her, catching it with her other leg in the air. Her foot was planted on its roof, denting the metal but leaving it otherwise in tack as she held it there propped up on its hood.

Next was him and the girls, a bundle of bodies he chained together with little protest and grappled to the nearest branch, pulling them down and landing with buckling knees. "You have the honor for old time's sake," he muttered, dusting himself off as the other two girls got up from the branch.

Isabella gave a good look at the familiar vehicle. "I can't imagine a better way to end it."

Lauren pulled Christina close. "Put them out of business but not their misery."

Bella liked the girl more and more. She smiled, her own appetite might have been full but there were still mouths to feed and the hunger was palpable. It churned along her skin like a trail of ants making her hands tremble and eyes quiver. Her skin was hot and burned to the touch with the solar heat in her grasp. They could see the heat simmer off her hair as it snaked and started to rise with a viscousness. What better company to eat with than in the presence of family and friends? She thought in sensations vividly sweet and reminiscent of the potent contradiction to the violence of her presence.

"CCC cutting in to cut it out." The LEVIATHAN had descended from its perch of high altitude towards them. It hung in the air with a screaming drone, placed miles before the tops of the tree and turned slowly. Its turbines shrieked with a united roar so its open hangar door could face them on the lengthwise side. Only a single sailor girl was left in the vacated ship's bay. It was holding a TV with the blue CCC avatar talking chipper as always.

"Tandem Tantrum Toys and Co. business is in mass production." She smiled. The screen cut to only her eyes, wide open and encompassing. Viewing the efforts of ants. There was no reflection of the world before her, only its tailor made and focus group tested perspective.

"Did you really think it would be that easy? We have policy standards to follow after all."

The turbine's roar was loud and not stopping. That's when it set in. On the flanks, far off in the distance but fast approaching, were familiar blocked shapes. Oh, the group gasped. The realization was shared.

"Triplets."

CHAPTER 12: THE JUNGLE

The group did not freeze. Bella, Eve, Christina, and Lauren may have stopped in fear, but the group did not freeze.

Not all heads were accounted for, after all. How could they be still when the tree itself that they stood on rocked with energy? There was a rumbling within San Anlos still, but the enemy was above. The stampede of thousands from a false ecology paraded its way en masse. The leaves curled with anticipation as a few stray streams of butterflies broke through the canopy first.

And then, all at once, the swarm of life came geysering out of the treetop like a fountain's stream, shooting upwards around the very place that they all stood with a velocity strong enough to carry them with it. Avians, insects, arachnids, flowers, mammals, and reptiles alike ascended upwards into the sky. The creatures filled the sky with colors of all varieties, painting the blessed blue canvas like impressionist dots before they started the plummet downward and collided against the leaves like rainwater in a rainforest during rainy weather and rainstorm.

It was unnatural this time of year, but San Anlos had a tendency for the unnatural. So really it had become a natural occurrence at this point.

At the end of it all was Marcus standing next to them, eyes glazed over in a solid green, small vines and branches sneaking before him to gather at his very feet so that he didn't mistake a placement and fall downwards.

"There is no place in this life for the likes of you."

He spoke with the rather feeble and quiet voice of his toward the hulking metal approaching them. It was his normal unimpressive voice that fluctuated at the wrong parts and leveled out when it shouldn't, making for uneasy listening, but it didn't matter. His voice ran along the earth, echoed throughout the trees, rippled across the ocean, collided with the city, and reverberated along the mountains and valleys, sending shockwaves with each syllable.

The LEVIATHANS' approach were constant, but not fast enough.

They were stupid in making a home here in San Anlos. It was a mistake to think they could build a city atop this, to think that they could produce the air they breathed, manufacture the mornings they awoke to, package and sell the days they amassed.

San Anlos, where the unnatural was natural. San Anlos was not a city you could build around and scheme. A city like San Anlos doesn't build, it grows. San Anlos was a jungle.

So in the end there was nothing odd about the unnaturally natural means by which destruction existed. Marcus lifted his arm, his eyes washed over green and saw a perspective far greater than his. In the same breath, two massive vines writhed and unlatched themselves from the tree. More and more strands of greenery wound themselves like rope until they were continual roots raised similarly high into the air.

Marcus brought his hands down and clenched them with an unnaturally natural strength. It was less like he had clenched them and more like someone had closed them for him.

The arms of the jungle shot forwards, covering the distance over the hills and ocean in both directions as they wrapped around and ensnared the two oncoming LEVIATHANS far off in the distance. Countless vines snapped at the tension of the action but they were encompassed and incorporated back into the mix. The wind picked up from the movement sending waves off into the ocean and currents to collide against the mountains like storms.

Bella kicked the car up in the air and caught it with her one hand, tossing a look over to the girls quickly after. "It'll be blunt. Make sure to enjoy it."

She didn't need to do anything new. It was a familiar motion to send the destruction into motion. One that she was adept at. Her one hand gripped the bumper, letting the metal screech and bend in her grasp the way things she held onto tended to do. She spun around, letting her body pick up momentum, her hair trailing after her and ensnaring her figure like a vines of the very tree they stood on. Slowly but surely, the energy picked up and continued until it was at a crescendo of waves overtaking her body. And when she had reached the apex she stepped forward with one leg raised high into the air and brought it down, putting her whole body in the motion, and hurled the car.

Less than a second. It took less than a second before the explosive laced car was toppling the lone sailor and retreating into the inside closure of the closest LEVIATHAN with nowhere to escape. Lauren opened her mouth to speak, but Christina was already on it, shooting a single sentence over her shoulder.

"In the end, we don't uhh... we don't get to uh see the uh fireworks."

Isabella turned as the constant crackle of pyrotechnics went off inside.

"There are more important things to see, aren't there? Who would have thought?"

Bella returned to where she dropped her briefcase to retract a single philips screw. She stopped for a moment and let her eyes peer through the leaves and branches to far below, not quite the city floor, to see the false animals still in a free fall.

"Dazzling."

The animal fountain had stopped, but the commotion didn't. The mass of metal droned in place while one explosion after another burst. It stayed in the air trying to remain calm, but the turbines and boiler rooms were sent into a shriek, unable to maintain the false homeostasis. The force of the chain reaction erupted out as the beast lurched forward, dipping into a descent that the group could not allow.

With a single flick of her hand, Bella sent out a standard screw ready to eviscerate and mold the hunk of now uselessly falling metal into a tinfoil ball. The little screw flew forward, shredding anything within its vicinity, tearing up leaves along the way, and heading straight for the metal beast.

Marcus had managed to wander before the very group and stood ahead and the tree lines edge looking at the open expanse of the world. The screw tore past him right over his shoulder, but no further. It stayed there in the air next to him. With his one hand he had caught it and plucked it from its course in the air. From behind him Isabella shouted something but he couldn't make out the words because he wasn't trying to. Somewhere next to her, Christina and Lauren tried to placate him, but he didn't hear them either. There was something else he was listening to. It was inside of him, pleading with his muscles and bones. It came from his chest and demanded for the rest of his body to listen to it.

He was running. He was running where there were no more branches underneath to catch him, but regardless the jungle leaned to one side and expanded rapidly to rise up and meet his feet, letting him push onwards.

"Just a bit further. Just a little more."

He was developing an appetite. He was famished really. It started in his gut, but there was nowhere else for it to go. He was never one to think many intricate thoughts. So it stayed there in his stomach and waited for things to come.

The small screw flashed brightly for a moment with his reflection inside before beginning to be set into a swirl. He had to be the one to set this movement into action. Within his own chest, he shoved the screw and turned it with his hands. It was hard, agonizing even at first. His body was like lard and didn't want to move but he made it.

"Just a moment more."

Life had fallen down around him in all colors. Suddenly the colors were captured and pulled back upwards. They were warped in the air and shone brightly like strands of gelatin caught in a vortex being pulled by his near liquid being. Parts of him evaporated into the forming globule above him as well.

He was wrong in fact.

He was wrong about many things in life, but this one in particular. His huger did not sit in his stomach. It started in his stomach and climbed out his throat in a roar. The wildlife around them was caught in the vortex of his scream.

Something pulled his lips back and made them snarl. It was a hunger evident in the way tree branches and vines were pulled upwards and incorporated into the now gelatinous combination. His hunger poured out to be at his fingers aching to act. The jungle pulsed with a life and reached a height greater than before, arching far above the city. He was very hungry in fact. Hungry enough that it festered into an energy along the back of his jaw and desired for the muscles to clench and chew. His breath steamed from the emotion. His mouth salivated.

The combination expanded into a golden idol, potent and bright. Its very own sun as the head of the jungle, connected by vines, tree limbs, and leaves holding it up. As it lurched forwards miles into the air the two massive vines retracted, hurtling the two LEVIATHANS towards him.

Marcus stood there in the in-between of the golden glimmering jaw, underneath the serene noise of the world. Between brown eyes and glimmering ears. All around him, smells. All around him, taste. All around him, San Anlos. All around him, muscles pulled back in the face for a snarl and then a roar.

"You have come to the jungle for gold, but you have found the maw of the jaguar."

Marcus was hungry, so he feasted.

STCKR: platonic panic - 558

STCKR: platonic panic - 560

STCKR: platonic panic - 561

ACKNOWLEDGMENT :

First and foremost, I want to thank anyone who took the time and resources to buy the book and actually read it. This book has been three years in the making and there have been many times where I thought I was never going to finish. It means the world to me to have another person willfully make the effort to try to listen and make sense of my nonsense. Ever since I was a little kid I have always wanted to eventually write a book. Well. I guess I kind of did it now. It turned out to be a lot longer of a story than I had initially intended to tell, but in the end I think I am really proud of the work I have created. If there was anything I would change it would be my horrible grammar. I have immense gratitude for anyone who managed to persevere for the story until the end, I hope you can look past all its undoubtable mistakes within. This has been a passion project that has been thought of, written, rewritten, edited, and ultimately proofread just by me and a little bit from my brother if he gets around to reading it at the time of writing this. Regardless, I hope the story was one that you greatly enjoyed as well and that your time with the book was interesting at least. This experience has been deeply rewarding and I look forward for the next time I can say I have finished a book, hopefully one that is a lot less long than this one. :)

-Andrew Touchette-
@whetdhogshoup

CPSIA information can be obtained
at www.ICGtesting.com
Printed in the USA
BVHW031358300523
665083BV00015B/983

9 798218 126025